THE FALLEN

A NOVEL

ROBERT DON HUGHES

BROADMAN & HOLMAN PUBLISHERS
Nashville, Tennessee

Printed in the United States of America

Published by Broadman & Holman Publishers,
Nashville, Tennessee

Book Design, Steven Boyd

4261-38
0-8054-6138-8

Dewey Decimal Classification: F
Subject Heading: GOOD AND EVIL—FICTION
Library of Congress Card Catalog Number: 94-35264

Library of Congress Cataloging-in-Publication Data:
Hughes, Robert Don, 1949–
The fallen / by Robert Don Hughes.
p. cm.
ISBN 0-8054-6138-8
1. Imaginary wars and battles—Fiction. I. Title.
PS3558.U389F35 1995
813\.54—dc20
94-35264
CIP

For Ruth Naomi Williams Hughes
my mother.
Of all my writing teachers, Mom, you were my first—
and you taught me the most.

CONTENTS

Chapter One

Flying over the bay

Halloween hovered over San Francisco like a hungry demon. The cool night air bore the sweet, seductive fragrance of sin. . . .

Or is that just the smell of pollution floating in off the bay? Jack Brennen wondered to himself. He tried to rein in his imagination, but that was hard. Jack never drove into this city without sensing something wicked lurking down every alleyway. And tonight was All Hallows Eve, with all its lurid promises! How could he fail to feel a tingle of terror dancing gleefully along his spine?

He glanced down at his wife, who slept with her head on his right thigh. It was a puzzle to him how she managed to get comfortable, wrapped as she was around the Mustang's floorshift. She must be, however, for she'd been sleeping peacefully in that position ever since they'd passed Livermore. *My darling,* he thought to her with a playful smile, *you're missing all the wonderful charms of Oakland.* She would certainly *not* appreciate him waking her up for *that.*

San Francisco, now—that was another matter. They both loved the dramatic beauty of the city. He paid the toll and drove onto the Bay Bridge, and as always looked off to the right. There was the Transamerica Pyramid, pointing its needle at the sky as if to proclaim, "Look down, stars, and see: This place is the crossroads between ancient Egypt and the Age of Aquarius—the capital city of alchemy!"

Indeed it was. On this Friday night in 1975 it seemed to Jack that the whole nation was glancing sidelong at San Francisco, following its lead like an awkward teenager modeling himself after the Fonz. "If you want to know what America will be like in two years," went the common phrase, "just look at California. And if you want to know where California's going, look at San Francisco."

That's probably not entirely *true,* Jack thought to himself as they rolled off the bridge and swung south of the downtown area. He'd grown up in southern California. He knew well that Hollywood was the foremost preacher of the values of this new age. Yet ever since Haight-Asbury had become the mecca of the Woodstock generation, since the hippies had gathered in Golden Gate Park for the "summer of love," since Anton LeVey had located his Church of Satan here, and Patty Hearst had been very publicly kidnapped, San Francisco had sneered at its smoggy southern rival. American values careened toward chaos, and this city proudly led the way!

Still, San Francisco is also the center of the Jesus Movement, Jack thought to himself as they headed across town toward the Golden Gate Bridge. Though they were but two young people in the midst of a world rushing headlong toward hell, he and his wife counted themselves members of that children's crusade. Jesus Christ gave them hope. Although the church they served as pastor and wife was only a tiny congregation threatening to expire at any minute, Jesus Christ gave them hope. Although Jack and Gloria were very different people with enormously different backgrounds, and the culture shock of this time and place put terrible stress on their love for one another, still: Jesus Christ gave them hope. *And,* he smiled ruefully, *even though I have a Hebrew test on Tuesday I'm certain I'm going to fail,* still: *Jesus Christ gives me hope! Now if the Lord would just give me a* sermon *for Sunday. . . .*

Jack's leg ached where Gloria's head rested, and he shifted position slightly to put the pressure at a different point. He was weary. They were still a half-hour's drive from the Marin County seminary campus where they lived, and he struggled to stay awake. He thought about waking Gloria up for company, but she looked so peaceful resting there. Her beautiful profile was almost hidden from him in the tangle of her black curls. With her long, black eyelashes and deep-tanned face, she looked like a mysterious, exotic princess from some European resort kingdom—that is, until her stopped-up nose made her sniffle and shift position. She'd been telling him all day she was afraid she was getting the flu, and he really hated to disturb her. He turned on the radio instead.

News reports blared from the speaker. "Invasion!" they proclaimed—and he grinned in instant recognition. These were 1930s-style news flashes, and the invasion was from Mars. That fit: It was Halloween night, and some local station was rebroadcasting Orson Welles' classic radio drama, "War of the Worlds." Having grown up watching "The Twilight Zone" and reading *Galaxy* magazine, Jack considered himself an avid science fiction fan. He'd even tried his hand at writing it during college. And while certain that his seminary classmates frowned judgmentally whenever he brought up the subject in conversation, he refused to see any inherent contradiction in a preacher liking science fiction. What was wrong with looking expectantly toward the future? Wasn't the Book of Revelation *filled* with exactly that? After all, they'd all liked Hal Lindsey's *The Late, Great Planet Earth!*

Once again Jack's imagination engaged. His lean, white Mustang became a starship as he glided out over the bay once again, this time on the Golden Gate Bridge. He settled back in his bucket seat to listen to the invasion from Mars, now afraid that they would arrive home before the program ended. They soon left the brilliant lights of the orange bridge behind them and started up the incline toward the rainbow tunnel—

He sat up suddenly, bouncing Gloria's head on his thigh. Had something just flashed over them? Something bright and fast and . . . *saucer*-shaped?

"What is it? What's wrong?" Gloria mumbled anxiously, still half-asleep. She often jerked awake thus, instantly ready to cope with any problem.

"Ummm—nothing," he mumbled. *Just my hyperactive imagination again,* he thought to himself, *responding to the images from the radio.*

Gloria needed no further explanation. She sank back down into her place and returned to dreamland. Jack smiled self-consciously and glanced at the rearview mirror. It was ridiculous, he knew, but he worried that some other driver might have seen that idiotic notion streak across his mind. As they flashed through the lighted tunnel and out into the dark night above Sausalito, he remembered the mocking news reports of the last week. Unidentified Flying Objects had been reported in increasing numbers from San Rafael to Novato. Jack snickered to himself. He turned the radio off, chuckling in embarrassment. "Flying saucers!" he whispered derisively under his breath. "Better to start thinking about that sermon—or that test!" He tried to rein in his imagination, but that was hard. That was always hard for Jack Brennen. . . .

Sunday was a lonely day. Gloria had indeed caught the flu. It seemed to Jack a far better way of expressing the facts would be to say that the flu had caught Gloria. She'd certainly done her best to elude it. Sick as she was, he'd had to leave her at home in bed and go on to church alone.

The morning drive across the bridge and down the peninsula had been totally uneventful—mornings usually were. San Francisco was an entirely different place in the daytime. Jack had paid no attention to his driving, for the little white Mustang seemed to know the way on its own. He'd concentrated instead on reviewing his hurriedly studied Sunday School lesson.

There'd been thirteen in Sunday School. Usually they had fourteen, but of course usually Gloria was with him. Four others had come to worship, making a grand congregation of sixteen to hear his sermon on the prodigal son. Once again, he'd gotten that feeling in the middle of his message that he was preaching to people who *weren't* there instead of to people who *were.* He'd really wished Gloria had been present to hear it. His wife was both his biggest fan and his sharpest critic, and he felt blind, somehow, without her.

Their little church was located down the San Francisco peninsula in a bedroom community not far from Stanford University. Since it was much too far to go home in the afternoon and then return for evening services, Jack spent the between-service hours the way he usually did: visiting the sick and the shut-ins, then taking a nap on a pew. *Fortunately,* he thought as he dozed off, *they are padded.*

Jack woke with a jerk and immediately sat up straight. His heart pounded. He glanced quickly around the darkened sanctuary, then glanced at his watch. Six o'clock—the sun was going down. In the pit of his stomach he felt that eerie sensation he'd always experienced in a darkened church building, ever since he was a child growing up in the church his father pastored. He called it the "Samuel syndrome," after the boy who'd heard God calling him by name as he slept in the temple. His seminary professors had given Jack a technical name for the feeling. It was the "in-break of the numinous," what Rudolf Otto described as "a dark abyss which is not accessible to our reason." Whatever it was called, it was always at these moments that Jack felt most keenly both the presence of God—and his own guilt.

Oh, it wasn't for any sin in particular that Jack felt guilty. In fact, he was probably about as caught up on his personal confession of wrongdoing as he'd ever been any time in his life. No, this was more that non-specific guilt of never feeling like he'd done enough, never feeling adequately prepared to preach, never being quite able to experience the fullness of God's grace himself, despite the fervor with which he preached it. "Lord?" he whispered to the darkness. In moments like this, Jack would not have been surprised to hear an audible answer.

None came—and he sighed. Then he asked himself: Was he sighing with disappointment, or with relief? What if God actually *did* speak to him? What if he were to see an angel? Gloria always said she longed to see an angel, but Jack wasn't so sure. After all—what would he say?

He got up and quickly turned on the lights—and the queasy feeling disappeared. He smiled a private, ironic smile. Nothing like chasing away the presence of the holy with a little garish fluorescence! He walked past the piano into the men's restroom and studied his reflection in the mirror. His hair was sticking up funny, and he ran some water on his comb and tried to correct that. He straightened his tie, then examined himself again: big nose, high cheekbones, bloodshot gray eyes, brownish-blonde hair, the bull neck that was his one legacy of playing college football. Yep, that was him. *If I were one of my congregation,* he thought to himself, *would I pay any attention to this guy?* Didn't matter, he shrugged. He was all they had. "All we can afford," he grumbled, imitating old Mr. McCoy's voice and mannerisms.

He wandered out to the fellowship hall to arrange a table for the after-service snack. He was not looking forward to it. Gloria wouldn't be here, and she was so much better in social settings than he. As he started setting up folding chairs he began to review the points of his evening sermon. Then he glanced at the window across the room and froze.

A stranger peered inside, his nose pressed flat against the glass. Evidently he hadn't yet seen Jack, for when their eyes met, the stranger froze too—then dropped out of sight. Jack ran to the window, but couldn't get it open far enough to look out. He could, however, hear the sound of running feet.

His heart was pounding again. *A thief?* he wondered. That's what old Mr. McCoy would surely think were Jack to tell him about this. Mr. McCoy was certain *every* student at the large high school across the street was trying to break into this building. "They're all drug addicts at that school," he would growl, "every one of 'em. Look at 'em! You can tell!"

It seemed to Jack that Mr. McCoy spent far more of his time thinking up new ways to keep people *out* of this church than he did encouraging people to come *into* it. Jack wondered if that wasn't a big part of the reason they only had fourteen who regularly attended. Then again, Mr. McCoy wasn't the first Christian Jack had met who thought that way; and he guessed if he remained in the ministry, Mr. McCoy wouldn't be the last.

No, he decided quickly, he wouldn't tell the old man about the face in the window. Next thing he knew they'd be voting to spend the missions offering on a new security system.

Nine people showed up that night, Mr. McCoy included. Jack stood up in front and led the singing, trying to show as much enthusiasm as if he were directing the choir at a Billy Graham crusade. Then he began his message, a continuation of the prodigal son story, focusing on the negative attitude of the older brother. He was wondering whether Mr. McCoy was even listening to him when the stranger walked in the back door.

The congregation sat numbed by shock. No one but church members ever came to evening services. No one. And the boy didn't sit down, either. He just stood in the back of the sanctuary, looking at Jack expectantly.

Jack stopped preaching. No one was paying any attention to him by then, anyway. They were all staring at the boy—especially Mr. McCoy. And yes, Jack had to admit, the kid *did* look like the stereotypical addict. His hair was long and greasy, he wore sunglasses and round-toed boots, and he'd zipped up his black leather jacket all the way to the throat. Jack noticed the boy had his hands in his pockets, and the barest hint of fear flickered through him. Did this teen have a gun hidden in there? Was he about to rob this whole congregation, then shoot them and leave them for dead?

"You have no cause to be afraid of me," the boy said, his eyes meeting Jack's levelly.

"We're not afraid of you," Jack lied in that unctuous, pious-sounding tone of voice that made himself sick whenever he found himself using it. "Can . . . we help you?" he asked, struggling to get more honesty into his statement.

"Can I talk to you privately?" the boy asked, and Jack quickly scanned the faces of the congregation.

"Sure," he answered, confident that at least the majority of the group would support this sudden change in worship plans. Most of them, after all, really did care about people and genuinely wanted to help others. Here was an opportunity for real ministry that had walked right in their front door! "Come on," Jack said, motioning for the boy to follow him into a Sunday School classroom.

Was he a boy? He looked to be about thirteen or fourteen, but Jack knew he was terrible about guessing ages.

"I'm fifteen," the boy volunteered.

Jack struggled to keep from looking startled by the statement as he joked: "You read my mind. I was just wondering about that."

"I know," said the boy. "I can do that."

Jack hesitated. "Do what?" he asked.

"Read minds."

Jack licked his lips—then said, "Oh."

"That's why they're after me."

"Oh," Jack said again. He'd already had the course in pastoral counseling—"holy psychology," someone in class had called it. And here was this strange-looking teenager whose name he didn't even know making paranoid statements about people being out to get him—

"You have no *need* to know my name, and I'm *not* paranoid," the boy said brutally. "And as for those who pursue me, I don't remember saying they were people. Did I?"

A chill began to crawl slowly up Jack's back, and for the first time he wished he was still out there preaching a boring sermon instead of sitting back here with a young weirdo who claimed to read—

"I don't *claim* to read minds. I *do* read minds, Mr. Brennen. Oh, excuse me," the boy mocked. "I suppose that should be 'Reverend' Brennen, shouldn't it?"

"Brother Brennen is what my people call me—"

"Oh, you're a 'brother,' are you?" the obnoxious boy said in the same sarcastic tone of voice. "And you have your own people? My, my. Do they know they belong to you?"

Jack let his pastoral demeanor sag and frowned. "What do you want?" he asked sharply. To his surprise, the tough kid winced at his words. Had they been that harsh? "What?" he asked more gently.

The kid peered at him a moment, then suddenly announced, "You know, you're genuinely kind, despite all your cynical doubts about yourself. I need a gentle mind near me for a few moments. Is that okay?"

Jack was—in that one single instant—complimented, perplexed, concerned, and suspicious. There were probably even a few more reactions in there as well. He was so busy trying to untangle all of them that the only word of response he could muster was another, "Oh."

"Don't try," the boy sighed, propping up his head with an arm on a knee and turning his gaze slowly to the window.

Jack couldn't help himself. He tried anyway: "Who *is* after you? *What* is after you?"

"Doesn't matter," the boy said wearily. Jack suddenly had the impression that—in some ways, at least—this lad was even older than old Mr. McCoy. "They would never think to look for me here. Besides," the boy added with a grim smile, "they can't come into a church."

"Hmmm," Jack nodded as he pondered. That meant the boy couldn't be pursued by demons, he thought cynically to himself. There'd been plenty of those present in *every* congregation he'd ever belonged to, and he could certainly vouch for the fact they were active in *this* one. The boy laughed aloud and studied Jack's face with an amused curiosity that Jack found slightly embarrassing. "What?" he asked.

"You have a very low view of your own congregation, did you know that?"

Jack shrugged—a bit defensively. "I have an *honest* view of my peop—my congre—this church," he finally finished. Incredible as it seemed, this boy really did seem to be reading his mind, and Jack didn't like it.

"Nobody does," the kid sighed, slumping back in his chair and rolling his blue eyes up toward the ceiling. Jack couldn't prevent himself from thinking that the boy looked like an orphaned waif at that moment. He felt genuinely sorry for the kid. Suddenly the boy's gaze darted down from the ceiling to stab aggressively into Jack's. "Don't pity me!" he snarled.

"Is it pity to care about somebody?" Jack responded calmly. Threatened as he was by this stranger's apparent ability to read his thoughts, he was nevertheless a minister—a "caregiver" they called it at school. And though it was a new idea to him, Jack was already beginning to imagine just how frightening possessing such a "gift" could prove. Why, the CIA would probably *love* to get hold of—

"Them and every *other* organization of spooks on this godforsaken planet!" the boy growled bitterly. Jack tried to shield his disapproval, but there was nowhere to hide his thoughts: "Yes, I *did* say godforsaken!" the mindreader said savagely. "Look around! What Viet Nam hadn't already destroyed in this country has been ruined by Watergate! People are being butchered in Cambodia! The Symbionese Liberation Army isn't the first blossom of racial revolution in this country and it won't be the last, and yet you want to stand up in front of 'your people' and tell them that there's actually a God, and that He actually cares about people?"

Jack heard this respectfully, but there was no question what his reply to the angry tirade would be. *Yes,* he thought quietly—honestly. He realized his eyes had drifted down to the linoleum-tiled floor, and he glanced quickly back up at the boy's face. The kid was staring at him, apparently incredulous. "What's wrong?" Jack asked, a slight smile tugging up the corners of his thin lips. He thought he knew . . .

"What do you call that?" the mindreader asked.

"Call what?" Jack responded, still certain he knew.

"That ability you have to simply dive from the grim realities of this horrible planet into . . . hope." The boy said these words with a sober gravity that bordered on . . . what? Respect, maybe?

No, spiritual pride, Jack reminded himself, plunging quickly onward to answer, "Faith. We call it faith."

Mr. McCoy couldn't have chosen a worse moment to pound on the door. Just as this powerfully gifted young man was about to be challenged by the claims of Christ Jesus as reflected in Jack, the suspicious old deacon spoiled the moment by shouting "Are you all right in there, preacher?"

"I'm fine, Mr. McCoy," Jack called back, trying hard to keep the frustration out of his tone of voice. He was watching the boy's face. The mindreader grinned sarcastically.

"He thinks I'm a drug dealer. He thinks I'm going to stab you and steal your money."

The thought leapt into Jack's mind unbidden: *On what this church is paying me,* what *money?* The mind-reading teen read the thought immediately and gleefully cackled. Jack felt his face flush, then clamped his teeth together to keep from saying what he was thinking. The boy cackled harder.

"Are you certain you're all right, preacher?" Mr. McCoy demanded, pounding on the door again for emphasis. "He sounds to me like he's having a trip or something—like he's high!"

Jack sighed deeply, and rolled his eyes around to the door. Back in the summer during Vacation Bible School some rambunctious local child had kicked a hole through its veneer into its hollow core. Four months ago—and they'd not found the money to fix it yet. Nor would they, he knew—for there were a dozen other similar scars upon the building that had gone unpatched for ages. Every time it rained the flat roof over the sanctuary collected standing water, which then proceeded to leak through onto the pews. Somehow, at this moment, Jack saw that hole in the door as symbolic of all that was wrong with this church. These people would never let their own houses look this ramshackle. Mr. McCoy washed and waxed his Cadillac every Sunday afternoon—that's why he could never go visiting. And yet the congregation seemed oblivious to the state of this house of God. Jack saw it as a symptom of something deeper, a spiritual problem he'd not been able to get his people to engage. Why did they even come to this place every Sunday? Did they really care? "I'm all right, Mr. McCoy," he called, forcing an unfelt cheeriness into his voice. "Really, I am. We'll be out in just a minute." *And what am I going to tell them when we do?* Jack thought. *That this scruffy-looking teenaged boy can read minds and is being chased by the CIA?*

"You could tell them what they want to hear," the boy smiled grimly. "That I'm a drug dealer being chased by my connections, and that I've run into your ugly little church to get 'saved.' That *is* what you were getting ready to try to do a minute ago, isn't it? 'Save' me?"

"Do you really know what we mean by that word?" Jack asked, trying to be as direct as possible.

"If I wanted to," the kid snarled, "believe me, I could read your mind on the subject." He sat back in the child-sized chair, laced his fingers behind his neck, and closed his eyes. The boy's shift in position caused Jack to notice something he didn't want to notice, that he didn't want to think about—but did. How long had it been since this kid had bathed?

"Yeah, I stink," the mindreader growled. "You think your people would find me a suitable prospect to get 'saved' in your church?" Jack didn't have to answer. The boy already knew. *How many minds could he read at once?* Jack wondered to himself. With his eyes still closed and his head leaning back, the boy answered, "Only one at a time, but I can shift from mind to mind at will." Suddenly his eyes fluttered open, and he fixed his unsettling gaze upon Jack. "Why don't you tell them what they want to hear? If they want to think me a drug dealer, let 'em. It's true, in any case. Here." He reached into his pocket, and once again Jack fought the fear of being stabbed or shot. "I told you," the teenager scolded, "I'm not going to kill you. Well, I guess you *could* kill yourself with these—if you wanted to," the boy mocked. He held up three marijuana cigarettes, very neatly rolled with the ends professionally twisted. The kid grinned. "How is it, Mr. Preacher, that you know when a reefer has been well made?"

Jack flushed. There were aspects of his past life that he had never revealed to his congregation. "Haven't always been the pure little preacher's kid, have you?" the mindreader grinned.

"If you really think *any* preacher's kid is pure," Jack said flatly, "then you sure haven't read many of their minds." He pointed to the neatly rolled joints. "What do you plan to do with those?"

"I'd planned to smoke 'em," the boy growled. "But if you want to take them and flush 'em down the toilet, that's all right too." His eyes sought out Jack's and he murmured, "It's true, you know. I really would *like* to get 'saved.' I simply don't believe you or your Jesus can *do* that."

And I believe Jesus can, Jack thought, wordlessly taking the marijuana cigarettes from the boy.

"That's exactly why I'm sitting here with you instead of somewhere else," said the mindreader. "Because I know you really do believe that. What I don't know is whether *your* believing it can do anything for me."

That was a problem. Jack didn't know either. He and several other students had been debating the differences between Calvinism and Arminianism last week, arguing the theological merits of free choice versus predestination. Growing up, he had always been pretty Arminian, he guessed—if *you* chose to be saved, God would save you. But he'd had a friend in college who had convinced him that not everyone can "have faith." Some people, it seemed, just didn't have the capacity to believe. Was this the central fact of Calvinism—that God only gave the gift of faith to His elect?

All of this raced through his mind before he realized he was thinking about it. Once he caught himself, he gazed wide-eyed at the mindreader, to see if the boy had caught any of it.

"I don't even know your terminology," the boy grumbled, shaking his head. "Give me enough time and I could figure it out—but weren't you trying to figure out what you were going to tell the man outside?"

"I guess so," Jack nodded.

"Look, I'm going to need some help getting out of this area. Couldn't you tell them you're taking me to a drug treatment center or something and then let me go home with you?"

"Go home with me," Jack repeated without expression. Immediately his mind shot to Gloria, sick in bed—how could he bring home a guest? Worse, his mind raced on, he knew nothing about this stranger, what if he should—

"The worst thing I'd do to you is leave a ring around your bathtub," the boy said sarcastically, interrupting his thoughts. "Never mind. I can see there's nothing to all that Christian baloney about my being a stranger and you taking me in. If you'll just give me a ride to the other side of the bay, I'll find other lodgings for the night."

Other thoughts now tumbled through Jack's mind—thoughts of entertaining angels unaware, of Tolstoy's story of Jesus' visit to the cobbler, of past guilts for not having been more of a good Samaritan to people in genuine need. "Of course you'll come home with me!"

"I'm not an angel, believe me," the kid snickered.

Jack glanced back at the marijuana in his hand. "Are you sure you want to give these up?" Jack asked, and the min-dreader shrugged.

"Small price to pay for a clean getaway," he grinned, and Jack studied the boy's eyes, still trying to decide whether he dared help him.

Yes, he *did* dare. Jack stood up and opened the door. Mr. McCoy met him with a frown, which turned into a knowing smirk when Jack held up the three joints. "I told you," he said gruffly. Jack didn't want to hear whatever the boy might say to Mr. McCoy about the contents of his mind. He brushed past the deacon into the hallway and stepped immediately into the sanctuary.

The saintly ladies who were the backbone of this tiny church were gathered before the altar, doing exactly what he'd expected they would be. They were huddled in a circle, their arms linked and their heads bowed and prayers flowing fervently from their lips. At that moment, Jack felt bathed in blessing. Yes, it was a tiny, struggling church, and he had to wonder sometimes why the Lord hadn't provided more in the way of male leadership. But there was a sweet spirit here—there always had been—and the reason why could be clearly seen. These ladies knew how to pray.

They looked up as they heard him come out the door, and he greeted them with a smile and held up the drugs like a trophy. He felt just a little hypocritical doing so—after all, the boy had been rather flippant, and there really hadn't seemed to be any repentance for any action involved. Still, the young man *had* voiced a real interest in the faith, and that had to count for something. Certainly he spoke no untruth when he announced, "He's asked me to flush these down the toilet and to take him to a drug rehabilitation center."

There was an explosion of joy from the ladies of prayer that he didn't join. Instead he headed on past them to the restroom, closed the door behind him, opened the lid—and hesitated. For the briefest of moments he heard the Evil One's tempting voice—*Why not keep them and smoke them yourself?* Then he laughed aloud and dropped them into the bowl as he flushed it—hard. He heard answering laughter from the other side of the wall. Yes, the mindreader had heard.

This is terrible, Jack thought. He was smiling, for he could see the irony of being forced by this stranger to be totally honest with himself in this place where he constantly preached about integrity. But the fact was that no one could stand to have their every thought exposed to the light of day! *Is this what judgment is like?* he wondered as he watched the last of the weed disappear with a swirl. Once again the thought flashed across his mind. Was this an angel, come to test him? Again, he heard laughter through the wall.

Jack came out of the restroom beaming brightly and announced, "It's past eight o'clock, and I think this experience has certainly been far more thought-provoking than the sermon I'd prepared for this evening. I'm going to take our friend on with me into town—"

"You're going to let him ride in your car, preacher?" Mr. McCoy demanded; and while he didn't go ahead and add the words, his tone of voice added them for him: *Are you crazy?*

"I sure am, Mr. McCoy, but there *is* something I would like to ask of all of you. You've been in a spirit of prayer while this boy and I have been talking. Would you continue to pray for us as we go?" Without awaiting a reply, Jack grabbed his Bible off the podium and motioned for the mindreader to follow him. They were out the door and into the foyer before anyone had a chance to respond, and Jack was already fishing his keys out of his pocket. The mindreader lingered in the doorway while Jack jumped into the Mustang and started it. The boy then ran to sling open the long, low door, and hopped in and shrunk down out of sight—easy to do in those bucket seats—as Jack wheeled out of the church parking lot and up the main avenue toward the freeway. Within moments they were flying up the peninsula on Interstate 280, fleeing from—what?

"You don't want to know," the boy said laconically.

"I beg your pardon, but I do," Jack replied.

"You *think* you do." The boy had crawled up from the floorboards by now, and gazed stoically out the front window. "Believe me, you don't."

"Why not?" Jack argued. He was letting his pastoral demeanor slide away, leaving in place the cockiness of an A-rank graduate student—they were very different personas.

"Because the more you know, the more trouble you'll be in for helping me. Come on, you've seen enough spy flicks to know what I'm talking about!"

That was probably true. Jack *had* seen a number of spy movies. The trouble was, he had naturally imagined himself in the role of the spy, dashing about the world, saving it for democracy. His enjoyment of that genre sometimes made him wonder about his sense of calling to the foreign mission field. In some odd way, did he see missionaries as God's super-spies, making the world safe through Christ Jesus?

"You have a big imagination," the mindreader announced flatly. Jack threw back his head and guffawed. "Why is that funny?" the boy asked.

"If you only knew how many times I've heard *that*," Jack grinned, shaking his head. "There are those who don't consider it 'seemly' for a preacher to have an imagination."

"Then there are those who think *all* preachers must have *enormous* imaginations already, to swallow all this God garbage." Jack winced inwardly, but said nothing. "Sorry if that offends you," the boy shrugged. "Actually, I've cleaned up my language a *lot* just to avoid offending you." The kid rolled his head around to look out the side window and down on the lights surrounding the inner bay. "You really believe that there's some God that cares about all those idiots down there—knows every one by name—and worries that they're committing adultery with their neighbors, or cheating on their income taxes. I find that amazing."

Jack thought a moment. "And I find it amazing that you can read my every thought, yet apparently don't seem to wonder where this special gift *comes* from."

"Hmm?" the boy said, looking around at him with apparent surprise. "Now that's a new line of thought for you," he said, a slightly mocking edge to his words. "Where do *you* suppose it comes from? God? The angels?"

"Where *does* it originate?" Jack asked back, just as mockingly. "Do you have any idea?"

"Of course I do."

"But you're not saying?"

"No." There was a long, empty pause between them.

"For my own good, I take it?" Jack sneered. The further he got from his church field, the less unctuous he became. He liked himself better this way—it was more honest. He wished church people allowed more honesty from their preachers. . . .

"Yes," the boy said. "It's for your own good. Take the next exit."

"What?" Jack said, sitting up in his seat. "That's not the way to my house—"

"We're not going to your house. At least I'm not. Turn NOW!" the boy commanded, and there was so much authority in his voice that Jack did just that. Jack had run up and down this road for years, and he thought he knew the area well. The fact was, however, he only knew that narrow strip of asphalt. Once they were off the freeway Jack wasn't certain exactly where they were. He certainly didn't know where they were going! Gloria would kill him—

"She'll forgive you," the boy growled, and then he barked, "Turn left here!"

Jack did. He glanced in the rearview mirror—was somebody following them? No . . . Not that he could see. . . . Then a chill scampered up his spine as he recalled that UFO he thought he'd seen flash above him near the Golden Gate Bridge just two nights—

"Would you cap your vibrant imagination and *drive?!*" the kid demanded with a sudden, strange desperation. Jack didn't appreciate being spoken to like that—especially in his own car—but he said nothing and drove. This curious adventure would all be over soon.

After twisting and weaving through the streets of south San Francisco, they evidently were approaching their destination. Jack's odd passenger seemed to be relaxing. "Next street," the boy said quietly, "turn right." Jack shrugged and signaled. The boy asked, "Do you know where you are? Nineteenth Street is that way," he pointed. Jack nodded, feeling a sudden weariness that seemed to seep all the way down into his bones. He glanced around at the neighborhood, trying to place it. Hadn't he been here before?

"Here's the house," the boy said, his hand already on the handle. Jack slowed to a stop at the curb. "Thanks. See ya." The kid bounded out of the car then, and charged up the walk toward a huge, foreboding house all painted in black—

Terror seized Jack; it gripped him by the throat and threatened to crush the breath from him. Yes, he'd been here—on a mission tour with a class from the seminary, but that had been in broad daylight, and even *then* this black-painted house had made him shudder. It was the home of Anton LeVey—the international headquarters for the Church of Satan.

He hit the gas and got a wheel from the feisty little Mustang—the first time he had *ever* done that! He steered madly back toward 19th Street and the roads he knew, his heart pounding, his hands quivering. "Oh, honey," he mumbled to Gloria under his breath, "here I come—"

It would be another twenty minutes before he could get home. Until then he cruised the radio dial for some news, hummed along with Crosby, Stills and Nash as they sang of the whales in "Wind on the Water," and tried his best to clear his mind of the haunting image of that house—sitting there, just like any other, upon a San Francisco street. And he prayed.

"Lord, Lord, Lord," he hollered, rolling down the window to let the frosty night air smack him in the face. "What was *that*, what *was* that, *what* in the world was that!" A demon, certainly—wasn't it? Didn't it have to be? "Lord, what *was* that!" He was heading past the Presidio now, on the approach to the Golden Gate, about to shake off this pervasive sense of dread that had seized him. He was on a road he knew, heading home—he'd be there soon. . . .

He crossed the bridge on the fly, studiously avoiding looking out to either one side or the other. There could be a whole fleet of flying saucers behind him, but if they wanted him to see them they'd have to sit down on that white line on the road.

At last, he turned in to the seminary campus, drove up to his apartment, and stopped the engine. He took a deep breath, rolled up the window, grabbed his Bible, and went inside.

"Hi, Sweetie," Gloria called from the bedroom as he locked the door behind him. "How was church? Did I miss anything?"

"Not much," he said.

Well, how was he ever going to *explain a thing like that?*

Jack put the episode out of mind. So well, in fact, that he managed to forget about it for twenty years. . . .

Chapter Two

Into the wardrobe, down the rabbit hole, over the rainbow, and through the looking glass

On Saturday morning Dr. John Brennen drove his van toward the center of Louisville—to the seminary. This was unusual, of course. He preferred to spend his Saturdays—the early part of them, anyway—in bed. But he'd agreed to lead a seminar at the annual missions conference on "The Calling of God," so here he was in his uniform of suit and tie, winding his way toward work.

They'd lived in Kentucky almost a decade now—more, if he counted his time in the Ph.D. program. In fact, apart from the two years they'd spent in Africa as missionaries, Jack and Gloria had lived here most of their adult lives. After years of living in a small house near the campus, they'd moved to the outskirts of town about a year and a half ago. It was a much longer commute, but it did give Jack a few minutes of quiet contemplation time before arriving for class. This was usually sufficient to help him get his thoughts focused on the first class of the day.

Today he was mentally reviewing the notes he'd prepared for this morning's conference when something happened that shocked him upright in his bucket seat. He had suddenly passed a hitchhiker on the side of the road. Jack realized immediately that this was the mindreader who had walked into his Bay Area church nineteen—or was it twenty?—years before. And he was still a boy! Dr. John Brennen wore bifocals now, and though his hair hung down in his face, there was a lot less of it to hang. The mindreader, however, still looked fifteen—the same apparent age as he'd been the last time Jack had seen him.

He gulped in shock, surprise, and some degree of understandable fear. After all, his previous encounter with this person had left him anxious and afraid. He drove on past, pretending for a moment he hadn't seen what he'd seen. But if Dr. John Brennen had learned anything in the years it had taken him to reach forty, it was that he never did himself any good by trying to lie to himself. That had been the mindreader back there, certainly. And there must be a reason.

Jack sighed deeply, turned the van around, and went back. When he stopped, the hitchhiker immediately climbed into the front. Jack couldn't bring himself to speak. He just hit the accelerator and started forward.

Why are you following me? Jack thought directly to the mindreader. "Isn't that a little egocentric, to assume I'm following you?" the boy retorted.

Then this is a coincidence? Jack thought accusingly.

"Why not?" the boy shrugged, crossing his arms across his chest and leaning back.

Jack thought, *You don't look a day older than you were when I dropped you off in front of the satanic church.*

"Maybe I just live right," the kid smirked. Then he added, "The years haven't been quite so kind to you!"

Jack couldn't prevent himself from reviewing the long years that had intervened since their last meeting—and for the first time, he spoke aloud. "No, I guess they haven't."

"Still 'trusting Jesus'?" the boy mocked.

Yes, Jack answered in his mind—and he meant it. It had been a difficult life at times—particularly the two years spent as missionaries in Nigeria. The years prior to that had been easier, certainly, but they too had seemed hard at the time. Graduate school, examinations, dissertation writing, missionary training—each had been difficult in its own way. But through it all there had been this one constant: Yes, he and Gloria trusted Jesus. Maybe they'd missed the Lord's guidance a time or two. Doubtless they had failed Him in various ways. Certainly there were attitudes they each held that wouldn't be pleasing to the Lord. But they trusted Him. God had, after all, blessed them with places to live and places to serve and with a beautiful daughter who seemed daily to grow in grace. Yes, they had been blessed by God. And they would keep on trusting Him.

The boy's cocky, caustic manner seemed to melt away. "I can't believe it," he muttered.

I can *believe it,* Jack thought toward him. *Not only can I . . . I do.*

"All right, all right," said the kid, waving him off and looking out the window. "Where are we going?"

"I'm going to the seminary to lead a conference on God's calling. Do you want to come?" He really didn't mean it when he said it. This boy frightened him. The fact that he didn't seem to have aged in twenty years gave him the creeps. And he really couldn't quite buy the idea that this second meeting was a coincidence. To his surprise—and discomfort— the boy shrugged and answered:

"Sure."

So it was that Jack brought a young guest with him to the Saturday morning missions conference—a teen dressed in jeans and a leather jacket, his shades perched on top of his greasy hair. He listened as Jack spoke from the Book of Genesis about Joseph, who told his arrogant dream to his brothers and as a result ended up flat on his back at the bottom of a pit. Jack felt there was a good reason the Holy Spirit had directed him to these passages. The missions conference was often attended by bright, "promising" young college students who were examining their sense of God's leadership in their lives. From his own experience Jack knew that being spiritually promising was far from being spiritually mature. As God matured Joseph through trouble, Jack preached, so God matures us through our difficulties—if we let Him.

The mindreader sat on the front row throughout the conference, silently taking everything in. While Jack found the boy's probing gaze to be extremely unsettling, he managed not to let it bother him too much. He focused his attention on his college-aged listeners instead, trying to make certain that they understood every point of his message. Would the boy understand too? Only by the grace of God and by the power of His Holy Spirit. Jack knew full well that he couldn't convince anybody to believe anything. Only God could change a person's heart.

At the close of the conference there was a line of prospective students to meet and greet, and Jack forgot about his odd guest as he tried to focus on each new student individually. But after the last one had apparently gotten every question answered and left the room, there was the mindreader, still seated on the front row, watching. Jack took a deep breath, scratched the back of his neck, and said, "I'm on my way to my office. Coming?" Without a word, the boy followed.

As all of his students knew, Jack Brennen's office was a maze of stacks of books, periodicals, file folders, and videotape boxes. Jack tended to file by pile and only excavated his desk when he was afraid he didn't know *which* pile contained something he expected to need soon. Otherwise, he was content to let the sediment accumulate; it seemed to provide him with a sense of permanency. He expertly navigated the piles toward his chair and flopped into it, then gestured at the one place someone else might sit without fear of a stack toppling over onto him or her. As the boy sat, Jack laced his fingers behind his head and said, "I've thought of you many times over the years."

"But only long enough to put me out of your mind," the kid answered. He was, of course, correct.

"I had the impression that's what you wanted me to do," Jack responded honestly. "Ahh—do you have a name? It's a lot easier for me to remember people when I have a name I can attach to their faces."

"You can call me Ben," the boy answered flatly. He, too, laced his fingers behind his head, leaning back to study the patterns on the ceiling.

"So, Ben," Jack asked, his weariness from the long week and this early morning conference making him feel both relaxed and a little daring, "are you running from 'them' again?"

"Who's them?" Ben asked.

"I don't know. You never told me." Jack smiled slightly. "You implied it would be safer for me if I *didn't* know."

"Still would," the boy mumbled. Suddenly he stood up, fixed his eyes on Jack and said, "Look, I can't do this, okay? I'm sorry. You'll never see me again."

With that, he turned on his heel and swept out of the office, the speed of his departure leaving papers fluttering everywhere. For some reason, Jack really didn't mind.

He had a deep sense of relief, as if he'd just dodged an onrushing truck, or been passed over as a potential victim by a mugger. Still, he couldn't help but pray for the strange boy who had just walked out of his office and—apparently—his life. "Take care of him, Lord. Protect him from them—whomever *they* are."

Sometimes, of course, God uses us to answer our own prayers. . . .

* * *

The summer seemed hotter than usual. It was certainly wetter than usual for those unfortunate folks who lived along the Mississippi River. Yet the record flooding that spilled out over the Midwest seemed almost commonplace in a year that had seen record damage from hurricanes in Florida, Louisiana, and Hawaii; record rains in southern California; and record damage from snowstorms in the Rockies. Dr. John Brennen peered through his bifocals at the television, watching CNN recount the damage and shaking his head. It was weird. The youth at church were already organizing another relief drive. It seemed the world had needed so *many* such drives this year. . . .

In Louisville, Kentucky, it had just been hot. Not as hot as Nigeria, of course—but it was hot enough, certainly. The farmers needed rain. They would have happily taken some of that precious water that flooded the Mississippi valley. *The neighbor's tomatoes could use some too,* Jack thought, absently rubbing the back of his neck. It was tense and tight from sitting hunched over a computer half the night writing Bible studies for young people. He was excited about the new formats being developed for use with teens and felt honored to have the chance to write for them. It was hard to break through to that age group in this decade. Then again, hadn't it always been so? He knew his parents' generation had had a horrible time getting through to his own. "And now we baby boomers are trying to get through to the MTV generation," he said to the television. The lady who was reading the news didn't acknowledge his comment: She just kept on reading, exactly the same copy she'd read half an hour before, and the half hour before that. . . .

"And if I sit here any longer," he told her, "I'll hear you read it again in another half hour." He hoisted himself out of his arm chair, stretched, and made his way upstairs to where Gloria napped. He thought he might lay down and nap some himself. One of the wonderful things about being a teacher was the opportunity to spend long, lazy summer days in rest and reflection. Of course, since he also served a small country church as part-time pastor, few of his days went *completely* unscheduled. He had to smile at the term "part-time pastor." Anyone who'd ever been in the ministry knew no church staff position was anything but *full* time to the folks. Still, the Lord had blessed him with more than enough days to linger after breakfast and enjoy the morning.

He decided he *would* lie down again later, but right now he would take a walk in the woods. Something about the smell of pine needles on a warm summer day reminded him of happy days as a kid at church camp. Usually his daughter would walk down to the woods with him; but since she liked to stay up far into the night painting or listening to the radio, he felt certain she wasn't up yet. He would just go by himself today.

He slipped on his walking shoes and went over to his sleeping wife to tell her where he was going. Since their years in Nigeria, they had made a pact to stay in constant contact with one another. When he was on the road, he usually called her two or three times a day. When he took a walk in the neighborhood, he always told her first. "Honey," he murmured, and she shifted in bed and opened one eye to look at him.

"Hmmm?"

A wisp of black hair hung down across her face, and he smiled and brushed it aside. Sure she was getting older—who wasn't who was alive? But she was still a doll. He told her quietly, "I'm going to walk down to the woods."

"Okay. Lock the door, would you?"

"I will. I love you—"

"I love you too," she said.

He kissed her cheek. In the days and nights ahead he would often feel a melancholy joy that those had been their last words to each other.

He closed the door behind him, locked it with the key, then set out across his neighbor's backyard toward the little forest. They were relatively new to this subdivision. While Gloria had been more interested in the house itself, the thing that had drawn him to this place was the "city park." It consisted of a creek meandering through a small, wooded valley on its way to the Ohio River. Small as it was, bounded on two sides by rows of houses and on the other two by expressways, still it seemed to him one of the most peaceful spots on God's earth. Its edge was a brisk, half-mile walk from his back door, and on a warm day like this he loved to plunge downward into the trees. To Jack it felt more refreshing than a dive into a pool.

He snapped his fingers in momentary frustration. He'd forgotten again to bring a trash bag to pick up the beer cans some insensitive lout had discarded along the paths. He and his daughter had seen them a few days before, and she had blamed certain local teenagers. If it were up to her, she had informed him, she would skip being a teenager entirely. He'd only listened and smiled. To be honest, he wasn't in any hurry for her to grow up. If she wanted to walk down here again in the late afternoon, maybe they could remember to bring a trash bag then.

There were three paths down to the creek, all of them steep enough to force him to lean backwards and clomp his feet down carefully to keep from falling. Once he reached the meadow at the bottom, however, the park flattened out. Then it became an easy stroll along the tickling brook, which was bridged at intervals by plank walkways. At this end of the park the water hadn't yet joined the main stream, and it was choked with large, flat lily pads. He couldn't remember where, exactly, but sometime during one of the family vacations of his childhood he'd seen a pond covered with lily pads. It lived on in his imagination as one of the most exotic sights he'd ever seen. He stood for a moment on a bridge looking down into the dark water, listening to the birds chirping against the backdrop of the brook's gentle trickle. He realized that he was happy, and thought that this particular morning seemed like a little preview of heaven—

Then he looked up, and there was Ben. "Ben," he blurted out. The old anxiety churned in his stomach once again. "I . . . I hadn't expected to see you again. . . . "

Something in the look on Ben's face told him the boy felt just as anxious about this meeting as he did. "That's what I told you, I know," the teenager nodded, "and I want you to know I'm sorry."

"You're sorry for what?" Jack asked, but the twisting tightness in his gut told him he didn't really want to know.

"You've been chosen—and I'm sorry."

"Chosen for what?" Jack frowned. He really had no plans to wait for a reply. He was about to sprint off the other end of the bridge and up the pathway, to run back to the safety of his house and his wife and his bed, and to take that nap he should have already been taking! Unfortunately, his legs wouldn't move. It was as if they'd suddenly forgotten how.

"You've been chosen to be taken," Ben sighed. Then he added, "And since you seem to think so highly of confession, I'll confess it to you: I'm the one who chose you."

"But . . . what . . .?" Now his legs *were* moving, carrying him toward Ben and off the bridge. No, that wasn't quite accurate. He glanced down to see his legs remaining just where they'd been, frozen in position. Instead, he was floating along about an inch above the planks. He was sorry now he'd looked down, for the very realization made him sick to his stomach.

Ben fell in step beside him as Jack floated—and Ben walked—down the creek towards the "green." Here the city elders had cut a swath in the trees to open up a spot large enough for community picnics and family reunions. It was about thirty yards across, roughly circular—and right now it was occupied by what could only be described as a flying saucer. Not that it was currently flying: Jack simply assumed that such a machine couldn't have gotten here any other way.

As if he was an outside observer monitoring the reactions of a stranger, Jack watched himself respond to this incredible occurrence. The most remarkable thing he noticed was just how ordinary everything seemed. The birds sang, the creek babbled, a slight warm breeze rustled the treetops, and he floated aboard a UFO. After all, such things happened every day, right? He always read the covers of those silly newspapers in the checkout lanes, and from what his inquiring mind had observed, he figured he must be in the minority of Americans—those who *hadn't* been abducted. Up until this moment, that is. . . .

He floated up the corny-looking gangplank, thinking just how much better Hollywood props looked than the real thing. These creatures needed to hire Stephen Spielberg as a design consultant. He managed to shift his head around enough to look at the hull of the vessel, and marveled at how dull and ordinary its surface looked.

"Titanium-silicon weave," Ben told him, sounding just a touch defensive. "Far lighter—and stronger—than it looks."

Jack nodded, just as he might have nodded to a tour guide giving him this information as he walked aboard a new attraction at Disneyland. Still, he couldn't help but feel strangely let down. He would have expected something a little more spectacular.

"That's like looking at unexploded fireworks and saying 'I'm not impressed.' You haven't seen it at night, Jack. They can make it look like *anything*: a dancing triangle, a whirling disk, a pulsating, organic blimp—even a stupendous city."

They were aboard now. Jack heard the door close behind him with an electric buzz and a final *thunk* as it slammed shut. He wasn't afraid, exactly. . . .

Actually, it was worse than that. Jack was not allowing himself to even *think* about how much this all terrified him. The turmoil in the pit of his stomach, however, reminded him that his body already *knew*.

Delaying his inevitable panic just a little longer, Jack's eyes devoured the insides of the spacecraft with the avid curiosity of a ten-year-old. For such a comparatively small vehicle it appeared to have a hugely complex interior. Several passageways branched off to either side of this one, their purposes clearly labeled above their doorways in illuminated pink lettering. He couldn't read it, however. It was written in no alphabet he'd ever seen. Jack considered himself widely read in the area of ancient languages—he'd passed both Greek and Hebrew, even if he *couldn't* read either one without a lexicon—yet he felt certain that no civilization in recorded history had ever used such symbols. As he gazed up at one such sign, his terror finally engulfed him.

He was lost. He was trapped. He was captive on an unidentified flying object, and he would never see his beloved wife again! "Gloria!" he screamed, as loudly as he could—to no effect. He really could hardly even hear himself yell. The acoustics within this craft totally dampened the sound of his voice. Despite his terror and helplessness, some part of him couldn't help but be impressed. Jack grabbed his ears and shouted at anyone who might be listening, "What are you doing to me?" He realized it was a stupid question, not worth answering. It was quite obvious what they were doing to him. They were abducting him. "Why?" he shouted, turning around to look at Ben, discovering as he did so that his feet again touched the ground—or at least they touched the surface of the flight deck. "Why!" he shouted again, and this time he reached out to grab the boy by his collar and lifted *him* off the surface for a change. That was a mistake. He knew it immediately.

Pain coiled around his chest and stung him all the way down to the hips. He dropped the boy and doubled over, crossing his arms to hug himself as he crumpled to his knees. As quickly as it had come, the pain abated, leaving only tingling nerve endings. For several moments thereafter they continued to tingle, as if asking one another if they'd *really* just experienced what they thought they had. When Jack managed to clear his watering eyes and look up, he saw Ben being hustled down one of the corridors and out of sight by an alien. Another alien stood before him, peering down at him.

Yes, an alien. Well, what else would you call a spindly, gray-skinned creature with an enormous bald head and huge, insect-like eyes? A "bug-eyed monster"? That's what they would have called them in the politically incorrect 1950s. Now, of course, given the public relations campaign Hollywood had been aiming at the world since the middle seventies, he knew exactly what to call them. These were aliens, of course. Or perhaps he should call them "extra-terrestrials"?

He had been prepared for this moment by all manner of media—by *ET* and *Close Encounters of the Third Kind*, by Whitley Strieber's *Communion*, by *Star Trek* and *Star Wars* and *Chariots of the Gods* and *In Search of . . .* , by television and cinema and newsmagazines and books, by dorm-room conversations and editorial cartoons—and by his own dreams. Yes, he had dreamed of this moment. While in junior high school, around the time of the Cuban missile crises, he'd begun to have dreams of the great invasion from the sky. In this recurring dream he would awake one morning to find mountain-sized black spaceships hovering over every major city in the world. And when they landed their ships and opened the doors, the aliens had looked exactly like—devils. What a shock it was to him, years later, to find that Arthur C. Clarke had invaded his dreams and written out this exact scenario in *Childhood's End*.

And now—? Now he crouched on the flight deck of an alien spacecraft, gazing up into the obsidian-black eyes of one of its unearthly occupants, feeling reminded of yet another movie: *Jaws*. Jack had never stared a shark face-to-face, but he was happy to take the word of those who had when they testified that a sharks' eyes were black and empty and dead. These eyes—praying mantis eyes, it seemed to him—stared at him without blinking, reflecting nothing, looking empty, dead, and evil. And now it spoke to him: Not with words uttered on sound waves, but by thoughts aimed directly to his mind: "Relax, my friend. Everything will be fine. Nobody is going to hurt you."

"Wrong," Jack blurted out. "You've *already* hurt me!"

"We prevented you from hurting yourself," the alien replied.

"Garbage!" Jack grunted. "You prevented me from hurting *Ben*."

"Which would, ultimately, be hurtful to you," the alien argued smoothly. "Please be at ease, Dr. Brennen. You'll find that if you behave in a civilized manner, we will be very civil in return."

"You call kidnapping civil?" Jack asked. "Just where is the civility in that?" But the alien had evidently lost interest in debating him, for he made no further telepathic response. Instead, he levitated Jack off the floor and floated him under the pink lettering and down one of the branching hallways—a different branch from the way Ben had been taken.

"Is this when you're going to give me my pre-abduction physical?" Jack snarled over his shoulder at the creature. Near the end of the Viet Nam War he had come within one day of being inducted into the service. His army physical lived on in his memory as one of the most humiliating, dehumanizing episodes of his lifetime. Naked, helpless, lacking any control over his own destiny, he had been poked and prodded and ordered around by strangers. That's exactly how he felt right now.

The alien's huge black eyes never blinked as he made only this telepathic reply: "You read too much science fiction." That was it. Jack was glided into a room, the alien left, and a door closed behind him. Gravity returned beneath Jack's feet, and as he dropped to the floor he was already whirling around to examine his surroundings. He found himself locked in a tiny cell—alone. Struggling to control his panic, Jack studied the room. The cabin was oddly shaped—probably because it was built to fit into a flat, oval-shaped craft. The bulkheads were rounded, bowing out at about his eye level and then back in. He presumed this was one of the cabins on the outside rim of the saucer. The walls seemed to be made of plastic, and they glowed like an LCD screen. They were the only source of light within the room, but they did provide that light quite effectively. There were no windows.

He had to get out! Jack charged the doorway and slammed his shoulder into it, hard. It gave a little—it really did feel like it was coated with plastic—but of course, it didn't break open. He guessed he'd not really expected it to, nor did he expect to have any more success the second time he slammed his body into it. Why, then, did he try? Because he had to do *something*! He was trapped—locked in—a captive! He had to take some kind of *action* in the face of that horrible reality, no matter how senseless and stupid the action might be!

"Oh, Lord," Jack murmured. "What is going *on* here!" This was *not* a rhetorical question. He was not one of those who invoked the Lord's name without thinking. This was the beginning of a heartfelt prayer, and as was his custom, he closed his eyes and bowed his head. Jack prayed long and hard. He didn't know how long—under the circumstances that hardly mattered. Still, when he opened his eyes and looked around again, he found himself right where he'd been. He licked his lips and sardonically quoted to himself, "'Give thanks in all things, for this is the will of God concerning you.' Lord, I sure do hope the lesson on the tail end of this experience is worth it. . . ."

Jack had become accustomed to learning through experience. He'd learned difficult lessons through his time in Africa—lessons about spiritual pride, personal failure, and dependence upon God. He'd learned some difficult lessons as a teacher. He was certain he'd learned far more from teaching seminary students than he'd ever taught them in return. And he'd learned something new about how to be a good pastor from every church he'd served. Still, he'd never been *eager* to learn difficult spiritual lessons. He'd realized long ago that it always costs something to learn something. Quite often he'd been most unwilling to pay the price of tuition. He'd paid it, just the same—time and time again—for when God decides school is in session, that's the way it's going to be.

As he glanced around this cabin he struggled to accept the fact that he was about to have to pay again. For while there had been times in his life when he'd felt so locked in that he could certainly identify with how a prisoner might feel, never before had he actually *been* locked up.

There was a bed in this cell—a human-shaped bed. Jack sighed and sank down onto it. Was Gloria missing him yet? he wondered. Were she and his daughter hunting through the woods for him? Would he ever see the two of them again? "Of course!" he grunted to himself. Any other answer would be intolerable! Difficult as it was, by an act of will he forced his mind to address this problem from a spiritual perspective. This was an old muscle, built up by years of practice, and it served him well.

The apostle Paul had been a prisoner many times. *How had Paul handled it?* Jack wondered. After all, Paul was a seasoned traveler who seemed to relish the journey. How had he managed those years in prison, first in Caesarea and then in Rome? "Dependence," Jack murmured to himself aloud. Paul had depended upon God, which was exactly what he needed to do right now. . . .

He noticed he was trembling. *That's understandable,* Jack thought to himself. He was in a state of shock. Anyone would be. His mind was working overtime to adjust to a radically different reality from the one to which he was accustomed. Aliens. He'd been abducted. Abducted! Kidnapped! Trapped!

He wondered if these walls themselves could display the scene outside if he just knew how to work them? You could do that, he knew, in spaceships invented by science-fiction writers. Were these aliens up-to-date enough to have the latest in imaginative technology?

The thought simply wouldn't stay away. "Gloria," he murmured to himself, and his heart ached. What would she think when he didn't return? What would she do? If he could somehow get a message through to her to tell her he was all right . . . .

That would be a lie, of course. He *wasn't* all right. Not at all. Other concerns began to tumble through his mind—trivial concerns, perhaps, but he was hardly thinking straight. Who would teach his classes? Who would preach for him Sunday? "God!" he shouted, panic seizing him again. "What are You going to *do* about this?"

"What do you expect Him to do?" said a voice behind him, and Jack nearly jumped through that door after all. It held, of course. He whirled around and flattened his back against it as he searched the room for the source of that voice.

A girl who hadn't been there before was suddenly sitting on the bed. No, she wasn't a girl; she was a young woman. Maybe not even so young. Where had she come from? How had she gotten in here? Who was she? Was she real? Was he going crazy?

These thoughts rushed through his mind as he heard his lips responding stupidly to her question, "I don't know. Something."

"Like what?" she asked.

"Like . . . break the door down, or open up a hole in the floor, or . . . or transport me back to my bed and let me wake up from this horrible dream!"

"Does God usually do those things when you ask?"

"Of course not!"

"Then why would you expect Him to now?"

Suddenly Jack was exploding, pouring out on this woman all of his anger and frustration at this terrifying situation. "I don't *expect* Him to now, I just *WANT* Him to! Don't you understand? There's a tremendous difference between the two!" Jack looked away, took a deep breath, and looked back. No, she hadn't disappeared. She was still sitting there watching him. "Who are you? How did you get here? *When* did you get here? How did *we* get here? What is going on? *Answer* me!"

The woman seemed not at all threatened by his emotional outburst. She didn't even seem to blink. "You've obviously been taken captive by something that is outside of your experience—something that doesn't fit into your definition of 'natural.'"

"What do you mean *I* have?" Jack snarled. "Are you saying you *haven't?*" Suddenly he realized the implication of his own words, and his gray eyes narrowed. "Are *you* an alien?" he asked stiffly.

She ignored his interruption. "You could hardly be blamed for considering all of this a 'supernatural' experience. It's not surprising that you wonder if you're not dreaming."

"Have you been put in here to analyze me?" Jack asked, smiling grimly.

"I've not been put in here at all, Jack," said the woman.

She'd said Jack. She knew his name! "Then why are you here?" he asked. There was no longer any demand in his voice. He was begging for a response.

The woman shrugged and met his gaze evenly. "You tell me."

Jack was utterly at a loss as to what to say next. He wanted to shout, "I asked you first!" but he didn't. Instead he sat on the bed, took a deep breath, and addressed the walls of this tiny cell. "My daughter is an expert on Lewis Carroll," he told her. "She and I have talked through those stories again and again, and . . . somehow . . . right now I'm feeling like Alice lost in Wonderland, or trapped on the other side of the looking glass. Is this all a dream?" He shook his head, then pounded his hands on it. "It's got to be a dream! I ask for answers, and all I get back are riddles!"

"Ask me whatever you want to know," said the woman kindly, "and I'll try to tell you what I can."

Jack looked at her, utterly baffled, then shrugged and began, "Why don't you tell me how you got in here?"

There was never an opportunity for an answer. The door opened behind him, and when he whirled around again he found himself face-to-face with the alien. Jack was jerked out of the room by a mere thought, the door whispered shut behind him, and once again he floated down the hallway at the alien's bidding.

"Ben told us you would enjoy watching this vehicle travel," Gork said inside Jack's brain. Gork wasn't the creature's real name, of course. Of that Jack felt certain. This was instead Jack's mental nickname for the alien: the way Jack thought of him. He just seemed like a big old Gork. He would have made a perfect villain for one of those old "creature features" Jack had watched every Saturday night through the early sixties.

"I would enjoy watching *Ben* travel right now," Jack grumbled, not at all kindly. He was imagining booting the boy in the backside, preferably off a high building. He doubted if the people in his church would consider that a very preacher-like thought, but it was how he felt.

"You really ought to feel more charitable toward the boy," said Gork inside his mind. "He's chosen you, you know."

"So he told me," Jack growled. "Am I supposed to feel *appreciative* that I'm a member of your 'elect'?"

"Many of your kind would. Many do. Why are you so resistant to that idea?"

Jack snorted derisively as he was propelled through another intersection of branching walkways. "Call me old-fashioned, but I think people ought to be *asked* if they want to become a member of a club."

"This is a very select body," Gork told Jack's brain directly. "*The* most select organization in the history of your race. Open your mind, Dr. Brennen."

"Apparently I don't need to," Jack snapped. "Both you and Ben appear to have easy access to it whether I close it or not."

"Why not simply relax?" Gork soothed—quite literally. As the creature placed this thought in Jack's mind he apparently underscored it by sending soothing, pleasurable sensations throughout the man's body.

Drugs! That's what this felt like. Jack had once had a kidney stone, and the doctor's first response to his horrible pain had been a shot of morphine. That shot had been wonderful—indescribably so. It had been a revelation to him, for he'd learned in a single instant how a person could be seduced into heroin addiction. That shot was what this felt like. A numbing, soothing, yet thrilling dose of elation seemed to instantly block every negative thought from his mind. He struggled to battle it, even as the reasons why he should slipped away. "Why is it so important?" Jack mumbled, his head lolling onto one shoulder.

"We want you to be happy," Gork smiled inside Jack's head. That's how Jack perceived it. He couldn't see the alien—indeed, his eyelids had grown so fat and contented that he couldn't see anything—but he could feel the creature smiling. It felt like nothing he'd ever experienced before, but something he wanted to experience every moment from now on. Of one other thing he was vaguely aware: He was no longer in control of his own thoughts. Something about that bothered him, but he just felt too good at the moment to worry about it.

"This feels great," Jack mumbled after a moment. He managed to raise one droopy eyelid enough to see that he was drifting into a large, circular room. The part of his mind that still struggled to care interpreted this place to be the control center for the craft. It was occupied by a host of aliens, and there were screens on every wall graphically displaying technical information that he found meaningless. That was okay, though. He didn't need to understand it, so long as these wonderful friends took care of him. All he really wanted to do was grin stupidly.

"Are you all right?" someone asked him. Before he could rouse himself enough out of his bliss to look that direction, the voice asked Gork, "Is he all right?" Now Jack had managed to roll his head that way, and he saw that the speaker was Ben.

"He's fine, Ben. He's quite happy. Aren't you, Jack?"

"Hmm?" Jack said, forcing his eyelids open. Had he just taken a quick nap?

"You're fine, aren't you?" Gork sang again in Jack's brain, and Jack grinned more widely and sang back:

"I'm fine! How're you doing, Ben?"

While the jolt of joy had severely hampered Jack's critical faculties, it hadn't closed them down completely. He recognized Ben's expression. There was disappointment there—accusation—perhaps even a little contempt. Even as he recognized this, Ben's expression changed, and the boy explained quickly, "That look wasn't intended for you, Dr. Brennen. It was meant for . . . for *Gork* here!"

"For whom?" the alien asked.

"For you!" Ben roared, and he faced the creature. "You promised me you'd let him be himself! You promised me you wouldn't dope him!"

This was an interesting turn of events, Jack managed to think. Feeling blissfully stupid, he turned to listen to Gork's reply. Gork, however, *made* no reply—or if he did, Jack wasn't privileged to hear it.

"You let *me* choose him!" Ben argued, obviously enraged. "Your interference with his perceptions makes him of no use at all! If you're going to dope him, just let him go!"

This is puzzling, Jack thought. They were talking about him, obviously. It was probably really important that he understand what they were saying about him. For one thing, what was a *Nargzz,* and how did he become one? Still, it was difficult to get excited about any of this. For some reason that he couldn't quite remember, he couldn't seem to hear the alien's end of the conversation. Hearing only Ben's arguments was a little like listening to a person talk on the telephone. He'd just ask Ben later what it had all been about. He felt sure the boy would tell him. After all, Ben had always seemed such a nice kid—

"Stop it!" Jack heard Ben shouting. "Putting your distortions into his head will ruin him!" Now Jack felt a little disapproval of his own growing, aimed at the boy. After all, he wasn't ruined. Far from it. In fact, he felt great! But the boy just kept on acting up, sounding more and more like a spoiled brat. Jack felt mildly incensed. How could he behave so spitefully toward these excellent interplanetary visitors who had cared so nobly for him? "I promise you," the bad-tempered youngster taunted, pointing an impolite finger at this honorable extraterrestrial, "If you don't release him right now, I won't help you!"

Ben's face suddenly twisted, as if the boy was in pain. Could it be that the alien was lovingly disciplining him? Jack felt tugged between two reactions, the first being that it served the insolent teenager right, the second that it all seemed so unnecessary. Why couldn't the boy just relax, as he had? Why, the lad ought to count himself amongst the luckiest people alive to have been accorded such an honor. To be chosen as a member of the Ultrastructure! Why, hordes of humans had begged to be so privileged, had competed with one another, had lied, cheated, stolen, betrayed their families or their nations of their race itself to be allowed such intimate access to the Majestic Ones. "Behave yourself, Ben!" Jack smiled benignly. "After all, look where we are! Glance around!" He gestured to the marvelous technology that surrounded them, then fixed his eyes firmly upon the boy. "Ben," he announced in his most preacherly tone, "I fear you owe these incredible creatures an apology!"

Ben squirmed on the floor of the command deck, gripping first one part of his body, then another, tears forming in his eyes. And yet, all the while he kept on sneering up into the face of his tender supervisor, who was only trying to help him understand clearly his role in life.

"Jack!" Ben cried out, and now Jack saw that the boy was peering up at *him*. "What about your *God?*"

God? Jack thought—and for a moment he felt slightly dizzy. *What about God? What did God have to do with this situation?*

"Didn't you say your God rescued Joseph? Didn't you preach that your God was sovereign over *all* creation?"

"Yes," Jack answered. "Of course He is." Jack immediately wished he hadn't answered that question. It seemed that when he spoke the back of his neck knotted up with tension, and his throat ached. He rubbed his neck and wished he could clear this smoky confusion from his mind.

All the aliens seemed to be surrounding them now, watching. Jack noticed that they seemed to be taking particular interest in Ben's pain. "You idiots!" Ben was screaming at them. "What good am I to you if I'm only reading *your* thoughts placed in some poor fool's mind!"

What does he mean by that? Jack wondered. Was Ben saying that *he* was a fool? Was he thinking someone else's thoughts? Hard as it was, Jack forced himself to knit these ideas together and tried to extract their implications. These ideas proved as elusive as fish in a tank, but he kept swinging his net after them until he caught one, at least: Yes, he was thinking foolishly. He appeared to be trusting, even *exalting* these porcelain-colored figures, when only minutes before he'd been raging at their injustice in kidnapping him—

"That's it, Jack!" Ben grimaced, twisting on the floor like a strip of bacon in a frying pan. "Keep thinking!"

Jack kneaded the back of his neck and slumped down onto the floor himself, first on one knee, then all the way down to sit. "It's hard," he grunted.

"Think about your family! Think about your church! Think about whatever you were thinking about while you were in the cell!"

Jack really did feel sorry for Ben now—and he also felt a little sorry for himself. The triangular white faces loomed over them, peering down at them, harassing them with their controlling thoughts.

"That's it!" Ben shouted.

Controlling thoughts, Jack at last understood. These creatures were controlling his thoughts. Of course he realized that at heart they were very kind creatures, and that if they were indeed guiding his thinking it was probably only to some worthwhile, humanitarian purpose—

"Fight it, Jack!"

"I *can't* fight it!" Jack yelled back, frustrated by these multiple intrusions into his mind. "There are too many of them in here!" That's what it felt like—like a squadron of thought police had invaded his personality—a cohort, a legion—

My name is Legion, for we are many.

That verse just seemed to leap into his brain, as if placed there by another, far more powerful mind than these.

"Yes!" Ben screamed.

Of course, Jack thought. *The Holy Spirit.* "Lord," he prayed, "please release my thoughts from the control of anyone save Yourself."

Jack woke up. At least, that was the sensation he felt, as the minds of several of his alien oppressors suddenly snapped out of his own. His head ached, but his thoughts were free, and he felt as fully alert as he had been when these creatures had kidnapped him.

The creatures, however, seemed dazed—stunned, as if a flashbulb had suddenly gone off in their pitch-black eyes. They seemed to be wobbling about on their spindly legs. Jack didn't think twice about what to do next: He bolted to his feet and toward the door. Old football reflexes served him well as he stiff-armed one alien into the bulkhead and threw his elbow into the face of another. It landed with a satisfying crunch, then he was into the doorway and down the hall like a tailback into the secondary. Although he knew the door of the vessel wasn't open and really didn't even know where it might actually *be* at the moment, there was an adrenaline rush in merely being *loose.* If he could just pick his way through this maze of curving passageways, perhaps he could at least—

The craft plummeted suddenly into the void.

Chapter Three

Alien logic

"Are you all right? Dr. Brennen, are you all right? Dr. Brennen?" Jack opened his eyes then squinted them shut again to block out the white-hot light above him. He threw a hand over his face.

"Oh, is that too much? Here—" The light dimmed immediately. Jack warily tried again, still holding his hand above his eyes as a visor. "What a relief!" the woman behind his head said. Woman? Where was he? "We were afraid we might have been too late, but apparently not."

Too late for what? "Where am I?" he asked, trying to sit up.

"No no, not yet," the woman said, and he felt her hands pressing his shoulders firmly back down to the bed?—table? floor?—and then placing a cool cloth across his forehead.

That was nice, he decided. He realized that his head ached. The cloth was definitely nice.

"Where am I?" he asked again, with a little more strength and little less panic.

"You're safe—now."

Jack reviewed the last events he could recall. They included his abduction, and his attempt to break away, then a terrible fall into a deep, black hole. . . ."Safe from what, exactly?" He wanted to pull the cloth off his face and look around, but not just yet. It felt *so* good.

"From the Grays," the woman answered matter-of-factly. "It was quite a struggle, but we won."

"Who are the Grays?"

"The beings who abducted you."

Jack recalled those huge, triangular faces with the almond-shaped black eyes, and shivered. "They're the Grays?" he murmured. "They certainly looked white to me. "

"Oh no," said the woman as she removed the cloth from his eyes and bent her face down over his. "We're the Whites."

He didn't scream. He did, however, bump his head on the table, trying to jerk himself away from the wrinkled rolls of fat white skin that swathed her lizard-like visage. Fact was, he couldn't scream. His voice had abandoned him.

The woman—the female creature—didn't seem at all wounded by his reaction. *Of course,* Jack thought to himself, *if she had frequent dealings with homo sapiens she must have become accustomed to that kind of response.* She moved her head away to allow him to breathe, and continued her explanation: "We're much whiter, don't you agree?"

Jack thought about it. *Yes—come to think of it, the other aliens* had *seemed to have a bit more gray tint to their whitish skin.* Even so, it reminded him of the time in Nigeria when an Ibo student had referred to a Yoruba classmate as "That dark-skinned man." Jack cleared his throat. "Yes . . ." he managed to say.

"Those Grays," she muttered reprovingly as she busied herself on the far side of the room. "They are so *barbaric.* We prefer to make gentle contact, but they go thrusting their noses into whatever seizes their interest at the moment."

"What noses?" Jack muttered, more to himself than to the woman. Despite her horribly alien appearance, he simply couldn't prevent himself from regarding her as a woman.

"Well, now, that's true," the large White female agreed, nodding her leathery head. "They really *don't* have noses, do they? How about—'thrusting their big heads into whatever grabs their attention.' They do have big heads, certainly—in more ways than one!"

Jack was amazed that this . . . this *creature* could know so much about American idioms and expressions. "You know our language so well," he murmured. The alien woman peered down her own enormous, wrinkled, almost elephant-like nose at him and responded:

"I've been around. I may not look like it, but I'm actually rather old by your standards." Her eyes—by far her most human-like feature—seemed to sparkle. Was it mischief he saw there? Was she joking with him? For certainly, if she knew his race well enough to speak the language so effectively, she must also know that her wrinkles and white skin made her look either extremely old—or dead!

"How—old *are* you? By my standards, I mean."

"Ohhh," she said coyly, "pretty old." She shrugged her shoulders as if to say that was all the information she was going to furnish on the subject, and it would be most impolite for him to pry any further. She reminded him of a lot of southern ladies he knew.

"What about the Grays—how old are they?"

"*Definitely* very old. That's why they're so conceited. They think they own the whole planet!"

Something in that statement made Jack shiver. "Ummm . . . *do* they? I mean, among alien races . . . ?"

"Of course not!" Miz White snorted. "Why, this planet has been regarded as open territory for more than—" She stopped herself. "I shouldn't be telling you this, of course." Suddenly she busied herself once more on the far side of the—room? cabin? ship? Jack seemed to have too many questions to get them all answered at once. Where to start?

"Where are we now?"

"In relation to what?" Miz White responded cautiously.

"Ahhh . . . the earth?"

She contemplated this a moment, then shrugged, setting all the fat in her folds of flesh jiggling. "Twenty-seven point eighteen of your American miles, I'd say. That's just a rough estimate."

"Then . . . we're in space?"

"Oh, you mean *that!* Yes, of course. Sorry—I thought you knew!"

"This is *not* the ship that abducted me, though," he asked by way of statement.

"Why would we want to travel in one of those flimsy little saucers?" frowned Miz White, wrinkling her—*further* wrinkling her nose, in apparent disgust. "They break apart, you know. They're forever crashing. Then again, those crazy Grays *will* race them about at top speed, won't they!"

"They do?" Jack prompted, hoping to draw out more information.

"Constantly! Racing with jetliners, turning flips around fighters, buzzing police helicopters—you'd think they'd find something better to do! They've given the rest of us such a bad name among you humans! Unfortunately, they seem to be quite happy with their sport."

"It's sport to them?" Jack asked.

"Apparently so. Oh, I know I shouldn't criticize. I mean, I'm certain that *our* actions would probably be regarded by some of you humans as equally inexplicable, and the other races are just as odd."

"*Which* other races?" Jack asked, his anxiety soaring—but not yet as high as his curiosity. Were there also "blues," perhaps? Or better yet, "little green men"?

Miz White sighed deeply, and her flesh-rolls bobbled. "Of course I shouldn't tell you this, but . . ." She seemed to be contemplating whether or not to continue, then she sighed again and began: "There are nine races currently visiting your world. At least, we consider their visits to be current, although some haven't actually shown themselves since before your recorded history. All come from various sectors of the galaxy, of course, although some seem to be *everywhere*—the Grays, for instance. You could say they're like ants at a picnic! Just about as welcome as ants, too. We believe they came from Zeta Reticuli/Three, but who knows? They were here before us, and we've been visiting for eighteen thousand of your years."

Eighteen thousand years! Jack was horrified by the white alien's words. Terrified! And she shared them so frankly, with such obvious sincerity, it really didn't occur to him to doubt them. After all, why should she lie? "And . . . the Grays have been here longer?"

"I'm afraid so. Long enough that they claim to have invented you people. Of course, we keep looking for evidence to refute that."

"Invented us?" Jack asked. His voice sounded very flat, he thought, for such a critical question—very hollow. Then again, inside he was *feeling* very hollow.

"Yes. You know, through genetic manipulation. They claim that they constructed you by splicing the genetic material of the African apes. That's why there's no missing link, you see. Or at least, so they say."

Jack laid upon the surgical table, thunderstruck. He couldn't respond. He had built his life upon his faith. In just a few short words this alien creature threatened to shred it. "No," he announced. "No, I don't believe that."

"Well of course you don't!" Miz White soothed, walking back over to rub the metallic-looking cloth back across his head. It immediately comforted him. *What* was *that thing*? Jack wondered. "We don't believe it either," she continued firmly. "That's part of the reason why we continue our own genetic research on your planet's various species. Of course, *we* don't stick instruments down you, or up you, or *through* you, as those insensitive Grays tend to do. You see, since they claim they made you they also think they *own* you, and that gives them a perfect right to experiment! We don't see it that way, of course, so we do most of our research on *other* mammals. It does terrify your farmers, I'm afraid, since we tend to have to completely eviscerate certain of your domestic beasts for the purpose, but we try to be humane about it. Get it?" Miz White grinned hideously. "Us? Humane?"

"Oh," Jack nodded, getting it—he guessed. He was thinking of all the reports of strangely mutilated cattle he'd read in the papers over the years. "So you're the ones who cut up cows."

"We're quite sanitary about it, of course. A *lot* of farmers have figured that out by this time, and they don't report our . . . interventions at all. Smart lads, since they'd certainly lose *all* profits then. Instead, they take the butchered carcasses back to their barns and package them for direct sale to people's freezers. Why, you may have some meat in *your* freezer that I actually cut up, right there on that table!"

Jack got off the table—quickly. "I . . . I don't know what to say. This is all so . . . so . . . incredible to me."

"Why, of course it is," Miz White said sympathetically, coming toward his head again with that marvelous metal hanky. This time, however, he brushed it away. He couldn't help but wonder how many poor cows she'd put to sleep with that thing before—

"Do you mind if I take a look around?" Jack asked, feeling a little ill.

"Of course not!" Miz White beamed, gesturing expansively. "Go wherever you like. May I suggest the Vista Deck, just above us? You can get a wonderful view from there. The

. . . well, what I suppose you would call an 'elevator' is right behind you."

Jack mumbled his thanks, then turned around to step through the open elevator door. Without his instructions its door closed and it bore him upward. He was lost in contemplation of why he'd thanked this ugly alien who had just devastated his world view, and now was apparently carrying him thousands, perhaps ultimately millions of miles from his home. Would he ever see Gloria again? he wondered. Then the door opened.

Jack stepped into the most marvelous panorama he'd ever viewed. The observation deck of this craft was covered with a see-through bubble. Once the elevator sank back into the floor behind him he had an unobstructed view fore and aft, port and starboard, and of the limitless heavens above. It was as if he rode in an open crow's nest while this vessel plowed the ethereal seas of space. Behind them loomed the earth, a gorgeous blue and green ball doing a slow ballet against a velvety black background. Brighter than the fullest of full moons, it made him utterly homesick. If only Gloria could stand here beside him so they could view the universe together!

He glanced over his shoulder and caught his breath in delight. The moon! They were flying to the moon! Instantly he remembered that evening when, as an eight-year-old child, he learned from the television that an American spacecraft orbited this silvery sphere. He had run outside and gazed upward, hoping he might see that tiny projectile looping around it. He hadn't, of course—not even through the spyglass his mother had bought him at Woolworth. But in his imagination he had made this journey many times. In all his trips to Disney's theme parks he'd tried never to miss going on the "Trip to the Moon" ride. Of course, after men walked on the moon they had to change it to a "Trip to Mars," and he'd—

A question flitted across his mind. *Couldn't Disney's "imagineers" fabricate just as authentic a space-travel experience?*

"Beautiful, isn't it?" said Miz White from behind him, and his flicker of doubt evaporated as he whirled around to face her. He hadn't noticed when she'd joined him. "I often come up here myself, just to commune with the stars and celebrate the magnificence of what *you* call 'Mother Nature.' Yes, I suppose you could even say I worship Mother Universe. Not that I believe she's an actual *person*, as *you* apparently do."

"What do you mean?" Jack asked, turning to look back at the growing moon—even though it was clear exactly what she meant.

"This archaic 'God' you humans believe in. Don't you find it a rather useless superstition in the face of modern realities? I sometimes wonder how long your race will continue to cling to its various tribal viewpoints—especially since they cause such obvious problems between you."

Jack felt distinctly uncomfortable. He certainly didn't want to participate in any theological discussion with this fat, wrinkled, grotesque alien.

"Tell me, Dr. Brennen. Do you believe your God created *me?* Look at me. Do you think your God could *love* me? Please, tell me. I really am quite curious to know how you might explain my presence—and my appearance."

"How should I know," Jack responded lamely. He felt embarrassingly unprepared for such a question.

"But aren't you supposed to know? Aren't you a fervent believer in your God—an evangelical, in fact, out to change everyone else's point of view? To get them 'saved'?"

"I am," Jack nodded. Remembering Paul's urging to always be ready to give a defense of the faith, he decided to give it a shot: "I believe God created the universe. Therefore—yes, I do believe God created you—*and* me, despite whatever these so-called Grays might say! And yes, I believe God loves you."

"Ugly as I am?" the white alien asked with a mocking sadness. She appeared to be playing with him, goading him for some reason. But Jack had heard *this* mocking tone many times before. It only encouraged him to continue:

"I believe God loves *all* His creatures. And since He made us look like we do—and I'm sure I'd look as bizarre to your race as you would to mine—then God must have wanted us to look this way. As for salvation . . . " Jack paused.

"Yeeees?" Miz White asked, her voice rising on the end in a perfect imitation of human sarcasm.

"I know only this. Jesus Christ died to save humanity from our sins—from our fallen state. As to what that would mean to another race from another world . . . I don't know."

The alien laughed. It was a long, spiteful, venomous laugh, as demeaning and contemptuous as any Jack had ever heard. Then, suddenly, it stopped, and the alien turned back into the solicitous being that had seemed so caring and sensitive only a little while before: "I'm sorry if I seem so callous, my human friend. It's just that I've heard that argument from so *many* of your kind for so *long* that . . . well, I'm afraid I've grown a little cynical. And now that I've listened to your little 'witness,' how about you listening to mine, hmmm?" Jack made no answer, but she continued anyway. "You are an organism—highly evolved, certainly, but still just an organism—who is a product of the life of a tiny planet circling a tiny sun in an out-of-the-way corner of a small-sized galaxy on the edge of an unimaginable huge universe which doesn't care a *fig* about you, or about what you do. I know this, for I am also an organism, the product of an equally tiny planet. I do have this advantage over you, however. I've traveled. Widely. And I've existed—far, far longer than you have. I've had plenty of time to meditate on this question: 'If there's a God, why would this God have created so much misery and suffering?' You can't tell me you've never wondered the same."

Jack just looked back at her, and she smiled smugly. "I thought not. You're a logical person. So why continue to believe all of this God nonsense? It can only hinder you from achieving your true destiny!"

Jack frowned. "Which is what?"

Miz White looked at the floor, as if she was again trying to decide just how much to tell him. When she at last spoke, it was in a different tone of voice. "Throughout this experience, haven't you been wondering 'Why me'?"

"Of course."

"And what have you come up with?"

Jack grunted. "I *haven't.*"

"Right. Because you have this inbred low opinion of yourself which has been reinforced upon you by all your religion's talk of 'sin.' It isn't true! You're not a 'nothing,' as your preachers and teachers would lead you to believe! In fact, you deserve to be honored!—to be elevated to a position of responsibility! Why you? Quite simply, this is why: Neither we nor the Grays engage anyone without first *choosing* them for such an encounter. You, my friend, have been *chosen.* Now, why don't you lay this religious garbage aside and start asking exactly what you've been chosen *for?*"

For a long time, Jack didn't answer. In fact, he *didn't* answer. He continued to gaze moonward for several minutes before asking, "Where, exactly, are we going?"

"Where does it look like?" Miz White replied affably. "You just wait, Dr. Brennen. Wait until you see the floating city on the far side."

Floating city? "You mean some kind of space station?"

"Just wait," the alien grinned, and Jack realized why he found her smile so disquieting. Her teeth were all pointed and appeared needle-sharp. He looked back at the moon and followed her instructions.

It blossomed now, growing enormous before them until its lower edge disappeared underneath the deck and its upper edge loomed above them. "We're going to crash!" he shouted, and Miz White laughed, for before he'd even finished the sentence they'd veered effortlessly "down" and "under" the rocky surface of this almost-planet. Now he craned his neck upward to study its features, staggering a bit at the enormity of it all.

"There *are* chairs," Miz White murmured, and a moment later he felt her hand guiding him backwards until his calves touched the seat of one. It was really more of a recliner than a chair, and he sprawled back into it on faith alone, never taking his eyes off the spectacle that continued unfolding above. He barely noticed the alien shuffling toward the forward-most point of the bubble. "Look here," Miz White commanded, and he ducked his chin to look over his toes toward her.

She was pointing at something, and he narrowed his eyes to search the black sky for it. Then—there. He saw it. And he gasped.

It was indeed a city, an enormous city in space. He'd seen images of a hundred like it on science fiction covers, in comic books and on film; but unlike those, this was . . . real. It was still small in comparison to the celestial object they circled, and yet he could already tell from this distance that it must be the size of Manhattan Island—and it had just as many windows and lights. Jack was stunned. "How . . . how could this be here!" he finally stammered out.

"Well it didn't just spring up overnight," the alien answered calmly. "It took millennia to construct. Or rather, it is *taking* millennia." She sighed. "I sometimes wonder if it will ever be finished."

"Your people built it?"

"Are building, yes," she said, gazing out at it herself. "Not us alone, of course. The Grays also built a part of it, and the Reezerts, and the Klemings, and I think another couple of races played a role in it four or five thousand years back. Mostly, though, it's been we four."

"But . . . but . . . but why haven't our astronauts ever seen it? How have you managed to keep it from us?"

The white alien turned slowly around and regarded him with a bemused gaze. "You realize, of course, that you just asked *two* questions, and not one."

Jack frowned. "You mean—"

"The astronauts *did* see it, of course. We told them they would, before they embarked. As for how your government has succeeded in keeping it from you? I suppose you'll just have to write your congressman about that."

"I don't believe this," Jack muttered, but he kept on staring, and Miz White smiled toothfully and said:

"Seeing is, as they say, believing. Well, I'll leave you to your 'heavenly visions,' Dr. Brennen. When you've seen enough, just call the elevator and it will come back to fetch you."

Jack tipped his head all the way back to see that the elevator had once again ascended, and it waited with open doors to swallow up Miz White and take her down to the—shudder—surgical deck. He looked into her terrible grin—upside down, now—until the doors closed, and the machine soundlessly bore her away. Then his eyes rolled back to gaze upward. They were now "below" the city, which now appeared so close that they could land on it in moments.

"Then ask them to," said a voice beside him, and Jack jumped and looked toward it.

"You!" he gasped, for he had seen her before—on the other alien ship. The dark-haired woman who had been with him briefly in his cell laid on a recliner next to him. She didn't look comfortable. "Where did you come from?" he demanded. "Where did you go, before? Who—or *what*—are you?"

"I could be a Reezert, I suppose," the woman said sardonically. "Or perhaps Klemings can appear and disappear at a whim, hmmm?" She seemed almost angry with him—disapproving, at the least. She also looked so *familiar* that he felt like he'd known her all his life.

"I . . . I don't know. Maybe."

"Or maybe," she said, "I, *too*, am an illusion."

"What do you mean?" Jack asked—but already he was beginning to see. Like the Cheshire cat, she was fading away. Already she appeared sheer enough to see through.

"Ask her to dock and show you around that impressive city. Just ask." These last words came out of nowhere. The woman who spoke them was gone.

Jack swiveled his head around to look down at his feet. He waggled them from side to side, watching intently. He had a purpose in this. He had the same purpose in pinching his right thigh. Yes, it hurt. But all of this still felt too, too much like a dream to be real. He got up from the chair and walked toward the bubble, putting his hands out before him. He really expected them to pass right through it, but they didn't. He rapped on the plastic, or whatever this was. It bruised his knuckles. He turned his eyes upward once more to the city floating above them, and nodded. "Elevator?" he called out. The elevator rose from the floor to greet him with open doors.

"You're back," Miz White smiled when Jack stepped back into the surgical unit. "Tired of watching the universe go by? Ready to find out more about your place in it?"

"I'd like to tour it."

"The universe?"

"The city. I want to see it for myself."

The alien's eyes were so *very* human-like—enough to clearly register first surprise, then alarm. "But . . . why?" she asked, smiling again.

"Why not? If this is to be my destiny, if I've been chosen to be a space-farer, then let's get on with it. Dock us to it, and show me around. I want to meet a Reezert."

"Sorry," Miz White smiled, "but there's not a Reezert in the galaxy who wants to meet *you*."

"What are they doing here, then?"

"I don't know," she shrugged. "There's not a Reezert in the galaxy who wants to meet me, either!"

"Fine, then introduce me to a Kleming."

"All in good time, my friend," the white alien chuckled. "When we get back to Earth will make sure you—"

"I want to see this city first. That's not a problem, is it? Your ship *does* have the capability to dock, doesn't it?"

"Well of course it—"

"You haven't brought me all the way out here for nothing, have you?"

"You're beginning to act like some of your more insolent fellow—"

"Why can't you show me around it? That seems a simple enough request."

"Well, quite honestly, there's no provision upon the floating city to meet your physical requirements for oxygen and heat—"

"You're telling me this little vessel, and those flimsy little saucers of the Grays, are fully equipped for shuttling humankind about through space, but this floating city that has taken millennia for you all to build together has not one place suitable for human visitation?"

"You're forgetting," the alien said as she cocked her blubbery head to one side, "that we took you away from the Grays. We really can't take you aboard the city without risking further struggle over you."

"One question," Jack said, holding up an index figure. "What do Klemings look like?"

"Ah," Miz White nodded, apparently relieved that he'd changed the subject. "Well, they're shorter in stature than the Grays, and there's a decidedly greenish tint to their flesh, due to their biological dependence upon chlorophyll."

"Little green men, then," Jack said, and the alien White smiled and nodded in agreement. Definitely *not* dark-haired, human-looking females who could appear and disappear. "I don't think you *can* dock with the floating city—"

"Oh, we're back to that, are we?"

"—because I don't believe it's really there."

The alien sighed deeply. "Dr. Brennen, we've already said that seeing is believing—"

"*You've* already said that. I didn't. In fact, from my point of view believing is *not* dependent upon what you see, for often the truth is not visible at all."

"Look around you!" the alien snarled—and Jack thought he recognized the voice. "Look!" The alien knocked on the wall of the cabin, and it made a heavy thumping sound. "It's real!"

Yes. Now Jack was *certain* he recognized the voice. "I have no question that this cabin is real—any more than I question the reality of the submarines at Disneyland. But you know what always disappointed me on that 'Trip to the Moon' ride, or the 'Trip to Mars'? It's that they would never let you get out. So if you want me to believe there's actually a city floating on the back side of the moon, you'll need to dock this ship and let me get out and stroll around."

The alien glowered at him. "You're a fool," it said at last.

"And you're no Miz White," Jack answered. "You're Gork in disguise."

"Who?" the alien snarled, but already his head was taking on that triangular form of his previous appearance. Those human-appearing eyes that had caused Jack to almost trust the so-called "White" were elongating into the sinister, slanted eyes of a "Gray." Yes. This was definitely Gork.

"I'm still aboard the saucer, aren't I," Jack asked. "You somehow knocked me unconscious, then set up this charade to gain my confidence. Why? Why me?"

"You are shrewd, Dr. Brennen," Gork responded, stretching his long neck and wiggling about, as if his lengthy performance in the role of Miz White had made him sore. "But not all of what I said was—as you call it—a charade. You still have been chosen—"

"By Ben, right? Where is Ben, anyway? If he chose me, shouldn't I be with him?"

"You'll be with Ben when you come to your senses! First, you must acknowledge the idiocy of your so-called 'faith,' and accept your nomination to become a part of the Ultrastructure. It matters nothing who chose you. What matters is that you are here, and that you are wasting precious time by being so intractable. Don't be a fool, Dr. Brennen! You certainly can see by this time that we have the wherewithal to force your submission to us. Why require us to resort to such measures? You're a logical, reasonable man. You've won the lottery! You're in the circle! You've been offered the opportunity to be a player! Why not embrace your good fortune and let us get on with the real business at hand?"

The "real" business. Whatever could that be? Once again, Jack's curiosity had been piqued. Why was this alien creature so adamant that he reject his faith? Why should that be so important? Given that it certainly *appeared* he had been abducted by alien beings, did the aliens treat all their abductees in this manner, wringing from each of them some recanting of their beliefs? Or was it possible that Ben had chosen him, specifically, *because* of his faith, and Gork was attempting to poison that in him before allowing the boy to come near him? For the moment, that seemed the most sensible explanation to Dr. John Brennen. If indeed he had been *chosen*, it certainly couldn't have been for any other reason *than* his faith—for that had been his lifelong reason-to-be. And if young Ben had enough influence over these creatures to force them to pick him up, even though it was clearly against their purposes, then the boy must be extremely important to them. Doubtless they were making some use of his "gift"—and that was the "real business at hand." But what that business was, or what Ben wanted of him, apparently would have to wait until he did something.

Something duplicitous. He would have to lie. Now, Jack Brennen had grown up as a preacher's kid. Jack firmly believed that few experiences in life could better train a person for being two-faced. Growing up in the expectation-filled environment of highly committed Christian families meant that a kid who both loved his family and yet wanted to find out about real life simply *had* to lie. At least, that's the way it had happened for *Jack*. He fervently hoped it would *not* be the way things had to happen for his daughter. . . .

It was the thought of his daughter that cinched it. He had to do something to get back to his family. "Suppose—" he began, and Gork looked at him intently. "Suppose I were to accept your offer to become a part of—what was it that you called it? The Ultrastructure?"

"That's what those who are in it sometimes call it," Gork acknowledged.

"Right. What . . . exactly, I mean . . . would I need to do?"

The alien smiled. Apparently he wanted to believe he had made a convert.

* * *

Gloria woke up and looked at the clock. Was Jack back? She called out to him, thinking he might be up in his office. He didn't answer. She looked at the clock again. *It really hasn't been all that long,* she thought to herself. *He'll be back in a minute.*

In another place—in another *time*—one could even say years before—various groups gathered, responding to a strange calling. It was a summons they could not understand themselves, nor really even explain. They responded for many reasons—some of them altruistic, others ambitious, others simply greedy. For whatever reason, they assembled. And although he had no way yet of knowing it, Jack was on his way to rendezvous with them.

Chapter Four

All these things . . .

How long will we allow this to go on?"

"Until He decides to stop it."

"That would be so easy . . ."

"And it would be so permanent. Not yet."

"That nearby star . . . a single flare . . ."

"It isn't time."

"They're destroying time!"

"We are to report and wait."

"Then let's report!"

"You think He doesn't *know?*"

"I think it's getting *late.* I think we should *advise.*"

"We are to *report* and to *wait.*"

"I disagree."

"With Him?"

Silence. Then, "No."
"Then watch."

* * *

"Now we're getting somewhere!" said Gork inside Jack's head, and he grinned. The sight revolted Jack, but he managed to smile back anyway. He was determined to find out what this "Ultrastructure" was all about.

The alien glanced around at the surgical deck, his soulless black eyes reflecting back the brilliant light over the table. "Let's find a more comfortable place to talk, shall we?" he said, and his long, stringy arm pointed at a wall. It opened away from them, and Jack saw—

Not space. He saw instead a large, inviting den, with oak-panelled walls and leather-bound chairs and plush maroon carpet on the floor. It looked like it had been lifted directly out of *Lifestyles of the Rich and Famous.* He felt a little thrill course through him—that "I'm so special" thrill which he and God had spent a lifetime battling inside him—and recognized it immediately for what it was. *Temptation,* Jack thought to himself. Stepping onto that carpet, walking over to sit in one of those deep leather chairs that smelled as luxurious as they looked, he had to acknowledge to himself that these creatures knew how to push his buttons. Gork followed him into the den, and the wall closed behind them. He saw that it, too, was paneled. The whole place reminded him of a movie set.

"Drink?" Gork asked, walking over to a glass-enclosed cabinet filled with decanters. "Cognac? Sherry? Jack Daniels?"

Jack had to smile to himself. He'd immediately thought of young Daniel in the court of Babylon, who had avoided the king's rich meat and wine and consumed only water and healthy foods. Drink didn't tempt him. Perhaps these creatures *didn't* read him all that well.

"Or would you prefer a soft drink over crushed ice?" Gork seemed to smile.

Now that *was* tempting. He'd started his walk this morning on a hot summer day in Louisville, after all, and a cold drink—No. He couldn't afford to eat or drink anything in this environment. Daniel's model had been a good one—and so had that of Jesus in the wilderness. "No thanks," he answered cheerfully.

Gork looked at him carefully, then nodded that wedge of a head. "Very well. Tell me if you change your mind." The alien then wound his elongated body down into an obviously human chair, and leaned back in it. "So," he began, "you want to know about the Ultrastructure.

"It has always been among you. Haven't you always guessed that? Haven't you always thought that there were those special few, the initiates, who by virtue of their inside information controlled all the events of the world?

"It's true, of course. The conspiracy theories are all correct. A small group controls the world. They're not the leaders of nations—some are, of course, but in many cases the leaders of nations lead nothing. The chosen of the Ultrastructure are the kingmakers, not the kings—the shoguns, not the emperors. A few of them are highly visible, because we need some visibility at times to accomplish our purposes. Most, however, are as unobtrusive as we can make them—for obvious reasons. Why should we expose our operatives to media scrutiny by allowing them to focus attention on themselves? We try, in fact, to maintain a stable of status-seeking, camera-loving celebrities who *think* they are on the inside—but are not—for your hero-hungry society to watch and adore. We tease others of your race into believing *they* are the controllers, and give them secrets to hide, then allow your human conspiracy buffs to ferret them out and 'expose' them. It's all a great game to us, Jack—and so amusing at times. You have no idea how wonderfully the news media of this present age have cooperated with us in this charade. We feed them something new about once a month, a new scandal to 'investigate,' a new 'outrage' to 'deplore,' a new celebrity to fawn over and ultimately destroy. The new pantheon of gods and goddesses is a *far* more effective blind than the old gods of Olympus and Valhalla *ever* were. But I'm getting ahead of myself, aren't I?" Gork grinned.

Jack said nothing. He just settled back deeper in his chair and listened to the alien's thoughts take shape in his head. It was more like watching a documentary than hearing a speech—more like interactive CD ROM than reading a book—for Gork not only placed words in his mind but pictures as well. Each concept was illustrated by images of persons, places, and events that were, to Jack, immediately recognizable.

"Didn't you always assume, Jack, that the rich and famous ruled everything? They think that, too. That's what makes it so ironic, my friend. For in fact, the Ultrastructure is composed of ordinary, work-a-day citizens like yourself, who nevertheless influence events upon this planet at the highest levels. The controller of your region *may* be a quiet tobacco farmer, or a local dentist, or even a particularly busy stay-at-home mom. Sound incredible? Of course it does! We want it to be incredible!

"Of course, we *do* take care of these people. They aren't poverty-stricken, by any means. They *are* 'civic-minded,' convinced that what they do is all in the public interest. And just as you don't know who they are, they don't know one another either—or at least, not as members of the Ultrastructure. They know their immediate supervisors, of course, and they know those whom they supervise. Beyond that, they only know—as you do now—that they are participating members of the most exclusive club in history, and that membership has its privileges. You do believe me, don't you Jack? Or do you find this all just too incredible to absorb just yet?"

Jack thought about that. "No," he answered softly.

It was a calculated answer, spoken in a tone designed to hide the whirling of his mind. It was also, at least in some measure, true. Jack was not surprised by the story Gork told.

He'd heard and read many conspiracy theories, and this was but one more. He wouldn't be surprised to hear Gork linking this conspiracy soon to particular organizations of "civic-minded" citizens he had known. But at the moment that wasn't really the point. The point was that this creature—whatever it was—was clearly attempting to seduce Jack into *something* that reeked of the ancient "mysteries." He was being tempted to enter into—and *believe*—a "special knowledge, available only to the anointed few." It was gnosticism—perhaps linked directly with first-century gnosticism. It was cultic—and Jack had to wonder if it had been others who'd had this same experience with Gork who had planted the profusion of cults exploding across the spiritual landscape. He wondered what his own response might be had he not been firmly grounded in the Scripture and the faith, and once again he questioned in his own mind if that might not be exactly why Ben had chosen him. But the biggest wonder he felt was at the apparent fact that—while Gork could place his thoughts directly in his head—this alien could *not* read his mind, as Ben could. How could they rule the world, as Gork claimed they did, without being able to be certain of the loyalty of their agents?

Through Ben, you idiot! Jack said to himself, annoyed at not having seen the obvious immediately. And since that was apparently the fact, he could see now why Ben was so exceptionally important to them. Ben—and Ben's gift—was the key to all of this. He had to get to Ben—

"Are you listening, Dr. Brennen?" Gork inquired. There was an edge of sarcasm in the alien's thought projection. Strange, Jack thought, that Gork could telepath not only human speech, but human inflection as well. "Perhaps you are tired? Needing a rest?"

"No no," Jack protested, waving his hands. "I . . . I guess I just got lost in thought there for a moment. I guess in fact your story *is* a bit difficult to absorb immediately, but I'm ready now to go on. How long has this Ultrastructure existed?"

Gork gazed at him, those flat, featureless eyes seeming to peer right through him. Then the creature glanced away, and blinked, and answered:

"Ever since we made you, of course. Ever since we determined we needed a worker pool to develop this virgin planet, and chose your ape-like ancestors to be our research rats." Gork's eyes came back to Jack's, boring in fiercely. "I wasn't lying a while ago, when I played the 'White.' Oh, I bent the truth about the number of races here. That's a little fiction we maintain to allow us multiple disguises when necessary. I could appear as a Kleming for you, if I chose—I do, sometimes, when it is necessary to play one group of humans off against another. But given our superior technology and our comparative immortality, do you think we would permit any *real* competitor race to interfere with our experiments? Of course not. We would wipe out any challenger."

Immortality. As Gork had "spoken" it he'd illustrated it with a thread of images that hung potently in Jack's mind. "Are *you* immortal?" he asked flatly.

Gork's facial features changed little. The sneer was in his projected thought: "You are, to me, as a mayfly is to you. You're here today, gone tomorrow."

Jack thought on that a moment, then asked, "Are you saying that you, *personally*, were involved in the . . . ahh . . . 'experiments' that resulted in the human race?" He wasn't buying it, but it *was* a fascinating tale.

Gork smiled. "I incubated your ancestors. Yes."

"I see," Jack nodded. After a moment, he asked the obvious. "Why?"

"Ahh!" Gork exulted. "The purpose question! The favorite puzzle of your philosophers! Isn't it crystal clear by now? Your purpose is to serve *us*."

"I see," Jack nodded again. Once again, he asked "Why?"

"Why what?" Gork snarled.

"Oh, you can answer that any way you want. Why should we *want* to serve you, why do *you* want *us* to serve you, why did you go to all the trouble and expense, what do you *get* out of the relationship with us—you can answer any of the above."

"I *could* give you the answer demanded by your ridiculous religion," Gork responded, sneering again. "Because we . . . *I* . . . am your God, and I *love* you." The creature's tone of thought dripped with sarcasm as he mocked all that Jack had built his life upon. "I wanted to have *fellowship* with you, to build a personal *relationship* with you. How's that, Dr. Brennen? You believe such garbage from your little black book! Why not believe it from a little white alien?"

Jack thought a moment, formulating his answer carefully. When the alien had referred to a little black book, he'd placed the clear image of a Gideon Bible in his mind. "My little black book, as you call it, does not presume to tell me the ultimate purposes of God. I understand it by faith, not by logic. You, however, imply you're speaking to me rationally—you leave no room for a faith-based understanding. So why don't you give me some rational reason why I should believe you by giving me some logical explanation for your presence here on earth?"

"You're very demanding for a mayfly, Dr. Brennen," Gork answered. "Nevertheless—since you've asked so nicely—I'll give you the answer you seek: Greed, Jack. That's why we're here. We control an enormous chunk of the universe—but we want *more.* We own the planets in a thousand galaxies, but we want to own the planets in *ten* thousand. We're greedy, Jack. We want possessions and power. Surely you can understand that."

Yes, Jack thought, he could understand that. It was the driving force behind all the strife he had ever witnessed, all the pain he had ever seen inflicted, all the jealousy and spitefulness he'd ever been a party to—all sin. And it was utterly devoid of that one thing that made human experience at all bearable—the very love Gork had mocked. Did these creatures feel no love?

"There it is, Jack," Gork said, uncoiling once again from the chair and rising to his feet. "In a nutshell, the reason *you* are, the reason I'm here—the reason for the Ultrastructure. We've discovered, you see, that what makes you people work is the same thing that made us make you. Quite frankly, we made you that way. In our image, I think your phrase is? We harness your greed to work for us. Now, granted, I've given you none of those high-flown moral ideals your leaders have concocted to get you to win wars for *them*, to gain territory and power for *them*—none of the lofty platitudes that made the church the single most wealthy institution on this earth. But—it's the truth. And as someone I once knew often said to His disciples, 'the truth shall make you free.'"

Jack caught the reference immediately. John 8:32. "You knew Jesus?" he asked. He really didn't want to hear the answer—or see Gork's sacrilegious images. But he did.

"Of course I knew Him," Gork replied, a grin back in his voice. "Now there was a wild-eyed cult-creator if I ever saw one. Better than David Koresh, better than Jim Jones, better than Hitler—well, obviously. You can see that by the wonderful success He had! And the organization He formed? Marvelous! We've pulled some of our *finest* agents from the ranks of your religion, Jack. You're just one more in a long line. See the truth, Jack. Let it free you."

But it wasn't the truth. Not the truth as Jack Brennen believed it. It was the opposite of the truth. Surely young Ben knew that! Was that what the boy was hungry for? The freeing truth that denied this self-absorbed conspiracy?

"What do you want from me?" Jack asked. His emotionless tone had been carefully chosen. He pretended resignation, although he was resigned to nothing this creature would propose. He just wanted to get away—to get *through* Gork—to Ben. In the language he had been taught to use to explain such things, Jack felt *led* by God to do this.

"Simple," the alien answered, doing an exaggerated imitation of a human shrug. "Just play along with the boy. Talk to him. Tell him all the holy nonsense you want. I assume you will, since that's your chosen profession?"

Jack waited a moment, then said "But . . . "

"Excuse me?" the alien mocked.

"Where is the 'but' in your instruction?" Jack asked. "Obviously, if you'd just let me be with Ben without all of this 'orientation' I would have done just what you say. So what is it that you either *don't* want me to do or *do* want me to do that made all of this display necessary?"

"Oh, that's simple," Gork said, actually chuckling. Once again he fixed those huge black eyes on Jack and said, "Doubt."

Jack frowned. "What?"

"We want you to . . . doubt. Doubt the truth of what you tell him, even as you 'witness' to him. Doubt yourself, and the way you've spent your adult life. Doubt God, doubt Jesus, doubt your church, doubt what your parents taught you, doubt all those Sunday School lessons—that's all, Jack. We just wanted you to doubt. And you *will* now, you understand. You will. You won't want to, I feel certain—but the seed has been planted. You'll have to. And Ben will read that in your mind. Let him read your doubt, Jack, and he'll grow tired of you, and then we can take you home. Hey, how's that for a motivation, hmmm? Just let him see you doubt, and we'll take you back to your wife and child and make certain you never want for anything. Just show him the truth, Jack. Show him your doubt."

Despite his wish to pretend resignation and defeat, Jack couldn't prevent himself from snapping, "What makes you think this one little encounter with you will change the way I've believed all my life?" Then Gork said the most frightening thing Jack Brennen had heard since his abduction began:

"Experience. I told you, you come from a long line of church leaders we've used effectively down through the centuries. Experience tells me that, no matter how high you set your standards and no matter how hard you try, you'll fail. So, make it easy on yourself. Go ahead and fail, Jack. Then you can go home."

There it was. Jack's greatest fear and his greatest temptation merged into one offer. He was terribly weary, and more than anything he wanted to go home—to snuggle up next to Gloria and forget any of this had ever happened. And all he had to do was give way to the greatest fear of his life—the fear of failure.

When he'd been a young man it had seemed a fate worse than death—or perhaps the same *as* death. Irrational, he knew, but in the early part of his ministry he'd felt that if he failed he *would* die. He'd lived long enough now for God to free him from that misconception. He'd had enough failures in his life—and survived them—to realize along with Peter that after every dark night of denial comes a new resurrection morning, and a new chance. He'd learned that he couldn't really accept *God's* forgiveness without also forgiving himself.

But to *plan* to fail? To purposely deny his faith so that Ben would lose interest in him and he would then be released—how could he forgive himself for that?

"Once again, Dr. Brennen, you appear lost in thought. While you ponder, could I interest you in a beverage? Perhaps something to eat?"

"No thank you," Jack answered, waving the thought off as he struggled to hold his mind on his dilemma.

"Perhaps you think too much, my friend. Relax," the alien coaxed him, and once again Jack struggled to wave away the thought. It dawned on him—slowly—that he was having more and more difficulty stringing coherent ideas together—

"Or perhaps you'd like to tour the floating city after all?"

The floating city? Oh yes, Jack remembered. The city that "Miz White" had shown him positioned on the far side of the—where? Where was he?

"Relax, Jack. You worry too much. Let it go and relax."

His mind was flooding with unrelated thoughts—memories, ideas, images—all his own, but all of them unrelated to whatever it was he'd been discussing with this creature. It was—it was as if the thoughts were beads he'd been trying to string together in logical patterns, and now the beads had spilled and were bouncing, bouncing everywhere. He couldn't seem to catch any one of them to string it with. Jack shook his head, trying to clear it, and blinked his eyes repeatedly. His usually fluid mind seemed to be like gelatin setting up in the refrigerator. He tried to get his focus back by staring at Gork, and noticed that Gloria was standing behind the alien. No, not Gloria—the woman who'd appeared and disappeared on the observation deck. She just *looked* like Gloria. A *lot* like Gloria. And now, suddenly, she too was speaking inside his head:

"The Holy Spirit, Jack," she said. "Greater is He that is in you than he that is in the world."

Yes, Jack remembered. That was Scripture—although he couldn't recall the reference at the moment. Besides, they weren't *in* the world right now.

"Of course you are," Gloria's double snapped. This was clearly a rebuke, and Jack felt jolted by it—jolted enough to remember that the verse was 1 John 4:4, and that its purpose was to encourage its readers to test the spirits—

"You're trying to control my thoughts again, aren't you, Gork?" Jack said flatly—and now the alien looked stunned. Behind him, Gloria's double disappeared.

"Why are you calling me 'Gork'?" the creature snarled inside Jack's mind. His frustration was clear—and so, too, were Jack's thoughts once again.

"I don't actually know," Jack responded. "What would you prefer to be called?"

"Since the time of the ones you term ancients, your race has called me *many* names. I've been Baal to the Philistines and Gungun to the Yoruba! I've been Shiva and I've been Thor! I've been—"

"Beelzebub?" Jack interrupted. "The 'Lord of the flies'?"

Gork's words and images stopped. The alien stared at Jack, motionless.

Then Gork laughed. "*Now* I see!" the creature cackled, and he filled Jack's mind with echoes and images of his mirth. "You are trying to *demonize* me! Of course! That's what someone with your background *would* do—try to make me into a spiritual bogeyman! I tell you, Jack. Even after *eons* of dealing with you creatures—after having *designed* you myself—I still am sometimes amazed at the limited grasp of your ridiculous little minds. Oh, but don't let me stop you, my friend. As if I could!" Once again mirth flooded through Jack's thought waves, and while it forced him to smile back, it also made his head ache.

"Tell you what!" Gork volunteered cheerfully. "How about if we break out of this little shell and go and tour the city!"

"What city?" Jack asked. Instantly the image of that humongous floating space-city orbited again through his mind, and he said, "I thought you told me this craft couldn't dock with the floating city—that it wasn't equipped for human habitation?"

"You think I'm a demon, Dr. Brennen!" Gork responded, still giggling. "Why would you believe anything I say?" As he said this the alien gestured toward the paneled wall opposite to the one they'd come through, and now it opened away from them—opened onto a busy avenue, clogged with the movements of all manner of creatures—including humans. Yet this was clearly not an exterior setting, but an interior. It was lighted like a shopping mall. Jack stepped toward the empty wall to get a better view upward. The ceiling above them peeled away just as the wall had done, opening onto the soaring interior of a construction so enormous it gave Jack vertigo to look up at it. Panic gripped him. He grabbed for the back of the chair he'd been sitting in to keep from flying off the floor—for he recognized where he was, or rather, what he was inside. The enormity of the implications robbed him of his ability to breathe.

Jack had often talked with friends of the "sub-genres" of science fiction. While an outside observer might decide that all science fiction covers looked so much alike that all the stories must be the same as well, to the educated reader there were a number of specific categories: space-opera, psychological stories, cyber-punk, alternative histories, etc. Ever since he'd read Larry Niven's *Ringworld* and Arthur C. Clarke's *Rendezvous with Rama*, Jack's favorite had been "artifact" fiction. The central theme of such tales was the discovery of some ancient, non-natural artifact—a ribbon-like ring that completely encircled its sun, as in Niven, or as in Clarke, an enormous, hollow space vessel, large enough inside to contain huge seas and the remains of manifold civilizations—large enough to have its own weather. What Jack gazed up into was that second kind of artifact—a huge tube, so big that human-sized creatures could live on its interior walls like microbes live on the inner surfaces of a drainpipe. Miles above his head Jack could see the other side of the tube, and from its surface hung Tinkertoy shapes he knew were buildings at least the size of the one he was in. There were tiny spires he knew could be vast office complexes, and little gray bubbles that could be the size of domed stadiums.

"You can let go of the chair, Dr. Brennen," Gork gently mocked him. "You'll not fly off the surface. As you've probably already guessed, we spun the tube eons ago to give us gravity."

Jack did let go, but he still felt dizzy, wobbling unsteadily on his feet as his eyes and ears and mind struggled to make sense of this totally unnatural perspective. "And . . . and this is the floating city?" he managed to stammer. When he'd first seen this place from the observation deck, it had appeared to be more a galactic squatters township composed of a jumble of unrelated construction. This, however, bespoke centuries of careful planning.

"This is it," the alien answered, with a touch of justifiable pride in his voice.

"But—" Jack began, then paused in dismay several moments before being able to get out, "why have we never seen it?"

"You mean from Earth of course," said Gork. "Well it *is*, as I showed you, in synchronous orbit designed to keep it always on the far side of the moon from Earth. Until we allowed you enough technology to get off the ground and off the planet, we really didn't need to worry about your looking *behind* the moon to see us, did we? In any case—if your military can perfect stealth technology while your 'Star Trek' writers imagine a so-called 'cloaking device,' do you think it would be all that difficult for us to play hide-and-seek with you?"

"B-b-but . . . " Jack stammered again, still scanning that far distant wall, trying to make out details in the construction. "You told me I . . . I couldn't go inside the city . . . that it wasn't suitably equipped for human visitation—"

"I've tried to take it easy on you, Jack," Gork scolded. "Really I have. We've learned that it's not healthy to expose humans' eyes to more than their minds can encompass. I've tried to stretch you, gradually, to help you understand the enormity of what it is you're now a part of. You simply must let go of your archaic notions of God and faith. The *Chariots of the Gods* are real, Dr. Brennen, and you've ridden in one today. It may be humiliating to consider that you are products of the gene-splicing of ancient astronauts, rather than the 'children' of some unseen creator. No more difficult though, perhaps, than coming to regard yourself as the outcome of your parents' sexual union rather than a bundle delivered by a stork!"

Jack was only marginally aware that the other walls were now disappearing as well, and that Gork was pacing away from him. As the alien widened the gap between them, seemingly enlarging the space where they'd been standing, Jack consequently felt smaller and smaller. "Hear me, John Brennen!" the alien called to him. "Embrace the new millennium we, your makers and mentors, are at last prepared to allow you to experience. Look!" The spindly-armed white figure gestured skyward. "What else do I need to show you to convince you of what I'm saying?"

The lights of the city high above him twinkled on and off, as the myriad inhabitants of those distant buildings went on about their business. Who were they, these hordes of space neighbors from the far side of the moon? Were they all near-immortals? Was managing the race of mankind their primary business, or was that merely a local affair, and meaningless in contrast to administrating a galaxy? Had all of them at one time or another visited earth? Or were they, like humans, of such widely differing interests and personalities that, to some, the thought of popping over to the planet for a visit seemed banal?

Jack at last had to rest his neck, and he rolled it forward and looked toward Gork. Panic seized him. Neither Gork nor the furniture was there any longer! Had he been left alone upon this alien street corner?

"Behind you," Gork said, and Jack whirled around to see his abductor sitting inside a bubble. "A tour, I think you requested?" the alien said, and Jack realized that this bubble was some sort of conveyance, and that he was expected to get into it. He did so, the bubble sealing closed around him. Gork explained, "This apparatus will enable you to relax and breathe while we take in the sights. You may not have noticed it in your astonishment, but as soon as I opened the room, breathing became very difficult for you. My people are rather indifferent to oxygen, I suppose. Our bodies can function in a wide range of atmospheric types and can endure extremes of hot and cold. That's what I meant about this place not being equipped to cater to your whim. However, in the interests of allowing you to see the truth—are you ready?"

Without awaiting Jack's response, the bubble began moving, floating about five feet above the surface as it started up around the curve toward those buildings Jack had been studying. He looked to his right, then past Gork to his left, sighting down the length of the tube in both directions, but he couldn't see either end. Meanwhile the bubble careened up the wall at an increasing speed, and Jack had to sit back and grip his stomach to keep from vomiting. Gazing "ahead" was difficult, for it seemed they were constantly going both upwards and back. The closest feeling he'd ever had to this was sitting in a roller-coaster as it climbed toward the peak of the rail. He kept waiting for the bottom to drop out of his stomach. It already *had* dropped out of his world.

"I know it is impressive, Dr. Brennen," Gork said solicitously, "but understand that, to us, it is nothing but a way station. Such as it is, to our race it is rather like a convenience-mart in the desert, halfway between Palm Springs and Phoenix. We find your science-fiction epics rather amusing, picturing yourselves, as they often do, astraddle a mighty galactic empire. For us, it's rather like you watching a baby pompously clumping around in Daddy's shoes. It's *our* empire, Jack. And perhaps—if you're cooperative—we'll let members of the Ultrastructure travel through it. You'd like that, wouldn't you? Haven't you always wanted to zip from galaxy to galaxy?"

Jack had managed to control his nausea by leaning back in his seat and taking deep breaths. Now he expelled one of these and asked, "How can you travel faster than light?"

"Quick as a thought, Jack, quick as a thought. If we can think it, we can go." Gork seemed to be thoroughly enjoying himself.

Jack contemplated this response. What did Gork mean? After all, in his imagination Jack, too, could visit other galaxies at the speed of thought. What was real, here? What really was the truth? He addressed the alien: "Sir—Baal, or Zeus, or whatever it is you want me to call you—"

He heard the creature's pleasure in his mind. "Call me whatever you like. Call me Gork if you wish, so long as it's a title of respect."

"Gork then . . . I . . . I really think I've seen enough. I . . . I'd like to see Ben now, if I may."

"Ben?" Gork responded, sounding a bit concerned.

"Yes. Obviously I've had a very distorted view of reality. I'd like to talk all of this over with him, if I could—? Maybe correct a few misperceptions that the young man may have picked from my mind?"

The bubble stopped moving. Inside his head Jack could hear Gork beaming as he answered, "That can certainly be arranged. We'll let you talk on our way home."

"Home?" What a payload of hope rode upon that word: Were they returning him to Louisville?

"To Earth. To meet with some friends at a rock near Albuquerque."

New Mexico? That was hardly home. But it was certainly better than this place. A moment later the saucer-craft that had abducted him swallowed their bubble whole, and he was once again being hustled down hallways beneath signs glowing pink with an alien script.

Chapter Five

Ben's story

A door slid open, Jack was pushed forward, and the door slid shut again behind him. "I've been through this before," he muttered to himself as he glanced around the room. Once again he found himself in one of the oddly-shaped, bulkhead rooms of the saucer—alone.

He turned around and hit the door once, shouting "Hey! Hey! Where's Ben?" But no one responded to his calls. "These creatures can't be trusted," he growled, and he decided to make the best of the situation.

Maybe that won't be so bad, anyway, he thought after taking a good look around the room. There was a table on the far side of it, and he realized now that it held a buffet of fruits, breads, meats, and sweets—and a half-dozen cans of soft drinks, cooling in a bowl of ice. Suddenly he felt ravenous, and he raced over to grab up a slab of roast beef and slap it between two slices of bread. Before chomping into it, however, he had that brief moment of doubt. Should he do this? Could Gork and his buddies be doping him?

"Wake up, Brennen!" he snarled to himself. "If they can get into your mind directly and manipulate your thoughts, why should they need to rely on chemicals? Eat!" *Thank you, Lord,* he prayed silently, and with that he took a huge bite.

The sandwich tasted wonderful. He grabbed a soft drink and popped the top. Then he sat on the edge of the bed to chew and drink and swallow. For the next few minutes he thought of nothing but his hunger and his corresponding pleasure in eating. After several return trips to the table he sat down again on the bed and sighed. He didn't remember lying back on the wonderfully comfortable mattress. He didn't remember falling asleep. For a time, he didn't remember anything.

* * *

Gloria stood at the back window, watching between two neighbors' houses for Jack's return. She glanced again at the clock. She'd been glancing at it every forty seconds for the last twenty minutes. Where *was* he? He'd been gone almost two hours—usually he stayed in the woods no more than one. She tried not to worry. She'd told herself over and over that she was being silly, that he'd just gotten into conversation with a neighbor and lost track of time. He did that, of course. That's where he was, surely.

Could he have fallen asleep down there by the creek? Not likely. On the other hand, it couldn't hurt to check. She stepped onto the landing and called up to their daughter's room, "Honey? Walk down to the forest with me and let's find Daddy." As she heard her daughter stirring around above her and getting dressed to go, she relaxed. There was relief in action. They'd find him in a minute.

* * *

"I thought you wanted to see me," Ben grumbled. "Why don't you wake up?"

Jack dragged himself to groggy awareness and opened his eyes. Ben stood over him. The boy looked impatient. "Hi," Jack mumbled, struggling to remember where he was.

"You've been abducted. You're aboard an alien vessel. And yes I'm impatient, because I've been waiting for you to wake up for a dozen hours."

"I slept for twelve hours?" Jack said, then he yawned. "I don't do that unless I really need to."

Ben's response held no sympathetic understanding. "There's no time to waste. We're on our way to a contactee convention, and before we get there we need to learn as much from one another as we can." Ben plopped himself down at the foot of the bed, and Jack felt obliged to push himself up and sit against the wall.

"I'd hoped this might all turn out to be a dream," he murmured, blinking his eyes to clear them. He was hungry again, and he glanced toward the table to see if the food was still there. Instead there was a new buffet—a breakfast buffet including sausage, bacon, biscuits, eggs, hash brown potatoes and hot coffee. Pleased, Jack thought to himself, *I could get used to this!*

"No you couldn't," Ben corrected him gruffly. "After a while it'll feel like a luxurious prison to you. It does to me."

Jack thought that would probably be true—but he was still hungry. He climbed out from under the covers—and stopped. Where were his pants? Who had undressed him and put him to bed?

Again, without waiting for Jack to voice a question, Ben answered "Your pants are in your closet—along with a new wardrobe. Your size exactly."

Jack felt a tremor of panic. What had they done to him while he slept! "How did they know my size?"

"The same way they knew you like roast beef sandwiches, sausage biscuits, and coffee. I told them."

"You . . . read my mind," said Jack, thinking as he said it, *I don't like that.*

"That *is* my gift," Ben nodded. "And of course you don't like it. No one likes to have their privacy invaded."

"But you do it all the time—"

"Just like you *see* whenever you have your eyes open. Apart from closing your eyes, how do you 'not see' what is around you? And I can't close my mind, Jack. I can't *not* read your thoughts."

Jack mulled this over a moment as he got up, went to the closet, and selected his own pants from the row of garments hanging there, and got into them. "I don't remember thinking about my waist size, or my tastes in food. Can you read my *memory*, as well?"

"Good question, Jack!" Ben grinned, and he got up to fix himself a plate as he answered: "I can't, no. But you'd be surprised how many things run through your mind that you *don't* give direct attention to at the moment, and don't even remember you thought about. And I've been aware of you for a while, Jack—listening to your thoughts, if you'll forgive my saying so."

Jack blushed, and Ben went on hurriedly, "Sure, I know you've thought some things that you wouldn't want to advertise. But believe me, compared to many minds I've been inside, you've got a pretty clear conscience and a genuinely kind spirit. I wouldn't have chosen you if you didn't."

"Oh yeah," Jack nodded, coming to the table to fix a plate himself. The boy's comment had been a compliment, he knew, but Jack had never been good at accepting compliments. Instead he would move on to other questions. He had so many—

"Ask away," Ben shrugged, his mouth full of chocolate donut.

"What exactly have I been chosen *for?*" Jack asked. He sat down on the other side of the bed to listen intently while he ate.

"To be my . . . confidant," Ben responded after a moment. "My friend, my companion—yes, my playmate, if you want to put it that way."

That *was* what Jack had been thinking, of course, and he found the idea somewhat humiliating. "Not that I don't like you, or consider that unimportant," he explained, knowing that Ben had heard his thought. He was starting to get the hang of this.

"I understand," Ben smiled. "But you know, it might turn out to be more significant than you think."

"In what way?" The trick was just to say the first thing that came into his head. There was no point in trying to hide it, and this way he at least felt he had a *little* control.

"*I* may turn out to be more significant than you think," Ben said a little smugly, and he finished his donut before he went on. Jack waited as the teen licked his fingers, purposely keeping his mind as blank as he could. "I may turn out to be the most significant person in history. Apart from Jesus, of course," he added, for he'd heard that thought pop into Jack's head. "And who were the Beatles?"

Jack smiled slightly. This kid *was* young. "They were a singing group from Great Britain that was very popular when I was . . . about your age. When you just said that, I remembered when John Lennon said, 'We're more popular than Jesus Christ.' Sorry my thoughts interrupted you, but I can't help it, you know. Go on."

Ben stood up and paced around the room. Suddenly he looked back at Jack. "Your room is so small. Why don't you grab your cup of coffee and come on to mine."

Jack's eyes widened. "Can I?"

"Of course," Ben shrugged, and he looked at the door. "Door—open." The door slid wide, showing them the hallway beyond. Jack immediately jumped up and followed Ben's suggestion, pouring a cup of coffee before following the boy out.

"Would it do that for me?" he asked, looking backward.

"Try it."

"Door—close," Jack instructed. The door obeyed. *Then I'm not a prisoner,* he thought, and Ben answered:

"Not of your room, no. But you *are* a prisoner of George and the gang."

"George?"

"That's what *I* call the creature you call Gork. But I'm thinking I might switch to using Gork myself. It seems to fit." They had walked down the curving hallway to another door, this one apparently on an inner wall of the saucer. "Door—open," Ben said without breaking stride, and Jack followed the boy inside.

Apparently Ben was, indeed, very important to the aliens. In any case, he had a far nicer suite than Jack did. It was filled with gadgets—

"Toys," Ben muttered.

—and its walls, which made a full circle about twenty feet in diameter, were decorated with posters of comic superheroes.

"They're the only people I can identify with," Ben snarled, throwing himself onto his bed. This was larger than Jack's—although he really couldn't see the need. After all, the boy was alone: painfully, tragically alone.

"Yeah," Ben agreed. "That's where you come in. Have a chair."

Jack sat in a large recliner, leaned back, and sipped his coffee. "I don't mean to feel sorry for you—"

"I feel sorry for myself, so why should I be upset when you do, too?" The boy rolled over onto his back and put his hands behind his head. "Now where were we? Ah, yes. Why I'm so important to these critters."

Jack wondered how they would feel about being called "critters."

"Doesn't matter what they think. They can't read minds, and I can, so they need to humor me."

"I noticed that . . . uh, Gork . . . couldn't read *my* mind. But he sure can manipulate it when he wants to!"

"Oh yes. That's their favorite trick. I won't let them mess with mine, though—and while I'm around I won't let them mess with yours, either."

"Why . . . thank you," Jack said, a bit amused at being protected by a boy.

"Listen, Brennen," Ben snarled, "You *need* my protection, so don't make light of it when I promise to give it to you!"

"Sorry," Jack muttered. He truly was. And grateful. "Thank you for doing what you can."

"I can do a lot," the boy said, flipping over again onto his stomach. "I wish it weren't so. If it *weren't* I wouldn't be here—but it is. That's why I identify with comic strip heroes. They're prisoners of their gifts as well."

"What else can you do, besides read minds?"

The boy paused. "Well . . . that's all, really. But that's plenty." He sat up and looked at Jack. "I can read any mind, any time, any distance. That's why they have this ship, you know."

"Why what?" Jack said, surprised.

"It's a special saucer. Passes through solids. I gave them the formula to make it work."

Jack gasped. "You invented a formula for making solid matter pass through other matter?!"

"No!" Ben scolded. "I just read the mind of a man who did and told them about it. They were thrilled. Not as thrilled as when I picked the brain of the lady who had the key to time."

"The what?"

"That's what I called it. She didn't call it anything. Fact of the matter is, she really doesn't know how she does it. They had me studying her for weeks and translating her thoughts for them, and sure enough, there it was: the key to time travel."

Jack stared.

"Yeah, I'm serious," Ben nodded. "And *now* you know why I appear to be the same age I was when we first met—back when you were twenty or so. As far as I'm concerned our first encounter just happened last month."

Jack Brennen was stunned. He laid back in the chair, happy that it reclined with him, and let the implications cascade over him. "So that explains it," he muttered.

"Yep," said the boy. "That explains it. They had me reading minds of computer geniuses in the San Jose area. They were so intrigued that they broke into the offices of a government contractor doing a top secret project—and they got caught. Quite honestly, Jack, for all their bragging they really aren't that smart."

Jack nodded slightly, and waved his hand. "Go on."

"They were all scrambling back to the saucer. I saw it as my chance, so I broke for freedom. The MPs caught me, which I figured was as good a way of escaping as any. Naturally, they wouldn't believe my story. I mean—would you?"

"Not without seeing it for myself," Jack agreed.

"Right. But they'd caught me in a government complex, stealing government secrets, right?"

"Right—"

"So they turned me over to the feds. The FBI guys didn't believe me either, but they *did* believe that something weird was going on, so they decided to give me to this other top secret agency that existed back then, with offices somewhere in the Pentagon. They'd taken me to the airport in San Francisco to put me on a plane to Washington when I gave them the slip." Ben chuckled, relishing the story as he told it: "They didn't cuff me, see—after all, I'm a kid, right? Besides, I kept thanking them for taking care of me, protecting me, being nice to me after I'd been abducted by aliens—all that stuff. I picked their brains for their hobbies and interests, and used the information to make them like me. I waited until I was certain they'd relaxed and taken it for granted I was thrilled to be with them—then I bolted. Oh, they were quick, and good at their jobs, but despite their quick reflexes it only took me a second to get lost in that crowd. And because I knew precisely where they were going to look for me, I managed always to be somewhere else. It was easy, really. Getting out of the airport was a breeze. I got a ride from a Hare Krishna guy in a VW who thought I was going to let him shave my head. I got away from him at a gas station in Belmont, then I just went looking for . . . a friend. I found you."

Jack tried to remember back to that night so long ago. He couldn't. Too many other nights had intervened—nights Ben, apparently, had never spent. "Why me?" he asked.

"Because you believe in God." Ben said this somberly. He'd obviously given it a lot of thought.

"A lot of people believe in God," Jack began, but Ben cut him off.

"A lot of people *say* they do. You really *do*. That's the reason I picked you, Jack. Because you really believe there is a God, and that He cares." Ben sighed. "Only one thing can get the world out of the mess I've gotten it into, and that's gotta be God." Ben looked at Jack. "You *do* believe that still, don't you?"

"I do," Jack nodded. He could see, now, why Gork had worked so hard to make him doubt. But this boy's confidence in him—and in his character—was enough to challenge him to resist all of Gork's manipulations—

"What did he do to you?" Ben demanded, suddenly very agitated.

Jack was surprised. "Don't you know?"

"Know what? You've been asleep since the moment we came on board!"

"I have?" Jack asked. "You mean that trip to the moon and the tour of the floating city was all a dream?"

"What?" Ben shouted—then he grew very silent. It seemed to Jack that his face grew whiter.

"Are you reading my memories?" Jack asked, for he was, indeed, reviewing in his mind the encounter with Gork as Miz White, then the tour.

"Time," Ben murmured. "That's it."

"Hmm?"

"They know they can't hide your thoughts from me, so they hid you in time. And I didn't even know they did it."

Ben was apparently talking more to himself than to Jack. "Could you let *me* in on your sudden insight into time?"

After a deep sigh, Ben said, "Okay. I've told you that I helped them find the way to travel through time. We do it all the . . . time . . . now. This saucer is more a time machine than anything else. But I had thought the saucer itself was necessary for time travel. I didn't think they could go without me. . . ."

"Are you saying that Gork took *me* for a time trip and left you here, and then brought me back to drop me down into the same second I left you in, so you wouldn't miss me?" Jack's head was starting to hurt.

Ben nodded soberly. "If all those things happened to you—yes. No wonder it's taking so long now to get turned around. You see, after each time jump it takes the computers several hours to recalibrate and to lock into the next time and place. They're working on speeding that up—even say they have historical evidence that they're going to succeed, if you can believe them. But if they made a jump without me, then it's going to take twice as long for us to get to Albuquerque." Then suddenly the boy frowned. "They never took *me* to the moon!"

I wonder if they really did me, Jack thought to himself. The woman had suggested as much.

"Really? That *is* a possibility," Ben nodded. Suddenly Ben froze, and then around to stare at Jack. He looked terrified.

Jack looked back at him, puzzled. "What?"

"Who's the woman?" Ben demanded.

What woman? "Oh, you mean the woman who looks like Gloria? I don't know. You mean you don't know her either?"

"How would I know who she is?" Ben blurted out. "Where did she come from? How did she get on board? Where did she go?"

"Wait, wait," Jack soothed, holding his hands up before him as if to push the questions away. "Actually, I'd wondered if I'd made her up."

"Your *mind* doesn't think you made her up! Who *is* she? *What* is she?"

"Evidently we can rule out her being one of the aliens," Jack responded, thinking aloud. He figured he might as well think out loud. Ben would hear regardless. "Since you don't know her, and *I* don't know her, but she apparently knows me, I've wondered if she might be an—"

"Angel," Ben finished for him, and the boy shivered.

"By the things she's said to me," Jack shrugged, "I have to believe she's *some* kind of messenger from God. And since that's the literal translation of what an angel *is*—" Jack smiled. "Maybe so. Wouldn't that be something! Ben?" He realized that the teenager was shaking. "What's the matter?"

"I'm . . . t-terrified!" Ben hugged his knees to his chest and rocked on the bed.

"Look, there's no need to be frightened," Jack began. "I admit I've never seen an angel before either—if that's what she is—but I'm not afraid of her."

"Of course not! She won't do anything to *you!*"

"Are you afraid she's going to do something to *you,* Ben?"

"You don't know what I've done, Jack! You don't know what I've unleashed! It's gonna take *God* to be able to put it all back together again, and what is He going to do to *me?* Jack, I *caused* this!"

"You caused what?" Jack said, sitting beside the boy and putting an arm around his shoulder to comfort him.

"All of this . . . this mess! They've used my gift, and I've given them what they want—Jack, I've betrayed our history, our world—I've betrayed our *race!*" Ben buried his head in his knees, and it was obvious that he was hiding tears.

Jack didn't know quite what to do. On the one hand, he firmly believed that there was no sin so terrible that it could separate one who longs for God from the Lord's love. On the other hand, he'd never before counseled a mind-reading super-boy while sitting on a flying saucer preparing to take another trip through time and space! Nor had *he* ever been visited by an angel before—if indeed that was what the Gloria-like woman really was. Still, he had plenty of comfort to give to the weeping teen. As far as he understood it, the Bible excluded *no one* from God's plan. And if Ben believed—

"That's just *it,* don't you see?" Ben snarled, raising his red-rimmed eyes to gaze at Jack and pushing himself away. "I don't know *what* to believe! That's why I had them kidnap you, but now you say they took you off and manipulated *your* mind! How can I know that anything you say might not have been put in your mind by *them?* They've ruined my confidence in you, don't you *see?* Any minute you might suddenly tell me you've been gone again, maybe for a day-trip around Jupiter, and how am I going to know that you're the same Jack Brennen that I was just talking *to?!*"

"Hmm," Jack said, stroking his chin. He noticed that it was stubbly. How long had it been since he'd shaved? "I can tell you this," he said softly, "and you can read my mind to know if I'm lying or not. As far as I know there's nothing that can separate me from the love of God. Romans 8:38–39 says, 'For I am persuaded that neither death, nor life, nor angels, nor principalities, nor powers, nor things present, nor things to come, nor height, nor depth, nor any other creature shall be able to separate us from the love of God, which is in Christ Jesus our Lord.' You called Gork and his gang 'critters,' remember? If God created them—and I believe God created everything in this universe, regardless of how big it truly is—then they can't separate us from God's love. Right?"

"They can't separate *you* from it, maybe. Me?" Ben said bitterly, "I've never felt it."

Jack couldn't keep his thoughts from running accusingly to Ben's parents. Who were they? Where were they? What kind of preparation had they given their son for life?

"You haven't figured it out yet, have you Jack," Ben growled. "You don't know where—or *when*—I'm from."

"Nope," Jack agreed. "You haven't told me, and I can't *read* minds."

"Very well," the boy said dramatically, getting off the bed to pace around the circular walls. "I was born in San Francisco. My parents were cult members. At least, my mother was. I didn't know my father. The cult elders always told me I had *many* fathers, and if father means the man who sleeps with your mother then I guess that's accurate. None of them took credit for impregnating my mother, though. They all believed I was conceived upon the altar by my mother and 'the Lord Satan' during a black mass—"

"The Satanic Church?" Jack interrupted. He remembered now that that was where he'd dropped the boy off so many years ago— "Wait! 1975 was the year I *met* you!"

"You got it, Jack. You gave me a lift *home* that night. Ah, there's no place like home, right? And there was certainly no place like *that* home! I wonder. Would you have given me a ride that night if you'd known who—or *what*—you were transporting?" Once again the boy's bitterness spewed out like bile.

Jack frowned to himself. "I . . . think I would have—"

"You would have taken me to the Satanic Church to murder myself?" Ben demanded, and Jack just rolled his eyes and sat back on the bed.

"Sorry," he muttered. "I won't interrupt again."

"Good! Then listen to me! I knew exactly where I was going that night! I was going back to the cult who had raised me to try to find that baby I had been and strangle it to death! Pity I didn't succeed, Jack—isn't it? Then I would never have grown up to be the monster I am, permitting these creatures to do through me what they've done!"

"Doesn't sound to me like it's your fault," Jack said quietly.

Ben smirked at him. "I thought you said you wouldn't interrupt." Jack nodded and closed his mouth. "And it *is* my fault. Oh yes, they trained me well for my task. The elders didn't exactly know what that would be, but they knew I was 'gifted' and that the gift was not of human making. It wasn't until I went back that night that I learned these creatures who own our planet and control our lives had done a little embryonic experiment—and that I was the result. They were waiting for me. Gork had somehow guessed I would come back there to try to kill myself. He may not be able to read minds, but Gork understands evil. Even if he *hadn't*, though, I still wouldn't have been able to get close to my infant self. From that point in 1975 at my conception until they took me away, the creatures had *always* had one of their number hidden within the cult. To 'protect' me, they said. To protect their investment is more like it!"

Jack swallowed hard. "And . . . when did they take you away?"

"June 8, 1988. My mother and her current boyfriend had taken me to settle with *another* cult in Oregon. I was going swimming with some kids I liked—I never let them know I could read their minds, so they liked me too—and suddenly there was the saucer, and there was George—Gork—and that was it."

"But then . . . you ought to be twenty-one by now—"

Ben hooted. "Sure! If I'd lived the intervening years straight through! Instead, I've been jetting around with these jerks for what *feels* like sixteen months. No—no it *feels* like sixteen *years*."

Jack tried to think of something he could say to this young man—something comforting or encouraging. He couldn't. He knew, of course, that some wounds simply cannot be comforted.

"Thank you for that," Ben said, looking directly at him.

"For what?"

"For not trying to comment on what you don't understand."

Jack nodded. The floor beneath them shook. *Earthquake!* he thought.

"No," said Ben. "It just means the computers have cranked the engines. Next stop, a bunch of crazy contactees. Hang on."

Jack gripped the arms of his chair and waited for the saucer to touch down. Strange, he thought. Suddenly they had started to move, and he had the clear impression they were going *up*, not coming down . . .

There was a grinding, twirling sound, then the craft seemed to launch free, up and out, and then quickly back down. "Who did you say we were going to meet?" Jack asked Ben.

"Contactees—people who've had experiences with UFOs. Think *Close Encounters of the Third Kind*, Jack. I sometimes wonder if Spielberg hasn't been visited himself."

The door slid open, and there in the hallway stood Gork. "I wonder, gentlemen," his words entered Jack's mind, "if you would accompany us to greet a few of our fans?"

"As if we had any choice," Ben growled. Then he picked something up off the table and handed it to Jack. "Here: Don't forget your comic book."

Jack started to ask, "What comic book?" but something in Ben's pleading eyes stopped him. As they followed Gork out into the hallway, he flipped open the front cover. There, scrawled in pencil above the title of the first story, he read:

SAY NOTHING. WATCH ME AND FOLLOW MY LEAD. WE'RE GOING TO ESCAPE.

Chapter Six

Worshipers at the rock

Jack rolled up the comic and stuck it in his front pocket, then followed Gork and Ben out into the hallway. "What is it you want us to do at this gathering?" he asked, and Gork stopped and looked back at both him and Ben.

He evidently telepathed a question to the boy, for Ben responded, "I didn't think he needed to."

"I didn't need to what?" Jack asked.

"I had asked young Ben to explain the purpose of this gathering to you, and your role in it," Gork explained directly to Jack's mind. "Apparently he doesn't want you to know."

"It's not working out with this guy," Ben complained as he gestured toward Jack. Jack was startled by this statement—perhaps even a little hurt. He thought they'd hit it off wonderfully well, and— "I want you to throw him back and give me someone else," Ben went on, his voice childishly petulant. Then Jack understood. If they were really about to attempt an escape, it wouldn't do for Gork to think they were already getting too close. He played along:

"If you would stop whining and start *listening* to me, son, perhaps you would learn something!" He looked at Gork. "But as for sending me back, I assure you that would be most welcome. I certainly hope you will consider it."

Gork looked both of them over carefully, his huge head swiveling on its spindly neck, his black eyes searching their faces. "I'm afraid that's quite impossible, Dr. Brennen. We've already invested far too much in your training to release you immediately. Besides, as I'm sure you realize, you know a bit too much." Those eyes turned back to Ben, and evidently said something to him about Jack having been his choice and now being his problem.

"Maybe he is, but I'm *your* problem," Ben snarled. "And you'd better think about how to please me if you don't want me to become *more* of a problem!"

Gork's eyes seemed to glitter, and the creature leaned his head in toward Ben as the boy suddenly cowered away. A threat had obviously been issued, and whether the boy was genuinely frightened by it or was just doing a good job of pretending, Jack was certainly convinced. The alien spun around and walked on down the corridor, and the two humans had no choice but follow after. As had happened on the day of his abduction, Jack was being floated above the floor. This time, however, Ben floated too.

"So will *someone* tell me the purpose of this party," Jack growled, "and what role I'm supposed to play in it?" He was pleased by the way that had sounded—gruff and bad-tempered.

"We're about to be displayed to some UFO groupies," Ben snarled back, sounding just as bad-tempered as he. "They'll ooooo and ahhhh over us, and consider us the luckiest people on earth because we've been 'permitted to fly with the gods.'"

"What gods? You mean Gork and his gang?"

"We're going to a conclave of 'ancient astronaut' crazies. They worship anything that comes out of a saucer, no matter how ugly it looks."

Gork spoke to both of their minds at once: "The attitudes of both of you become quite annoying." Suddenly Jack's head hurt so badly he thought for sure he was having an aneurysm. He was only mildly comforted when Gork continued, "Allow this to remind you both that we *can* practice behavioral modification—and *will*." Jack managed to twist his head around to see that Ben, too, appeared to be squirming against the pain. As abruptly as it had begun, the pain stopped. Both humans were also dropped back down to their feet, although this came as such a shock that neither Jack nor Ben could keep from crumbling on down to the floor of the corridor. "Dr. Brennen, please be advised that we have established positive relationships with this particular collection of humans, and we would prefer that they maintain a high opinion of us. Your positive comments and smiling visage will help us build rapport."

Still on his hands and knees, Jack leaned his head back to look up at Gork. "And if I *don't* smile and say nice things, you'll zap my head again."

"I'm simply urging you to take full advantage of the opportunities offered," Gork answered. "Now if you'll excuse me, we're about to make planetfall."

Jack looked over at Ben, who sat against the corridor wall rubbing the back of his neck. "I didn't really think they'd hurt you, too."

Ben blinked, true fear now obvious in his features. "I didn't either," he gasped. "They haven't in a long time."

"Was this my fault?" Jack asked, climbing to his feet.

"Of course not!" the boy snarled. "This is *their* fault! They're the ones doing this! And nothing has changed. Stay close to me. I have a plan."

Jack didn't argue. He certainly had no plan of his own. And although the prospect of more of such alien headlocks frankly terrified him, the thought of freedom from these monsters thrilled him more.

The ship rocked from side to side, then seemed to settle. Jack looked at Ben. "Planetfall," the boy explained.

Funny, thought Jack. It had felt just then that they were going *up* instead of coming *down.*

"It *did* feel like that, didn't it?" Ben nodded, still sitting against a corridor wall. "Curious. Oh well." He extended his hand, and Jack grabbed it and pulled him up. "Let's go meet our admirers."

Jack hadn't seen any alien but Gork since right after his abduction. Now the pink-lit corridor filled with them—dozens of them, all looking so much like Gork that Jack wondered how they ever told each other apart. They herded Ben and Jack before them toward the door. A moment later that portal opened, and Jack gasped with joy at the simple sight of the natural world. How long had he been inside this machine? He wanted nothing more than to race down the gangplank and kiss the earth—but he couldn't. Once more he had been swept off his feet, and now he was being floated down toward the waiting faces in a stately, he guessed respectable manner. The aliens couldn't prevent his eyes from scanning the horizon, however, and now that he actually *saw* where he was he began to question if they were on the earth at all. The landscape looked more lunar than earthly. Everywhere he turned, whorls of black lava jutted up into the sky. Beyond the silhouettes of the lava flows, however, was a sight that welcomed him home. He floated above the gangplank, gazing enraptured at a gorgeous, salmon-pink sunset. Or was it dawn?

"It's dawn," Ben commented from behind him. "These people have been waiting all night to see us."

Jack looked down now to meet the gawking stares of the elated onlookers. It didn't take Ben's gift to read their minds. Most of them were in an obvious mood of religious ecstasy.

Jack could read their beatific expressions: They were the privileged few being allowed to witness a close encounter of the third kind. And as for Jack and Ben—yes, the boy was right—they were being regarded with that mixture of awe and jealousy usually reserved for lottery winners.

What Jack found most remarkable in the onlookers was just how much they all looked like throwbacks to the sixties. Long hair, granny glasses, beads and braids, and leather fringe were everywhere—and not on just a stubbornly retro few. *Everyone* in this group looked like refugees from Haight-Asbury at its zenith. "Curious," Jack murmured.

"It is, isn't it," Ben responded with a dry smile. Then they were engulfed by the crowd. A stringy-haired, bell-bottomed blonde grabbed him by the foot and literally jerked him down off the gangplank.

"Who are you? What are you? Where are you from? Where did they pick you from?" she demanded, all in one breath.

"Ah . . . Louisville—"

"Where?" she frowned, wrinkling her nose.

"Kentucky?" he answered, though it was really more of a question.

"Why?" she demanded. Clearly she couldn't imagine why the aliens would stoop so low as to pluck someone from such a backward place.

"They . . . haven't really told me—" Jack told her honestly, and she dismissed him and darted past him to get to Ben. Meanwhile a very large, black-bearded man had grabbed him by the shoulders.

"What can you tell me about the Roswell incident?" he whispered, drawing Jack away from the saucer and into the crowd. "It's true, isn't it? It happened!"

"What? What happened?" Jack mumbled, wondering if Gork or another alien was watching him, wondering how far they would let him move into this crowd before "gently" compelling him to return to the ship.

"The saucer crash! The alien bodies recovered! July 8, 1947! The Air Force has been covering it up for more than twenty years!"

"It has?" Jack frowned.

"They recovered bodies! Alien bodies just like these!" The man gestured back toward the saucer, and Jack looked over his shoulder. Gork and the others were still on the gangplank, but they were obviously communicating with the admirers that clustered around them. He realized with some shock that he was beginning to be able to read their expressions. He had no trouble figuring out what their messages were, even though none of them happened to be telepathing into *his* mind at the moment. They were saying *We come in peace to all mankind* and *We love you* and *We've come to save you from yourselves.* Naturally, the crowd was buying it. After all, they'd come all the way out to this black-scarred desert to hear it. The bearded man jerked him around again and once more was in his face: "They've got the bodies on ice in a super-secret hanger at Wright-Patterson Air Force Base in Ohio!"

"Oh," Jack nodded. Then he shrugged himself free. "If you say so," he said as he thrust past the man and pushed still deeper into the crowd. He was looking around for Ben when he was grabbed once more by yet another pair of hands. This time he was spun around to face a man who looked to be about his own age—but who was acting like someone much younger. While most of those around him wore single strands of sixties love beads, this man wore ropes of them. While those around wore tiny, round, John Lennon-type glasses, this man wore huge, orange, octagonal shades Jack might have expected to see on Elton John. And while those around might have braids woven into their otherwise unkempt hair, this man's gray locks had been teased and tangled and braided into a hair helmet of immense proportions. Jack wondered how the guy slept at night. This aged wannabe-freak fixed Jack with his unblinking blue gaze and, smiling, asked:

"Is von Daniken with you? He is, isn't he?"

Jack recognized the reference. In the late 1960s a Swiss writer named Erik von Daniken had sold millions of copies of *Chariots of the Gods*, a book purporting to prove that humanity was the offspring of "gods" from outer space. "Documentary" films had been made to illustrate his viewpoints—Jack had seen them on television years ago. But hadn't the man pretty well passed from the scene? "I think you're a little behind the times, friend."

"Maybe he's not, Jack," he heard Ben say from right behind him, adding, "They're not watching us. Head for that level spot off to the left."

The gray-haired hippie was still smiling benignly as Jack dodged past him and headed left. He could see now that this flat spot in the lava bed had been turned into an impromptu parking lot. There were vehicles parked every-which-way across a small rise—and again, Jack found them a very curious sight. Not only curious, he realized; this was downright unsettling. While there were at least a few psychedelic-painted microbuses, most of these cars looked factory-fresh—yet not a single model dated from the 1970s or later. Jack felt a chill, but Ben wouldn't let him think about it. Instead the boy put his palm in the small of Jack's back and pushed him forward murmuring, "The gray-haired guy left his keys in his Firebird. Let's *go*."

"You mean you want us to take his car? Ben, that's grand theft auto!"

"If you ask me it's simple survival!" Ben said, now racing past Jack toward a blue Pontiac. Suddenly fearing being left behind with these creatures and the crazies who worshiped them, Jack pursued him. The boy dove into the passenger side, shouting, "Because I can't drive!" to Jack's unasked question. Left without any other option, Jack hopped in the driver's seat and turned the key, expecting any minute to feel a bolt of alien lightning shaft through his brain. Instead, he got a gust of hot air from the air conditioner, and a blast of sitar music from the radio. *Sitar?* he thought as he quickly turned it off. "This is crazy," he told Ben. "It's like we just dropped in on a post-Woodstock 'happening.'"

"Not post," Ben advised. "Pre-Woodstock. By about eight months."

Jack's heart suddenly was trying to claw its way up into his throat. "What are you talking about?" he gasped—even though he knew. "Woodstock was in the spring of 1968—"

"August of 1969, actually," Ben corrected. "Look, would you please drive?"

"But . . . I was a sophomore in college in 1969—!"

"Fine! Then let's head for California, *right now*. Maybe you can find your younger self and warn you to stay away from me!"

Jack managed to keep his trembling hands on the wheel as he steered the car toward the obvious tracks these hundreds of vehicles had made getting *to* this deserted place. He glanced in the rearview mirror—nobody was chasing them. Yet.

"He's not chasing us," Ben advised. "Trust me. The guy is stoned. While I was in his mind I could barely make any connection at all between one sentence and the next."

"It's not him I'm worried about," Jack grumbled. He glanced again at the rearview, watching the saucer.

"They're not coming either. In the first place they haven't missed us. In the second place they're trying to deal with a problem they didn't expect."

"Oh?"

"Two FBI agents posing as freaks just snuck on board the saucer."

"But . . . won't they need you to read their minds?" Jack worried.

"Not to deal with these two. They're already in the process of manipulating the agents' senses. There's no way the feds will even remember this experience. Meanwhile—there's the road!"

Jack hit the accelerator and raised a plume of black dust behind them. He was trying to figure out where they were—

"Albuquerque, remember?" Ben grunted. "A little west of it, actually. We're south of Grants."

Of course, Jack thought to himself. He knew he'd seen these lava flows before. When he was a child, every other summer his parents had made their bi-annual trek eastward to their old homeland, and he'd ridden through these forbidding black rocks every time. Somewhere north of here they would cross Interstate 40—or old Route 66, one. It didn't matter which. It would be a road away from here.

The tank was full. The car was new. Jack "drove like Jehu" until the highway came into view up ahead. "East or West?" he asked.

"You're driving," Ben said, sinking down in the bucket seat and leaning his head back. He looked like he was getting ready to go to sleep.

Jack thought about it. If this truly was pre-1970s, then he would know *no* one east of the rockies. He *would* know California, however—if he could remember it. When they got to the concrete ribbon he put the dawn behind them and put the pedal to the floor. After all, if this was pre-1970s then it was also pre-55-mile speed limits!

Then he thought better of it: What if they *should* get stopped by the police? What would a cop make of his Kentucky driver's license with the color picture and the 1996 expiration date? And what if it were reported that they were driving a stolen vehicle?

Another thought crossed his mind. He *did* have his wallet, and it was full of plastic—1993 plastic, with hologram IDs certain to make his credit cards conversation pieces anyplace he tried to use them. Besides, weren't they still calling his VISA a BankAmericard in 1969? "Ben," he murmured. "Have you got any cash with you?"

"Plenty of it," the boy mumbled, his eyes still closed. He turned his face away from Jack and yawned deeply. "You want some?"

"Might help," Jack nodded, and Ben pulled out his wallet and handed it to him. Jack kept one eye on the road while he flipped open the fat wallet and thumbed open the money pocket.

Inside were greenbacks—thousands of dollars worth. Hundreds, fifties, twenties—yes, the boy had come prepared. "I didn't have any money that first time I got away," Ben explained without opening his eyes. "I determined I'd never let *that* happen again."

Jack nodded appreciatively and looked back up at the road. He suddenly had an idea. Ben obviously was reading his thoughts as quickly as he could think them, for the boy groaned. "I don't wanna ride the bus!" he whined, but Jack's mind was already made up.

"That's the only way we can get rid of this stolen car and still make it to California. It's not so bad. I've ridden the bus across the country before." Indeed he had. Had embarked from a station somewhere near here, actually, in the summer of 1970—from Sante Fe to North Carolina. As he remembered it had been a terrible trip. Then again, he'd been alone that time. This time he was traveling with company.

"But not *good* company," Ben grumbled. "Not if you're going to make me ride the bus!" Jack made no reply—he just watched the speedometer, the rearview mirror and the highway markers. It took them twenty minutes to get to Grants, three minutes to get directions to the bus station, and another fifteen minutes to park the car at the other end of town and walk back to the station. Jack left the Firebird locked, with the keys and a twenty-dollar bill in the glove compartment. Ben told him he was crazy several times as they made the trek back to the station. Jack paid him no mind. He was worrying now about how long it would be until a bus came through.

They were lucky. An hour later they were riding westward through the desert toward Gallup. There was nothing more Jack could do about aiding in their escape—the aliens either would or would not think to look for them on a Greyhound.

Since Ben had been up all night waiting for Jack to wake up, the boy slept.

With no one to talk to and very little to look at, Jack had time now to reflect on far more troubling issues. What was he doing stuck in 1969? He no longer had any question that he was. He'd glanced at the date on a discarded paper in the bus station—January 18, 1969. He'd bought a *LIFE* magazine at the tiny newstand: It contained stories of the coming transition of power from LBJ to Richard Nixon, of the continuing war in Viet Nam, and about the Apollo 8's trip to the moon and back. It took him a minute to remember that this was also pre-Neil Armstrong's summer walk on the moon—and he shivered. He'd just been around the moon himself!

"Time travel," he muttered to himself as he gazed out at the empty landscape. Jack had never been much of a fan of "Quantum Leap" on television. He really wasn't the nostalgic type, for one thing, and besides, that show went in and out of time so easily and so often that it really all became meaningless. He'd loved the *Back to the Future* movies—even the middle episode that had confused so many of his friends. He remembered how much time he'd spent explaining that movie to others who couldn't quite get the parallel time tracks thing untangled. As an intellectual puzzle he'd always enjoyed such. Now he had his own dilemma to resolve. Not having a time-traveling Delorean stashed away anywhere, how was he ever going to get home? That's when it struck him: He would never get back to Gloria without the aliens' help.

That was the only way. He turned his head to glance at Ben, fearful of the boy's reaction to his thoughts. But Ben slept peacefully on. Were times of sleep his *only* time of peace? Jack wondered. What was in *his* mind, the head of this boy who knew far too much? What dark secrets had he read—indeed, what dark secrets had he *not* read? Jack had been a minister for over twenty years, long enough to know that *every* mind harbors dark secrets. What a weight for this youth to have to carry, forced to know the blackness of *every* person's soul?

More to the point, what dark intentions for this world lurked in the minds of the aliens and their "Ultrastructure"? If Ben remained with Gork and the others, wouldn't they continue to use him to manipulate time and space, and to suck the good out of God's green earth? Then how could he let the boy go back to them? Worse thought still, could he *ever* contemplate betraying Ben into their hands, just in order to win passage for himself back to his own time and place? Somewhere on the road west of Gallup, Jack tumbled into a pit of black despair.

* * *

"Linda? Hi . . . this is Gloria. How's George? Did he get over that stomach thing? Good. Yes. Yes we did. I'm so glad. Yes, we'll keep on praying. And that's why I called you. Oh no, that's okay. I just called to ask for you to be praying for Jack. No, it's not that—he's just kind of . . . well . . . missing.

"No, no, now don't do that. I'll call them myself when I think it's absolutely necessary. Right now I'm hoping he's just in some neighbor's garage or something, but I have to admit, I'm concerned. He went down to that creek behind our house—you know the one? Yes, well he hasn't come back. I walked down there but I didn't see him. No, the car is here. I'm sure it's nothing, but . . . I just have a really bad feeling, Linda. I've already called Janice and Rebecca to get them praying, and I know I can depend on *you* to pray too.

"No, no, not yet. I'll call you back if I feel like I need to do that. He'll *probably* walk through that door in just a minute or two, and I'm probably being silly—

"Well, thank you. Thank you. Let's just pray, can we? Then if you'll continue? I know you will. That's why I called *you.*"

After the two women prayed together over the phone, Gloria fixed a light lunch and sat down to eat it—her eyes on the door. "Bring him home, Lord," she prayed silently. "Please bring him home. . . ."

* * *

It took only a few stops for the pattern of bus travel to become numbingly routine. They would ride, then stop at a station for half an hour to stretch their legs and buy something to eat, then climb back aboard to ride some more, only to stop again and go through the exact same motions. Ben complained frequently, quietly reminding Jack that while it *was* 1969, there *were* still jet planes. Jack didn't reply. He didn't need to, since the boy knew what he was thinking anyway.

He felt better. He had no idea what was going to happen next, but he *did* feel better. As they'd rolled through Flagstaff sometime in the middle of the night, he had been reminded of Jesus' promise: "I am with you always." Always. That certainly covered "now"—whenever "now" really was. Comforted, he did his best to keep his mind free of frustration by focusing on God's purpose for him here. Surely there *was* some purpose. God works all things together for good to those who love Him, the ones He has called. At this point Jack didn't even feel particularly impatient to *discover* that purpose. Often it only showed itself clearly after the fact, in any case. He'd frequently preached that *doing* God's purpose didn't require any special knowledge, just faithful obedience. That he could do.

At about 5 P.M. he woke up and looked out the window. They'd passed through Barstow and had turned south toward Los Angeles. Sometime this evening he and Ben would be safely locked inside a motel room in the city where he'd grown up. There would be no cable television—wouldn't UCLA's basketball team be devouring opponents right now?—and all the people he knew would be twenty-five years younger. He was still debating seeking out their help. His present appearance would surely blow them away. Of course, he could pose as his own uncle, visiting from back east. . . . Then again, he could also go see his dad—

Ben was asleep again, and didn't see the sudden tears spill down Jack's cheeks. He quickly wiped them away. His dad had died a year ago—or rather, a year before this adventure began in Louisville. He still missed him so much. He suddenly remembered playing the role of the stage manager in a high school production of *Our Town.* Among his lines had been those warning the dead Emily not to go back in time to witness a birthday or any special day. The most mundane day, fully relived and remembered, would be enough to break her heart. No. He couldn't do that to his father. He couldn't do it to *himself.*

"So what *do* I do?" he said to the window.

Ben wasn't asleep after all. "Are you asking yourself? Or God?"

Jack looked over at him. "I don't know," he answered honestly.

Ben leaned back against the headrest and stared into the seat in front of him. "I'm sorry."

"For what?"

"For your dad dying. For separating you from your family. For getting you into this."

"You didn't get me into this," Jack said softly, expressing a conviction that had grown throughout the waking hours of the night and through this day. "God did."

Ben turned his head and looked at him, as if to say, *Do you really believe that?* "You do, don't you?"

Jack sighed, and nodded. Then he smiled. "I'm looking forward to that motel. Can't wait for a shower!"

"They'll find us, you know." The boy's voice was morose—hopeless.

Jack was shocked. Why this sudden change? He silently reminded himself that, for all of his experiences in and out of time, Ben was still a teen—

"Don't patronize me!" the boy snarled, and he shifted position to gaze angrily out the window. "I may be young, but I've got a very old mind. Very old—and very tired."

Jack tried to hear this without reacting—without thinking of anything but the most hopeful, helpful response: "Don't give up, man," he encouraged. "After all, this was your idea, remember?"

"Yeah," the boy sighed, watching the desert slide past. "A monumentally stupid idea."

Jack forced a smile. "We haven't been caught yet, have we?"

"How are you ever going to get back to your family if we *don't* get caught?"

Jack heard this, but chose to ignore it. "We'll need to get some new clothes—"

"Why not face facts?" Ben demanded. "Is that a part of your religion too—that ability to ignore the facts whenever they're unpleasant?"

Jack answered softly: "Sometimes they aren't really facts. Sometimes they're just fears, and lack of hope turns them into facts."

"Lack of hope," Ben echoed thoughtfully.

"Sure," Jack nodded. "That comes with a lack of faith. You know I believe in God. That's faith. And I believe the Bible when it says that faith is the assurance of hoped-for things, the certainty of things not yet seen. It also says that God's perfect love casts out fear. So—why not ignore those things which *could* happen, but haven't yet, when there's still hope that they won't?"

"Because there's *no* hope that they won't happen," Ben said flatly.

"I wonder," Jack began, "if this long trip hasn't made you too weary to be *capable* of hope. That happens sometimes."

"They'll find us, Jack," Ben said again. "They have spies everywhere. There's no one you can trust. I don't *believe* that. I *know* that."

Jack's forehead creased in a frown. "Let me ask you this. Can't you read the mind of people I *might* trust, to *see* if they can be trusted? If you tell me you're certain they cannot, why, I'll believe you. But if you *can't* be certain of that, then—could you trust my judgment?"

Ben rolled his eyes, then flopped deeper into his seat and leaned the headrest back. "Sure, Jack. Whatever you say." Somehow, he didn't sound convinced.

Jack Brennen looked back out the window. The landscape was still the same—sandy dirt and olive-drab scrub-brush stretched off into the distance. A line of pinkish-brown mountains ranged across the horizon, while above them floated wispy pink and gray clouds. The tans, the browns, the olive-greens, and the grays were all the standard colors of the California high desert. The pinks, however, were the gift of the sunset. Suddenly Jack caught sight of the moon and turned his head to study it. It was a full disk of brilliant silver, even out here on this bright desert. That was the orb Borman, Lovell, and Anders had just circled—the moon two other crews would have to circle before Armstrong and company touched down—and suddenly it registered. Did their presence in 1969 have anything to do with the frequent moon missions of that historic year?

"Bingo," Ben muttered.

"What?" Jack shifted all the way around to face the boy.

"You heard me. You guessed it. Gork and the gang are fascinated by America's moon visits."

Jack took a deep breath. "Because of their floating city."

Ben looked at him carefully. "I guess so."

"You don't know?"

Ben pursed his lips. "Not for certain."

A question had been bothering Jack, one he'd meant to ask earlier but hadn't seemed to have the chance. "You told me you could read any mind, anywhere, at any distance. Can you read the aliens' minds too?"

Ben contemplated that question for a full minute before carefully responding "Yeees . . . "

"But what?"

"But I don't do it."

Jack frowned. "Why not? I thought you couldn't prevent yourself from reading minds, just like—"

"—you can't prevent yourself from seeing without closing your eyes. Right. But I don't read alien minds for two reasons. One, I *don't* want them to know that I *can.* Jack, they'd kill me, no matter how useful I am to them alive. After all, I would know their secrets, right? And the second reason is I . . . " Here the boy paused, and seemed to struggle to get breath.

"What?"

"I . . . I can't stand to be in there with them." Ben leaned his head down to whisper, "They are either so *different* from people, or else so *horrible*, that reading their minds is like being in hell!"

"Hell? Do you mean that literally?"

"What I *mean*, Jack, is that they are utterly inhuman in all their views! *That's* why they can abduct people without compunction and subject them to the most horrible of tortures! They may convince their devotees that they do it in the name of science, or research, or some such. Truth is, Jack, they enjoy our pain. To them, it's like . . . candy."

Jack noticed his lips were suddenly very dry, and he licked them. He wasn't sure if he wanted Ben to go on—

"Then I'll stop," the boy said flatly, leaning back in his seat.

"No, no! I want to hear," Jack told him. "I *need* to hear." Ben read his mind and knew that it was true.

"Okay. They enjoy human suffering. Maybe the suffering of the cattle they mutilate too. I don't know. I just know that it's certainly not *greed* that drives these creatures—or at least not greed for money."

"Then Gork lied to me," Jack murmured.

"Gork always lies. They all do. They've got all the *things* they want—or that any *human* could want. That's how they buy governments. No, what *they're* after is simple *power*—control. They want the freedom to continue to do to us whatever they choose. They want to be able to continue to control our world through our government leaders. They want to continue to encourage wars and injustice, because those things result in cruelty and death and missing persons, and I'm convinced they harvest their own victims from every conflict. And they want something else too. . . ." Ben paused.

"What?" Jack asked breathlessly.

The boy looked at him with utter seriousness. "I don't know. I can't figure it out. But whatever it is, it is *the* most important thing to them, and they would gladly sacrifice all of humankind to get it."

"And . . . you have *no* idea what it is?"

"No. Except for this: It has something critical to do with *control*."

"I see," Jack nodded. He really felt the need to tumble the thoughts around in his mind some, polishing them up a little before speaking them. Since that was impossible with Ben, however, he just shrugged his shoulders and asked, "If they would sacrifice our race to get it, why haven't they already?"

Ben smiled to himself—a smug, "I-know-the-answer-and-you're-a-fool-for-*not*-knowing!" kind of smile. "God," he said simply. "That's why not. God won't let 'em."

Jack raised his eyebrows, then nodded. "I understand." He turned his face forward and sat back in his seat, folding his hands in his lap. *So you're not faithless at all*, he thought toward Ben. *In fact, this is a very powerful faith indeed.*

Chapter Seven

Men in black

Night, crossing the desert. No oncoming traffic. No reading lights on in the bus. The moon had long since set. With numbing regularity the long white stripes of the lane markers leapt up out of the distance into the headlights, then slipped swiftly off to the left and underneath them. They were alone—utterly alone in this long empty desert on the way to L.A. Jack dozed.

Then suddenly he was wide awake and screaming at the driver, for three brilliant white triangles had flashed across the road in front of them. He plastered himself against the window, looking up, following their trajectory as they looped over the bus, then flashed back around into its path and hovered there. The driver, terrified, swerved from side to side, and Jack was screaming at him to stop, to let them off, or else to jump off the road and drive headlong through the desert sands to get away. The huge vehicle screeched to a stop, careening sideways in the process and throwing them into the aisle. Just that quickly the doors were opened—or did they open at all? It happened so fast, it almost seemed as if Gork had suddenly appeared, standing over them in the aisle, and Jack could hear Ben shrieking as the gray monster thought-crushed his brain, and then he was himself screaming—screaming—screaming—

"Would you *wake up?* Wake up!"

Jack came awake in bed someplace, and groaned a sigh of relief. A dream. It had all been a dream—

"Not all," Ben said, and he flipped on a light.

Jack sat up, burying his eyes in his hands to keep the light out of them, fighting to remember exactly where they were.

"Motel room. Long Beach, California. 1969." Ben furnished these details crisply, efficiently. *Great,* Jack thought. *He's been inside people's brains so much he even sounds like a memory.*

"You were dreaming."

"Right," Jack nodded. "And were you reading my nightmare?"

"Of course. Terrifying."

"Right." Jack got up out of the bed and padded to the window. He pulled one drape aside and peered out. "It's daylight."

"Close to 11:30. But we didn't get in here until 3:00 in the morning. Remember?"

"It's starting to come back," Jack nodded.

"Good," said the boy. "Especially since this was your idea."

"What was?"

"To grab the local bus to Long Beach. To take a room in this motel. To contact your friends here. You *do* have friends here?"

"I did in 1969," Jack muttered, rubbing the back of his head. He looked around the room. They certainly couldn't have found a room more barren and gray than this. Gloria would never stay in a motel room like this.

"It was the closest motel to the bus station, and neither of us cared what it looked like as long as it had a bed for each of us. Is it *still* coming back?" the boy asked sardonically. After all, he was monitoring every single thing that Jack was thinking. He could certainly tell just how fuzzy-brained his companion felt.

"Maybe a cup of coffee would help," Jack mumbled.

"There's no room service here."

"Isn't there a coffee shop somewhere close?"

Ben winced. "You mean you want us to go walking around outside in broad daylight?"

"Why not? They don't know where we are."

"How do you know that?" Ben demanded.

Jack swallowed hard. "*Do* they know where we are?" he whispered.

"They know we took the bus west from New Mexico. They *think* we went north to San Francisco—they know our mutual connection there, of course—but they have Men in Black scouring California for us from the Bay Area all the way to San Diego."

"Who?" Jack frowned.

"Men in Black. *Men in Black.* Honestly, Jack, haven't you ever read any serious UFO literature?"

Jack smiled slightly. "Sorry, Ben. I've obviously been spending too much of my time in Ephesians. So tell me, who are the Men in Black?"

Ben took a deep, perhaps overdramatic pause, then began his explanation: "In September of 1953, three men dressed all in black appeared to Albert Bender, the founder and editor of *Space Review*, and told him something so terrifying that he left the field of UFO research. He told his closest associates that they were agents of the United States government, but years later he changed his story and said they were actually aliens disguised as humans. Ever since, there have been many visits by the Men in Black to various UFO fans. Most have claimed to be too frightened to talk about it later—although it is interesting that they weren't afraid to say they'd been visited."

Jack raised an eyebrow. "So who *are* these 'Men in Black,' really?"

Ben frowned. "There *are* those who think they are demons . . . ."

Jack blinked twice, hiding the chill that chased down his spine. "Are they?" he asked. He was wondering where that woman was—the one who looked like Gloria who'd kept appearing on board the saucer like an—angel. If they were at war with demons he hoped she was close—

"With what you already know, you have to ask who they are?" Ben scolded. "They're the enforcers of the Ultrastructure, obviously. They're agents of whatever government service they belong to, true, but more importantly they're agents of the aliens. It really doesn't matter what service they are attached to, they all function in exactly the same way when questions related to the defense of the Ultrastructure arise. And there are Men in Black salted through every military, police, and intelligence organization you can name. Regardless of their national loyalties, they function in concert with one another at the direction of their Gray masters. If they happen to be wearing the uniform of a military service or a police force, they change out of that into the nondescript black suit, white shirt and black tie of their 'other' employers. They're everywhere, Jack. Everywhere."

Jack sat on the edge of his bed, his hands clenched between his knees. It took him several deep breaths before he was ready to talk again. "So. What you're telling me is that we're being pursued by an organization that has access to the files of the CIA, the FBI, the Joint Chiefs of Staff, plus every major police agency and every national intelligence agency *in the world?*"

"Right," Ben nodded. "Because they are in effective *control* of each one. Understand me, Jack," Ben went on, having read

Jack's unasked question, "this doesn't mean those agencies *know* they are being controlled, and *every* one of those agencies would deny to the death that they are in any way linked with the other. The fact remains: The Men in Black *know*."

"Then why haven't they already found us?" Jack demanded. "I would think through their computer networks—"

"1969, Jack, remember? The infancy of computer networks? If this were 1995 we'd never have reached Arizona. The bus company will have computerized ticketing by then."

Jack mulled this over. "So we're still a needle in the haystack of California? Don't just give me your best guess, Ben. Read their minds and find out!"

Ben shrugged, nodded, then closed his eyes in thought. Jack could only assume he was sending his mind out on a sweep of the state, sampling the thoughts of all those he already knew were hunting them. Ben opened his eyes. "They've narrowed it down to southern California. They know we got off the bus in downtown L.A. last night."

"We've gotta get out of here!" Jack yelled out, and he grabbed up the phone and started to dial. Then he slammed it down and peered at Ben. "Are the phones safe?"

"In this decade, yes. Which one are you going to call?"

Jack heard this question with an exasperated grunt. He had been thinking of two possibilities for help, but hadn't decided yet which friend to involve in all of this. What bothered him now was the fact that he'd told Ben about neither, yet Ben knew of his internal debate. This lack of any mental privacy was beginning to really annoy him!

"Sorry," the boy said, and he got up and paced around the room, pretending indifference. Jack knew better—but he appreciated, at least, the boy's gesture. Now—which one to call?

His best friend in 1969 had been a college classmate—a seeker of wisdom who had explored every occult book shop on the Sunset Strip and Hollywood Boulevard, and had visited every non-Western place of worship in the region of southern California. Baptized an Episcopalian as a baby but a self-identified agnostic by his teens, Jeffrey had been the perfect foil for Jack's naive evangelical faith. They'd had long talks, taken long drives, engaged in one never-ending discussion of the nature of truth, the existence of God, and the possibility of ever really *knowing* anything. By the present—no, by 1995 Jack corrected himself, uncertain where, if anyplace, *now* could possibly be on any time line—Jack had lost track of Jeffrey completely. But in 1969 he knew exactly where Jeffrey could be reached—living in his parents house in Riverside.

And how would Jeffrey respond to a cryptic call from the future? With fascination, probably. With some degree of critical incredulity. He would doubtless begin immediately to run the time paradox questions. He would probably want to meet Gork himself—

"Then don't call him!" Ben said from the bathroom door, jerking Jack out of his reverie. "Sorry to pry, but the person you've just described to yourself is exactly the type that Gork and his buddies most enjoy talking to. If you love your friend"— naturally, that's exactly what Jack had been thinking of in response to Ben's statement—"then you won't permit him to get entangled in this affair in any way. They'll seduce him, Jack. Believe me."

"Very well then," Jack muttered, turning his thoughts to Ferguson Potter. He sometime wondered if many of Ferg's problems weren't directly related to the fact that his parents had given him that name. Not that Ferguson was a *bad* name, especially—it was simply . . . odd. And Ferguson Potter, too, was . . . odd. A fun-loving, round-faced guy with a good mind and zero ambition, he'd come from an Appalachian hill family that had moved to California to escape utter poverty. Strong believers, his parents had raised Ferg in the "nurture and admonition of the Lord," and that's why Jack knew him. They'd grown up together in church—Jack a preacher's kid, Ferg a deacon's kid. To be honest, *each* of them had been a bad influence on the other, despite *all* their respective parents tried to do. Oh, Ferg was a believer all right—a strong believer who wrestled regularly with the possibility that God had called him to full-time Christian service. When majoring in fraternity at college caused him to flunk out—and subsequently get drafted—that sense of calling had led Ferg to seek appointment as a chaplain's assistant. He'd received that assignment on the strength of his good mind and strong convictions, then lost it when he inexplicably went AWOL just before being shipped overseas to Germany. Instead, he'd spent the Viet Nam War dodging bullets as a desk clerk in Saigon. Ferg was a character.

"Sounds like he has possibilities," Ben called from the bathroom. There was great tension in the boy's voice, and Jack wondered if he—"I'm terrified, that's why!" Ben snarled. "We've got to get out of here! Call this Ferguson person!"

That was a problem. Where was Ferg in 1969? College? Or had he already flunked out? Was he still living at home? One way to find out. Jack looked up the number in the phone book, and called the Potter home.

"Jack? Is that you?" Mrs. Potter grinned into the phone at the sound of his voice. Of course she knew him. She'd been his Sunday School teacher, after all . . . . Fortunately, she couldn't *see* him. He felt certain she was hearing a long-haired kid wearing love beads and leather fringe, instead of a graying father in bifocals. That was fine—

"It's me. You all right?"

"Just working," she answered. That was normal. Ferguson's folks really did nothing *but* work. Maybe that was why Ferg had such an aversion to it himself?

"Looking for Ferguson. Is he there?"

"You're in luck. He got a weekend pass." *So—he's already in the service,* Jack thought. "I'll put him on," she said, but she didn't put him on—not immediately. This, too, was normal. "How's college?"

Oh dear. He struggled to remember: "Ah . . . it's fine. Lots of . . . of papers due. Too many!"

"Well I know you'll do fine," she said, still smiling into the receiver. She'd always been proud of him. In a sense she counted him her own son, almost as much as she did Ferguson. "Are you dating anyone?"

"Ah . . . no. Not . . . not steadily. . . ." This had been true of 1969—and how could he tell her the truth? Ben stepped around the corner from the bathroom and looked across the room at him, grinning. Jack pointed a warning finger at him and said, "Is Ferg dating?"

"Oh, I think you know better than *that*," she replied, sounding just a touch exasperated. "I don't think that boy will *ever* give me grandkids. But he *did* get his appointment as a chaplain's assistant, did your parents tell you?"

"I . . . had heard something about that," Jack responded. Patience, he told himself—and Ben.

"I'll let him tell you. Ferguson! Ferguson! . . . " She left the phone, and Jack said a silent thank You to the Lord. A moment later Ferg picked it up, answering in his characteristic:

"Yellow."

"Ferg," Jack smiled, genuine affection in his voice.

"Jack, my man. How's it hangin'?"

"Got a problem, Ferg. A bad one. Need your help."

"Oh?" The voice shift was both subtle and sweet. Ferguson had just dropped from his goofy goodfellow personality into the posture of a serious listener. He would have made a *good* chaplain's assistant, Jack mourned silently. He would have made a good *chaplain*. "Tell me."

"I can't, really. I just need you to come get me without saying anything to your mom about it. I'm at the Best Western motel downtown on Long Beach Boulevard, just off the Harbor Freeway. Room—" Jack glanced at Ben.

"106."

"Room 106."

"Gotcha. Be there in a sec." And with that, Ferg hung up. Jack held the phone away from himself and looked at it. He was thinking that maybe the angel was still nearby after all.

"I wish you wouldn't think about her," Ben said, shivering. "Gives me the willies!"

"Stay out of my mind," Jack shrugged, "and you'll be fine." He hung up the phone, got up and put on his pants, then stretched out on the bed to wait. One thing about Ferg. If you asked him to drop every responsibility and chase after an adventure, you could count on him to *be* there.

Still, it took Ferg half an hour to get to them from his parent's home in Lakewood. That was plenty of time to worry about the approach of the Men in Black. "Where are they now?" Jack asked nervously for the dozenth time.

"They've got two cars at the bus station here," the boy muttered quietly. He described the unfolding events much like a golf announcer on television—barely speaking above a whisper, but managing to convey with every succeeding sentence his own growing tension. "There's a third on the way down from L.A. The locals are asking about our arrival last night—but no one working now was on duty at 3:00. They're talking in the men's room. Now they're coming out. There are six of them, and they're fanning out—three groups. They always work in pairs. They're about to begin checking hotel registries in the area."

"Ferr-gu-son," Jack sang anxiously, his hands behind the back of his head, his eyes searching the ceiling. "Come on, Ferg . . . ."

"One pair is about three blocks from us and walking this way."

"Oh, come on, Ferguson, how long does it take to get from—"

They heard the noise of a puttering engine pull up outside the door, and Jack was off the bed, onto his feet, and at the peephole before the car shut off. "It's him," he mumbled in relief. "Grab your stuff." He did as he'd instructed Ben, scooping up his own baggage—which amounted to two brown paper bags. They contained the few changes of clothes they'd managed to find time to buy during bus stops—one bag for new, one bag for dirty. The dirty clothes bag was fuller.

Thus equipped, he threw open the door before Ferguson could knock on it, then stepped back to give his friend a good look at him before saying anything.

Ferguson's big, goofy smile froze on his face. His eyes grew wide—very wide—and he said, "Whoa." Quickly, he recovered enough to say, "Let me guess. You're doing a movie, right? And this is an *extremely* realistic age makeup."

"Nope."

"Ahhhh—you've been experimenting with LSD and got some *really* bad acid. I've warned you about that stuff Jack—" Clearly Ferguson knew something was radically wrong. Humor was his manner of coping with it.

"Sorry, Ferg."

"You got caught in a time warp and it took you twenty years to find your way back?" Ferg was grinning, the laugh lines around his eyes crinkled up in merriment. Whatever it was that had caused his friend to age so precipitously, Ferguson was bound to find a joke in it.

"That's getting a lot closer, my friend—"

"Look, could we do this in the car?" Ben asked from behind Jack. "They're five doors down, grilling the clerk this very minute—"

Jack needed no further urging. "In the car. Quick." He dashed past Ferguson for the passenger door of the bottle-green VW, threw it open, and hustled Ben into the backseat. Ferguson wasted no time in following them, and by the time Jack was himself in and had shut the door, the old Beetle's engine had coughed to life.

"I take it we're avoiding those two guys in the suits?" Ferg said casually as he backed out of the parking space. Then he jammed down the clutch and threw the Bug into first, and they were out the back entrance of the motel in a screech of tires. Jack peered out the tiny rear window to see the two Men in Black sprinting after them, but Ferguson just patted him on the knee between second and third and said, "Don't sweat it. We've lost 'em."

Ben gave a disdainful snort from the backseat, then shouted, "They know what we're driving!"

"So what?" Ferg frowned. "We'll just spin by the house and swap this out for my dad's car."

"No!" Jack barked—with far more authority than Ferguson had every heard from him at nineteen. His friend rolled his big eyes around to peer at him curiously.

"Is that really *you?*" Ferg asked as he glanced in the rearview mirror and made a sudden turn up an alley.

"Not as you ever knew me," said Jack.

"Oh yeah," Ferg grinned again. "Time warp, right?"

Jack twisted around to look back at Ben. *How much should I tell him?* he asked the boy silently. Ben winced, shrugged, and said, "The less he knows—"

"The less I know, what?" Ferg asked, gunning the VW through some garbage cans and sending them bouncing.

"The safer you'll be," Jack finished, his eyes on the end of the alley.

Ferg pursed his lips and nodded as he switched back onto a main street and floored the accelerator. In a VW Beetle this certainly didn't produce actual *speed*, but it *did* make a lot of earnest noise. "You mean from the bad guys back there."

Jack turned back straight in his seat and looked out the windshield for the first time. "You got it."

"Right. Ahhhh—they *are* the bad guys, right? I mean, *we're* not the bad guys or anything?"

"We're the good guys, Ferg," Jack answered quietly, closing his eyes and reaching back to rub his knotted neck with both hands. "Believe it."

Ferguson concentrated on his driving, zipping the tiny car back and forth through the streets of downtown Long Beach, working his way north and west toward the ghetto. Ferguson had many black friends—he was the first white guy Jack had ever known who kept his car radio tuned to the "soul" station—and he felt at home in that section of town that other whites went out of their way to avoid. He was thinking their white pursuers would be as uncomfortable as most, and would quickly give up the search.

"Don't count on it," Ben said ominously from the back seat. It took a minute for Ferguson to realize the boy was talking to *him.*

"Don't count on what?"

"Don't count on losing the Men in Black in the ghetto. They have African-American agents too."

"African-Ameri . . . you better not let the brothers hear you calling them that," Ferguson warned. "These folks are *black*—and *proud* of it."

"Whatever we call them in 1969, your strategy won't work."

"How do you know that was 'my strategy?'" Ferg frowned. He was thinking that he wasn't sure he liked this kid.

"That's okay, nobody else likes me either."

Ferg turned his frown on Jack in a mute demand for an explanation. "Ferg, this is Ben. Ben reads minds."

Ferguson blinked. "Really?"

"Really. And if he says your strategy for losing the Men in Black won't work, listen to him. He's reading their minds too as they chase us."

Ferguson's eyes popped, and he faced forward and drove. "Weird," was all he managed to say for several minutes as he angled them toward Signal Hill.

Jack twisted around in the seat to look at Ben again. "Any suggestions?"

"We need to get out of the city and get to some deserted place by nightfall. In the daytime they can only pursue us in ground vehicles. At night—?" He looked at Jack and raised an eyebrow meaningfully.

Jack understood. At night Gork could hunt for them by saucer. He rolled over in his mind the possibilities of deserted areas within a half-day's driving distance. "We could go to Big

Bear Lake," he murmured, letting Ben view the place through his memory pictures.

"That looks as good as any," the boy said glumly. "This was a stupid idea. We're never going to make it." With that announcement Ben slumped down on the uncomfortable backseat.

Jack looked over at Ferguson, who's round face was now utterly serious. He had already started heading toward a route that would take them the back way toward Riverside, and on beyond it to the mountains. After a few minutes of silent driving, Ferguson took a deep breath, then said, "Seems like it might be a good time to tell me what all of this is about."

"You're probably right," Jack sighed, and he began to try to explain. Many questions, a number of murmured "Whoa's!", and two hours of driving time later, they were in the foothills above San Bernadino.

"Okay," Ferguson said airily—and he laughed.

"Ah . . . what's okay?" Jack asked.

"Just—okay," Ferg shrugged. "I mean, if somebody you knew were to drop in on you twenty years later and tell a story like that, what would you say?"

"You don't believe me?"

"Sure I believe you!" Ferg laughed. "Sure I do. Now where do you want me to take you?" They were already headed up the "Rim of the World" road, and would be at the lake in twenty minutes—assuming the VW would make the climb. It seemed to be crawling up the mountain.

Jack called back to Ben. "*Does* he really believe me?" When Ben didn't answer, Jack twisted around to look at him. That's the first time he noticed the expression on the boy's face: He was white with terror—as white as an alien. "What is it?" Jack demanded quietly. "Is Gork brain-crushing you?"

Ben trembled. "No," he managed to squeak out.

"Ferg, take us anywhere you can think of. Something's wrong with the boy. What is it, Ben? Where is your mind? What are you reading?"

"I . . . I . . . can't say . . ." Ben stammered. Whatever it was, Jack thought, it was terrible.

* * *

Dead babies. Mutilated bodies. Images of the victims of serial killers. The confessions of rapists. Napalm in Nam.

These were the images Randy Anderson kept rolling through his mind, at the direct instruction of his supervisor. Occasionally he would interrupt them with the thought, *Are you listening, boy? You want some more? How's this?* Then he would shift to yet another grisly mental picture of some horrible thing he'd witnessed as an MP in Southeast Asia, or as a cop in the heart of Los Angeles.

Vice-squad busts. Abused children. Suicides. Pit bull attacks. Fire fights in a rice paddy. Fear. Hatred. Gore. *Are you getting all of this, kid? Are you enjoying my mind?*

As instructed, he was maintaining radio silence, keeping the green VW at least a mile ahead of his ram-charged Dodge—which wasn't easy. He had some questions about the "violent mental-image" thing—did anyone really believe that a kid in that car could be reading his mind?—but he swept them from his thoughts whenever they popped up. Certainly he didn't voice them, for his supervisor was sitting right next to him—a cold-eyed, pasty-faced old warrior in silver wrap-around shades. Except for the sunglasses he looked for all the world like an undertaker in that plain black suit—

Undertakers. Morgues. Dismembered bodies. Natural disasters. Perversity. Lu—

"They just turned off," his supervisor muttered.

Indeed they had. Private driveways branched off this whole section of road, dropping down or climbing up into the forest on either side to thousands of tiny cabins. Which driveway had they taken?

"Look for dust," said his supervisor in that same, quiet monotone he'd used for every sentence Randy had ever heard him mutter. Silently they both scanned the private drives on either side of the road for plumes of dust. After a couple of wordless miles, the supervisor—Randy had never heard his name—muttered, "Retrace." They turned around.

* * *

Ferguson let the VW bounce down the dirt trail, whipping the wheel from side to side to avoid trees. "Watch out!" Jack was screaming, but Ferguson only gave a grim-faced chortle.

"You wanted to get away didn't cha? You told me to go wherever I thought to go!"

"But Ferguson!" Jack shouted, clinging for dear life to the strap behind his right ear, "this is a *bike* trail!"

Ferg gave a little mock-frown of disbelief. "Really?" Then he cackled. "It's also a back path to a place I know. Some of the brothers and I had a party up here last June, and I *think* this bike path will run into the driveway to the cabin we used. It's a renter. Maybe we'll luck out and nobody'll be there."

A moment later they twisted around another sharp turn and—sure enough—there was a dirt drive twenty yards below. The only trouble was—this was where the trees were thickest, and the path the most narrow. Ferg hit his brakes and they slid on the pine needles toward a close-set pair of tree trunks. At the last possible moment the vehicle stopped—and Ferguson was able to thread it between the trees. He grinned triumphantly. "Try doing *that* in anything but a VW!"

Jack knew he was as white now as Ben *had* been. He took a deep breath, then shot a glance at the backseat. The boy was cowered down in the floorboards—and yet he looked, if anything, *less* terrified than before.

"It's a long story," Ben muttered. Then Ferg was making a sharp, skidding left onto the dirt driveway, and Jack looked back out the windshield. They were heading up a little incline toward an A-frame cabin. There were no cars anywhere around it. "Well," Jack managed at last to mumble. "Maybe we'll at least have enough time for you to tell it."

* * *

"And now?"

"We watch."

"Watch and wait. Watch and wait."

"You challenge His wisdom?"

"Never. I grieve at the liberties they take! I mourn the losses He permits."

"He permits them. Not we."

"And so we wait."

"And watch. . . ."

Chapter Eight

Old friends

Two unmarked police cars, one black Oldsmobile with government plates, and a CHP cruiser all blocked the private drive to the cabin. They were awaiting further instructions from the supervisor, who for some reason had gone up to the town of Big Bear. Meanwhile they followed orders, not talking to one another, focusing their minds on things twisted, sordid, perverse. Some of them did so easily—for supposed lawmen, perhaps *too* easily. And—as they'd been told to do—they punctuated their thoughts with mental insults aimed at the boy they were tracking. It seemed stupid to most of them to do so, but hey. . . . They were each dressed in black suits. They'd each done *plenty* of stupid things dressed this way.

This was not a heavily-traveled road. Still, they kept a rotation of two men out on the highway on either side of the drive, discouraging rubber-necking with long, fierce frowns as they waved any traffic past.

About an hour after they'd located the drive, Randy Anderson's black-and-white Dodge came back down the mountain, and pulled in behind them. The supervisor stepped out. Slowly he removed his sunglasses, and placed them on the seat of the car.

Those in the group who had never seen him without them were surprised to see how small his eyes were. From his white shirt pocket he pulled a pair of thick, glass-lensed bifocals, unfolded them, and put them on. At the same methodical pace he slipped out of his black coat and laid it on the seat of the car. The black tie came off next, and he unbuttoned the top button of his oxford-cloth shirt. Then he opened the back door of the cruiser, and got out two large pizzas and a six-pack of soda. It was then that Randy made the connection in his mind—the person the supervisor most resembled. He looked like Dr. Doolittle. Not Rex Harrison, from the movie—the little round doctor in the books.

The assembled force tried not to stare as the supervisor turned around to look at them. He spoke three words—only three: "That is all."

They waited for a moment, looking at him expectantly, but he said nothing more. Then Sheriff Randy Anderson threw his car in reverse and backed out of the drive. The others responded by jumping into their own vehicles, and soon all of those powerful engines had roared to life.

The supervisor—pizzas perched on one hand like a waiter, six-pack of soda dangling from the other—waited for each of them to leave. Then he began his casual stroll down the driveway toward the cabin.

* * *

"Yep!" Ferguson called from the other side of the porch. "Here it is!" He came walking back around to the front door holding up a key. "It was right where it was before." As he placed the key in the lock and turned it, Jack clutched his shoulders and shivered.

"Are they expecting snow up here tonight?" He knew it often snowed at this elevation in the winter.

Ferguson looked at him as if he were crazy. "How should I know?" Then he pushed the door with his shoulder, and they were inside.

The cabin had been recently occupied. *Very* recently. In fact, for a moment Jack felt a little like Goldilocks breaking into the three bears' house. He even glanced at the table to see if three bowls of porridge were cooling. "I'm feeling really nervous about this, guys," he said. "What if the owner comes back?"

"Key was hanging in the safe spot, right?" Ferg argued. "It's Monday afternoon, right? Somebody *was* up here, a renter probably, but they went back down the mountain to work and left the key where they were supposed to. Let's look around. Maybe they left some food." Ferguson was the only one to follow his own suggestion. As he started going through the refrigerator and cabinets, Jack and Ben tumbled into a couple of old, dusty couches and looked at one another. *I wonder if they know where we are,* Jack thought to himself.

"Yes," Ben responded, but he didn't elaborate.

"All right, well, we didn't do too badly," Ferguson was saying as he walked back into the living room area. "We've got part of a box of cereal and a little milk. We've got some tea bags, salt, and a half a box of spaghetti. So—what'll it be?"

"I'm not really hungry," Jack murmured. There was a knot in the pit of his stomach so huge it would hardly permit space enough for food. "Ben, are you?"

The boy shook his head.

"Good!" Ferguson grinned. "Then the cereal's mine!" He went back into the kitchen to find a bowl.

Ben's morose expression prompted Jack to ask, "How long before they come get us?"

"I don't know," the boy said, his eyes studying the cabin's plank floor.

"That's . . . a little unusual, coming from you. . . ." There was a question in Jack's words, and Ben knew, of course, exactly what it was.

"What happened in the car?" he began glumly. "They blocked me, that's all. They're doing it now."

"Blocked you? How? I didn't think that was possible."

"Or you would have done it yourself?" the boy snarled. There was no use denying it. Jack just shrugged. "You couldn't do it, anyway. You don't have it in you."

"Why? What'd they do?"

Ben took a long, deep breath, then exhaled it slowly before answering. "They all filled their minds with the most horrible, most repulsive thoughts a person could think—all of them!—and they kept rotating those thoughts over and over in their minds. Jack, some of the things they imagined couldn't be described in words. I couldn't get any thread of their intentions toward us because they kept shuffling those thoughts under this bombardment of evil! And all the time they kept . . . well . . . taunting me, asking me if I was enjoying their disgusting imaginations! And here's the thing that really got to me, Jack. These horrible things they were imagining doing? Some of them were imagining doing those things to *me*." The boy couldn't prevent himself from tearing up as he said this, and for the first time since he'd met him Jack saw Ben as the fearful fifteen-year-old he really was.

He remembered back to when he was fifteen, and felt nothing but admiration for the way Ben had handled all the pressures of his young life. "Thank you," Ben said, plucking the compliment from Jack's mind as he wiped his tears away on his sleeve.

"One thing I don't understand, though," Jack frowned. "Have you not been with these people—creatures—whatever—long enough to have heard *many* such thoughts?"

Ben nodded, now almost fully in control of himself. "Yes. It's just that they were never doing things to *me* before. That makes a difference."

Jack prevented himself from smiling as he nodded and said, "It usually does, yes."

"And these are the people who are about to *grab* us! I tell you, if I could get a message to Gork right *now* to come and get us, I would!" Jack felt a cold chill run down his spine at those words.

Ferg walked back into the room, bowl in his left hand, spoon in his right. "How is it?" Jack asked.

Ferg wrinkled his nose. "A little stale." He took another bite, and chewed it reflectively. "I was just thinking," he said after swallowing. "Maybe I should go hide the VW under the trees? They could be looking for us with choppers. . . ."

"Ben says that—" Jack began, but the boy cut him off.

"That's a good idea. Why don't you do that?"

Ferg nodded, took another bite of the cereal, then—mouth still full—said, "I think I'll do that," and headed out the door.

Jack frowned a question at Ben.

"I just wanted a chance to talk to you without him hearing," the boy answered. He looked terribly depressed. "Of course I'm depressed!" he snarled. "Look at this mess I've gotten us into! You, your friend—it's all my fault!"

Jack thought about that. "I thought you told me it was all *their* fault? The aliens."

"They're not aliens," the boy grumbled, and Jack sat up straight on the couch. "Look," Ben continued. "You've got to send your friend away. He's already in deep trouble, and it's getting deeper every minute he's gone."

Jack thought he'd understood what Ben was talking about. Now he wasn't sure. He *did* have an uneasy feeling, though. "Trouble? Besides the trouble *we're* in?" The boy nodded, and nodded again as he read Jack's next thought. Jack sat back in the couch. Along with the knot in his stomach he now had a pang of guilt. At that moment Ferguson came back in the door. There he stopped, and looked at the two of them.

"Well, *this* is a cheerful bunch!" he grinned. "I just *know* we're in for a fun afternoon together, right?"

"Ferg, are you AWOL?" Jack asked.

Ferg's eyes widened, then narrowed, then he grinned sheepishly. "The kid really can read minds, can't he? Ah . . . sorry about all the things I've been thinkin' about ya, kid."

"No problem," Ben said expressionlessly.

Jack sighed deeply. "You never did get a chance to tell me about the chaplaincy program."

"Yes I did. Two weeks ago. Oh, I know that was twenty-some *years* and two weeks for *you*, but it was just two weeks ago for me. Seemed kind of repetitive to bring it up again, y'know?"

"And now you're AWOL."

"Yeah, well—things like that happen sometimes. They'll get over it. My commander likes me."

Jack looked at him and shook his head.

"He *doesn't* like me?" Ferg asked, his tone of voice lightly mocking.

"They don't get over it," Jack said sadly. "You get busted, you lose your appointment and your orders for Germany, and get sent to Nam instead."

Ferguson just looked at him, then he blinked twice. "You *know* all this? For certain?"

"For certain," Jack nodded. "The one thing I didn't know—because you never told me—was *why* you went Absent Without Leave. I never had any idea I was responsible."

Ferguson thought a moment, then scratched his head. "Well I guess you *weren't* responsible—*then.* I guess you are now." He picked up the bowl of cereal and took another bite. Then he made a face. "Yuck. Soggy."

"Don't worry," Ben said glumly. "Pizza's coming."

"What?" Ferg frowned, then he looked at Jack. "You phoned in for pizza?"

Jack gave him a blank look and a shrug, and they both turned to stare at the boy. Ben had shifted around to lay on the couch, his hands folded on his stomach, his eyes fixed on a point somewhere on the ceiling.

For all his nonchalance, Ferguson clearly hadn't gotten away from what was, for him, Jack's prediction. "One question," he asked as he put the bowl on the table. Then he looked Jack in the eye. "Do I survive?"

Jack nodded and smiled, happy at last to be able to give some good news. "You do."

"Whew!" Ferguson gasped, and a new smile lit up his face. "Then I'm fine! The only reason I applied for chaplain's assistant was 'cause I didn't wanna get shot at! By the way—do we win?"

"Win?"

"In Viet Nam."

"Oh. No."

"Humph," Ferg grunted, frowning. "Bummer."

There was a knock on the door. Ben was the only one who didn't jump in fright. Jack looked at the boy, but Ben wouldn't look at him. "Come in," he called out nervously.

A man in white shirt and black pants opened the door—and smiled.

Jack knew the smile well. This was, indeed, his friend of long-standing, the guy he'd roamed all over these mountains with. "Jeffrey!" Jack shouted, rejoicing.

"It is indeed," the supervisor replied, smiling his Dr. Doolittle smile.

Jack hesitated before speaking again, quickly running the implications of his friend's appearance in this place, at this moment, through his mind. "Are you . . . " he began, but he faltered. This was Jeffrey, his best friend—and Jeffrey was a "Man in Black"?

"Am I one of 'them?'" Jeffrey said, still smiling enigmatically. "Why not ask the boy there?"

But Jack didn't need to—not now. He'd noticed Jeffrey's lined face, and his gray hair. Jeffrey was at least as old as he. That awareness passed over his eyes, and his old friend noted it and nodded. Then he turned to Ferguson, who was staring at them both.

"You're Ferguson—is that right? We met—oh, years ago, for me, though I dare say it was less for you. Here—" Jeffrey said, handing one of the pizzas to Ferg. "Have a pizza." Ferguson accepted the box, but still said nothing. This was all beginning to get to him. "Tell you what, Ferguson—why don't you take that one with you and eat it on your way down the mountain? Oh, and there's some drinks on the porch, too. Get yourself a couple."

Ferg gazed at him blankly. "You mean I can . . . go?"

"No one will stop you," Jeffrey said warmly. "I can guarantee that."

"But . . . how will they . . . how will they get—"

"To where they're going?" Jeffrey asked politely. He had always been the most *correct* person Jack had ever known. "I'll take them there. It's surely clear to you that where they're going, *you* can't take them . . . ?"

"Ah . . . sure, but . . . " Ferguson looked at Jack for help.

"Go ahead, Ferg. Do as he says. We've already messed up your life enough today."

Ferguson looked back and forth between their faces, then a relieved smile crept over his own. "Well . . . okay then. Oh, shoot," he added, frowning in apparent consternation.

"What?" Jack asked, worried.

"I'd wanted to see a flying saucer!" Ferg explained, then he cackled.

"That *can* be arranged, I assure you!" Jeffrey said, laughing along with Ferg—but Jack could only see that as menacing now. His old friend, menacing? This was becoming a very sad day indeed.

"Well," Ferg shrugged, and he stuck his hand out to shake Jack's. "I'll see you."

"You will," Jack nodded, and he gripped Ferguson's hand firmly. The only trouble was, he didn't know if he would ever see Ferg again. He wrapped him in a sudden bear hug, until Ferg broke away saying:

"Hey, come on! None a' that stuff. Jeffrey, my man, take care," he continued, shaking the supervisor's hand. "Oh, and you might try some Grecian Formula on that hair. See ya' kid." He waved at the couch, then opened the door.

"Don't forget the pizza," Jeffrey reminded him, and Ferg grinned and grabbed up the box.

"Toodleoo!" he said. Then he was gone.

A moment later the VW coughed awake again, and they all listened silently as it puttered away.

When the sound died, Jeffrey glanced at the other pizza box and said, "Aren't you hungry? You've been on the run all morning."

"You've been chasing us all morning?"

"I came in on it late, actually. As your friend apparently noticed," he said, running fingers through his gray mane, "I really don't belong in this year any more than you do."

"What year *are* you from?"

"1995. And you?"

"The same," Jack nodded. "I guess that's the point time has progressed to—"

"Meaningless idea," Jeffrey said, shaking his head. "If time travel exists, then the old saying 'There's no time like the present' takes on a new and very literal meaning. There's no time like the present because there *is* no present. Right, young Ben?"

The boy had said nothing since Jeffrey had come in. He still said nothing, choosing instead to stare into space.

"Well, he's understandably frustrated," Jeffrey said. "And what about you, old friend? Are you also frustrated?"

Jack thought about that a moment, then he took the pizza box and opened it. "I'm confused," he said, picking up a slice of pepperoni.

"And why wouldn't you be?" Jeffrey responded, helping himself to a slice as well. "You've been ripped out of your own time frame, dragged away from your wife—how is Gloria, by the way?"

"She was fine when I left," Jack shrugged helplessly. He really wished he could call her. He knew the number of her parent's home—it hadn't changed since the day he met her. That was the trouble. In 1969 he hadn't *met* her. What would he say? *Hi! This is your future husband calling, just to say I miss your voice and I love you!*

"I'm sure she still is, then. One of the nice things about time travel is that you really needn't miss *any* time, in any age. If we can get all this straightened out, then the Pleiadian Siblings can drop you right back down where they found you. Chances are you won't remember a thing. Happens all the time, you know."

"The who?" Jack asked, suddenly remembering Ben's earlier comment. If they weren't aliens, what were they?

"Our big brothers," Jeffrey smiled. "The Pleiadians—people of the Pleiades. They're the ones who took you, and who dropped you down in this decade. Or at least, I assume it was they. Wasn't it?"

"That's not what they called themselves to me," Jack mumbled. His eyes were on Ben, who had at last risen from the couch and was walking past them. "Where you going?"

"Upstairs, to take a nap. No, I *don't* want to stay here and listen to you two! You're going to tell him what *you* believe, and he's going to tell you what *he* believes, and I already know what you *both* believe, and believe me, it's not worth *listening!*" Ben brushed on past, then, and climbed the A-frame's stairs up to the loft.

"As I said," Jeffrey murmured as they watched him go, "he's frustrated. And I'm certain he's confused, too. Wouldn't you be, if you spent your time in other people's heads all day? It's a wonder he even remembers who he is."

Jack gazed at Jeffrey. "How do *you* know who he is?"

Jeffrey smiled that old, patient smile of his and said, "Why don't we get the drinks, have a seat on the couch, and talk all of this through, hmm?"

That seemed a sensible plan to Jack—as sensible as anything he'd seen or heard this day, at least—and so a moment later they were plopped down on either end of one of the couches, the pizza between them, picking up a conversation they never really had finished.

"It's this belief system of yours," Jeffrey was saying. "It prevents you from seeing any alternative possibilities. It always has. You're terribly closed-minded."

"My father used to warn me not to be so open-minded my brains fell out."

"And I remember you quoting him saying it. Look, this whole problem can be settled empirically! You've seen the saucers. *I've* seen the saucers. You've seen the Pleiadian Siblings, and *I've* seen them too—"

"Wait a minute. These 'Pleiadian Siblings'—very politically correct name, by the way—"

"Of course," Jeffrey smiled.

"What do they *look* like, exactly?"

Jeffrey sighed. "Ahh, well, let's see. They're shorter than we—shorter than *you*, anyway," he added. He had always been a bit self-conscious about being short. "They have white skin and almond-shaped eyes, and . . . why am I describing these people to you when they *brought* you here?"

"Because they told me nothing about any 'Pleiadian whatever.' Because I've had occasion to see one of the creatures who *did* bring me here in . . . costume, I guess. As a completely different alien species. Ugly, with a long nose."

"Oh yes, they do that with the new folk."

"The new folk?" Jack frowned, wrinkling his nose as if he smelled something peculiar in Jeffrey's words.

"Until they can trust you. They've told hundreds of different stories, with no continuity between what they tell you one day and what they tell you the next, until you've demonstrated to them your loyalty. *Then* they'll allow you to see the truth."

"The truth," Jack grumbled. He'd heard *that* word on this trip before.

"Yes, the truth. That religion of yours, the one that binds your mind—doesn't it say that you shall know the truth, and the truth will make you free?"

"Of course it does. How many times have I said that to *you?*"

"But it didn't make you free, Jack," Jeffrey smiled. Sometimes that expression almost became a smirk. . . .

"I think it did. I think it *does.* Question:"

"Yes?"

"If these creatures whom you worship—"

"No!" Jeffrey corrected him quickly. "Not worship. Appreciate, yes—treasure, yes—serve? Most definitely. But logically—with purpose. Not illogically, as you serve your 'Lord Jesus.'"

"If I may finish—if you know these creatures knowingly lied to you in the past, why in the world would you *believe* them *now?*"

"Because I've seen the planet, Jack," Jeffrey said smugly. "I've *been* there. And can you say the same about your 'celestial safety valve?'"

"You mean heaven?"

"What else would I mean?" Jeffrey grunted, picking up another piece of pizza. They were going through it pretty quickly, Jack noticed. Maybe he should save some for Ben?

"I told you, I'm not hungry!" the boy roared down from the loft.

"I thought you were asleep!" Jack called back up.

"How can I with all those *thoughts* flying around down there?" the boy snarled. "Very profound, you two, I can tell you that."

Jack shrugged and took another piece. "No, I haven't seen heaven."

"Then how do you know your God isn't lying to you about it?" Jeffrey asked. "Of course, you *don't* know. But you *believe* in heaven, right? You *believe* that there's a God, and that He made the world, and that He cares for you personally. And of course, I never did."

"You do now?"

"I've *met* the *gods*, Jack! I've eaten with the council that designed our bodies, the scientists who perfected our race in the genetic laboratory!"

Jack rolled his eyes. "Oh yeah. I've met Gork too."

"Who?"

"Gork. Top alien? Carries a lot of influence?"

"I'm talking about Ruzagnon, the Maker of Man! Jack, don't you *see?* Why would you cling to your puny evangelical faith when you've heard these wonderful space brothers explain how you came to be? Why would you question any of this when you've seen *evidence* of the power of these creatures?"

Now that *was* a good question, and Jack knew it needed a proper answer. He got up from the couch and paced to the largest window in the front of the cabin. It faced Los Angeles—why anybody would *want* to, Jack couldn't figure, but there it was. The sun was setting in the West, turning the smog-choked sky as red as rust. "Mayb e. . ." he began, "maybe because I've seen *more* power displayed by the One *I* worship."

"Here it comes," he heard Jeffrey groan behind him.

"And I *do* mean worship, Jeffrey. I do worship Him."

"And this is a surprise?" his friend chortled. "Listen. We've been all through this, years ago. I, too, saw evidence of something, some . . . *force*, some *energy* that permeated relationships and enabled—miracles."

"You never called them that."

"You always wanted to claim them for your God, that's why!"

"Well—"

"But I *did* see the power. And I knew, if it was *real*, that it could be tested, used—"

"Controlled," Jack offered. "That's why you investigated magic."

"All right. *Controlled* is fine. If an energy, a force, is real and available, then it's a resource, right? To be managed."

"And that's always been the difference between us. I wanted God to manage my affairs, and you wanted to manage God's affairs."

"I wanted to *understand*, Jack. To understand all that we *could* understand. So I searched, yes, in the ancient writings of Thoth, *The Book of the Dead*, the *Bhagavad Gita*, the *I Ching*—"

"Even *The Art of Zen Motorcycle Maintenance*, if I remember correctly," Jack said.

"There's a lot of good in that book!" Jeffrey argued. "You should read it!"

"And the bottom line is, you decided that since all of them were talking about similar things in different languages and terms, then they all must be talking about the *same* thing."

"Precisely," Jeffrey nodded. "None of this parochial 'my religion is best because my Mama told me so' business."

"The old 'One Mountain, Many Pathways' idea."

"And I was *right*," Jeffrey concluded, his tiny eyes glowing with a light Jack recognized easily. It was the light of a "true believer," one who is so certain he's right that anyone who disagrees with him is obviously either a fool or a liar. He recognized it because he could remember many times in his life when he must have had just such a light in his own eyes—even when he proved to be dead wrong.

"And how do you know that?" Jack sighed. "Because Gork told you so?"

Jeffrey frowned. "I really wish you wouldn't use that guttural term for a being so august as Ruzagnon. Of course, he's had many *other* names and titles that would be equally appropriate—Loki to the Vikings, Prometheus to the Greeks, Baal to the Phoenicians, Ahura Mazda to the Persians—"

"Yes, yes, he already told me some of those."

"And you don't believe him."

Jack snorted. "It's all Gork to me!" Jeffrey groaned and laid back on the couch with a hand to his forehead. "You asked me why I couldn't trust the alien's demonstrated power." Jack went on, pacing toward the window and looking out toward the blood-red sky. "Here's why. Because I've seen that power do things I would *never* expect my God to do. Things in fact I would only expect to see the *devil* do—" Jack paused. He frowned. Could all of this be . . . ?

"Bingo," Ben called down quietly from the loft. After a moment, Ben added, "For a so-called man of God, it took you long enough."

Jack whirled around. He expected to see Gork sitting in the place of Jeffrey—but no. His old friend just laid there on the couch, pinching the bridge of his nose between his thumb and forefinger. Then he sighed, took his hand away, and turned his small eyes onto Jack once more. "You still don't get it, do you, Jack?"

"Get what?" he asked—although he wasn't at all certain that he *wanted* to get it.

"Satan, God—they're the same."

"No," Jack said firmly.

"They're the same, Jack. Always have been, since the beginning of our race. Not 'all-powerful'—not at all. In fact, in some cases their attempts to help us have really been all-*pitiful*, like that Prometheus episode when they entrusted mankind with fire and he burned down their laboratories with it."

"Gork told you that?"

"And like the devil, since you bring that particular manifestation up. Oh, they've taken *hell* out of humans on that one. Yet when they thought him up, their only purpose was to try to get some *balance* into a world view, so we would have someone to blame their *failures* on. I guess they got their wish, huh? We believed that one *too* well! Ended up *killing* a lot of our own, and some of *them* as well, trying to stamp the idea out!"

"Some of us still feel that it's the devil who bears the responsibility for much of that killing—"

"Of course you do," Jeffrey nodded. "It's what they wanted you to think. But look, Jack—there's no more need for that! Just understand that all the roads, all the spiritual pathways, all the religions were only *analogies*, many of them culturally bound, to help each of us reach the same level—"

"The level *you've* attained, right?" Jack had never felt comfortable with talking about "levels" of spirituality, even when it was couched in Christian terms. Jesus had seemed particularly unimpressed with the spiritual "levels" attained by the Pharisees. And the more Jeffrey talked, the more this sounded like a new gnosticism to him—a "secret knowledge" with Gork and the whole lying gang right at the heart of it.

"It's the level all religions were designed to attain," Jeffrey answered confidently. "The platform to understanding the *true* mysteries, implanted in us genetically by our Siblings in space. You see, the historical religions are all like the peelings, the shells. You don't eat an orange for its peeling, Jack—you tear that off and throw it away. It's not the peeling of the banana that is refreshing and nourishing, it's the fruit inside."

"So are you telling me that our good buddies from space are going to make all religions taste like bananas?" Jack mocked. He couldn't help himself.

"No," Jeffrey said, with the infinite patience of one who believes themselves spiritually superior. "I mean all religions will prove to be nourishing and good."

"To use your analogy, you don't think maybe some of these 'fruits' might possibly be poisonous?"

"Jack, Jack," Jeffrey chided. "They all came from the same source! How could they possibly be hurtful? Shiva, Kali, Buddha, and Baal—peel each one of these and you find truth inside!"

"Satanism too, I suppose?"

"Why not accept it, Jack? It's really not so different from your own church. The rituals are much the same."

"Borrowed from my faith and perverted, weren't they?" Jack argued.

"Why be so judgmental? Why not come to a meeting tonight and see for yourself?"

"Come to a—" Jack started, then he stopped. Chills raced down his spine. He felt, rather than saw, the saucer suddenly come to hover outside the large window. A moment later its glow inundated the room with light. "Ben!" he called upstairs, and the boy answered:

"I see it." Ben's feet hit the floor with a thud, then he stoically made his way down into the living room. By that time Jack had turned to look at it, holding his hand up to his face against the light. As suddenly as the glow had blossomed, it disappeared, leaving an afterimage on the inside of his eyelids. When he opened them again, the ship was but a black silhouette against the multiplied millions of lights that lit up the night in the L.A. basin. He tried not to feel it, but he couldn't help himself. He felt—relieved. That mysterious object out there was his only means home, and its occupants—be they from Beta Reticuli, or the Pleiades, or hell itself—were the only creatures he knew who could operate its controls.

Chapter Nine

Outside the ring of darkness

Congratulations, Jack," Ben said as he walked to the window and looked out at the hovering saucer with him. "Now you can go home."

Jack's cheeks burned. "I tried to help, Ben. I really did."

"As best you could," Ben agreed. "Southern California wasn't the right choice, I don't think, for hiding. Think about it. We're fifty miles south of Edwards Air Force base, where President Eisenhower supposedly viewed the bodies of dead aliens in the fifties. We're only a few minutes west of Vandenburg Air Force Base by jet; Camp Pendleton is due south; and to the east of us is Rancho Mirage and March Air Force Base."

"Don't forget Norton Air Force Base," Jeffrey added helpfully. "Bush closed it down in 1988, but at *this* point in history it's just a few miles that way—" He pointed to the east.

Jack sighed. "Then why did you let us come this way?" he asked Ben.

"I knew it was your home in the late sixties," the boy shrugged. "I thought maybe you had—I don't know—some real contacts that might have been able to help us escape. I thought . . ." The boy paused. "Oh, I might as well say it. I thought your *God* might get us out of this mess. I mean, you kept thinking you were talking to angels!"

"Angels?" Jeffrey asked, his curiosity piqued.

"One angel," Jack mumbled, more to himself than to the others. Suddenly he looked accusingly at Ben. "If you knew all along we were dealing with demons, why didn't you tell me?"

"Demons?" Jeffrey laughed. "Come on now, Jack. I've *told* you who we're dealing with here and it's not—"

"Because I knew you wouldn't help me then," Ben snapped. "You'd be too afraid."

"I would have been terrified, of course," Jack argued, "but I still would have helped you!"

"Friends—" Jeffrey tried to interject.

"Oh, yeah, right!" Ben snarled. "You would have sat in your cabin and *prayed* instead of taking any real *action.* That's what most of you Christians *do* when confronted with real evil! You pray for God either to take it away or take you *out* of it, instead of trying to *do* anything about it!"

"You may be right about a lot of Christians," Jack agreed grudgingly, but he argued on: "Still, that's not the true nature of prayer. I don't pray to try to change God's mind, I pray for God to let me *know* His mind!"

"If I could—" Jeffrey tried again.

"You forget, Jack!" Ben spat out, with all the venomous sarcasm that only a teenager could feel the freedom to unleash, "I can read *your* mind! You think I didn't hear you in there in your cabin, asking your God to rescue you from these *terrible* circumstances that *I* had gotten you into? You never even *once* prayed for *my* welfare—and I can tell you with certainty that you never prayed to have God's mind, either!"

His cheeks flushing a deep red, Jack narrowed his eyes and glared at the boy. "You may have noticed that I was not talking to *you* at the time, Ben! Did anybody ever tell you that it is incredibly rude to eavesdrop on other people's conversations?"

"Sorry," said Ben in a tone that communicated that without question he was *not* sorry at *all*, "but you'll remember my entire life's experience has taught me that listening to other's conversations is precisely my purpose!"

"Would it be possible for us to—"

This time it was Jack who cut Jeffrey off. "And who *taught* you that was your purpose, hmm? If you recognize the nature of these creatures to be demonic, how can you accept *their* definition of your purpose in life?"

"What other *choice* do I have?" the boy raged.

"You have *God's* choice! It's God who gave you this gift, not them!"

"And who's going to tell me what *God's* purpose for my gift might be? *You*? Just a reminder, Jack. You haven't spent much time praying at *all* on this trip. Not at all!"

Feeling terribly convicted, Jack tried a deflection defense. "But you just said you didn't *want* me praying, you wanted me to *act*—"

Ben's response was bathed in acid. "Is there some *law* you Christians have written down some place that you can't act and pray at the same time?"

How could he argue with someone who knew the motivation for his every argument? Still Jack tried— "You think if I'd known we were dealing with demons I wouldn't have been praying without ceasing from day one?"

"We are *not* dealing with *demons* here, people!" Jeffrey roared over both of them, forcing them both to look his way. His normally pasty face was purple with frustration, and he'd clenched his jaws in determination. "We are dealing with creatures from an entirely different star system who have *imitated* gods, demons, angels, and fairies from the days they gave our ancestors consciousness! I am about to give you both a demonstration of that fact! And if the two of you will not cease this ridiculous bickering and accompany me willingly outside to the ship, then I'll simply have to force you!"

And he did. Jack learned to his great remorse that Jeffrey, too, had the power to clench his brain in a crushing vise. Or was that something Gork was doing from inside the ship, perhaps at Jeffrey's request? In either case, Jack didn't hesitate. He hastened out of the cabin onto the porch, swiftly pursued by Ben who clutched his head and howled. Jeffrey followed after at a more stately, dignified pace. They ran under the dark shape that hung silently over the treetops and waited, their heads splitting, for Jeffrey to saunter up. Then the craft's bottom opened and dropped around them. They were lifted from the ground—the deck closed under them—then they were dropped to the floor as the brain-lock was simultaneously released. They both curled up there, cradling their aching heads in their hands, as Jeffrey looked down at them and said tonelessly, "I'm sorry that was necessary. Please don't require me to use such methods again. I find them personally distasteful." He turned on his heel and disappeared up a corridor.

The saucer shot into motion, leaving Jack's stomach far behind. In what seemed like an instant they were slowing down again, and Jeffrey stepped back into the central deck. From his place on the floor Jack could see that his old friend still wore his black, wing tip shoes and black pants, but now he'd donned over his other garments a thick, blood-red robe. Jack rolled his eyes back to take it all in, and saw the robe had a heavy cowl hanging down the back. It looked like it had come direct from the rack in Central Costumes marked "Satanic Rituals."

"Well," Ben mumbled, "we *are* near Hollywood, y'know."

Indeed they were, Jack thought. Certainly no shortage of demons around here. "In fact, they run the place," Ben agreed.

"I don't know what you're talking about, young Ben," Jeffrey said archly, "but I would request that you keep your views to yourself. Now I want the two of you to stand up and come with me." When they didn't immediately move, he added for emphasis, "Please?" The menace in his voice was unmistakable. They got up and followed him back up the same corridor to a room much like that Jack had occupied. Was this the same ship? The design was identical, certainly, but neither Gork nor any of the other Grays were in evidence. Jeffrey stepped to the closet and produced two more cowled robes—for Jack, a green one—"Novice level," Jeffrey explained—and for Ben a richly brocaded robe of black satin. "The highest plateau," Jeffrey smiled at Jack as he handed the boy's robe to him. Jack frowned a silent question at Ben.

"It wasn't by *my* choice," the boy grumbled, taking the garment and slipping expertly into it, "anymore than *you* chose to be born a preacher's kid. Besides, in '69 I *wasn't* even born yet."

Jack looked back and forth between the two of them. "Did you know each other before today?"

"Oh, no," Jeffrey said cheerfully. "I'm of a completely different branch of the Brotherhood. Ah—" he corrected himself "the Siblinghood. And I didn't attend *this* function when it originally occurred *myself.* I heard about it later from friends, though," he said, his small eyes glowing with the anticipation of an archaeologist who's just discovered a dinosaur fragment. "And tonight? I see for myself how the Siblings have related to a living faith!"

Something about the way he said that made Jack shiver. Considering a coven a "living faith" seemed to bring full circle all of those discussions of "universalism" and "salvation for *all,* regardless of their creed." How could all religions be universally valid when some of them literally worshiped the *opposite* of the Truth? No wonder the believers of the New Age considered all truth relative. That was another way of saying that all truth is *meaningless.*

Jeffrey led them back into the circular deck in the center of the craft. "Now when we get there, I want you both to be utterly silent," he instructed as they walked, sounding somehow like an aged schoolmarm prepping her class for a field trip. Ben rolled his eyes around at Jack and nodded. He'd apparently caught the image, and agreed. "We're there to observe, not to interact. We'll keep to ourselves, and well to the side. Fortunately," Jeffrey added with a wry smile as he turned to face them from the far side of the deck, "I don't think the people down there in Topanga Canyon will be in much shape to *remember* a lot of what goes on!"

Oh yes, Jack remembered now. The late sixties in southern California. Sex, drugs, and rock and roll. And there he'd been, in the midst of it. *Lord, forgive me,* he added. *I did know better. And please bless Ben,* he went on, remembering what the boy had said about his lack of a consistent prayer life the last few days. It suddenly occurred to him to wonder if that was the reason he hadn't seen his Gloria angel recently.

The saucer dropped out of the sky and deposited them on the ground in an instant, and in the next instant shot back into the sky and away. They were standing near a large group of revelers under a starless, smoggy California night. Bonfires burned all around them, adding plumes of stinking smoke to the choking mix, and within moments Jack's lungs started to ache. People in various states of dress and undress, some robed and some in street clothes and some in not much at all ran from one fire to another, or laid on their backs in the grass, or stood in groups and laughed and drank and pointed first over here then over there, then somewhere else. Their faces all seemed to Jack to wear the same glazed, stupid expressions, and he was reminded once again of where the expression "dope" originated. These people looked like dopes.

If any of the party-goers noticed the three of them standing there, they quickly forgot them when the chanting began.

Jack saw now that they stood in a kind of natural bowl, and that downhill from them a large circle of robed and hooded figures had started to form. Jeffrey jerked his head that way, and Ben and Jack dutifully followed him to take a position just outside the circle.

What they were chanting Jack couldn't make out. Didn't really matter anyway, he decided. Gork and the others were already planning to put in an appearance regardless of however they were "invoked." From what he could gather, whether they were Jeffrey's "Space Siblings" or Ben's demons, they would answer *any* call couched in such terms. Maybe this was why cults always seemed to manage to get enough "spiritual" affirmation to hold their adherents, and why sorcerers always managed to summon up *something*. In fact, Jack thought as he threw a shocked look uphill over his shoulder, if the *chants* didn't bring down the demons then the *activities* surely would. Some of the things he saw taking place in the hellish firelight would surely have been standard practice in pre-destruction Sodom. Jeffrey bumped his shoulder with his elbow, and directed his attention back toward the center of the circle.

They were building an altar. Jack now saw that each of the hundred or so robed celebrants in the circle had at their feet a cubical brick about the size of a basketball. Now, as if on cue, each person was leaving his or her place in the circle to pick up their brick and carry it to the center of the circle. There a group of about a dozen hooded figures wearing black brocade like Ben's received the bricks and worked to stack them in rows. An altar grew out of the grass—about six feet long by four feet wide, climbing in four rows up to about three feet high. As the last brick was put in place, still others from the circle muscled a large, flat wooden slab out to the leaders—this was placed lengthwise across the top of the stack of bricks. Then the black-clad leader-group—Jack counted thirteen of these, to be exact—joined hands around the altar and began pacing back and forth around it, first clockwise, then counter-clockwise. They were once again chanting some mumbo-jumbo Jack felt *certain* had some meaning to *them*—but had absolutely none to him.

It did attract attention, however. The party-goers up the hill had finally caught sight of what was going on, and they brought their bottles and their joints down to enlarge the perimeter of the ring of watchers. Suddenly Jack was surrounded, and as drunken people shoved up behind him and around him, he felt a kind of dizziness, a vertigo, as if his body was trying to say to him, "What in God's name are you doing in the midst of *this* crowd!" The robed circle had picked up the chant now, and the sound of all those voices together sent chills down his spine. Those who circled the altar moved faster now, their feet picking up the rhythm of the chant in a chaotic dance. Back and forth they went, rotating around the altar faster and faster, and now the outer circle, the watchers, began to clap in rhythm.

As the volume level of the noise increased, as the crowd behind him pressed forward on his back, as the circle of thirteen grew frenzied in their dance, Jack felt a flood of emotions rise inside of him. The first was pure panic. He was surrounded by a mindless mob being manipulated by the drugs and the noise and the drama to a peak of excited sensation. The next was temptation. "Join in!" the vibrations of the sound demanded, and indeed the strangers that had crowded in on either side of him started grabbing now at his hands to try to pull him into participation. Then up from his gut came disgust—sheer hatred of the noises and the smells and the chaos that assaulted all his senses.

He jerked himself free from all grabbing hands, straddled his legs apart to give himself a wide base, then began wildly swinging his elbows from side to side in a clear signal to those around him to back off! Strange—for now he saw that people all around him were writhing and jumping and flailing their arms about. In the center of the circle they were doing the same, and the chant had turned now into a thunderous litany of names—some of which, he realized with a sick feeling in the pit of his stomach, he knew well:

ASH-TER-OTH! AZ-MOD-E-US! CHE-MOSH!
BE-EL-ZE-BUB! ISH-TAR! AZ-E-EL! MO-LOCH!
LUC-I-FER!

The robed circle repeated this over and over again, each time a little louder, until the crowd that danced around and behind him picked it up and began repeating it with them. There was much laughter along with all of this—as if the drunken revelers who joined in saw all of this as a harmless party-game, a theater piece that encouraged audience participation. But as the chant grew in intensity and volume, gradually binding more and more of this congregated mob into the single-minded focus Jack knew was the chant's purpose, it seemed the already oppressive night became blacker. Evil itself hung in the air like smoke.

ASH-TER-OTH! AZ-MOD-E-US! CHE-MOSH!
BE-EL-ZE-BUB! ISH-TAR! AZ-E-EL! MO-LOCH!
LUC-I-FER!

His head pounded, throbbed, ached, threatened to explode open. His body shook with tension. His nails cut into the palms of his hands as he clenched his fists, and his teeth ground together as if his jaws had suddenly locked up. And just when he would have joined his screams of pain with the orgiastic cries of frenzy he now heard all around him, a voice inside him said, "Why?"

Why indeed. Why participate? Why be swept away by all that surrounds you? Why not pray?

Jack prayed: *Lord. Bless these poor, confused, mistaken people all around me. Bless them, Lord. Bless them. Oh—bless them.* It was a silent prayer, but honest. And now another feeling swept up from inside him. Grief. He turned around where he stood, full circle, a single, calm, silent figure in the midst of a writhing sea of people—and wept. He understood, in that moment, why Jesus had wept over Jerusalem. It had been a long time since Jack had wept over the state of the world. He hadn't done it enough in 1969 he knew—no, nor in 1995 either. He had accepted, instead, the argument that since he could do little to change the world, it wasn't his responsibility to *care* for the world. But there was the fault in the argument, he realized: He could indeed do something to change the world, but not *unless* he cared.

Finishing his full circle turn, he realized there was at least one other motionless face in the crowd. They'd become separated in all the pushing and shoving, but there, about six feet away, stood Ben. The boy was watching him. Ben wasn't smiling, he wasn't frowning, he was just . . . watching. Jack wondered how many others in his lifetime had watched him—perhaps taken their cue for how to live from him. Realizing anew how poor had been his example at times freshened his tears. . . .

The black sabbat continued. He felt strangely detached from it now, however. Maybe not so strangely. He remembered how Peter had walked on the water toward Jesus, then sunk down into it when he looked at the storm that raged around him. At this moment Jack felt so focused on Jesus that no storm could disturb his peace. But for all of these people around him . . .

The noise suddenly stopped, swallowed up in shocked gasps and excited whispers. That jerked Jack's attention back to the center of the dancing ring, and there he saw the reason for the hush. Gork stood on the altar.

Sure it was Gork. Oh, maybe he had on a different costume now, Jack thought to himself. In fact, Gork was doing his imitation of a goat, and it wasn't a bad one, either. He had huge spiraling horns and a whiskered chin, hair-covered legs that went down to cloven hooves and, behind him, a goat's tail. But it was Gork. Jack could tell by the eyes. In his human-like hands he brandished symbols of horror. In his right was a bloody knife, in his left a severed head. Jack beheld all this with revulsion, but not with fear. He did have to wonder, though—why would *anyone* want to venerate such a figure?

"We've never been able to understand that," said a voice to the side of him, and Jack turned his head to see who it was.

"Gloria!"

She looked every inch like Gloria. A classic, composed, perfect face, curly black hair, full lips, eyes that flashed with righteous incredulity at what she beheld. But she wasn't Gloria—Jack knew that. She was an angel.

"I've missed you," he said.

"I haven't been anywhere," she answered.

"I guess *I* have," he admitted ruefully, and she did not comment.

"Who are you talking to?" asked an anxious voice from the other side of him, and Jack turned his head to glance at Ben and explain, "The angel." He looked back at Gloria.

Ben craned his neck to look around him, then grabbed his left bicep with both hands and squeezed hard. "Jack, there's no one there!"

"Yes, she is," Jack smiled. He was, by this time, oblivious to the black celebration that continued all around them.

"No, she's *not!" Ben pleaded, still dragging downward on his arm. "I can see her in your mind, I can see you think she's there, but she's not! Jack, don't leave me here alone!"*

"I'm not going anywhere," Jack comforted Ben offhandedly. But he was wrong.

Chapter Ten

Within the ring of light

Light began to glow outside the ring of darkness. At first Jack thought it was the dawn. Then it struck him that it couldn't be any later than one-thirty in the morning. Besides, this light came not from the east, but from all around them, emanating from every direction except from within the dark circle itself. "What are you seeing, Jack?" he barely heard Ben pleading as the boy continued to cling to his arm. Try as he might, however, Jack couldn't answer. He kept swiveling his head from side to side, scanning the suddenly illuminated horizon, trying to make some logical sense of the messages his eyes were sending.

The light continued to grow in intensity and brilliance, as if this clearing was surrounded by klieg lights powered by a single, incredibly powerful dimmer circuit. Soon the light appeared far more substantial than did the figures gyrating crazily around the altar. The dancers began to seem less like persons than like shadows—ghosts, almost, as the light poured around their silhouettes. Then—impossibly—that same light began to pour *through* them, as if they'd suddenly become wholly transparent. Jack watched in amazement as the light continued to grow in luminescence and the dancing revelers continued to fade away. "Jack!" Ben begged once again, "Don't leave me!" But in Jack's eyes Ben himself had become both transparent and weightless. While he apparently still tugged at Jack's arm, Ben might as well have been a gnat jerking on a giant. Jack soon couldn't feel a thing.

At last they all just disappeared. Ben, Jeffrey, and the whole host of the devil's devotees were swallowed up in the brilliance that surrounded them. Long before they were gone, however, Jack saw clearly the reason why. The circle of darkness had itself been completely enveloped by a ring of shining beings. They were at once more beautiful and more terrible than any creatures Jack had ever beheld. They were gorgeous—each a human ideal—with perfectly-formed faces, powerful bodies gigantic by human standards, utterly composed—and all of them frowning. Jack knew immediately what they were—*who* they were: "A band of angels coming after me," he murmured in awe, repeating a line from an old song he'd sung as a boy at church camp. "Coming for to carry me home."

Angels. Thousands of them. Myriads, to use that biblical term. Like the host of heaven that encircled the army of Syria, this heavenly brigade surrounded the satanic revelers. And like the servant of Elisha whose eyes were at last opened to see them, Jack's eyes were truly opened. He trembled. He was going to heaven now. He was certain of it. He glanced over at the Gloria-like angel to his right and said, "It's my time, isn't it?"

"Your time for what, Jack?" Once again she had answered with a question, remaining as frustratingly noncommittal as ever, even in the face of this glorious vision.

Jack blinked. Then, "Why don't you ever give me a straight answer?" he demanded.

"Why do you ask so many questions?" the angel responded. She used that same cool, challenging tone of voice she'd taken with him since their first encounter.

Jack pondered that, then looked back out at the ring of angels encircling them, and struggled to hold his emotions in check as he answered, "Because I'm so absolutely, utterly confused! I'd like some explanations for all these events! I'd like to know why I'm here! But if I'm not *supposed* to know, if I'm not even supposed to *ask*, well then, fine. Just tell me I'm not, and I'll keep all my questions to myself."

Her face softened. "Ask whatever you like, Jack. I'll answer whatever I can."

Still the light grew around them, dispelling every shadow, until the angels themselves disappeared into the light they had brought with them—or which had brought *them*. It appeared now that he stood alone with Gloria in the daylight. The night was gone. The Satan worshipers were gone. The altar had disappeared. He felt embraced by an atmosphere of orderly calm. In place of the noise and the smoke and the chaos there was silence. He could smell that wonderful scent given off by pine needles when they've been heated by the summer sun.

He saw now that they stood upon grass of a rich, emerald green. It looked dry and inviting, and not at all damp. Jack sat down in it, and his angel followed his lead. She looked at him expectantly and waited. Was she finally *smiling*?

"Why do you look like Gloria?" he asked first.

"I don't look like Gloria," was her answer. "Rather, you *perceive* me as looking like Gloria. You humans see us as you expect to see us, projecting the image of your expectations upon us. By the way, it speaks very highly of your esteem for your wife that you would regard her as so angelic you would allow me to impersonate her."

Jack ducked his head, shrugged, and said, "Well, I . . . I just love her. You understand."

"No," the angel responded frankly. "I don't."

"You don't understand why I love my wife?" Jack frowned.

"I don't understand love, Jack—not, in any case, as an emotional response born of a relationship between male and female. Love as you understand it is a mystery to me—to all of us—one which we can see causes great pain and suffering for humankind, but apparently great joy and pleasure for you as well."

"What are you telling me?" Jack smiled. "Are you like . . . Spock, then? You can't love because you're entirely rational?"

The angel—he couldn't help but think of her as Gloria, even though she was clearly a far different creature from his wife—did not appear confused by his reference. Neither did she appear at all impressed by his cleverness: "This is not a trivial question, Jack, to be answered by analogy to a television character. We are different from you—created differently, at a different time in the cosmic history, for a different purpose. The relationship between yourselves and the Holy One is not the same as our relationship to that One. What is unknown to you is known to us. And yet, some things that are simple to you are equally a mystery to us. Love is just such an enigma. It's a mystery into which we all long to look, but one which apparently will not be revealed to us until the fullness of all things is also revealed to all of *you*."

Jack struggled to understand. "Are you saying—you can't love?"

"I am saying that we stand in a different relationship to the Creator. We *know*. You *believe*. Your faith, your trust, your hope—these are ideas that we comprehend, but don't experience. We are fundamentally *different*, Jack. That is why at times we cannot understand you at all. Human behavior is utterly baffling to us."

Jack raised his eyebrows, and nodded in agreement. "It is to us sometimes, too."

"We know that," the angel said flatly.

"Yeah," Jack nodded again. "I suppose you'd have to. But—does this mean you really don't love *us?*"

"Would you be disappointed if I were to say yes?" the angel asked, and Jack thought about that.

"A little, I guess . . . " he admitted.

"Because it is in your created nature to love and to wish to be loved. It is in our created nature to serve without question. Just as you might be disappointed that the angels do not love you, so we might be disappointed that you do not *serve* our Holy One."

"Ah," Jack nodded, not really wanting to get into this. He felt certain that this angel would find much to disapprove of in his daily living.

"We have all knowledge," the angel Gloria went on, "but knowledge does not equal understanding. We *know* you—far better than you know yourselves—but we do not understand you. We know the Holy One, but we do not understand why the Holy One permits what He permits—why He overlooks your lies and inconsistencies and yet still continues to love—"

"Then you admit that God loves us?"

"Why of course!" the angel answered, almost fiercely. "Why else would we be here watching over you, if not for His love?"

"But then," Jack pursued, "would you say that you love *Him*?"

"I understand your question," the angel responded patiently. "Do *you* understand that you can only understand my answer in your own human terms? I must state that your human words fail to carry the full meaning of our experience. We *worship* Him. We *serve* Him. We *obey* Him. Would you call that love?"

Jack thought that over. "I . . . I think I've *preached* that that's a demonstration of our love. Yes."

"Then call it what you choose. Knowing how loosely you human creatures use that word 'love,' however, I would prefer to call our response obedience. And *in* obedience to Him," the angel continued sternly, "we oppose those who oppose Him, those who have chosen to disobey Him."

"Sinners," Jack nodded.

"Failed humans, yes," Angel Gloria nodded. "And those who entice them to failure as well."

"The demons?" Jack asked.

"The fallen," the angel responded softly. Suddenly she was quoting: "'For thou hast said in thine heart, I will ascend into heaven, I will exalt my throne above the stars of God: I will sit also upon the mount of the congregation, in the sides of the north: I will ascend above the heights of the clouds; I will be like the most High. Yet thou shalt be brought down to hell, to the sides of the pit.'"

"I know that's Scripture," Jack said ruefully, "but I'm afraid I can't recall the reference—"

"The Book of Isaiah the Prophet, the chapter you call fourteen, verses thirteen through fifteen."

"The passage about Lucifer?"

"About Lucifer, about the King of Babylon, about *anyone* who sets himself up as a god over the eternal standard of the Holy One. Including those beings created with *us*, who chose *not* obedience, but disobedience."

"The fallen," Jack said. The angel nodded. Jack took a deep breath and looked around him. This idyllic meadow entranced him. He could hear birds chirping in the trees around them, and he could smell the sweet fragrance of summer. It reminded him of that summer morning when he'd begun this odyssey—how long ago had that been? However long, it had been just that much time since he'd felt this much at rest—and at peace. In a way, he really didn't want to go on with the conversation. It seemed to be moving into subjects he found discomforting. How much more relaxing it might be to simply sit here in the grass and bask in the glow of a thousand angels. But his curiosity compelled him. "How many . . . fell?"

"Myriads," the angel replied flatly. "Legions. A finite number, but far too many to be counted. Can you be satisfied with that?" she asked evenly, "or are you looking for a figure to enter into your calculator?" *Was there a hint of mockery in that response?* he wondered. Or could it be she was teasing him? Did angels have a sense of humor? Jack pushed those thoughts from his mind to focus on the major issues:

"And Lucifer is their head?"

"Lucifer. Beelzebub. Satan. He has many names. Call that one whatever you choose, he is the chief among them, the initiator of the rebellion, the one who determined in his heart to oppose the Holy One and who then seduced the others to follow."

"Is that Gork?" Jack asked, shivering. Did Angel Gloria smile?

"The one you call Gork is but one of many. He's a minion of Lucifer—but he's far from being the chief. Not that he wouldn't tell you he *is.* All of the fallen lie at every opportunity, to one another as well as to you humans. Most especially, they lie to themselves, believing somehow that if they are devious enough for long enough they might escape somehow their inevitable defeat. They're fools, Jack. All of them. The one you've met is merely one of many, competing with others of the fallen to be viewed as more powerful, more influential in evil than others."

"Is . . . all of this to win the . . . Lucifer's favor?"

"Who can understand their motivation?" Angel Gloria snorted, her nostrils flaring in contempt. "They are fools, these fallen. They have no center. They care nothing for one another, but they do *fear* one another. They are ruled not by obedience and servanthood but by terror and violence. They are haters, Jack. They hate the Holy One, they hate those of us who remain obedient, they hate the created order, they hate you humans, and they hate each other. They battle one another constantly for position within their perverse hierarchy, but whatever pleasure they gain from this is meaningless to us. They consume one another but are never destroyed, they harm one another and in reward are harmed by their superiors. They take pride and pleasure in inflicting pain on others, even as they weep and rage and mourn at their own suffering. They are devoid of any sense of obedience, Jack, which makes them incomprehensible creatures to us—and they are equally devoid of anything that you might call love, which *should* render them incomprehensible to you as well. The fallen are wrong-thinking beings, Jack. They have been since they first chose to disobey. But they *are* seductive—and they are clever.

"That is why they were imprisoned here upon this tiny rock of a world—to limit the spread of their destructive virus. We, of course, could not comprehend the Holy One's choice in that matter. Left to us, this pitiful little gravity well would have been incinerated long ago. Like a single, cancerous cell which could, unchecked, wreak havoc upon your human body, this tiny, rotten rock could infect the entire creation. Our choice would have been—would still be—to dispose of it, and its contagion, in a stroke."

"But God won't let you?"

"*Yet*..." said the angel. Jack found her fiery smile chilling.

"And . . . where do we fit into all of this? We humans, I mean?"

Once again, the angel's features softened. She looked at him with something approaching pity, or perhaps—despite her words—affection. "In some ways, that remains to be seen. Unto you has been entrusted the mystery of the plan of the ages, hidden from the beginning in God."

"Ephesians 3," Jack nodded, recognizing the reference.

"By the Holy One's design you wrestle with the principalities and powers, the rulers of the darkness of this world, empowered by the Holy Spirit and watched over by us. But that is what concerns us."

"What does, exactly?" Jack asked.

"You creatures are so inconsistent. You say one thing and do another. Even as you yourself preach, Jack, is it not almost with the assumption that your teachings will be heard but not obeyed, agreed on but not followed? Don't you ever feel this?"

Jack grunted to himself. "All the time."

"Picture it, then, in this way," said Gloria, rising from the grass to a majestic height to make her point. "We are like excellent athletes—or highly-trained warriors—who are not allowed to participate *directly* in the game—or in the war. We must instead be coaches, drill instructors to poorly motivated recruits, many of whom apparently joined up just because they feel they look good in the uniform. Does this image make sense to you at all?"

"Oh yes," Jack nodded, not meeting her eyes. It made too much sense.

"The instruction manual is clear," she went on preaching. "There are training facilities scattered all over the world—although most of them seem to be concentrated in your own country. But instead of training athletes or preparing warriors, your churches often seem more like weekly parades—and not even attendance is required, much less dedicated marching."

"Must be frustrating to you," Jack nodded. He knew there had been *many* times that had been frustrating to *him*, yet he knew as well that at times his own behavior was as inconsistent as that of those he led.

"It's more than frustrating," Angel Gloria said sadly. "It's tragic. For the creatures who seduce you, who struggle to wrest you away from the Holy One, only want to amuse themselves with your suffering, and ultimately to consume you. The fallen are awful, heinous, sadistic, conscienceless destroyers of all that has been created—and yet more of you creatures would prefer to listen to their lies than to hear the truth. You are like lambs inviting the wolves to supper. And because we are forbidden to force our way into your concerns, we can only wait and watch as you creatures cheerfully make reservations for eternal suffering."

None of this was news to Jack, of course. At the same time, he wondered how seriously of late he'd been taking the eternal implications of his own behaviors. "I can see a little better why you might want to rinse the planet clean."

"It's been rinsed clean once already," the angel reminded him. "I'm sure you've not forgotten Noah. Next time," she went on, "this festering wound will be cauterized." *The fire next time,* Jack thought to himself, and he shivered. "What can I do?" he asked honestly and directly.

"You can be faithful. You can be obedient. You can serve."

"I can love," Jack added quietly.

"Yes," said the angel. "Do that."

"But what can I do right now?" Jack went on, and he gestured around at the meadow. "I don't even know where I *am* right now—or when! Am I dreaming? Or am I really in a fully lighted meadow sometime past midnight in southern California in the late 1960s? What do these aliens—or whatever they are—want of me? And what do *you* want of me? Give me some answers, please. If you can't give me answers, at least give me some clues!"

"You are with the fallen," the Angel Gloria replied. "They have their own purposes for holding you, some of which you know. But part of their purpose in keeping you on board their vessel is to discourage us from destroying it. We have done such in the past, you know. As they've zipped about, deceiving your race, we've taken the occasional opportunity to knock them from the sky. Understand this, Jack—it is very important: When the Holy One imprisoned Lucifer and his minions on this speck of space dust, He also took away their wings. Figuratively, of course," she added glancing down at her own wingless shoulders. "We have the ability to travel wherever we are sent in the created order—the universe. They no longer do. That's why they need their machines. And the reason they need your scientists and technicians is that they cannot create these machines for themselves.

"Think of it, Jack!" she went on, warming to her subject. "You creatures were designed in the Creator's own image—you were created creative! We, on the other hand, were created to be *appreciators* of what the Holy One has created. Those of us who accept our function and perform it with joy don't envy you at all your gift. The fallen, however, envy your creativity *terribly.* Since they will not celebrate creation, but can only destroy it, they cannot create for themselves a way *out* of their predicament. Hence all through your history they've been stealing your technology in order to make themselves appear 'godlike' to your race. Like the little wizard of Oz, they hide behind their curtain of secrecy, manipulating your governments and your geniuses to advance their own designs, all the while promising rewards they can only deliver by further lies, deceit, and manipulation."

"So . . ." Jack said thoughtfully, considering the implications of all she had told him, "the creatures we encounter as 'aliens' are not space travelers at all, but evil entities who pretend to be 'space brothers' in order to gain our technology?"

"Precisely. The occupants of UFOs are not space creatures, although they would very much like to be. That is their purpose—to get off of this planet. And while in *this* generation they've pretended to be aliens, they've played other roles to seduce earlier generations of your race. They've called themselves elves, or fairies, or gnomes, or trolls, or any number of other names in differing cultures. Haven't you noticed that almost every culture appears to have a tradition of 'little people' of some kind, who kidnap humans and take them away on fanciful adventures?"

"Like *my* current trek," Jack agreed wryly.

"In an earlier time they convinced your forebears they were various gods and goddesses. They interacted with the various tribes of mankind, promising them protection and deliverance while taking from them their tribute and technology. They've played at being gods, Jack. They've convinced many. Now, they are seeking to seduce your race into playing at being gods yourselves."

"And it's all been a sham?"

"They are liars, Jack. Their leader is the father of lies."

Jack nodded, rubbing his chin. "Then as I guessed, my trip to the moon was all a 'simulation'?"

"You might call it 'virtual reality,' Jack—or you might call it lying with technology. There was nothing true about that trip. In those words often applied to magicians, it was all smoke and mirrors."

"And the critical events and 'close encounters' of UFO study—they are all a part of this same conspiracy to manipulate mankind?"

"All," the Angel Gloria said firmly.

"The Gulf Breeze, Florida, incidents that have received so much press in the United States?"

"Much of that has been revealed to be a hoax perpetrated by humans—but every time the fallen see the UFO fascination catching hold in a region they do their best to reinforce it by making their own appearances. They've convinced the armed forces of various nations that they are, indeed, whom Gork claimed to you that they were. Some elements in your own government truly believe they've made agreements with space aliens. There were even stories circulating in the American intelligence community at the start of the Gulf War that Armageddon had begun, and that Jesus was coming back to Florida *in a space ship* to reclaim His people. Half-a-dozen armed services intelligence agents went Absent Without Leave from their posts in Germany, just to come to Florida to be 'caught up in the air to meet Him.' Now, Jack," the Angel Gloria said with a dry smile, "does that sound *anything* at all like the end of the age prophesied by the New Testament?"

"No," Jack answered softly, feeling sad and embarrassed for Christian brothers and sisters so deceived. "I remember that in Matthew 24 Jesus warned against believing such stories. 'Then if any man shall say unto you Lo, here is Christ, or, there; believe it not. For there shall arise false Christs and false prophets, and they shall show great signs and wonders, so as to lead astray, if possible, even the very elect.'"

"That does seem very plain to *us,*" said the angel, almost growling in her obvious frustration. "Is it really that difficult for you humans to understand? He said clearly that His coming would be greater than the dawn—imagine, Jack, the light you saw blossoming in this meadow just a few minutes ago, only now coming from billions of beings like myself instead of just a few hundred? And in the midst of all of us, the *true* light Himself shining, the light that outshines all the collected stars of space and time? How could your brothers and sisters *miss* such a description? How could they possibly confuse that image with space ships and flying saucers?"

"I don't know," Jack shrugged. "I truly don't."

"You mention the Gulf Breeze sightings. How about the UMMO sightings in Spain, and the resultant cult that has sprung up around those events? Since the early seventies people around the world have reported seeing saucer-shaped ships with the name of the supposed planet 'UMMO' emblazoned on their undersides—most recently some credible witnesses within Russia. Tell me, Jack. If space brothers from another planet truly intended to come to this world and take it over in order to 'set it right,' do you really think they would advertise the fact for twenty-plus years without permitting themselves to be directly interviewed and videotaped by the worldwide media?"

"No," Jack had to agree.

"And yet that's the mythology that the fallen have spread in your generation. Not through legitimate, documented, news-gathering organizations, but through rumors, tabloid papers, and sensation-oriented television magazines and talk-shows. They cannot deliver on their threats: Even despite their agreements with various national intelligence agencies, the fallen don't have the hardware nor the unity to publicly and internationally seize the apparatus of all governments. Then again, why should they want to, when they already control all they need? It wouldn't be in their purpose to do so, Jack. It *is* in their purpose, however, to keep humankind wondering about them—and also doubting the Holy One's promises. They are liars, Jack. They are very skilled at taking the truth and destroying it."

"Then what about the Majestic 12 documents?" Jack asked. This was a series of supposed secret papers obtained by UFO researchers through the Freedom of Information Act. It described the organization—by President Truman in the early 1950s—of a committee of twelve scientists and spies appointed to investigate the "flying saucer" phenomenon.

"Those papers, too, have been proved to be a human hoax, but it's exactly the *kind* of myth the fallen want to encourage. The same is true with the Philadelphia Experiment, or Area 51—"

"You know about Area 51?" Jack asked, impressed at this angel's knowledge of the UFO phenomenon.

"Why wouldn't we know about that, Jack? 'Human-eating aliens, living in caverns under Arizona, working together with American scientists to perfect new space technologies'—with all I've told you, with all you yourself have seen, you might begin to guess that *some* of these stories border on the truth."

Jack felt a chill course through him, and asked, "Is that where I was, when Gork showed me the 'space city' simulation?"

"You *do* remember 'coming up' to the surface rather than 'landing' on the surface, don't you? And is that really so different from traditional images of the demons in hell that you've been familiar with all your life?"

Jack shivered. "And what about the Corona incident—the saucer crash in the late 1940s near Roswell, New Mexico?"

The Angel Gloria gazed at him evenly. "I already told you. We have, on occasion, knocked the fallen's little flying machines to the ground."

"And . . . *were* bodies recovered?" Jack asked quietly, almost reverently. According to UFO buffs, this was, after all, the biggest question of all.

Angel Gloria seemed to study his face for a moment. "Why do you want to know?"

Jack blinked. The reason, of course, was that he was simply curious. To have special, hidden knowledge, to be on the "inside," "in the know," a member of the initiated. He realized, with a blush, that this was the precise human foible the fallen had always exploited to entice people into their service. It was gossip. "I guess I don't need to know that, do I?"

Gloria's searching expression didn't change. "Subtle, isn't it? That temptation to possess supposedly godlike information?"

"Forgive me," he mumbled.

"I can't forgive," the angel replied. "All I am is a messenger. Only the Holy One can forgive—but contemplate, before you ask, what exactly you're asking forgiveness for."

"I thought you just said—"

"Is curiosity sin, Jack? Or is it simply part of that creative nature the Holy One gave you, which separates you from us? Do you want to know things to boast to others of what you know, or do you want to know things to think of new solutions to problems?"

"I . . . don't know."

"The one feature in you creatures that gives us hope is that you *can* learn. Sometimes you *do* learn. Knowing enough—but not too much—makes you inventive. But while the Holy One seems to take delight in your creations, the fallen delight in perverting them. The more quickly you innovate, the more rapidly the fallen pervert your innovations to their own ends. Now they are bending time itself."

"And that's not good," Jack nodded, concerned immediately for Ben, who provided them with the information that made that possible. He could imagine all kinds of historical events that the fallen would like to alter, given the opportunity to do so.

"Don't be overly frightened, Jack," the angel said to him softly. "The Holy One *made* the time-space continuum. They cannot go to any time or space where we cannot reach them. They cannot change any event that we cannot change *back*."

"Then—" Jack thought to himself for a moment. "Why do they try?"

The Angel Gloria gazed at him evenly. "You tell me, Jack."

He took a deep breath, then glanced again around the beautifully illuminated meadow. Were they still dancing here, the fools who did not see the truth? Still blinded by their self-absorption, did they still celebrate their own darkness? Jack stood up, and paced around the meadow, enjoying it. He felt a growing sensation that he wouldn't have the opportunity much longer. Finally he looked back at Gloria, who seemed to be patiently waiting on him. "So, it's all fixed. The outcome of everything is already known."

The angel nodded, utterly composed. "Your namesake—your real name *is* John, isn't it?—has already seen it all and written it down."

"The Revelation," Jack murmured to himself. Then he smiled crookedly, and looked at her again. "Can't the fallen read?"

"They'd rather try to rewrite it. They're trying now."

"So—what's next for me?"

"You've already said it, Jack—*John*. Be yourself. Serve. Be obedient. Be . . . *loving*."

"I can do all that," Jack nodded, "just as long as I know you're with me."

Suddenly, the angel looked distressed.

"Did I say something wrong?" Jack asked.

Gloria looked—perplexed. "This is the reason we don't reveal ourselves to you creatures more often," she said.

"What is?"

"You become dependent upon *us*."

"No, I didn't mean to say—"

"The Comforter is with you, Jack. He always has been. I'm only a messenger, sent from the Holy One to encourage and explain. But you mustn't expect to see me much more. Depend instead upon the Holy Spirit within you—upon what you've always believed to be the truth—upon the spiritual wisdom built up inside you by years of experience with the Holy One. And remember your favorite hymn, Jack . . . ."

"My favorite hymn?"

More quickly than it had come, the light departed. It was as if some heavenly circuit breaker just flipped. But he did hear the Angel Gloria's voice one more time: "Remember it, Jack." Then the darkness was complete.

Chapter Eleven

Rude awakening

"He's back," Ben said.

Jack opened his eyes. He recognized this room immediately. He'd awakened here before. It was the "surgical center" within the ship where he'd encountered Gork in the guise of "Miz White." He saw both Ben and Gork standing over him. Once again his fallen abductor wore the body of a gray alien. *What a comedown,* Jack thought to himself—*to fall from being one of those glorious creatures of light who had ringed the meadow, to this wrinkled, slimy monster. . . .*

"We were worried about you," Gork lied, smiling. "You've been gone a long time."

Jack rolled his eyes over to look at Ben. *How long?* he thought at the boy. Not that it made any difference in this time-jumping adventure. Jack thought he heard both relief and apology in the boy's voice as Ben answered, "Eighteen days."

"Eighteen days!" he gasped. It had seemed like only a few moments! Then again, as nearly as he could figure he'd been in heaven. As they say, time flies when you're having fun!

"We thought we'd lost you," Gork said, still smiling that ridiculous-looking alien smile.

"Really? I thought we'd lost *you*," Jack answered. "Wishful thinking, I suppose, right, Ben? I remember watching you doing the twist on top of the altar," he went on, mocking Gork. "Did everybody buy your act?" Jack saw Ben rolling his eyes in warning, but he didn't care. What did it matter, really, what this thing did or felt?

Pain suddenly coursed through him, and Jack remembered why Gork's feelings mattered. Soon he was screaming. Then, as suddenly as it had come, the pain stopped. Through it all, Gork smiled.

"Ben told me of your dream," the fallen then said softly—almost kindly. Jack, of course, knew better; he had the tingling nerve endings to prove it. "I need to remind you, however," the fallen went on, "that dreams are only that: dreams. I hope you'll not be so foolish as to convince yourself that any of that actually happened." Gork stepped away from the surgical table, allowing the bright light from above to glare down into Jack's eyes as he went on: "This, however, is reality. The hard, cold table under your shoulder blades, the light in your eyes, that terrible sensation of pain you just experienced—these are the real world. Welcome back, Jack," Gork finished—and his last word was almost a snarl. Then—thankfully—he left the room.

Ben still stood beside the table, peering down into Jack's face. He clearly still felt responsible for what was happening to Jack. Had he been worried that Jack wouldn't return?

"Yes," the boy answered quietly. "It appeared so beautiful there—so peaceful." Ben sighed.

"I was in heaven, wasn't I."

"I don't know," Ben answered softly. "Were you?"

Jack sat up and swung his legs off the side of the surgical table. "Seemed like heaven," Jack muttered, and Ben nodded. He tested the muscles of his arms against the table. Despite Gork's dose of agony, they seemed strong and fit—hardly what he would expect if he'd been in a coma for almost three weeks. "Look at this," he said, and he gripped the round edge of the table and pushed himself up and off of it. He landed lightly on his feet. His legs felt wonderful. "I feel better than I have in years," he murmured, and he looked at Ben and raised an eyebrow. "I have to tell you, Ben, it *felt* like heaven."

Ben nodded again, but said nothing.

"You don't believe me, do you? You don't believe it really happened."

The boy shrugged. "I believe *you* believe that it really happened."

"But you don't?"

"It's . . . hard, Jack," Ben answered. He obviously didn't want to be talking about this. If indeed Jack had been "away" for almost three weeks, what had the fallen done to the boy in the interval? Ben shook off the unasked question with pleading eyes, and went on quickly, "It certainly *seemed* dream-like to me."

The change in the boy was remarkable. Something had happened. He was obviously far more frightened of the fallen than he had been. "How much did you tell them of my . . . dream?" Jack asked.

"Enough that they know what you believe about it," Ben answered. Then he scanned the walls—and seemed to relax. "Even if I did believe it I wouldn't tell them I did," he whispered. "I've convinced them that I think you're crazy. That comforts them—my thinking you're crazy. If what the angel—" Ben stopped himself, then went on even more quietly "if what your *dream* told you has any truth to it at all, then you're safest as long as I continue to disbelieve."

Jack glanced around at the operating theater. "Can we . . . go somewhere else? I can't help but think of slaughtered cattle in this room. . . ."

Ben nodded, and led him out the door into a corridor. Jack remembered being very confused by his surroundings the first time he'd awakened in this room. He wondered if they were still on board the saucer. "Where are we now?"

"Underground . . . somewhere," Ben said evasively.

"New Mexico?" Jack asked, but the boy just shrugged. "*when* are we?"

"Ah—back in the present, I suppose."

"You're not certain?"

Ben couldn't restrain a chuckle. "Would *you* be?"

Jack brightened. "Then I can call Gloria!"

This time Ben didn't *try* to restrain himself. He laughed aloud. "Sure. If you can find a cellular phone in this place!"

"Oh," Jack murmured. "Right."

"The . . . uh . . . Grays are very angry with me right now," Ben said. "With you too. I don't think it would be a good idea to request phone privileges—if you understand my meaning?" Clearly, Ben was warning him. Would they kill him?

"They have in the past," Ben answered Jack's chilling thought offhandedly.

As they continued through a maze of featureless corridors Jack forced his thoughts in another direction: "Why back in the present? Why not still in 1969?"

"Well . . . " Ben began as he led Jack into a room that had obviously been tailored to look like the generic motel room, "They—messed up."

"What do you mean?"

"They were trying to stow away on that first Apollo flight to land on the moon—remember? The Neil Armstrong flight?"

"Of course I remember," Jack snorted. "'The eagle has landed'—'That's one small step for man, one giant leap for mankind.' It was a Sunday afternoon in California, and we called off evening church because nobody came. Everyone stayed home watching the moon walk on television."

"Yeah." Ben grunted. "Well, they were trying to stow away on that flight, and they got caught. There were threats from the government and counter threats from the aliens and—oh, it was a real mess, Jack, believe me. You don't need to hear the whole story. I tried to tell them that it was a stupid idea, that if there was no history of them *doing* it then it *didn't happen*, and *wouldn't* happen. But, they're new to this time-travel thing. So, now were back in what we both remember to be the present time, and they're . . . " Ben paused. "Oh, never mind."

"They're what? What are they doing now?"

"Oh, just trying to steal a space shuttle is all." Ben grinned impishly and shrugged. "Who knows? Maybe they'll succeed!"

They can't, Jack thought to himself. *They can't be allowed off the planet. The angels won't permit it.* He belatedly remembered that Ben read his every thought, and searched the boy's face for his reactions. Ben just smiled at him—enigmatically, he thought. "Where's Jeffrey?" Jack asked, thinking of his old best friend, now a "Man in Black." Once again, Ben's answer was evasive:

"Oh . . . keeping busy."

* * *

Nighttime in New York, a little after 10:00 P.M., and the taxis in the street below him hurtled ever onward in their search for another fare or an almost green light. Ronald Pearson sat on the balcony of his East 68th Street condominium, gazing southward into the heart of Manhattan. This breathtaking panorama of tall buildings and tightly packed humanity had always been the best thing about this place—but it didn't stir him tonight. He usually enjoyed the Chinese food his wife ordered up from the little place around the corner, but tonight it just seemed to sit in his gut, arguing with him in Mandarin. Even his bourbon was doing nothing for him.

"You're rich, Ron," he told himself quietly, eyeing the lights on the pointed dome of the Chrysler Building. "So why are you so strapped for cash?" he mumbled bitterly, draining the liquor from his glass.

He knew why, of course. He just couldn't say. No one at the office knew, or he'd be dead already. His wife didn't know, and he prayed to all the gods she never would. "Someday I'll be out of this," he lied to himself—but as good a liar as he was to other people, Ron Pearson had never been able to lie effectively to himself. And so the bourbon and the chow mein were having it out in his stomach—

His phone rang. He checked his watch—after ten. No one called him after ten! No one but them! He jerked his pocket phone out of his coat and hurriedly flipped it open. "Pearson," he grunted quickly.

"Is it done?" asked the voice at the other end.

Ron recognized that voice immediately—a man's voice, yet high-pitched enough to be a woman's. And it had behind it a sinister smile he'd seen only twice—but that was too much. He hated having to answer, "No. I need more cash!" Then he bit his lip, and winced at his own stupidity out at the Manhattan night.

The voice paused for what seemed like a full minute. "Calmly, my friend," it finally said. "Meet me there. Now."

Pearson frowned. "There? Meet you there? That's three hours away!"

"Then hadn't you better get started?" said the voice, and it hung up.

Ron cursed, and very nearly threw the phone at the tall building that loomed across the street—but he didn't. Instead he folded it up, shoved it back in his pocket, and slid open the glass door. "Gotta go downtown," he said as he hurried through the small living room toward the bedroom.

"Oh?" said his wife, with that one icy word conveying every possible inflection of contempt, bitterness, and suspicion.

"Don't start," he growled, and he was out of the room, able to ignore her snippy "Start what? What was ever finished?"

Back he came into the living room to pause at the entryway and throw the latch. "This will take all night. Don't wait up."

"Why would I want to wait up for—" The door slammed behind him, sparing him the rest of her sentence. Didn't matter. He knew what she was saying.

The elevator ride down from the twenty-second floor was uneventful. He waved off the doorman's offer to call for his car and ran out to the street to hail a cab. Park Avenue was clear down to 37th and the Ghanaian cabby drove it furiously, asking no questions. He got out at Madison Square Garden and quickly trotted down the steps to Penn Station. In fifteen minutes he was on the southbound train for Baltimore, gazing out the window as they rumbled through the dark tunnels under the river. He was wishing he'd never *seen* an alien, much less become a part of their clandestine organization. He was also hoping they were bringing him money. . . .

* * *

Jack sat on the bed in this pseudo motel room, wondering. He'd had plenty of time to do that in the hours since his awakening. Soon after avoiding his question about Jeffrey, Ben had excused himself. And while this place was in every other way like a motel, this room seemed not to have been equipped with a television. Or a phone. Or a phone book. Or literature of any kind. Most certainly, it had no Gideon Bible, for Jack had looked. Then again, why would it?

There *was* a curtain, at least—but no window. The door opened onto a blank corridor anyway. At least, the door opened for *others* onto a blank corridor. It wouldn't open for him at all. There was nothing to do but sit and wonder about things, and the main thing he'd been wondering about for the last half-hour was how he and Ben had *ever* gotten away from these creatures. He had about convinced himself that they had been *allowed* to escape when the door opened, and Gork walked in with a tray of fried chicken.

No, this wasn't Gork, Jack realized quickly. It was an alien "Gray," like Gork, but slimmer, and—somehow—friendlier. "Hungry?" the alien asked, and smiled. Strangely, Jack thought. Almost—flirtatiously! "Come on," the Gray encouraged, setting the tray on top of the dresser that ran the length of the wall. "I promise I had nothing to do with making it!" the creature giggled.

Jack was stunned. He'd not heard one of the pseudo-aliens giggle before. This being seemed somehow girlish. He remembered Miz White all too well, however. "Are you female?" he asked.

"I'm an alien," the Gray responded. "What possible difference could *any* alien gender make? We might have three sexes—or even four!" Once again she giggled, and Jack stared at her until she quit. Then, "Sit down, Jack," she said calmly. "Eat. You're bored, and I'm happy to keep you company."

He was indeed bored. And he hadn't eaten in weeks! Without further argument he did as she suggested.

* * *

At 2 A.M. Pearson got off the Washington-bound train under Baltimore's Pennsylvania Station and wrapped his coat up around his face. A chilly wind did blow down the tracks, but his primary purpose was to keep anyone from recognizing him as he climbed the steps up into the station. He was nervous. Would the Man in Black be in a car out at the curb? Or would he be left to sit alone on the wooden benches of this station, hoping to go unrecognized as he waited for further contact?

He walked purposefully through the lobby, trying to peer out the front door—nothing. His stomach churned. Then someone grabbed him by the elbow and hurried him along out the side door, and although in any other circumstance he would find that terrifying, at the moment he felt nothing but relief. Moments later he was ducking into the back seat of a car as his escort climbed in beside him, and they were off to cruise the streets of Baltimore as they talked.

"Very foolish," said the Man in Black as their driver cruised the quiet streets toward the waterfront. "You know better than to make such statements on an open line."

"You caught me off guard," Pearson grumbled. "I wasn't expecting to hear from you for two more weeks."

"And yet you say you need more cash. That suggests it might *not* be finished in two more weeks. Am I interpreting that correctly?"

"I cannot hide a project of this magnitude from my accountants!"

"Nonsense," smiled the Man in Black, his pasty face spreading into that long, thin smile Pearson found so unnerving. "You're the CEO. You can do what you like."

"You give me too much credit," Pearson mumbled.

"Apparently!" said the Man in Black, and he chuckled politely. "And yet, here you are asking for even *more* credit!"

"You have it," Pearson snarled. "You know you do."

"Of course. But what do we *receive* for our money? Give me a report. Is it nearing completion? What's the extra money for? Are you having any difficulty with materials? Are the authorities snooping?"

"No authorities. Not that I'm aware of. It *has* been rumored that we have a major new product in R-and-D, and certain ambitious accountants are making a game of finding out as much about it as they can—"

Jeffrey whipped a small notepad out of his coat pocket and flipped it open. "How many? What are their names and—preferably—their addresses?"

Ronald Pearson had anticipated this question, and had jotted their names down on the back of his ticket. He handed it to the Man in Black and was graced with that same threatening smile.

"Very good," said Jeffrey. "And you also remembered to buy only a one-way ticket. Excellent." He glanced into the rearview mirror, meeting the driver's eyes, and immediately the car wheeled around and headed out of town. "Naturally, these will be taken care of. For now—why don't you lean back and take a little nap? I'm sure you're very weary from your lengthy travels, and for the moment our business is finished."

Pearson didn't try to resist the suggestion. He knew he wouldn't be able to. He knew, too, that he was likely to wake up anyplace on earth. But when you partner with aliens, he told himself, waking up somewhere on earth was preferable to a number of other possibilities . . . .

* * *

Are you reading my mind, you little thought squeegee? Jeffrey was thinking as the sleeping executive was floated up the gangplank into the saucer. *That's your job, I know, soaking up the thoughts of others and pouring them out to our esteemed Sibling. I do wish I could read yours—perhaps just for an afternoon. Fair play, don't you think?* "Store him," Jeffrey instructed another of his black-dressed ilk, and Pearson's sleeping body was steered down a slanting hallway and into a cabin.

Jeffrey stretched and slipped out of his coat, then ambled into the smallish cell set aside for him. *I do wish we could at least converse by thought, young Ben,* Jeffrey's mental monologue continued as he stretched out on a well-used couch. *Two ways, I mean. But for the moment*—he fished Pearson's folded rail ticket out of his shirt pocket and read the names over slowly to himself. *Now then, Ben. If you are reading me—and you are, aren't you?—please have our esteemed Sibling dispatch a team to visit these inquisitive accountants, all right? Very good. Let him know, too—if you haven't already—that we're on our way to pick up Henry Ritter from St. Petersburg, and will be back in base by*—Jeffrey checked his watch—*by 4 A.M., your time. Give my best wishes to our faith-affirming friend, will you? Nighty-night.*

That done, Jeffrey leaned back more deeply into his couch, hands laced behind his head. Without bothering to untie them, he pried off his shoes with his toes and closed his eyes. He would have a few minutes of rest time before waking the drug king out of his sleep. Jeffrey's thoughts drifted toward the promise of the aliens—eternal life. What would it be like, he wondered excitedly, to roam the spaceways, himself a Sibling, long after the earth had become a fried cinder in the embrace of an expanding sun? He would live forever—or close to it—and not in some spiritual, other-worldly plane indistinguishable from a dreamworld. He would survive his own race—most of it, anyway—to become an adept, a ruler, a master in this very real universe.

Suddenly the saucer lurched sideways, pitching him off his couch and onto the floor. He knew immediately what had happened: They'd been spotted on radar, and jets had scrambled in pursuit. Still on the floor, he grabbed the well-secured couch and held on while the craft accelerated away. Fortunately, the technology of this vehicle still superseded that of its pursuers, but it wouldn't for long. Pearson's upgrade was needed *now!* As suddenly as the saucer had shot into motion, it stopped. They'd gotten far enough away to go to ground and, in effect, disappear. The fighters would fly on a ways, perplexed, then return to base to make a lame, laughing report about UFOs and try their best to forget about it. It happened all the time.

Jeffrey *did* wonder, from time to time, why the Pleiadian Siblings would not provide humankind with their *own* technology. He understood clearly, however, the reasoning behind that policy. Their technology was so far superior to that of the earth that no one on earth could comprehend it. Besides, how could a mother bird teach her chicks to fly without forcing them to use their own wings? The Siblings' purpose was to teach their younger, human counterparts to find their own means of leaving the planet—thus, the need for Pearson's new design, constructed to fit precisely into the cargo bay of an

American space shuttle. It was all human technology, of course, but brought together and empowered by the insight and influence of their Siblings from the stars. "And by human cash," Jeffrey said to himself as he climbed back up onto his couch. This time he took the precaution of strapping himself in.

"You spoke?" said a voice over the intercom.

"Not to you," Jeffrey barked back. "Just get us to St. Petersburg, *now*."

Once again the craft shot into motion, accelerating to its top speed, and within minutes it was gliding ten feet over the Gulf of Mexico, making a long circle over the white caps to approach Tampa-St. Pete from the sea. If they were spotted again tonight, it would only be by a Coast Guard vessel, which would regard them as either an impossibly fast hovercraft, or an inexplicable blip. Jeffrey relaxed, and at last dozed. He'd been a blip on a radar screen too many times to find it exciting any more.

* * *

The chicken was delicious. The company was—interesting. Jack ate and listened, tearing the greasy meat with his teeth as he watched Astra stroll about the room.

That's what she called herself: Astra. And regardless of what she'd said about genders in aliens, she was clearly as feminine a presence as Gork was masculine. As she giggled and glided about and waved her slender arms expressively, Jack saw clearly what she was attempting to do. She flirted with him. She was charming him—seeking to seduce him emotionally. The thing that bothered him most about all this was that he couldn't help but like her.

She suddenly sat on the bed next to him, boring into him with her enormous obsidian eyes. He instinctively shifted backward. She tilted her head to one side and said, "You're afraid of me, aren't you?"

"No."

"Oh, I don't mean you fear me the way you're afraid of Ruzagnon—"

"Who?"

"My . . . consort. The one you apparently call 'Gork.'"

"Oh. Him."

She giggled again, and it sounded so innocent and sweet that Jack had to look away from her and rub his forehead to keep in focus who—or what—was speaking to him. "Why do you call him that, anyway? He hates it!"

Jack couldn't help but be pleased. "Perhaps *because* he hates it."

"You're mean, you know that?" Astra teased, and Jack smiled. "Actually," she went on, lowering her voice conspiratorially, "I think it kind of fits him!" Then she giggled again, and closed the distance between them. Jack shivered, then stood up and moved to the other bed. He sat down and faced her again, and saw that she was gazing at him with a look of triumph. Then she pouted and asked, "Why do you keep moving away from me? Is it because of this ugly old alien skin I'm wearing?" Astra stood up and slid her long fingers down the length of her gray body. This was the first time it had really registered on Jack that all of the aliens went naked. "Wouldn't you like to see some of the *other* costumes I've greeted *mankind* wearing? Or not wearing?"

Frightened as she took another step toward him, Jack took refuge in a familiar defense—academic curiosity. "I *have* wondered how Gork—or whatever his name is—manages to change his appearance. I've seen him in three guises that I *know* of, but I've—"

"Would you like to see *me* change?" Astra interrupted him, taking another step closer.

"Ah . . . no . . . thank you . . . "

Now she stood directly over him, looking down on him. Her voice changed from the mincing, girlish tone she'd been using to a deep, powerful, and yet still clearly feminine sound as she said, "You *do* know who I am—don't you?"

Jack didn't like anyone standing over him this closely, but when he started to shift away again she grabbed him by both of his shoulders, and he knew he wasn't going anywhere. Her grip was more powerful than any weightlifter's—and her mere presence far more intimidating. He looked down at the tops of his knees and murmured, "I can guess who you're going to *tell* me you are."

"Guess," Astra commanded.

"You've . . . given me enough clues, certainly. You're going to tell me you're Ashteroth, consort of Baal—or Astarte, or Ishtar of the Egyptians—or Aphrodite, or Venus, or any one of a dozen other incarnations of the ancient goddess of love."

"You're so smart, Jack!" she praised him, her head hovering directly above his. She sounded genuinely pleased. "And is *that* why you don't want to watch me change into a more—shall we say—attractive form? Because you're *afraid* of your own reactions to the beguiling beauty of Aphrodite?"

He *was* afraid. More than that, he was embarrassed. Here he sat on a bed in a motel room with this . . . creature, and he could feel his blush climbing up his face to the roots of his hair. He would *never* permit himself to be placed in such a position in his ministry, never, and while he knew he had no control over this situation, he couldn't prevent himself from feeling guilty about it somehow. His guilt made him angry: Angry at Ben for leading him into this trap, angry at the fallen for manipulating him so, angry at . . . at God for allowing him to be plunged so swiftly from heavenly bliss into this . . . this . . .

Then he recalled the angel's words. "Remember your favorite hymn, Jack," she had said. Which *was* his favorite hymn? He loved so many—*Victory in Jesus; Because He Lives; Day by Day, and With Each Passing Moment*—actually, just thinking about any of those stilled some of his fear, dispelled some of his guilt, and relived some of his tension. But his favorite hymn?

A Mighty Fortress Is Our God. It was the one song he always said had to be sung at his funeral—and *all* of it needed to be sung, not the "first, second, and last verses" song leaders often tried to abbreviate hymns into. The third verse carried the phrase that meant the most to him—the phrase, he now realized, the angel had pointed him to: He spoke it aloud now, to Astra.

"And though this world with devils filled should threaten to undo us, we will not fear for God has willed His truth to triumph through us. The Prince of Darkness grim, we tremble not for him—his rage we can endure, for lo, his doom is sure. One little word shall fell him."

By the time he finished quoting the stanza, Astra had retreated all the way to the door. Her gray face had turned white, and her long, spindly body trembled with either terror or wrath. Perhaps both, Jack thought, for when he finished, from her alien mouth burst out such a flood of verbal sewage that he thought the room might actually begin to stink from it. The curses she spewed, the invectives she heaped upon him, the vile sounds that gushed from her mouth erased any wisp of the seductive web of attractiveness she'd been laboring to weave around him. Yet despite her proven physical prowess she appeared unwilling to cross the carpet between them and bodily seize him again.

Eventually she was forced to repeat herself—Jack was reminded again how limited a vocabulary four-letter words provide—and at last her tirade ground to a halt, and she just stood in the doorway glowering at him. But the moment Jack began to feel proud of himself for resisting her so effectively, she seemed to regain her poise. Astra laughed—not the giggle she'd entered the room with. This was a contemptuous, spiteful, scornful laugh, full of power and resolve. "You think you've won, don't you? You puny little believers, you always think you win! But you *never* win, Jack, for the game's never over. Watch yourself, Jack. The next time you see me you won't even *know* me—but I'll know you. And you, my little man, will want very much to know me then. Oh yes. And *more*." Astra reached behind her to turn the knob, and left the room with a dramatic flourish.

Jack sat on the bed with his hands between his knees. "Oh Lord," he murmured breathlessly. "What next?" How he wished Gloria was here. Either one of them.

Chapter Twelve

Nobodies

Even though she was now many hours and many miles away from Huntsville, Carrie Baxter continued to watch her rearview mirror. All the way to Chattanooga she'd watched it. Somehow, driving past Lookout Mountain, she'd been sure someone was peering down at her from the heights above, monitoring her progress toward Washington. Everything she'd read about the international intelligence community, about spies and secret societies and government corruption, had convinced her that there was no way they'd let her get away with this—no way at all.

But no one had stopped her yet. She'd planned this well—hadn't told a soul, although every Wednesday night for weeks she *had* pleaded with her little Alabama church to remember her unspoken prayer request. So earnestly had she prayed, in fact, that her pastor had called her twice to check on her, transparently giving her the chance to open up to him. But she wouldn't tell him. If he knew what she knew, he'd be killed.

As she still might be, Carrie thought to herself, once again glancing behind her. Didn't she recognize that silver car from several stops back? Had it been following her? She began immediately looking for a rest stop, some place to pull over to let this potential pursuer either go past her or identify himself. If they were going to stop her, it might as well be sooner as later. She knew she could never run away from him in her overheated station wagon.

It was piled full of suitcases and clothes hampers. She wanted anyone who passed her to assume she was a poor, single woman, moving to a new city. The suitcases were cheap looking, bought secondhand mostly, but only one of them contained any clothes. And as for the hampers, if anyone peeled off the top layer of towels they'd find reams of documents in each one—copies of documents she'd made and removed from her company near the Redstone Arsenal—what outsiders called the Space Center at Huntsville. She'd copied and removed two or three documents at a time over a period of months. The bigger the stacks had grown on the floor of her bedroom, the more she'd realized she couldn't just cart them off to Washington in file boxes. But she'd had plenty of time to devise means of disguising them and carrying them away to her rescuer, to the man who would get to the bottom of all this. After all—she'd had to help get him elected, first.

Now he was. Finally! Congressman Ralph Wilkenson! That title had such a wonderful ring to it! And while she certainly wasn't solely responsible for his election, she *had* poured hours and hours of volunteer work into his campaign, along with many more hours of prayer *for* it.

Ever since she'd stumbled onto this secret, she had known she would need to find some God-fearing, Christ-loving person in government to reveal her story to. Now she had him! Not that Mr. Ralph really knew her, of course. Carrie was far too quiet a worker at *whatever* she did to receive any notice from the really important people. Even though she didn't wear glasses, she looked like the kind of person who *should.* Her sunken chin and sober expression rarely attracted a second glance from men. She was routinely dismissed as the "smart librarian" type of girl—efficient and hardworking, but otherwise invisible. Carrie was wise enough to recognize that this was why she could learn what she'd learned and get away with it—why apparently no one within the conspiracy had as yet discovered that she'd put together all the pieces. Still, Mr. Wilkenson would surely remember her face from the campaign office well enough to give her the hearing she so desperately needed.

"And what if he doesn't?" she worried aloud to herself as she finally spotted a reststop and pulled off the interstate. Carrie worried constantly about everything, and this was the one thing that worried her most. "What if he's forgotten the little people already?"

Carrie didn't have a very positive view of politicians in general. How could she, with the country in the mess it was in? It seemed every time some decent Christian person was elected to go up there and make a change in Washington, Washington changed him or her instead. She'd seen it happen before. She prayed that wouldn't happen with Mr. Ralph. The people needed him to be faithful. God needed him to be faithful. Carrie needed him to be faithful!

The silver car had headed onward to the northeast, never even hesitating even after Carrie began to signal. She realized now that she'd been holding her breath ever since she'd spotted it, and she just sat still for a moment, letting the engine idle while she collected herself.

For the dozenth time *today* she reviewed her plan for flaws. She could think of none. No one at work had appeared to suspect her. No one had questioned her when she'd asked for a week off to go visit her sister. In fact, her boss had smiled broadly and made some comment about how he thought she was never going to take a vacation. She liked her boss. She'd satisfied herself that he knew nothing about the scheme, that he was as much in the dark as anyone about the "special project in Building J." She hoped he wouldn't be hurt when she blew the whistle—even though she knew that whatever hurt the company would ultimately hurt everyone who worked *for* the company. In the earliest days after her discovery she had struggled to think of ways she could reveal what she knew without even losing her own job—a fantasy, she realized now. Several times in the last few days she'd had to stop herself from tearfully hugging her coworkers good-bye. After all, as far as they knew, she would only be gone a week. So, she had bidden a silent adieu to each of them and had cried her tears at night.

"Gotta put that all behind me," she told herself as she pulled back out onto the interstate. Very soon now all her bridges would be burning behind her. She had to speed her way onward. Carrie Baxter had put her faith in Congressman Ralph Wilkenson. Oh—and God, of course. Always and ultimately God.

* * *

The tentative knock on his door assured Jack immediately that it was Ben. No one else in this place would knock. He even had a pretty good idea of why it was so tentative. "Come on in, Ben. All is forgiven."

The boy stuck his head in the door and said, "Are *you* reading minds now?"

Jack was laying back on the far bed from the door, his hands laced together behind his neck. "Not me, my friend. I can't even read my *own* mind at the moment."

"Sorry Astra came to work on you."

"Did you hear that conversation?" Jack asked, turning his eyes back to the bland, empty ceiling.

"Only a bit. I was . . . working."

"Anything you can to tell me about?"

The teenager sat on the other bed and rolled down onto it on his stomach. "I guess I could tell you whatever I want to. There's no one to stop me."

"I'm sure not in a position to report any secrets, that's for sure," Jack acknowledged. "So. Anything you *want* to tell me?"

"Only that you're free to wander around the tombs wherever you want to go."

"The tombs?" Jack frowned.

"That's what I call this place. You might have another name for it."

"Hell, perhaps?"

"I really don't think it's as bad as *that*. . . ."

"Of course not," Jack said, sitting up. "Are you certain I'm free? Every time I've tried the door it's been locked from the outside. At least, to *me* it's been locked. Everyone else seems to have unlimited access."

"The doorknob mechanism had been programmed to recognize your fingerprints and refuse to turn for you. Latest technology. I got them to change the combination and let you out."

"How?"

"I just asked. Well, and I threatened not to cooperate. I also told them exactly what you just said—after all, who *are* you going to tell?"

"Let's go then," Jack said as he moved toward the door, and Ben hopped up to follow him. Indeed, the knob turned easily for him now. Jack shook his head in amazement as he held the door open for the boy to pass through. "What I don't understand is how we ever escaped before. Did they just *let* us go?"

"I don't know," Ben shrugged as he waved for Jack to follow him down a long, deserted corridor. "I don't read demons, remember? But it may be that they just don't have this technology on the saucer—on any of the saucers. I've never seen it on any of them. They're getting old, you know."

"The saucer?" Jack remembered now how weather-beaten the craft had appeared to him the day he'd been abducted.

"The whole fleet of saucers. They're over six months old. That's why they're so anxious to get the new fleet finished."

The concept struck Jack as funny. "Wonder what kind of trade-in they can get on a *used* saucer?"

Ben smiled politely. "The new ones won't be saucer-shaped, though."

"Oh no? And what will the 1995 model look like? Sleek? Stylish?"

"Square," Ben answered, still smiling.

"Square?"

"Rectangular, really. Boxy, anyway. Designed to fit precisely into the payload bay of a space shuttle." Jack stopped grinning, and Ben raised his eyebrows and nodded. "I told you, Jack. The angel told you. They want off of this rock, and soon."

Jack shook his head, still trying to put all the fantastic notions he'd heard over the past weeks together with the facts of the American space program. "Why should . . . " he spluttered, " . . . why should they steal a shuttle? Why don't they just go ahead and . . . and build their own?"

"That's an interesting point," Ben nodded, a macabre grin on his young lips. "But I guess you can see by now that—to them anyway—they *have* built their own! We Americans just *thought* it was ours." He waited for Jack to respond, but then saw clearly the massive disruption in Jack's thoughts. "Sorry," he said. "I thought you'd already put most of this together."

"I . . . maybe I *should* have, but . . . "

"The head of the company who's building the new fleet is being brought in tonight. He's a major government contractor, fabricating components for the new space station. At least, they're *supposed* to be components of the space station. It's just that certain of those boxy 'habitats' will be outfitted with other special features. They'll include all the bells and whistles you've seen demonstrated by the current generation of saucers, plus a lot more."

"Time travel?" Jack asked.

"Of course," Ben sighed guiltily. "Wouldn't want to be caught somewhere out in the time-space continuum without the wherewithal to jump back at least a few minutes and correct your mistakes."

"Is this executive a part of the Ultrastructure?"

"Of course," Ben nodded curtly. Then he half-smirked. "Face it, Jack. Like it or not, *you're* part of the Ultrastructure!"

"I mean, does this man *know* what he's doing? Does he know whom—or what—he's building these things *for?*"

"To be quite frank, Jack," Ben replied, "the CEO and his company are building them for *money.* While he knows he's working for aliens—or thinks he is—he's really not all that concerned about who'll control these things after they're built."

"I still don't understand," Jack murmured. "With all the technology I've seen the fallen exhibit, it . . . it seems like it would be a *simple* thing for them to build a craft to get themselves off the planet."

"It does, doesn't it!" Ben grinned. "Makes you wonder if someone might be . . . stopping them?"

Jack's eyes rose from the gray floor of the corridor, and he turned to look Ben in the face. "You do believe the angel, don't you?"

Ben shrugged. "Not if Gork asks, I don't. And I'd suggest you not say anything more about all this either. I mean, they've only released you as a favor to me—well, and to demonstrate to you how utterly powerless you are. Ah—those are their words, not mine. But Jack—and I hope you'll take this without feeling any offense—to be honest, I kind of feel you're powerless too. I mean—maybe the angels will stop them, and maybe they won't. But don't you figure that no matter what it is people like us do, or how hard we try, ultimately it won't make a bit of difference?"

Jack reflected on that for a moment. After all, he was fresh from the presence of angels—and demons seemed to find his attitudes worth attempting to change. When he answered, it wasn't with his voice, but with his thoughts: *No Ben. Quite the opposite. I think what people like us do will make* all *the difference.* Then he spoke. "Why don't you show me where you do your 'work.'"

* * *

The new congressman had boxes everywhere. Boxes on the desk, boxes on the chairs, boxes on the floor, and more boxes on top of all of *those* boxes. And the trouble was, Ralph didn't know if he'd be able to find anything *in* any of the boxes, even if he could find the right box to begin with. He'd been in town only a few days, and had been amazed at all the public things he'd had to do that prevented him from doing any of the *private* things he'd been elected to do. Not that this was any real change from the campaign. During that, almost everything he'd done had been a public event. He'd become accustomed to it. *Too much so, perhaps?* he wondered as he cleared a box from his desk chair and sat down in it. Now that he was actually in office, all of those promises he'd made about what he would do when he got here seemed to be every bit as intimidating as all these piles of boxes. In fact, he guessed if he'd boxed up all his promises and brought *them* with him to Washington, they would have filled this room and overflowed into the hallway. And this office had *very* high ceilings. . . .

It had all happened so quickly. The grand old man of the opposing party had suddenly died in office, resulting in the need for a special election. His own party had *never* been competitive for this seat in Ralph's lifetime, and the opposition didn't think they could be competitive now. He'd been asked to run by a few concerned Christian laypeople who didn't mind "wasting their vote," as they put it, if it meant sending a message to the party in power. He'd agreed to run partly out of a sense of Christian duty and partly because he felt so honored they'd asked him that he couldn't say no. *Why me?* he'd wondered. Well, for one thing, with his high cheekbones, full head of black hair, and youthful expression, he guessed he was relatively good-looking. He always seemed to photograph well, anyway. And he had a background in advertising that helped him know instinctively what would and wouldn't sell to his generation. Not even *he* had known how good he could be at stump-speaking and handshaking. Certainly the opposition hadn't. So confident were they of victory that their candidate really didn't even bother to campaign against him. And now Ralph Wilkenson was the new congressman from his district, and the other party had put together a blue-ribbon panel to study its "failed election strategies."

Let them study whatever they want, Ralph thought to himself. He didn't have time for any more electioneering himself. He had to learn how to be an effective *lawmaker.* What he really needed to do was to crack into one of these boxes and start reading the materials he and his staff had pulled together on the various issues. Health reform—he'd have to find that box quickly. Welfare reform? Yes, that too. Gun control? There were so *many* basic issues he needed to spend so much time reading up on that he didn't know how he could afford to give time to anything else! And yet he already had an appointment on his calendar for today—a constituent, his secretary had told him, who'd driven all the way from Alabama to talk to him. Worked in his campaign too, she said—although from his secretary's description he really couldn't place who it might be.

He glanced at his watch. She would be here in ten minutes. He would need to clear a box off of some place for her to sit down, but he had a little more time to scan his notes on—

His secretary buzzed him. "Yes, Mary?" he responded through the intercom.

"Your appointment is here, sir."

Ten minutes early! Ah well, Wilkenson thought to himself. Better to get it over with quickly so he could really focus on these critical issues. "Be right out," he said. He cleared a spot for his visitor on the couch and went to open the door. "Miss . . . Baxter, is it?" he said, recalling the name Mary had neatly typed on his daily agenda.

"You remember me!" Carrie said brightly as she jumped up to meet him.

Ralph smiled his of-course-I-remember-you! smile as he welcomed her into his office, all the time trying to place the woman. It did seem he'd seen her before—stuffing envelopes, maybe? Once they both sat down he leaned forward, put his hands on his knees, and said, "You're my first constituent visit! How are things in Alabama?"

Carrie kept smiling at him, but any joy in her eyes died. She'd rehearsed this moment for weeks. She saw no reason not to cut directly to the point. "Not good, Mr. Ralph. And . . . and before I go on, I'd best tell you that you're going to find a lot of this story *hard* to believe. . . ."

Oh dear, Wilkenson thought to himself. *Whatever* tale she was going to tell him, Ralph was certain now it was going to take a long time. He sat back in his chair, crossed his legs, and put his hand to his mouth in a gesture of deep concentration. He was reminding himself that, after all, he'd asked for this.

* * *

Ben's workplace turned out to look much like a huge corporate boardroom. It was a long, high-ceilinged space with an enormous mahogany table in the center, surrounded by plush chairs. About half of the chairs appeared to be higher and thinner in shape than normal—designed, Jack assumed, for the comfort of the Grays who sat here at meetings. Indeed, one Gray was already present in the room when they walked in, seated at the far side of the table. As they circled the table toward him, the sound of their steps being swallowed up in the thick carpet, Jack scanned the creature's features, expecting this to be either Gork or Astra. The aliens—or these alien guises, anyway—still appeared so much alike to him that it was difficult to tell differences. He decided quickly, though, that this being was neither. Who was it, then? Ben read his question and introduced them: "Kundas, you probably already know of my companion Jack. Jack, this is Kundas, who is kind of the chief science and technology officer for the . . . visitors."

Kundas' shining black eyes scanned Jack's face quickly. Obviously unimpressed, his gaze returned to a massive blueprint unrolled before him. Many more such blueprints were stacked in a neat pyramid beyond the edges of this one. When Jack leaned slightly over the table to see what was outlined there, Kundas shot him a look of suspicion. A sudden shock of pain ripped down his spine, jerking him upright. Ben took his arm and hustled him back around the arc of the table toward the door, and the pain stopped. Startled more than he was hurt, Jack glanced back over his shoulder at the silent, brooding alien, who had returned again to the plans.

"He doesn't like to be disturbed," Ben murmured quietly.

"I'd guessed that," Jack grunted. He reached over his shoulders with both hands and rubbed his still-stinging backbone.

Still half-whispering, Ben explained, "You may know of him from mythology as Hephaestus, or Vulcan, who hated mankind and helped to make Pandora's box. Sorry I didn't have a chance to warn you, but whatever you do, stay out of his way. He despises people."

"I can see where the feeling could become mutual."

"Careful, he has great hearing—"

"Get out, Ben," the fallen creature said in a voice that seemed filled with bitterness and despair. "Come back when the guests arrive."

Ben escorted Jack back into the hallway, and shrugged. "You asked to see where I work," he grinned apologetically. "That's it."

"This is no kind of life," Jack murmured, more to himself than to Ben.

"It's the only kind of life I know—" Ben began, then he stopped and turned his head, as if listening to something in the walls of the corridor. He looked back at Jack. "They're here."

"The industrialist?"

"And several others. Your friend Jeffrey is among them."

Jack nodded uneasily. He wasn't sure how much of a friend he could count on Jeffrey to be, these days. Moments later a door at the far end of the corner burst open, and a number of figures pushed through. They were led by a fat, blonde-mustached man whose toothy smile and swaggering walk suggested he felt right at home in this place. His pink and orange shirt and the profusion of golden rings that banded each of his fingers up to the knuckles proclaimed that he was not a man to be ignored. Obviously assuming everyone present was a willing participant in this conference, he came straight for Jack and held out his big, multi-ringed right hand. "Henry Ritter, Tampa-St. Pete!" he boomed, and Jack had no recourse but to greet him with a smile.

"I'm . . . I'm Dr. John Brennen . . ."

"Glad you remembered!" Ritter boomed, and he laughed heartily. "Thought you'd forgotten who you were there for a minute!" he added, and laughed again. Meanwhile he was pumping Jack's arm mercilessly while seizing him around the neck with a huge left hand. Suddenly he quit and began pulling up the front of that hideous shirt. "Doctor John, huh? Say listen, I've been having a pain right here in my gut that I think might be—"

"I'm not a medical doctor," Jack said quickly—profoundly glad, at the sight of this man's white belly, that this was true.

Henry Ritter dropped his shirt and laughed. "Not the kind of doctor who can do anybody any good then, right?"

"Right," Jack smiled back, wanly.

"Ph.D.?" Ritter prompted, and, when Jack nodded, went on, "Posthole digger?" Then he laughed more loudly than before and clapped Ben on the back. The boy absorbed this stoically. Ritter stepped on past, pushing his way into the boardroom and permitting others to come up the corridor. Several men in black suits and dark ties brushed past without a glance at either Jack or Ben, then a man who looked at them furtively, as if fearful of being recognized. He, too, ducked swiftly into the conference room, followed by another pair of Men in Black. Then came Jeffrey.

"Jack!" he said, and his affection seemed genuine. "Glad to see you back amongst the living!" he put his arm around Jack's shoulders and muttered, "Ben and I were afraid we'd lost you." He stepped back then, his hand still resting on Jack's shoulder, and said, "Good to see you're still with us." Then he stepped past Ben and opened the door to usher the boy inside. He was pointedly excluding Jack, which suited Jack fine.

But not Ben. "He can come," Ben told Jeffrey, pushing Jack through the door before him. Jeffrey simply raised his eyebrows, and admitted both of them.

"Beside me, Ben," Kundas said wearily, and Ben went obediently to the open chair next to the alien. Jeffrey firmly planted Jack in the chair to Henry Ritter's left, then sat himself on Jack's left.

Jack was surprised to see that Kundas was the only alien present. The meeting hadn't started yet, and apparently would not until the creature had completed his personal review of the diagrams. The industrialist sat meekly beside him, waiting. Henry Ritter, however was not a man to wait. He turned to Jack and said, "So Doc, are you the physicist they've been talking about?" Jack shook his head, not wanting to risk the alien's wrath with any comment.

Ritter didn't seem worried. "Oh that's right, she's a woman isn't she. I'm the money man in this deal. Strictly cash. Believe me, I've got it! More than I can spend, of course, since the DEA is constantly watching my bank account. They know I'm pushing powder, but they can't ever find my boats or planes! That's because *these* guys are my boats and planes!" He gestured at Kundas and then at Jeffrey, and laughed. "Can you imagine what the feds would say if they knew my mules were space bugs!" He cursed expansively, then laughed some more.

It was dawning on Jack that Henry Ritter was *not* comfortable in this place—not at all. He guessed this jolly performance masked a terror of his Gray masters every bit as profound as that of the CEO who slumped in the chair next to Kundas. He glanced across the table at Ben, looking for silent confirmation, and the boy nodded. At that same moment Kundas uttered a command that made this relationship apparent:

"Shut up, Ritter," the Gray murmured without looking up.

Henry Ritter shut up. He clasped his sausage-sized fingers together and rested them on the table before him, and for the remainder of the meeting wore the expression of a perfect cherub.

There was silence in the room for about five minutes as Kundas pored over the diagrams. Abruptly he sat up in his alien-sized chair and looked at Pearson. "This is the problem, isn't it?" he said, stabbing a spindly finger down onto the plan. Ron Pearson scrunched down further into his own chair and nodded. It appeared to Jack that the CEO had been hoping the flaw would go undiscovered. "This *is*, of course, your responsibility and not mine," the Gray said icily, and Pearson nodded again, meekly. "Yet you come asking me for more money?"

Pearson embarked on a lengthy explanation of his cost overrun that Jack found far too technical to follow. The essence of it was clear, however. A design flaw would have to be corrected if the new vehicles were to be completed according to specifications, and more money would be needed—cash, from an invisible, untraceable source. Henry Ritter's angelic smile grew notably brighter through this exchange, but the big man kept his mouth shut until Kundas addressed him directly. Yes, he could provide all the cash needed, and yes he would be pleased to do so as his contribution to the larger success of the Ultrastructure and his Pleiadian Siblings. And when could he expect more "product" from the South American Brothers?

As details of names, dates, times, and transactions multiplied, Jack's mind began to fog. He had heard and believed Ben's description of this worldwide network of conspirators. He had listened to Gork's boasts of its control of international events. Now he heard names familiar from the evening news casually dropped in an intimate, authoritative way. He heard complicated world mysteries reduced to simple intra-Ultrastructure power struggles. He heard unimpeachable sources impeached, insiders revealed as outsiders, presidents reviled as puppets, and toppled despots portrayed as still-powerful players—and through it all he heard Ben's question repeated over and over again: "Haven't you figured it out that no matter what it is people like us do, or how hard we try, ultimately it won't make a bit of difference?"

How was it, Jack wondered, that he could be so certain of his convictions, yet only hours later experience such debilitating doubt? He chanced to glance up then at Ben, whose evident purpose in this conference was to insure that the human parties present never lied to their Gray master. He saw that the boy was looking at him—sadly.

"There's another problem," Pearson was saying as Jack hopelessly tuned back in to the conversation. "The technology you're demanding is based on science that hasn't even been developed yet! This lady physicist in Boston, whose brain we picked on the time thing. I can't get her to focus her attention on her research!"

"What's distracting her?" Kundas asked flatly.

"Oh, the usual—lack of funding and some new boyfriend. The money I can provide, now—but I don't know *how* we deal with the boyfriend—"

"Ben, you've been in her mind. What does she want? How do we force her back to work?"

Ben's eyes were still full of sadness. They drifted down to the polished tabletop as he pondered for a moment. "It's not the money. Not really. She thinks that because she's a female her work will never receive the honor and recognition it deserves—"

"Nor can we allow it to," Kundas snarled. "Her thinking is far too advanced to be permitted to enter general human distribution at present. It's costing us a brutal amount to suppress publication of her current papers. Any publicity she receives will make that far more difficult."

"Is it time to bring her in?" Pearson asked earnestly. "Set her up here?" *Kidnap her?* Jack thought. *Bring her down into these tombs and force her to work on secret projects? Incredulous, that these creatures would kidnap people and use . . . them . . . to . . .* Then again, Jack had to remind himself: They had abducted *him*. . . .

"She won't do her best work here," Ben argued. "You're wanting creative leaps of intuitive insight from her, not laboratory drudgery. She'll not think those thoughts in captivity. I guarantee it."

"Then tell me how she *will*, Ben," Kundas demanded, making it clear he was leaning toward Pearson's suggestion.

Ben sat back in his seat and folded his arms across his chest. "I'm telling you what *won't* work, Kundas. I can't tell you what *will*, but I can tell you this *won't*."

"Perhaps you overestimate your *own* insight, boy," the Gray sneered. "I've worked with hundreds of generations of these 'creative spirits.' I assure you that certain negative stimulants can prompt *great* focus of energies."

"What if you just brought the lady *and* her boyfriend here?" This suggestion came from Henry Ritter—much to Jack's surprise. "You know—you could make it like a honeymoon vacation. Give them everything their hearts desire!"

Kundas turned his eyes toward Ritter and cowed him into silence. "We *could*," the creature said softly, "simply remove the man from the picture. Cheaper and more effective. He'd be out of the way, and she could bury her grief in her work. Ben?"

"I thought you wanted this technology *now?* His death would throw her into such depression it might be *years* before she can think again—maybe forever."

"Did I say anything about killing him?" Kundas asked. "Have him break off with her. Break her heart, but make her angry as well. Let her plunge back into her research to prove to him how wonderful she is, and how foolish he's been."

"And how are you going to get him to do that?" Ben asked, but he said it with little energy. He knew Kundas had a method in mind.

"Set him up with some pretty little sophomore who thinks he's wonderful—and provide the new couple with plenty of money. Pearson, see to it."

"I don't know how I can give the time to that when I've got a Senate sub-committee serving me with subpoenas—"

"Jeffrey, see to it he does it. Take Ben with you. I really don't care how you do it, just get the woman thinking again on what *we* need her to think about. And keep her out of the press! The first story that runs on her, she disappears. You understand?"

"Certainly," Jeffrey answered. Jack felt a shiver run down his spine.

There was a momentary pause, as Kundas looked around the group. Then, in a human-sounding voice dripping with acid, the creature snarled, "Well?" The boardroom cleared out in a moment.

The whole troop was walking briskly down the corridor, Ben and Jack included. Ben was towing Jack along as Jack demanded, "Wait! Ben! Tell me where we're going!"

"Didn't you hear?" Ben answered. "Boston. You'll enjoy it. They say the leaves there are gorgeous in the fall."

As he followed the leader on down the hall, Jack was mumbling to himself. Was it fall already? He'd always wanted to take his wife and daughter to New England in the fall. . . .

Chapter Thirteen

Picking her brain

Ralph Wilkenson felt the hair on the back of his neck stand up. The more he heard, the more evidence he saw, the more convinced he became that everything that Carrie Baxter told him was true. The trouble was, everything she told him would also be perceived as absolutely insane by every news organization in the country—and, Ralph was certain, by almost all of his new colleagues in the House. On the one hand, he had an issue here that could get him front page coverage on newspapers across the country. On the other hand, he could already visualize the captions attached to his picture: "Newly arrived Congressman finds government full of aliens." While the first reports of this matter might be in the *Times* or the *Post*, he was certain all the follow-ups would be carried in those lurid, checkout line tabloids. Out of the corner of his eye he could see the piles of boxes awaiting him: the central issues of current political life in America—issues he *needed* to be studying. He also saw the suitcases and clothes hampers Carrie Baxter had brought to Washington—and the case they made was irrefutable. The question was what was he going to do about it?

He'd skipped ahead to the bottom line, of course. Carrie hadn't quite gotten to that question herself. She was still developing her case, building evidence through what was really less a paper trail than a paper *highway. Good gracious, she's thorough!* Ralph thought to himself. And every new piece of evidence—each new suitcase she went out to fetch in from her car—added still more fuel to the funeral pyre of General Aeronautic Industries and its president, Ronald Pearson.

At the same time—all of this was crazy! How could he bring himself to believe that a solid, patriotic American company would use a blind of government contracts to build top secret spacecraft for alien invaders of the planet? As the woman droned on into the third hour of her story, Ralph Wilkenson struggled internally with his first real crisis as a Congressman: Was he going to tell a truth to the American people that was certainly stranger than fiction? Or was he going to maintain a fiction that *appeared* on the surface to be much more believable, more trustworthy, more . . . true?

There was another problem—one of which Ms. Baxter apparently had no knowledge. At one point in her presentation she'd handed him an outline of the executive staff of the company, including the local managers of the Huntsville plant. These names, Ms. Baxter claimed, *all* had to have some knowledge of the activities in Building J, and while she was certain some of them were unaware of the criminality of the project, all would be implicated in any investigation. Wilkenson had quickly scanned the list. Most of the names he didn't know. Several that he did know—including Pearson—he'd already figured for stinkers. But two of the names on her list belonged to members of that group of Christian laypeople who'd first come and asked him to run for this office. What would such a sensational national scandal do to *their* lives, their careers, and—ultimately—to their churches?

It was a very troubled new congressman, then, who gravely accepted Carrie Baxter's documentation and promised to do whatever he could to see that it was exposed to the world.

"You will?" she said, almost in disbelief.

"I really don't have any other choice, do I, Ms. Baxter? This is the truth. The truth *will* be known."

Carrie wanted to hug him! Instead, she pursed her lips, and let the tears that she'd kept in check throughout this ordeal finally begin to fall. "Thank you," she stammered finally. Wilkenson was a bit shocked at the change in the young woman's demeanor. As she'd explained this complicated plot to him, she'd argued with all the skill and passion of a trained lawyer. Now, suddenly, it was as if the young woman was folding back into herself and disappearing!

"I want to tell you, Ms. Baxter," he went on, "that never in all my days have I seen anyone do a better job of organizing and presenting information. Your skills are formidable, and if there's any way I can help you, please let me know."

Carrie blinked once or twice. The tears were drying up, and the burden was lifted off of her. And this man, her hero, had just volunteered to help her any way he could! "Well," she said at last, and sniffed. "I'm afraid I *am* going to need a new job, and real soon—" Afraid now to meet his eyes, she was glancing around at the piles of boxes that seemed to sit everywhere in this otherwise bare office.

Wilkenson saw her look and put it together with her words, and a lump leapt into his throat. She was wanting to work for *him*, he thought, and panic struck him. Of course, she was a marvelous organizer, and could no doubt do a tremendous job of setting his files in order and researching whatever it was he needed. Certainly he needed a research assistant, and soon. But how could he use this young woman, with this terribly explosive story? "Tell you what," he said smoothly, reaching out to take her hand in one of his and to pat it with the other, "when you get back home you let me know, and I'll make a couple of phone calls to some people I know. Of course, I anticipate you're going to be very busy in the near future, testifying to committees and meeting with prosecuting attorneys. But I want to warn you, too: If indeed your story is true—and you've certainly provided every imaginable scrap of evidence to demonstrate that—then your life is in grave danger. It . . . ah. . . " He paused. Hadn't she told him she had a sister near here? "It might be good for you just to spend some time with your sister—not in hiding, exactly, just—out of the line of fire, so to speak. We wouldn't want to come to the place when you needed to appear before the Senate Arms Committee and learn you'd been abducted by aliens!" He chuckled at that—inappropriately, he realized immediately, for Carrie Baxter's eyes widened at the notion and then narrowed at his apparent disregarding of it. His campaign reflexes, still honed sharp by being so fresh from the fray, caused him to add a comment he hoped he would never have to be accountable for: "You know, of course, that these creatures *do* that . . . "

Ralph Wilkenson didn't believe this. But it was clear from Ms. Baxter's reactions that *she* did, for he saw the acknowledgment in her eyes. She started to turn away, heading Ralph toward the door, then she stopped and looked back at him. "Ah . . . before I go . . . can we pray?"

"Of course!" Ralph said, smiling warmly, and he led them in a prayer for Carrie's safety in travel and for his own wisdom in how to deal with the terrible conspiracy she'd discovered. He felt rather good about how he'd crafted the words. Ralph had often been told he prayed very eloquent prayers. After the Amen, he looked up at her with an encouraging smile.

Carrie Baxter gazed back at him with such appreciation and . . . well . . . adulation, that he was embarrassed. "I *knew* I could trust you!" she sang adoringly. Then she squeezed both of his hands, and turned for the door. As she grabbed up her purse she stopped, and looked back at him hesitantly. "Ah . . . about the suitcases . . . "

"Just leave them here," Ralph said firmly. "I'll see that all the information is appropriately filed and labeled, and I'll return the suitcases to you."

"Oh, that's okay," she said with a relieved smile. "I don't need them. So long as I know you're handling this." She smiled shyly, then said, "Thank you. You don't know what a *burden* you've lifted off my shoulders!"

As the woman left his office Congressman Wilkenson beamed a confident smile after her. As soon as she shut the door behind her, his shoulders drooped. "Oh, but I *do* know what a burden you're rid of," he mumbled to himself, stepping around a clothes hamper full of documents to get back to his desk. "Now it's on *me*." He sat down, sighed, and looked at his watch. 4:30. The day was gone, and not only had he not *solved* any problems, he'd inherited a whole new pile. "Along with another promise," he growled, almost groaning. He picked the list back up off his desk and regarded it one more time. For there was yet another problem he had that Ms. Baxter knew nothing about. Ronald Pearson, that name right there at the top, was also at the top of his list of campaign contributors.

* * *

While they were en route to Boston, they had two stops to make first. The trip to Florida from somewhere under the Western deserts took only minutes. Soon they were gliding in low over the Tampa Bay—or at least that's what Jack was told. He wasn't in any position to see anything.

"Set me down in my country house—you know the one," Henry Ritter had said. Evidently this was true, for no one asked Ritter any directions as he explained to Jack it was in the midst of a huge orange orchard about six miles southeast of the city. This was only one factoid garnered from the lengthy monologue Ritter had been delivering ever since they'd departed. The passengers had all begun the trip in the same couch-lined lounge, but as Henry continued talking, the others had found reasons to go elsewhere, leaving only Jack behind to play the role of audience. Other items Jack learned about this extraordinarily successful drug dealer were that he loved his grandkids, had been married to the same woman (his third wife) for fifteen years, and that through his car dealerships he sponsored no less than a dozen kids' athletic teams in various sports. "I even coach one!" he said grandly, then added a bit more quietly, "Of course, we always lose . . . "

Jack nodded. "I've played on some losing teams in my life," he said, remembering several spectacularly bad church softball teams he'd added very little quality to in the past. "What about your church life, Henry? Are you a Christian?"

The big man's smile disappeared. His mustache seemed suddenly to drape his mouth with a blond curtain. "What?" he said.

"I just asked if you're a Christian," Jack said again, noting the redness that started to curl onto the flesh of the man's neck. It looked like Henry Ritter was about to be angry—but then he wasn't. As abruptly as the flush had come, it went away. Instead, Ritter laughed and gestured around them.

"Have you looked at what we're *riding* in?" he said at last, once again grinning hugely. "This is a *spaceship*, Doc! What's that tell you about Jesus, huh? He was from outer *space*, man! Isn't that obvious?"

"Not to me," Jack answered flatly.

Once again Henry's neck reddened, and his mustache drooped, shrouding his smile. "Well, then you're crazy," he grunted. "But I still like you anyway," he added, and the grin slowly returned. He reached out one of those huge, balloon-fingered hands and clapped Jack on the back. It was a little harder pat than Jack could comfortably receive. At the same time he could see clearly why Henry Ritter could sell anything—from Cadillacs to cocaine. The man was a natural.

Suddenly the craft stopped moving, and Henry bolted up out of his chair. When Jeffrey stepped into the room, Henry was ready. As they shot quickly down the curving passageway, they were exchanging last-minute plans for how and where Pearson's needed cash would be picked up. Then the saucer was in motion again, and—as if by magic—the other passengers who had formerly populated the room began to reappear. Jack wondered where, exactly, they were headed now—

"Across Florida and out to the Atlantic," Ben explained without bothering to let his friend actually voice the question. "We'll travel directly away from the coast, keeping well ahead of any fighters that might spot us and scramble to intercept. Because we'll be outbound they'll quickly ignore us—this *is* near the Bermuda Triangle, you know—and then we'll circle counterclockwise over the ocean and head back in across Maine. We'll be moving so quickly they'll not spot us until we're inside the perimeter, and we'll disappear off their screens before they can react to the sight of us. Can I get you something to drink?"

Jack *had* been feeling a little thirsty. He accepted the grape soda without commenting to Ben that it was exactly what he thirsted *for*. "Why can we travel so fast, without noise, yet the researchers into supersonic jet traffic can't seem to solve the problem of sonic booms, or aerodynamic drag, or half a dozen other technical difficulties?"

"You've figured that out already," Ben replied—for Jack had. Still, Ben confirmed it for him: "The researchers probing that problem—or *any* scientific mystery—are the best of what's *left*, after the Ultrastructure has skimmed the mental cream off the top. You know, of course, that the average age when a scientist makes a major scientific breakthrough is under twenty-five. The Ultrastructure finds the *really* bright ones when they're *young*, then anonymously coaxes them through the international academy system. They know about everyone with promise—just like they knew about me."

"Funny," Jack grinned. "They never seemed to notice me—"

"That you're aware of. But weren't there various persons pointing you, challenging you, trying to encourage you into studying the natural sciences?"

"Of course, but you're not saying that every high school guidance counselor in the country is an agent of the fallen!"

"Of course not. But there are ways that the Ultrastructure can *monitor* every student—much like college coaches monitor and evaluate the progress of high school and junior high school football and basketball players. And when a sparkling, creative mind begins to shine in a particular field, they begin grooming that mind for future usefulness to them."

Jack felt a little uneasiness in the pit of his stomach. "And when that mind has—*made* its 'contribution'—had his or her intuitive mental breakthrough—what happens then?"

"Several possibilities," the boy shrugged.

Jack was reminded once again just how young *Ben* was. What a weight for a kid to bear, to know so much about the routine exercise of enormous evil.

"Thank you for your concern for me, by the way," Ben interjected with a sarcastic grin, and Jack came back to the point in question. "First, the prodigy might be consciously taken—as you were, Jack, or as I was. He or she would become, then, a member of the inner circle—which, as you've guessed, is a rather large group, internationally.

"Take this woman we're going to watch: Elizabeth Kingsley. Should she be taken, she might find herself offered the chance to head some prestigious research foundation somewhere, or might be allowed to set up a technology company with Ultrastructure funding behind her, or might be allowed to *receive* the honors she feels she deserves—in exchange for her cooperation. These things would come as a result of her agreement to *suppress* her true discovery—at least until the more pedestrian minds left behind in the scientific community are able to catch up."

"She could sell out, in other words."

Ben smiled. "They say everybody has their price, Jack. The key is in knowing just what it is people want."

Jack thought about this a moment, and Ben let him. "That's why you're so valuable to them," Jack said at last. "Because you already know everybody's bottom-line wish."

The boy sighed. "Yeah. That's part of it."

"And, I suppose you're also part of the evaluation process—determining the potential value of young minds?"

"Yeah. That too."

"Suppose she won't cooperate?" Jack heard himself ask—although in some ways he really didn't want to hear the answer. "Suppose she decides to go ahead and publish her papers, to push her theories out into the public record?"

Ben nodded. "Several possibilities there. The first is—she's laughed out of her discipline. This is not as difficult to achieve as some might think. Intuitive breakthroughs, after all, almost always run counter to prevailing theories, and—despite all their preaching about the sanctity of the 'scientific method'—the established figures in her discipline have a vested interest in rejecting new ideas that prove their *old* theories are inadequate."

"Typical," Jack grunted.

"At least *some* of those established scientists would know she *is* right," Ben continued. "But if they're Ultrastructure members themselves, they would be instructed to lead the charge against her ideas and to force her out of the area.

"She might then leave the field, embittered, knowing the truth but unable to get anyone to believe her—or there's another possibility. Told often enough and by important enough figures that her research is meaningless and her results flawed, she *might* become convinced that she was wrong. Then, while the Ultrastructure members privately take her ideas and expand upon them, she herself might well become a vociferous opponent of the very view she first expressed!"

"Insidious," Jack muttered to himself. "You're saying there's a whole different level of scientific awareness which the fallen have managed to preserve for themselves alone."

Ben picked up Jack's thread of thought and continued it: "Which the governments of various nations have become convinced is actually *alien* invention! Thus, they're willing to enter into secret pacts with beings they consider 'aliens' in exchange for that new technology. It's a great scam, Jack," Ben smiled without humor. "It's been working a long, long time."

"But suppose she *persists* in her crusade to sell her idea to the wider world audience. What then?"

"Lots of possibilities. The more she knows about the Ultrastructure and the more she tries to reveal that knowledge, the more easily they can smear her in the media as a lunatic. They may actually be able to get her committed. Then there are always auto accidents, heart attacks, acts of 'random violence' that might leave her senseless or dead. Or, she might just turn up missing. That's if they deem her mind capable of further insights and intuitive jumps, and they decide to put her to work in one of their own laboratories. She *eventually* may come around to their way of looking at things, and be allowed to rejoin the world—"

"As a loyal member of the Ultrastructure," Jack finished for him, shaking his head.

"You got it." Ben looked away then, that curious expression on his face that always appeared when he was "listening" to faraway thoughts. "We're almost to New England," he said.

Jack wore a faraway expression himself. "They're never going to let me go, are they?" he murmured. Ben looked back at him and shrugged.

"I don't know. I told you—I don't read demons." He glanced away again, then said, "We're coming in just south of Boston. Very low." Moments later they were settling down *into* the earth, and Ben excused himself. "Gotta go to work," he said quietly.

"Ben," Jack said, and the boy turned to listen. "Rather than destroying this woman's life, why not give her some positive feedback on what she's accomplished? For most people that's a strong stimulus to creative thinking. Then, if you want her to direct her brilliance to a particular detail in her theory, you could just *ask* her. All you need from her is a thought, right? Something that may even seem a trivial detail to her?"

"Right," Ben nodded.

"And if she thinks it, you can recognize it and pick it out of her mind?"

"Of course."

"Then why not just call her, pretend to be a physicist who might have read her paper, and *ask* her for what you need?"

Ben thought for a moment. "Sounds like it could work. I'll try to convince Jeffrey." He started out of the room—then he stopped and looked back, grinning. "Do you realize that in trying to preserve this woman's current life you may have just *enabled* the completion of the new, improved 'evil-wagon?' Had you thought of that?"

Ben didn't need to ask. No, Jack hadn't thought of that. He returned to his cabin and went to bed. He felt sick.

* * *

Elizabeth Kingsley left her lab and hurried toward her office, shrugging out of her white labcoat on the way. Bolting through the door, she tossed the white garment into the corner where dozens of other such coats already resided, awaiting liberation by Dr. Kingsley's classroom assistant. This graveyard for dead labcoats was not the only unkempt area of her office. In fact, the whole place looked like a dump, or the warren of a dozen packrats, or a teenager's bedroom. Elizabeth Kingsley didn't notice. At least a hundred other things were going through her mind at the moment. Neatness was not high on her priority list.

She was, of course, late to class—not that that bothered her. She was always late to class, but she was also always a scintillating and stimulating lecturer. They would wait. It *did* bother her that her hair wasn't brushed, for Gilbert was picking her up right afterward. She paused at the mirror on the back of her office door to fluff up her shoulder-length, dark-brown curls. Tossing the brush onto her cluttered desk, she tugged down the tight vest of her silvery silk suit and spun around to check in the back to insure that the calf-length skirt hung straight. Then she grabbed up the file folder of her class notes and darted out into the hall.

Her telephone rang. Back she went inside her office, mentally berating herself for taking the time to answer it instead of letting her voice mail do it. A moment later she collapsed, delighted, into her oversized executive chair, simultaneously throwing off her earring so she could cradle the phone comfortably next to her ear. Her class was forgotten, for *someone* had read her paper, and was astonished by it!

She didn't recognize the voice. That was curious, for through professional associations she thought she'd met most of the important figures in her specialization. And this voice sounded so young—almost boyish. Yet he'd obviously read and understood her theories. At any rate, he *seemed* to. Once or twice during the conversation he asked really stupid questions—incredibly stupid. But as soon as she began to explain he jumped ahead of her, giving her own explanation to *her* before she could give it to him. It was almost as if he was reading her mind! It was a *very* stimulating conversation—and so welcome, after all these months of trying unsuccessfully to publish her findings, or to find a venue that would even give them a hearing! But the call was also a bit unsettling, for this stranger began to push the conversation into territory she'd only begun to research.

Suddenly Dr. Kingsley felt suspicious. Was this some unknown research assistant out to make his own name on the back of *her* theories? Her mind began racing, trying to determine what exactly this character might be up to. She was tempted to hang up on him, but then realized that his questions had sparked new thoughts in areas she'd never really considered. "Just a moment," she interrupted, "I think there's someone at the door." She put him on hold and began to search frantically through the papers piled on her desk for a pen and a legal pad. Finding both, she jotted down three lines of notes and a simple equation, then turned back to the phone to—

The light on the dial was no longer flashing. He was gone. Chagrined, Elizabeth Kingsley sat back in her chair and swore at her nameless caller. She was certain now that she'd soon read a paper by some *male* claiming her theories as his own! Only one defense for *that*, she thought, the competitive juices flowing in her. That was to write yet *another* paper that expanded upon the practical applications of her theoretical model. There, on her legal pad, was the germ of that new paper—and it was brilliant, even if she had to say so herself. She sat still for a moment, reviewing the implications quickly in her mind, imagining the recognition she would receive when *this* finally hit the journals. Then she grabbed up her pad and went back to her figures, scribbling furiously for fear of forgetting something. Twenty minutes later she dialed her boyfriend and told him not to come, that she was onto something important and had to work. He'd said something sweetly encouraging in response, and they'd made a date instead for a *very* late dinner, whenever she was done. Elizabeth Kingsley sat happily back in her chair, propped her stockinged feet up on the edge of her desk, and let her thoughts flood out onto the paper. Never in her life had she felt so creative—nor so loved.

The saucer was already streaking for Alabama as Ben reproduced on his own legal pad the thoughts Elizabeth Kingsley was that very moment thinking. Jeffrey, smirking triumphantly, watched over the boy's shoulder. Nothing distracted Ben. He focused clearly on her every word. He knew that while he seemed to understand it now, once he was out of her thoughts he wouldn't comprehend a tenth of it. She was, indeed, brilliant—perhaps the brightest mind on earth at the present time—and he had been the one to find her for the Ultrastructure. Now he'd saved her *from* the Ultrastructure—or at least, he'd saved her for the moment. Later he might mull over the implications of this theft of her genius—how she would never receive the recognition due her, nor profit financially from her own brilliance. Later he would bear the guilt of that, for guilt there would be. But he intended to share it this time with Jack. After all, this had been Jack's idea! For the moment, however, he just kept on writing down equations.

Chapter Fourteen

Alabama highways

Jack woke up, and looked around. He found himself in the same place he'd been for weeks—his cabin on the saucer. It had become his home-away-from-home. Maybe he needed to simply consider it his home from now on. His participation in this bizarre conspiracy was beginning to look permanent.

He got up, showered, dressed himself from the closet the fallen had so thoughtfully filled for him the day they'd abducted him, and wandered out into the curving corridors of the craft. They were not moving. He wondered where they were.

He wandered down the hall to Ben's room. The door slid back to admit him, and he saw the boy curled comfortably on his bed, obviously sound asleep. Jack rubbed his hands through his own hair, scratched his head, and walked back into the hallway. *Were they back under the desert?* he wondered. From the way light hit the curving wall in front of him it appeared the hatch was open and the gangplank down. He ambled that way. . . .

And stopped to stare upward in disbelief.

They were in a huge hanger of some sort, its ceiling looming some five or six stories above them. It dwarfed the saucer, which apparently sat in the very center of the building. He stepped out onto the walkway and looked around. In every corner of the enormous structure there sat an identical rectangular box. And everywhere he looked he saw workmen scurrying about to complete the construction of these boxes, under the watchful supervision of at least a dozen Grays.

An incredible sight, he found himself almost dizzy from it. Then a familiar voice spoke from behind him:

"Three more days and they'll be finished," said Jeffrey. Though he wasn't looking at his face, Jack could tell he was smiling.

"Four of them?"

"Four. Each incredibly expensive—and I mean government contract expensive. Billions."

"But these are not for the government."

"Of course not," Jeffrey snorted, stepping up beside Jack and folding his arms across his chest. He was dressed casually today—white shirt and black pants, but no tie.

"Why do they need us to build their ships, Jeffrey?" Jack asked quietly. "Why can't they do it themselves?"

"They can do it themselves," his old friend responded firmly, but warmly as well. "But they've challenged us to develop our own abilities and technology. Surely we've spoken of this before?"

Jack looked around at Jeffrey and shrugged. "And I don't suppose we'll ever agree."

Jeffrey's smile broadened—a difficult task, actually, for one with lips so thin: "I don't know. I haven't given up yet." He walked down the ramp to step onto the concrete surface, and looked back up at Jack. "We're in northern Alabama, in case you hadn't put that together. You're familiar with the area, aren't you? Through Gloria?"

"I've been here before," Jack nodded. *If* this were actually northern Alabama. He'd made several trips through the region recruiting new students. He'd had a car break down not far from here.

"Tell you what," Jeffrey said, raising a single finger for emphasis. Given his generally unexpressive demeanor, this was the equivalent of most people waving both arms. "We've no reason to hang around this place all day. Why don't we find a car and drive around a bit. Perhaps even find a taco?"

Jack smiled. Finding a taco in Alabama could be a little like hunting for a needle in a haystack—but he gladly accepted the offer. Anything to see the outside world again.

He followed Jeffrey across the vast floor toward one of the corrugated walls, and moments later stepped into the sunshine. It felt wonderful on his face. He realized his spirit starved for a glimpse of something green. . . . Jeffrey commandeered a company car from security and hopped in the driver's side, unlocking the other door for Jack. As they passed through no less than four checkpoints on the way out of the complex, Jack noted the respect—perhaps even fear—Jeffrey engendered in the uniformed guards. Was he their boss? Jack wondered. Exactly what *was* his old friend's role in all of this?

"Let's try close to the university," Jeffrey suggested, wheeling the car onto a four-lane highway Jack didn't recognize. "I'm sure there'll be a taco stand *somewhere* near there." After a few minutes of silent driving, Jeffrey squinted his small eyes at the road ahead and said, "Ben tells me you helped us out. He says you suggested how we might get the physicist to do some creative thinking."

Jack turned his head to watch the trees fly past. After a moment, he responded, "I just didn't want to see you destroy *her* life, *too*."

"I understand that," Jeffrey nodded. "Very commendable, my friend—and very much in character. You have such a sensitive nature, so attuned to the 'human factor' in situations. It's doubtless the result of all your years of being a minister. All those committees you've had to work through, all those people you've had to counsel—you know human nature very well. Actually, you always have."

Jack shrugged, and said nothing. He was wondering where all of this was leading.

"It's a gift, Jack—you realize that, surely. To be able to read people correctly, understanding their inner motivations well enough to be able to prompt them to change behaviors? Truly a gift. That's why I'm hoping you'll decide to begin actively helping us, rather than continuing to allow your resentment toward our enterprise to smolder. Not that I expect you quickly to revise your low estimate of myself or our Senior Siblings. I know how firmly you hold to your convictions and how strongly you believe what is taking place is"— here Jeffrey allowed himself a chuckle—"devilish."

"But think, Jack. Through your wisdom and insight one young woman is free to pursue her life's pleasures and pastimes, while also feeling *good* about what you've challenged her to accomplish. What we do with the ideas she generated has no bearing on her life. She doesn't even know the contributions she's made. Nor, perhaps, do *you.* For as you've guessed, the Siblings have not always been so . . . subtle in their relationships to mankind. Understandable," Jeffrey added, "considering all that they've contributed to our race over the eons of time."

Jack still made no reply.

"I know this all appears a hideous, demonic plot to you. But think how your influence could alter our processes! Yes, we do 'play God' with people's lives. Yes, we do control information, and technology, and governments. These are facts, Jack, and I don't deny them. I know you're wise enough to realize that this is the way things *are*, like it or not. But I think you're also bright enough to see just how much you could *help* those whose minds and abilities we need! You could protect them *from* us, Jack—acting as a kind of ombudsman for the weak—"

"Sort of like a chaplain at Auschwitz, hmm?" Jack muttered.

Jeffrey laughed again, soundlessly, barely showing his small, even teeth. "Perhaps it isn't time yet to broach this with you. On the other hand, maybe it's something you need to keep in mind as you watch what's taking place around you. The decisions we make are in pursuit of *goals*, Jack—and hurting people is certainly not one of those goals."

"Certainly not," Jack echoed sarcastically.

"But we *do* hurt people," Jeffrey continued. "Sometimes we hurt them a lot. Sometimes we kill them. Think of it, Jack. You could help them." The matter-of-fact way his old friend confessed to murder chilled Jack far more than if Jeffrey had shown any glee in the admission. He spoke as a fisherman might of scaling fish, or a farmer of slaughtering a hog. His task occasionally required it, so he did it. Jeffrey was a true believer. It didn't matter what he was called upon to do to support those he called the Siblings. Whatever, he would do it. Yet the offer he was making to Jack was sincere—and, in its way at least, true enough. Jack *could* help people. Real people. So why then did this feel so much like a temptation to sin?

"You're offering to make me a 'Man in White' amongst the 'Men in Black'?" Jack said.

Jeffrey smiled at the road ahead of them. "Men in Black. There's quite a mythology built up around that concept, you know. Almost makes me want to buy a gray suit."

"Would that prevent me from having to buy a white one?"

Jeffrey chuckled. "You can dress however you like, Jack. Does that mean you'll join us?"

Jack thought on that for a minute. "No. It means I'm trying to imagine what life would be like—what my life *will* be like, since your 'Siblings' have stolen me from my wife and family."

"You can be returned to them, Jack," Jeffrey said eagerly. "That's easily enough arranged. You can even remain a preacher and seminary professor if you choose—just so long as you privately renounce all real belief in the 'God' your parents indoctrinated you into trusting. It was all a lie from the beginning, of course. Surely you realize that by now."

Jack felt sick to his stomach. Gork and Astra and the others—they just wouldn't let it go. "Look," he said suddenly, pointing to a familiar sign on the road ahead. "Would you settle for fried chicken? This *is* Alabama, after all."

"That'll do," Jeffrey answered, wheeling into the drive-through lane. "But let's not change the subject, all right? I want you to give serious thought to what I've suggested." Then he was rolling down the window, ordering into a speaker for both of them. Interesting, that after all these years he still remembered that Jack liked the dark meat best. . . .

* * *

Ralph cradled the receiver in his hands, trying to decide whom to call next. He'd spent the whole morning on the phone—after having spent the whole night reading through Carrie's copious files. How he would love to have that woman as a research assistant! She was dynamite!

But her research threatened to dynamite his legislative career right here at the beginning. His first calls had been to party supporters back in the home state. Without revealing any information, he had probed a chosen few about scandals: *Should* he find out something potentially damaging to party supporters, what was the best way to handle it?

"Keep your focus, Ralph," one old politician had told him. "We didn't elect you to go up there and chase rabbits—even if they are *dirty* rabbits."

But what if such a scandal could potentially compromise the security and stability of the United States of America?

"Be careful, Ralph. There's lots a crazies out here, wantin' to suck you into the awfulest idiocies you can imagine. I'm *assumin'*," the southern gentleman drawled ironically, "that this *is* all hypothetical. But if some hypothetical person should try to reveal to me a scandal of some sort, I think I'd do some strong checkin' on that individual's vested interests. Keep your focus," the old politician added, his voice almost a growl. "We've gotta get you reelected soon."

He *did* need to keep his focus, Ralph agreed. He'd been sent up here to help people, and aside from Ms. Carrie Baxter—whom he really didn't know from Eve herself—just who would be helped by his pursuing this bizarre conspiracy theory any further? Before he could mentally discard the matter, however, he had to check up on Ms. Baxter's credibility. If he could find someone who could give him just one little *hint* of her instability, he would feel justified in chucking her whole pile of suitcases into the dumpster!

Unfortunately, Ralph thought to himself as he continued to hold the receiver between his knees, he'd not been able to find a single soul who could call into question either Ms. Baxter's morals, her ethics, her patriotism, or her mental competence. He'd called all of her superiors, phrasing his questions in the guise of considering her as an administrative assistant. All had been astonished that he even knew her, but each person he'd talked to had given her glowing references. More tellingly, they'd all jokingly threatened him in some way if he should, indeed, hire her away.

The clincher, however, had come when he'd called the woman's pastor. He didn't know the man, actually, although he had met him at fund-raisers and knew his reputation. The preacher gave him nothing but glowing reports about Carrie's faithfulness and conviction. "I wish we had a dozen more like her," he'd said with obvious sincerity. Then he'd added, "I *do* know she's had some burden on her heart for a long, long time, but she's never even given me a hint of what it concerns. I'll tell you, Congressman, if you're looking for someone who can prayerfully keep a confidence, Carrie Baxter is the lady you need."

A burden on her heart for some time. The woman had used those exact words with him. And the evidence sat piled on the floor all around him—incredibly detailed, thoroughly organized. What could he do? He had no other choice. Ralph Wilkenson sighed, then buzzed his secretary. "Mary," he said, "please get me the FBI."

* * *

"How many Men in Black are there?" Jack asked between bites of biscuit.

Jeffrey finished swallowing, then fastidiously wiped his greasy hands on his napkin before replying. "It's hard to say. You understand, of course, that most of those who have been so labeled by the lunatics don't help us full-time."

"Ah yes," Jack nodded. "They belong to other organizations. Government organizations, mostly, in every country of the world."

"So I assume," Jeffrey agreed, "although I cannot verify it. Our group of Siblings is *not* the only group working. Others focus directly *in* South America, for example. You may have been told something of the UMMO organization down there. Others focus primarily in Europe, apparently keeping the Belgian Air Force occupied. Still others have functioned in the areas Winston Churchill christened 'behind the iron curtain.' It seemed best to the Siblings not to confuse the existing administrative and intelligence networks too much."

"Besides, it allowed them to play one government off another," Jack growled, tearing into another piece of chicken.

"There was some of that, certainly—but all for a *goal,* Jack, never forget about the *goal.*"

"Yeah. To perfect the technology to launch the fallen off this rock."

"The 'fallen,' Jack? I wish you wouldn't use potentially derogatory terminology. The Siblings never 'fell' from anything. And the goal of their competition with one another has been to push mankind *forward*, to help *us* get off this planet. They've succeeded, too. Spectacularly. And now that the two space programs are being linked together—"

"Then why time travel, Jeffrey?" Jack demanded. "Why is that important if we've already gotten off the planet? Don't you see that your precious 'Siblings' want it to try to alter human history?"

"Ridiculous!" Jeffrey smiled. "But hardly a surprising notion to come from you. Think, Jack! Space travel? Infinite distances to be covered, at speeds far below that of light? What we *need*, Jack, are not ships to *carry* colonists between the stars, but rather habitats constructed to *receive* colonists at the conclusion of the journey! Time travel, Jack. Our ship embarks in this century for the home planets of the Pleiades, and the colonists on board it jump forward in time to its arrival date! Controlling space *and* time we can seed the universe with humankind, each new planet's population watched over and guided by the Sibling who accompanied them there!"

Every demon his own god, Jack thought. *Exporting hell.* He shook his head in dismay. "Why see the universe with *us*, Jeffrey? If they've already done this before—why *us?*"

Before replying, Jeffrey picked up another piece of chicken and thoughtfully devoured it. Then he carefully wiped his hands and said, "Because they love us."

Jack's jaw dropped open, then he laughed. Given all their previous conversation about the interference *in* and casual ending *of* human lives, this response seemed utterly nonsensical. But Jeffrey obviously believed it, for Jack's laughter made him furious. "Why can you not *see* the *truth?*" Jeffrey snarled, his pallid cheeks turning red.

"I'm wondering that same thing about *you!*" Jack answered.

"Look, if you—" Jeffrey began, then he stopped. One finger went to his left ear, and he inclined his head that way as if listening to something. Jack watched as the blood that had rushed into his head drained swiftly away, and the man turned white. Then he grabbed the box of chicken up off his lap and plopped it onto Jack's, started the car with a roar and backed out of the parking lot like a teenager on speed. Without reference to *any* speed limits of any kind he hurtled the vehicle back down the direction from which they had come. He did not hesitate when an Alabama State Trooper jumped onto their tail, blue lights flashing. Instead he spoke into his left sleeve and kept right on speeding, and within moments the trooper backed off and turned off his lights. Jack began to wonder if there was *anywhere* Jeffrey could not go.

The checkpoint gates were wide open for them when they arrived, as was a vehicle door into Building J. They drove straight to the saucer where a dozen men in black suits and sunglasses awaited them. Jeffrey said nothing to them as he jumped from the car, but evidently the others already had his instructions. Jack's door was jerked open and he was hustled out and up the ramp. The craft's engines were already engaged.

Four of them dragged him inside and closed the door. Then they were gone, departing the building downward rather than up. Jack expected to be locked inside the cabin, but once inside and away the Men in Black abandoned him, pursuing Jeffrey into the control bay. Curious—and not a little pleased at Jeffrey's apparent consternation—Jack followed them.

He couldn't see either Jeffrey or Ben over the heads of the black-clad enforcers, but he could hear the conversation. "Who knows?" Jeffrey was demanding.

"The FBI is all—so far," Ben answered. "The congressman *is* considering informing NASA, military intelligence, and the Secret Service, but he hasn't yet. He's scared."

"Good," Jeffrey grunted. "And the woman?"

"Gork and—excuse me, Ruzagnon—and the others are in another saucer, hunting her."

"Hunting her?" Jeffrey barked. "Where *is* she, Ben?" Jack could tell it from Jeffrey's voice: Ben was about to be hurt.

"I don't know!" Ben whined. "She's . . . asleep right now! Drugged sleep, too, so she's not even dreaming. I can *assure* you, Jeffrey, that the minute she wakes up and gets her bearings I'll let you know! Meanwhile I think we can be confident she's somewhere near the D.C. area. We're to meet the others there."

"Standard place?"

"Of course!" the boy snapped. "You want a rendezvous between two saucers in downtown Washington in broad daylight?"

Jeffrey's voice was calm. "When this is resolved, Ben, I think you're going to have to be disciplined."

Jack heard no response from the teenager. He was certain Ben had already read Jeffrey's mind to know just what such "discipline" might entail. Feeling helpless, Jack wandered back to his cabin and laid down. Some things he didn't want to know.

* * *

"Mr. Wilkenson?" Mary's voice erupted from the intercom. She sounded very agitated. He understood why a moment later when four men walked coolly into his office without so much as a knock.

"Congressman Wilkenson," one of them said quickly, "sorry to alarm you and your secretary, but this is a matter of vital importance and we really have no time for niceties. Please forgive us." The man flashed his badge in Ralph's face so quickly he really didn't get a good look at it, but in any case his attention was focused on the others with him as they squatted by boxes and suitcases, swiftly rifling through the pages. "Is this the information you've gathered?" the spokesman asked, his blue eyes boring into Ralph's.

"Yes," he nodded, watching incredulously as the suitcases were closed, latched, and picked up.

"Very good, sir. Excellent work. And may I add, sir, that there's no *question* your swift attention to this matter will open new doors in government. Does your secretary have any idea what is contained in these suitcases? Any at all?"

This was all happening so fast that Ralph seemed to be capable of only one word replies. "No," he muttered.

"Even better," the agent smiled. "Even better. Now, this is plenty, of course, but I'd like to ask you if you would accompany us to the agency. We'll need a deposition from you immediately—also one from the woman who gathered all of this together. Ms. Baxter, is that right?"

"Yes—" Ralph nodded. Then, "How did you know?" he gasped. He had certainly told no one!

The blue-eyed agent smiled. "Impressed? Hope so. We're good at our jobs, Congressman. I know you and the country are grateful. Listen, would you mind setting your secretary's mind at ease? We've ruffled the little lady's feathers, obviously, and we don't want her to stay in a stew all day. Would you calm her, please?"

Had to be the FBI, Ralph thought to himself. They were the only ones he'd called! Besides those folks back home, of course. And yes, he had to say he *was* impressed, *indeed* he was impressed. He touched the intercom button. "Not to worry, Mary. These are men from the—" He stopped. Actually, the agent had stopped him by quickly placing his hand to Ralph's lips. Ralph looked up at him in shock, and the man smiled.

"Not too specific!" the agent mouthed. Then he took his hand away, and gestured at the men around him who held the suitcases and hampers in their arms, ready to leave. "This is all top secret," the agent whispered.

"Mr. Wilkenson?" Mary demanded, her voice strangled by anxiety.

"They're from the government, Mary. Important matters from the government." Then he added with a trace of a laugh, "We'll have to get used to this, Mary! Remember where we are now!"

The agent beamed at that, and gave him an enthusiastic thumbs up. Ralph was beginning to relax. Ms. Baxter had dumped her unwanted burden upon his shoulders a few days ago. Now he felt it being lifted off. He grabbed his coat off the back of the chair and followed the line of agents out of the office. The blue-eyed agent came out behind him, closing the door, and threw a smile and a wave toward Mary.

Still trembling from the intrusion, the woman sat back in her seat, waved both hands before her face to get a little needed breeze, then sighed. Somewhat mollified, she returned to her typing.

* * *

"Where is she, Ben?" Jeffrey demanded. He'd gone *way* past losing his patience.

"Why should I tell you?" the boy snarled back, his arms folded across his chest. "Ask this Wilkenson guy when he gets here. Ask your guys to do some *work* for a change."

"Where is she, Ben? Quickly."

"You have to promise not to do anything to me," Ben muttered.

"You know I won't do that, Ben. You know, *too*, that I'm only growing angrier, and it's only getting worse for you."

"Oh yes, I know that. I know that perfectly, Jeffrey." Ben yawned dramatically, then shifted positions and put his hands behind his head. "So what's the point of telling you what you want to know—what you *need* to know—if it's not going to do me any good?"

"Where is she? Tell me *now!*"

"First your promise."

"I lie, Ben," Jeffrey said flatly.

"And I can *read* your lies, Jeffrey," the boy said back. "Face it. You need what I know. You'll *always* need what I know. And I'll *always* know when you actually intend to keep your promise to me. So are we going to waste any more time, or are we going to get this resolved before we meet with Ruzagnon?"

Jeffrey looked over his shoulder at the pilot. "Time to base?" he snarled, then looked back at Ben.

"Three minutes," the pilot responded.

Jaws clenched, Jeffrey glared down at the obstinate teenager for a full minute before admitting—only to himself, of course—that he agreed. *But if you gloat about this before the others, boy,* he thought fiercely into Ben's eyes, *then I will seek any pretext to do you injury, and be justified in it!*

Ben nodded curtly. "She's in her car on her way back to Alabama."

"You said she was in a drugged sleep!" Jeffrey exploded.

"Turned out she was taking a nap at a rest stop. Look, the woman is exhausted!"

"She can soon sleep all she wants," Jeffrey growled. "Where?"

"Interstate, southwest of Bristol, Virginia," Ben replied lazily. Then he added, "You can't miss her."

Jeffrey turned to his lieutenants. "As soon as we touch, you four take this craft down that roadway! I don't care if you're seen, just find that woman and stop her. Ben and I will interview this Wilkenson, then join the Esteemed Siblings in the other craft and follow you."

"And if we're intercepted?"

"Take evasive. That's why we're coming too—one to search and one to play bogey." He waited then, silently watching the instrument panel until they arrived at their destination. "We're in," he grunted. "Go!" he shouted at Ben.

"What about Jack?" the boy asked as he rose casually from his chair. Ben smiled as he read the thoughts racing through Jeffrey's mind, allowing Jeffrey to watch him doing it.

Jeffrey's frown did not fade. *You're coming dangerously close, boy,* he thought. *Dangerously close.*

"You know that the Esteemed Siblings will want Jack with *them,*" Ben said with pretended innocence. "For whatever reason," he added with a shrug. He knew very well the reason. The fallen feared the angels.

"Get him, then," Jeffrey grunted, "and let's get on with it!"

A moment later Jack's door slid open and Ben bounded into his room. "We gotta run," the boy announced, gesturing for Jack to precede him down the corridor.

Jack didn't argue. While he had no idea what would happen next, he figured Ben must. He was willing to trust his young friend. Moments later they stood on the asphalt floor of an underground hanger, watching as the saucer that had brought them disappeared. Jack looked at Ben and raised his eyebrows.

"Do you really want to know?" the boy said. Something in his tone of voice assured Jack that no, he really didn't. . . .

Chapter Fifteen

Interrogation

Ralph Wilkenson had been escorted into the dignified gray building with all the pomp and circumstance of royalty. As he followed the other agents down the hallways and into the elevator, he was greeted by smiles and nods of recognition.

So grand had been his entrance that when they all got onto the elevator he was feeling quite proud of himself. As they rode downward into subterranean levels he was watching himself perform the role of the heroic congressman—and he liked what he saw.

"Mr. Wilkenson goes to Washington"—that's what he was thinking about. As the elevator door slid open and they exited down a marble-lined hallway, he caught a glimpse of his reflection in the glossy wall. He had to admit—he cut a formidable figure, striding briskly along the corridors of power, flanked by suited attendants. Yes sir. Ralph Wilkenson was going to make a *difference* in government.

An hour later he wasn't feeling nearly so grand. To his great shock and chagrin he was being grilled by a team of interrogators. He sat in a swivel chair in the center of a featureless, square room. A half-dozen dark-suited agents surrounded him, and while they would not answer his direct questions they certainly had many questions for him.

"Why were you seeking this information?" One asked again, gesturing at the stack of papers sitting on a table along the far wall.

"I was *not* seeking this information at all!" Ralph snarled, his pique growing steadily more severe. "As I've already told you, it was brought *to* me by one of my constituents! Before yesterday I had no awareness of this matter at all! Once I had the opportunity to review the material, I called you! Now what is your *problem?*"

"I don't believe I have a problem, sir. I believe *you* have a problem, since you've chosen to entangle yourself in this highly secret defense matter."

"I did not *choose* to become entangled in this . . . this *conspiracy!* It was brought to me and plopped onto my floor, and I did what I've sworn myself to do—represent the interests of my constituents and the greater good of the nation by seeking to get to the bottom of it!"

"And do you think you've gotten to the bottom of it, sir?" another agent asked him dispassionately.

"I believe I've opened a stinking *mess* is what I believe, young man!" Ralph twisted around in his chair to look at the agent who had behaved so courteously toward him back in his office. "Can *you* help me out here, friend?"

The affable agent wrinkled his brow thoughtfully, then scratched his jaw. "Sir," he replied, "I really don't know that I *can.* Not at this point. Sorry."

"What is *with* you people?" Ralph roared, masking his growing fear by finally loosing his temper. "I am a United

States Congressman, and this is a government facility, and I can tell you that I am going to get some *satisfaction* here or else there is going to be really, really bad trouble for this agency!"

"Unhunh," the young agent nodded, then said "and which agency is that?"

"Why . . . ahhhh . . . the . . . Federal Bureau of Investigation of course!" Ralph spluttered. As the young men exchanged restrained smiles he added, "Isn't it?"

"Sir, would you recognize the FBI building if you saw it?"

Ralph hesitated a moment. He was struggling as hard as he could to maintain his composure, but in truth he was feeling the deep waters closing over his head. "This isn't it?" he mumbled.

Another agent—or something—spoke up. "Do you really think your election entitles you to know *anything* you want to about this nation?

Again Ralph hesitated. "Of course not. Not *anything*. . ."

"Then you understand the need for secrecy in some matters, and the need to maintain that secrecy against the intrusive curiosity of the media?"

"Certainly," Ralph nodded vigorously. In fact he'd even campaigned against the pervasive influence of the media. "But you'll notice, young man, that I did not *call* the media. I called *you*, which is certainly the appropriate response in a case like this!"

"That's not the concern now, sir. The concern *now* is to prevent any further dissemination of this information. In that light, your stated intentions to 'get to the bottom of this' or to 'make trouble for this agency' are hardly encouraging, sir."

Ralph swallowed. Then he pointed to the boxes. "Those are not defensible government secrets! You *know* that those boxes contain highly inflammatory documents describing scandalous, potentially treasonous behavior. Those boxes contain evidence of a conspiracy *against* this government! Now let me be certain that I understand you: You *are* trying to intimidate me into just *forgetting* that I ever had any knowledge of this matter whatsoever—correct?"

The agents looked at one another in apparent surrender, and Ralph sat up straight in his chair, feeling he had scored. A moment later the door opened, and a man he hadn't seen walked in with a wireless telephone receiver. The other agents parted before him deferentially as he walked directly to Ralph and silently handed it to him. Ralph automatically put the receiver to his ear and said, "Hello?"

"There's no one there," the new man said flatly.

Ralph looked up at him. He had small, weak eyes and a pale, almost ghostly face. In contrast with the other men in this room he really needed to spend some time in the gym. He neither smiled nor frowned. He simply waited.

"Am I supposed to call someone?" Ralph asked, waving the phone.

"I'd suggest not," the man replied. "Then you might miss the incoming call."

"Oh?" Ralph sneered. "Am I about to hear directly from the White House?"

"Someone far more important to you personally, I judge."

"Who are you!" Ralph roared. "Where are we! I'm a United States Congressman, and—"

"I know exactly who you are, Mr. Wilkenson, and you do *not* know who I am. Which of us has the advantage in that, do you think?"

Ralph just stared at the man incredulously. The incongruity of all this had at last overwhelmed him.

"Let me share a little of what I know about you. You are a former school teacher turned businessman with a successful small business. You reside with your wife and two teenage sons in Huntsville, Alabama. You own your own home and carry a minimum of personal debt. You're a regular attender at your service club luncheon and functions of your party, and before running for office were quite active in the life of your church. You're a graduate of 'the University' at Tuscaloosa, and also have a twenty-year-old daughter enrolled there. Am I correct so far?"

Ralph licked his very dry lips. "Yes."

The man nodded and paced around the room. He showed no interest in the table loaded with documents, nor did he say anything further for a full minute. So focused was Ralph on this man's deliberate pacing that when the telephone in his hand rang, he nearly dropped it. Fumbling it up to his ear he blurted out, "Hello?"

"Daddy, is that you?" In that one sentence Ralph immediately recognized both his coed daughter's voice—and her terror.

"Tricia? Tricia, are you all right?"

"Oh, Daddy," she said, and she began to cry.

"Tricia!" he spoke sharply. "Tell me where you are! Have you been kidnapped? Are you all right?"

She sniffed herself under control and said, "I'm at the police station. Daddy, it wasn't my fault!"

"What? What wasn't your fault?"

"They didn't tell you?"

Ralph grabbed a ragged breath. "Tricia, I don't know anything that's going on. Tell me the whole story, please."

"I've . . . I've been arrested for . . . manslaughter! They're accusing me of drunken driving!"

Ralph fought for breath. Every vein, every artery, every capillary in his circulation system seemed to freeze. "Honey," he murmured, his tongue slurred by shock, "you . . . I didn't think you drank . . ."

"I don't! I mean . . . it's just . . . Daddy, it's been a really weird afternoon! None of this is my fault, I promise you, but the police here in—"

"You're at the police station? In Tuscaloosa?"

Before she could answer him, the round, pallid-faced man jerked the phone out of Ralph's hand. "Ms. Wilkenson?" he said warmly, almost cheerfully. "Could you just hold on there a moment while I speak to your father? Will you do that for me? Good. Now I'm going to put you on hold—" He pulled the set away from his head and touched a button. Then he took a long, deep breath—and smiled politely at Ralph. "I'm—almost certain that this is all a mistake. After all, Tricia is a fine, hard-working Christian girl with strong principles and a high motivation to help people. Social work major, isn't she?" Ralph nodded. He was trembling. "And, as you say, you *are* a United States Congressman. Of course, dismissing drunken driving/manslaughter charges is not quite the same as getting a speeding ticket fixed. Isn't there a mandatory prison sentence connected to conviction, even for first-time offenders?" The man glanced around at the other agents as if looking for confirmation. Then he looked back at Ralph. "Still, I'm certain that it *can* be done." He paused for a moment, shook his head sadly and said, "*Magna cum laude* from high school, wasn't she? And I took a look at *your* transcripts too, Congressman Wilkenson. You're no dummy either!" he chuckled—then his voice grew cool as he went on, "So I'm sure you already have a clear idea of what I'm about to suggest—and I think you'll see *immediately* that it's really the wisest course for all parties involved:

"Number one, we will instruct the arresting officers to drop all charges against your daughter, return her to her dormitory at the university and advise her that you, her adored daddy, through your considerable influence in high places, have arranged everything.

"Number two, we will arrange for the permanent disappearance of all of these records. We will also secure for Ms. Carrie Baxter alternative employment in another state and industry. You have heard, of course, of the witness protection program? For her own safety we will place her in that. We will assure *her* that you have begun a high-level investigation into this entire matter, and that ultimately it will all come out, but that she is to be patient and to rely on you to handle it.

"Number three, we will advise the CEO of the company in question of your awareness of this secret project and of your initial concerns about it; but we'll also advise that now that you understand it is a top secret, government-sponsored program, you will simply remain quietly proud to have it located in your district, providing jobs for your constituents. Think of all those jobs you'll save at General Aeronautics. And think of the embarrassment you'll save! Who would buy that UFO garbage, anyway? Do you? I mean, really!

"Number four, we will arrange for regular, totally legal contributions to be made by patriotic individuals to your campaign for reelection, and that as long as you share nothing of the events of the last two days with any living soul, these funds will never amount to less than half a million dollars per campaign until you choose to leave Congress—or, by some unhappy event, you are defeated. But we know that's not going to happen, don't we, Congressman! Especially with that kind of war chest?"

The man clapped Ralph on the shoulder, then walked a few steps away and continued, "Of course, *should* this matter continue to be of fascination to you, that money will *not* be available. More to the point: Did you know that your younger son—Carl Andrew, right?—is best friends with a boy who has drug paraphernalia in his school locker?"

Ralph didn't answer immediately. He was still shaking. Apparently an answer was required, however, and he managed to mutter, "No."

The round man shook his head with concern. "It's a tough world today for kids, isn't it?" Again there was silence in the room.

"Yes," Ralph said a moment later. It was as if he was acting in slow motion.

"We don't want to make it tougher, do we?" said the man—and he held up the phone to give Ralph a good look at it. "Do we?" he asked again.

Pause. "No."

"Good," said the black-suited man, sighing with relief. "I was really worried for Tricia. Ah—since it seems to be a bit difficult for you to speak at the moment—and I'm not criticizing at all, you understand, that's just an observation, and it's a perfectly normal reaction, believe me—I think I'll go ahead and tell her the good news, all right?"

He punched the blinking button and put the set back up to his head. "Ms. Wilkenson are you still there? Good. Please . . . please don't cry . . . please . . . listen to me . . . listen to me . . . good. That's better. I've been speaking to your father and, quite frankly, we *really* think there has been a *terrible* mistake made here. Is the arresting officer standing there by you? Yes? Would you put him on, please? Now relax, Ms. Wilkenson. Everything is all right. Your father has taken care of *everything*, all right? All right? Okay. Now put the officer on, please."

The man looked at Ralph and smiled brightly, then turned back to the receiver. "Officer? Is this Officer Carney? Excellent work, officer. Code green twenty-seven, and thank you, so much. I'll remember your work." He casually pulled the receiver back down and disconnected, then handed the phone to one of the other agents and looked back at Ralph.

"Congressman," he said, and now his voice sounded almost pastoral, "I realize that this has been a rough-and-tumble introduction to secret affairs in the capital. I want you to know that you did the *right* thing—the right thing. And I salute you for your honesty and integrity and high principles. Don't ever lose them, my friend. Hang onto them. Still, it's good to see that you're also a man of principle related to maintaining secret information. Now, you've heard a lot more already than most freshman congressmen hear, in fact most *veteran* members of the House hear for a very long time. But I hope you will understand that what's happened to you here today as a result of your conscientious attempt to do your job is really not *unusual* for such matters. So, if you feel any temptation to get down on yourself, please don't. You're here to *help* people, sir, and you *will* help people—*are* helping the people of your own district by allowing us to clean this up.

Welcome to Washington!" The man extended his hand. Although he didn't want to, fear forced Ralph to take the hand and shake it. "That's it, Ralph. Be careful now, you hear me? Someone is going to run you back to your office." With that, the man turned on his heel and stalked out of the room, followed by four other men.

Ralph just sat in his swivel chair for a moment. "Sir?" someone said, and he turned his head. It was the friendly agent, and the man smiled encouragingly. "Can I give you a lift?"

As he walked out of the square chamber Ralph didn't give the boxes and suitcases of papers another look. He never wanted to see them again in his life.

* * *

Jack and Ben had been transferred to another saucer by three Men in Black. Jeffrey and Ruzagnon had been in animated conversation at the foot of the ramp as they were brought aboard. Left to themselves the two found an empty cabin, and Ben explained what was taking place. "Do you realize," Ben said, "that you've stopped thinking of the Boss as Gork?"

Jack really hadn't noticed. Now that he thought about it, however, he realized that it had become increasingly difficult for him to view the leader of this crew of the fallen in that denigrating manner. Respect, or fear, or *something* was forcing him to revise his estimation of the creature.

"Give the devil his due, right?" Ben said softly, and Jack shrugged.

"I guess that's it. It's always dangerous to underestimate your enemy." And the dominant Gray was certainly the enemy. "Where did that name come from, anyway? Ruzagnon?"

"That's his 'Pleiadean Sibling' name. Sounds rather exotic, doesn't it? Extraterrestrial? I really think he'd be as happy with 'Baal' as any other. That or 'Prometheus.' He really liked being Prometheus."

Jack mulled the Prometheus legend over in his mind, wondering exactly what events had given rise to it. Had the angels intervened in his mischief, and somehow bound him?

"Who knows," Ben shrugged.

"Are you always listening?" Jack asked the boy and Ben shrugged.

"I'm always listening to someone, I guess."

"Then why don't you listen to Jeffrey and tell me what's going on?"

Ben shrugged again, and for the next half-hour he gave Jack a blow-by-blow description of the Alabama Congressman's ordeal. The man was being interrogated in a room adjoining this large subterranean hangar. Jack shook his head at the description of Jeffrey's manipulation of the Congressman, trying to find some explanation for how the friend he'd known in college had become this person. When he asked Ben if the fallen truly intended to relocate Carrie Baxter, the teenager just laughed. "To a graveyard, yeah!" From that point on Jack couldn't concentrate. He was praying.

Moments later there was action in the corridors as the Grays and their human agents came back on board the saucer. Its engines leapt to life, and they departed the D.C. area—under the ground.

* * *

Carrie was singing as she drove. She'd found a really good contemporary Christian station on her radio, and whoever had arranged the program liked the same songs she did. As one powerful message of praise followed another, she was able to release the burden of worry and fear that had oppressed her since she'd first left Alabama. Congressman Wilkenson had accepted the burden of the conspiracy she'd uncovered, and with it months and months of terror and grief. She'd gotten some sleep, finally, and while she knew she needed much more she could relax now in the anticipation of getting a *real* rest when she got home. She was off from work, and no one knew where she was. She could sleep for *days* if she wanted to, and that's exactly what she intended to do. Then on Sunday she'd go to church and share with her friends all that God had done. It would all be out in the open soon, so she could actually *tell* them what they'd been praying for all these months!

The more she thought about it, the sillier she began to feel for being afraid that someone would try to *kill* her. "Too many political thrillers, Carrie!" she told herself aloud. She was going to have to quit renting that kind of movie! Honestly, they would make *anyone* feel paranoid about our own government!

She drove straight through supper time, ignoring as best she could the sun in her eyes. As twilight came, then early evening, it seemed the traffic thinned out. Most people were home watching television by this time, leaving the road to just Carrie and the truckers.

She knew what her mother would be saying right about now, if Carrie were to call her and give her the chance: "Girl, you've got no business at *all* bein' out on those roads at this time a night! Honestly, a young woman by yourself and all! Get you a motel room, girl! You can find a cheap one . . . !" And, of course, Mom was right. She could have, but she didn't. She *really* wanted to get home tonight, and it wasn't that far now. She'd just taken her turn to get off the interstate. She dipped down into a familiar holler, leaving the lights of the four-lane behind—

There was a flying saucer in the road! Carrie hit her brakes and screeched to a halt, then realized it wasn't stopped at all—it was coming *toward* her! She slammed the gas peddle down again, making a wide U-turn to race back toward the lights of the four-lane, but by the time she was turned, the saucer had come up over her and blocked her retreat—NO! There were *two*, and one of them was trying to land on *top* of her!

"Lord Jesus!" she screamed, whirling the car into a spin, trying to steer it back toward Huntsville. Even as she did it she heard the vibrations coming from the alien craft above her, and soon it was shaking her whole car from side to side. She glanced in the sideview mirror and saw the other craft looming up behind her—and she was well aware of the fact that OBJECTS IN MIRROR ARE ACTUALLY CLOSER THAN THEY APPEAR.

All of the panic of all the months flowed back into her. All of her joy at God's provision evaporated. Carrie screamed out the name of Jesus over and over, but when her engine died and her battery went dead, her faith died right along with them. How many times had she dreamed exactly this? How many nights had she awakened in a cold sweat and listened for the inevitable sounds, certain that the ships of the evil ones had come to fetch her at last? *This* was the truth, she realized bitterly. Like all the tabloids claimed, the alien watchers were real. And what of the guardian angels she'd prayed to believe in? Where were they? She had herself documented evidence that proved the aliens were real—but never had a single guardian angel ever showed himself.

The car was rocking so hard now that the wheels were bouncing up off the ground—first the right side, then the left, higher and higher each time, until she was certain they intended to flip her over and drop her on her head. Coolly she checked to insure her safety belt was fastened—but Carrie was lost, and she knew it. Might as well stop fighting it. She lowered her window and craned her neck out, a spectator now to her own inevitable destruction. Whenever the left side of the vehicle bounced upward she saw clearly the saucer right above her. Then, abruptly, the rocking stopped. This was it, she thought, pulling her head in and facing straight ahead. Soon a beam of light or whatever would issue from the craft and zap her into oblivion.

Carrie was ready for it, she decided. She was tired of running and tired of the fearful dreams. But nothing happened. Patience, she told herself.

Still, nothing happened. What were they doing? Were they landing? Were the ugly, little lizard-like creatures disembarking? She felt rather than saw the figure rounding the back of her car. Were they going to come around to her door like intergalactic space cops and jerk her out with their slimy little hands? She closed her eyes, fearful of what she was about to see. Through her lowered window she felt a radiance on her neck, and without looking she quickly cranked it up. Still, she felt the creature's eyes upon her through the glass, and though she tried not to do it she whimpered in terror. Then something warm touched her shoulder—through the window! As she jerked away, her eyes flew wide to stare at . . .

The most beautiful man she'd ever seen. So achingly solemn and handsome was he that her heart fluttered with something far removed from terror. Gorgeous features, gorgeous eyes, powerful chin, perfectly-proportioned shoulders—he might have been the model for Michelangelo's David. And he glowed, as if his skin was translucent and he had a night-light in his chest. She looked down at her shoulder to see his perfect hand resting upon it—through the glass of the window, just as she'd thought. And she couldn't help herself. She reached over to place her own hand upon it and said with genuine wonder, "Are you *real?*"

The classic lips did not smile, but there was a change of the light in his eyes—almost a look of relief, Carrie thought. She realized with a sense of keen disappointment that that was *exactly* what his look meant, for now that he was certain she was okay he was withdrawing his hand through the window and turning his eyes skyward. "Don't go!" she whined, but already he was effortlessly ascending straight up. She frantically rolled down the window and stuck her head out shouting, "Wait!"

As she struggled to peer upward, a marvelous thing took place. She saw clearly the two saucers, hovering exactly where they'd been above her head. But now she also saw enormous humanoid beings of light ringed around each of them, gripping the two saucers between them as a circle of firemen might grip a safety net. Angels. They had to be angels.

Carrie twisted around on the front seat and nearly crawled backwards out of her window, watching with rapt attention the drama high above her head. "Her" angel had just joined the others, taking his grip on one of the saucers. Then, upon some signal Carrie neither heard nor saw, the angels *flung* the saucers—elsewhere.

Where, Carrie didn't know. The two saucers didn't fly up, or down, or sideways—any direction Carrie could see. They just went away. The angels continued to hang there in the sky, two awesome, radiant circles. But the saucers had just . . . disappeared.

Sitting now on her door, clutching the roof of her car to keep from falling backward, Carrie continued peering upward as the angels departed. One by one they flew off in every direction, as if they'd rallied to her aid from all points of the compass. Carrie wondered, then, how often they did this—how often in her *own* life they had rallied to "her" angel's aid? The incredible difference *this* time was that they had let her *see.*

Motionless, powerful, her own angel hung in the sky until all the others were departed. Then he inclined his head and looked down at her, and it was hard to miss the meaning in his stern expression. "Now," he was saying to her, "will you *believe* and trust God to care for you?"

"Yes," Carrie murmured. The sound of her own voice startled her. She realized that since the car had stopped bouncing, she'd not heard anything at all.

The angel turned, then, revolving effortlessly in the air as if he dangled upon a silver thread from heaven. Once she realized he'd turned his face toward Huntsville, Alabama, he majestically veiled himself from her view.

Carrie just sat there for a moment, looking up where he'd been, certain now that he was still *there*—waiting on her. Then she took a long, deep breath. "All right," she said, and she slid her upper body back inside the car and down behind the steering wheel. Her engine roared to life with a twist of the key. She would have sworn it was running smoother now than it had been the whole trip. "Let's go home."

Chapter Sixteen

Roswell redux

Ah—Ben?"

"Yeah, Jack?"

"You're there, then."

"I'm here. And no, you're not blind, I hope. . . ."

"You can't see anything either?"

"Not a thing. Here—hold my hand, would you?"

"Sure. Where are we?"

"Wish I knew."

"You don't?"

"Nope."

"Nobody around us does?"

"Nope."

"Nobody in the control center knows?"

"Nope."

"Where do they *think* we are?"

"In deep trouble. And I can assure them—they're right."

"What happened?"

Ben drew a deep sigh in the darkness. "I'm not sure. I can tell you what the woman was *seeing* just before whatever happened . . . happened."

"Okay . . . "

"Angels." Ben proceeded to tell him all that Carrie Baxter had witnessed and felt up to the moment they disappeared. As he spoke, a slow smile spread over Jack's face in the utter darkness.

"Well," Jack said when Ben finished, "so much for the 'Jack Brennen, good luck charm theory!'"

"You don't seem all that upset."

"Why should I? I *like* angels."

"Yeah, but what if they've thrown us into *hell?*"

Jack heard the terror in the boy's voice and realized now that Ben's hand was trembling. He pondered for a moment, then said, "I don't know where this is exactly, Ben, but I can tell you for certain it's not hell."

"How do you know?"

"In the first place, because *I'm* here, and I know for a fact I'm going to heaven."

"Oh, *that's* reassuring," the frightened boy snarled.

"Point two is, wherever hell is, God is not. And God is here with us."

"Where?"

"In me," Jack answered, his voice filled with confident comfort. "I think you know He's here, too."

"Why do you think that?" the boy grumbled.

"You saw the angels; I didn't."

"The woman saw them," the boy argued. "I just read her mind."

"And you don't believe her eyes? You don't believe *something* just threw this ship and everyone in it *somewhere?*

What's your explanation for all that, Ben? What's happened to us?"

The boy was very quiet. Jack just held his hand in the darkness and waited. Finally Ben said, "I know you believe this stuff, Jack. More than that, I know you believe that *I* could believe it with you, and by believing it could be just as certain of God's acceptance. But don't you figure Gork believes it too? And Gork's not going to heaven. Nor is Astra, nor Kundas, nor any of the other creatures who share this black box with us.

"Yes, Jack, I believe that God and His angels have opposed my boss, and all the other bosses of all the other demonic cells. But I've *helped* them, don't you see? I've *helped* these horrible beings *succeed!* How then could your God ever love *me?*"

Knowing the boy could read his thoughts anyway, Jack answered as quickly and as directly as he could. His response took no thought, really. He knew with certainty what he believed. "You're certainly not the first human who's been tricked into aiding the evil ones. All of us have—all of us *do.*

"These fallen and their evil leader are masters at manipulating our feelings and dreams—and don't think for a minute, Ben, that while you read other's minds your own mind goes unread. I don't know *how* he relates to his minions, I don't know where our hosts fit into his hellish hierarchy, but I *do* know this for sure: The Evil One knows you, hears you, and speaks to you, whether you are aware of that or not. And right now he's telling you every reason he can muster why God wouldn't care about you, Ben. But the good news of the gospel is simple: He *does* care, my friend. He *does.*"

Powerful forces suddenly rocked the ship, and they were both thrown sprawling in the darkness. A moment later they could see again, but it was not as if the lights had come back on in the saucer's interior, or power had returned to the generators. It was rather as if they'd been no place, and now were someplace again. Lying on his back on the floor between the bed and a bulkhead, Jack could see Ben's foot out of the corner of his eye. "Where are we, Ben?" he shouted. Just like that, the boy's answer shot back:

"Somewhere over the desert, somewhere back in time, the angels threw us into the past without benefit of computer computation, so everything's gone haywire. The guys at the controls are trying to read their instruments now. Ha!" the boy laughed. "Somebody's thinking they ought to buy a paper and read the date on it!"

Suddenly the ship seemed to waddle in flight, dipping downward and almost turning on its side. Jack found himself wedged even further into the crack between bed and wall, but he guessed he was fortunate. Ben was literally bouncing *off* the wall above him. "What was that?" he managed to call out.

The ship righted itself, and Ben fell back onto the bed. "It was a bad bump, that's what it was!" the teenager snarled. "Give me a chance to get my bearings, will you?"

"No rush," Jack sang, no longer trying to wiggle out of his uncomfortable position. He figured they might bounce through a few other exotic maneuvers—and he was right. Again, the ship nosed downward, then it seemed to turn sideways and do cartwheels on its edge. Jack took a deep breath and held it. Much more of this and he was going to need one of those bags they put in the seat pocket of airplanes. . . .

Like a top bouncing off the ground and righting itself, the saucer leveled out again and found its balance. After a moment of apparent normality, Jack decided to trust it. He emptied the held breath from his lungs and swallowed a couple of times to settle his stomach. He really wanted to know where they were, but he wasn't going to ask the kid again any time soon.

"New Mexico," Ben said wearily from somewhere up on the bed above Jack's head. "There's a rancher watching us, and I'm reading his mind. He's trying to decide whether to be afraid or not—he wonders if we're Japs who don't know the war's over. It's . . . it's 1947 here, Jack."

"Here *where?*" Jack asked, finally trying to unwedge himself from the crack.

"In the middle of the desert, really—somewhere near . . . *omigosh*," the boy whispered breathlessly.

"*What?*" Jack pleaded, dragging himself up onto the bed to stare at his companion's thunderstruck face.

"Roswell. Roswell, New Mexico, 1947. Actually, Corona is closer. Ring a bell, Jack?"

Ben knew it did. Jack had seen enough quasi-documentaries and spooky miniseries on television to know that Roswell was where a saucer crash was rumored to have taken place in 1947. It was famous. It supposedly caused President Truman to appoint the MJ-12 committee to study flying saucers. A report had actually gone out over the radio saying that the military had recovered a crashed flying saucer, and the report was then quickly corrected. Whitley Strieber had written a novel about it, and there'd been a host of "investigative reports" into the "Roswell coverup." "Isn't that where the military is supposed to have discovered the dead bodies of four little gray aliens?"

"You got it, Jack," the boy replied, his eyes glowing. "And Jack—the other saucer just crashed."

Jack blinked. "Were there Grays on it?" he asked, his voice hushed.

"Yep," answered Ben. "Four of 'em."

* * *

The truck bounced and bounded over rough terrain. The guys in the back of the troop carrier rocked from side to side, each clutching the long bench as best they could to keep from rolling over onto one another. Henry Widdershins' fanny was telling him they'd long since left the road. "Where we go-IN', Sar-ARGE?" Henry called out, his words misshapen by a sudden jolt over some rocks.

"'at's classified," the sergeant grinned, and the men rolled their eyes. Sarge loved knowing things they didn't know.

"Right, like we're gonna tell somebody between here an' where we're goin'," somebody grumbled.

"Like it matters, now the war's over," Henry added.

"It matters," the sergeant said self-importantly, still grinning. "Don't you guys read the papers? There's Japs who still think we're fightin'!"

"I think the *Sarge* still thinks we're fightin'," one guy mumbled to another.

"I heard that, Wilson," the sergeant snarled—but his grin was still fixed in place. This made Henry uncomfortable. Whenever the Sarge grinned like that, it was usually because he'd volunteered them for some really stinking detail.

"Come on, Sarge, you can tell us," Henry yelled in a bantering tone. "We're your best buddies!"

"We're Sarge's *only* buddies," Wilson said, and all those who dared to do so laughed along with him.

"You just wait, Wilson," the sergeant cackled, his grin growing dangerously wider. "Whenever we get there, I got a *special* task picked out just for *you!*"

Wilson cursed his own big mouth, and now the whole detail laughed.

"So what is it, Sarge?" Henry kept on. "What're we doin' bouncin' around on this desert?"

The sergeant turned his eyes on Henry now, and the whole group waited expectantly. He had that cat-who-just-ate-the-canary look on his face that let them all know he was at last going to let them in on the big secret. "You really wanna know, do you? Awright. We got wreckage detail." A chorus of expletives greeted his announcement, and he seemed to enjoy the curses as much as an actor loves applause. He cackled with genuine pleasure.

"Big crash?" Henry asked, his stomach already churning. He'd gotten in only on the tail end of the war in Europe, but he arrived in time to have to ship a lot of dead buddies home to their mamas. Big crashes meant a lot of bodies. . . .

"Don't know," Sarge shrugged. "Don't know what it is." Then he grinned again, about to reveal the biggest secret of all. "What I *do* know is—it ain't one of *ours!*" Then he sat back against the jerking canvas wall of the truck to enjoy their reaction. As he'd expected, he got nothing back this time but stunned silence.

"Japs?" somebody murmured at last.

"Russkies more likely," someone else said quietly.

There was another pause before Henry asked for all of them, "Did we shoot it down?" This was a question full of import. It could easily mean the start of the next war.

"Nope," the sarge answered. Then he corrected himself: "At least, that's what I'm *told.* That's it, guys, that's all I know. Somebody crashed out here, they weren't one of us, and we didn't shoot 'em down. We're supposed to pick up the dead bodies and parts of the wreckage, especially any pieces with identifying markings, and take them back to the base. We oughta about *be* there by now," he added, banging on the window behind the driver's head.

Half an hour later, the truck slowed down to a crawl, then stopped. The group piled out of the carrier, all craning their necks to a get a view of the wreckage. It wasn't impressive. Somebody made the observation that it looked like a wadded ball of tinfoil. That began a series of jokes about tin cans and sardines and trash, designed to cover over that unsettled feeling everybody shared about walking up onto someone's corpse. But no one was ready for what they actually found when they arrived at the sight.

What looked like tinfoil turned out to be some incredibly strong silvery material like nothing any of them had ever seen. The tiny I-beams they pulled out of the wreckage were as light as balsa wood—but too strong to be bent, or scratched. There were some markings, but nothing anybody could identify. They looked like pink hieroglyphics, in a language no one in the unit recognized. But what silenced them all were the bodies. Not the three human bodies—these were tagged and bagged like they'd been taught to do. It was the four *non*-human bodies that caused them to gasp and gag. They were gray and slimy—like slugs on the sidewalk after the rain—but they had big bald heads and huge almond eyes, which caused one man to mutter, "They look like those Japanese gods. " No one else said anything. What was there to say?

Once the bodies were loaded on the other vehicle and they climbed back into their truck, Sarge's face looked as chalky as that of any of the strange creatures they'd retrieved. Before he gave the signal to the driver to go, he looked around the unit and took a deep breath. "Boys," he said at last, "I don't know if you're thinkin' what I'm thinkin', but it looks to me like we got us one of those flying saucer things."

No one else said anything, so Henry Widdershins spoke up. "Sarge? You think they're from . . . Mars?"

The sergeant shook his head gravely. "I don't know. From there or Venus, most likely." Then his face grew steel-hard, and he glared around the circle. "Okay, listen up. This may be the first wave of an invasion force, and you know what that means: The first guy says *anything* about this to *anybody?* I'm not gonna bust you—I'm gonna *shoot* you! You got me?"

Everyone nodded. Sarge pounded on the driver's window, and the truck lurched forward once again.

* * *

As they angled down over the crash site, Jack's head was spinning. They'd made a quick trip to Washington D.C.—but not the D.C. of Freshman Congressman Wilkenson. At this point in history he was still in diapers in a tiny Alabama town. They'd gone instead to Truman's Washington.

Jack didn't learn this until they were leaving, of course. A minute after they'd reentered the stream of time in 1947 and learned of the crash, Ben had been fetched away to the control room to assist in planning strategy. He'd played a critical role in negotiating the intervention in and suppression of the saucer recovery effort back in New Mexico, but it had taken much of the afternoon to make the arrangements. Ben explained the situation to him on their way back across the country to Roswell:

"It took us a while even to make contact with the Ultrastructure people in this time period. In 1947 the organization had pretty well fallen apart—in this country, anyway. Seems like our fallen friends thought they had a winner in Hitler, and had backed him completely!"

Jack shook his head at this news. He'd heard enough by now about the Ultrastructure's activities that he felt he couldn't be shocked by anything. This news didn't even surprise him. "But you evidently *did* find somebody, since the government has managed to cover up the Roswell incident for almost fifty years."

"Finally, yeah," Ben nodded. He had a fifteen-year-old's excitement about his role in this sequence of events. He wouldn't worry about the implications of his involvement until later. "But we didn't get it stopped in time to prevent a report going out over the radio. That report has been cut off by now by the government, and they'll soon be holding a news conference to claim that the crashed saucer was really a weather balloon."

Jack had heard this story before, a dozen times in a dozen different forms. "What about the bodies? Are they going to be taken to that famous hangar in Dayton?"

"No way," Ben snorted. "We're going now to get them back. First, we've got to fly over the crash site."

"Why? Didn't you say the bodies were already at the base hospital?"

"Yes," Ben nodded.

Jack was puzzled by this—but it wasn't the only thing in this incident that bothered him. He'd not made any comment on it yet, however. He was afraid if he brought the question up it might hurt Ben's growing trust of the angel's explanation of events—

"Why don't you just ask me, Jack? It's not as if I don't know exactly what you're thinking in *any* case. Besides, it's *your* doubts that are really bothering you, not mine. You're thinking that if Astra and the Boss and Kundas are really fallen angels, how can their bodies die, right?"

"As you say," Jack growled, "it's not as if you don't already know my every thought. Since you *are* inside my mind again, why don't you give me an answer? *Can* the demons be killed?

"Those are two very different questions, you know," Ben answered.

"What are?"

"Can demons die, and can their *bodies* die? In just a few minutes you may find out for yourself the answer to the first one." That was an unusually cryptic statement, coming from Ben. Only moments later Jack realized exactly what the boy had been suggesting.

As they hovered over the crash site, Jack suddenly felt a terrible, overshadowing power enter their cabin and sweep over him. Perhaps others would not have been so quick to recognize the horrible weight of *evil* in this presence, but Jack did immediately—and he trembled. Before it could control him, however, he shouted aloud, "Lord Jesus, *no!* God help me!"—and the demon that had tried to occupy him bounced off.

Demonic possession had been a big subject in seminary in the 1970s—and nowhere more so than in San Francisco. Who can be possessed by a demon? How is one possessed by a demon? Can a Christian become "possessed" when he or she already has the Holy Spirit dwelling within? If a Christian cannot be "possessed," can he or she be "oppressed?" *The Exorcist* added fuel to the fire. Some Christians began "deliverance" ministries, while others opposed such ministries as *tools* of the devil, focusing the attention of believers on the Evil One instead of on the Christ. Jack had decided long ago that if Jesus could talk to demons and cast them into a herd of swine, then they must be real. He'd also decided early on that Christians who paid too much attention to the occult could get drawn into that fringe themselves. But of two points he had become most strongly convinced. First, he'd come to accept that there *is* evil in the world, and the power of the demonic is at least as good an explanation for *why* as any other explanation he'd ever heard. And second, if indeed such immoral immortals existed and interacted with people, only God could have the power to dislodge them and defend against them. It was that simple. Ever since the night of Black Sabbat and his own visit to Glory he had been thoroughly convinced that these creatures in alien bodies were, indeed, the fallen angels of an all-powerful God and that they could at least oppress Christians. They'd certainly oppressed him enough. Now he stood in his cabin trembling, just as convinced that apart from the name of Jesus Christ he would be experiencing possession himself, right now.

"Ben?" he said quietly.

"That's what it was, all right," the boy answered in a whisper. "And not just any demon, either. That was old bad-tempered Kundas himself. His body was one of those carried back to the base this afternoon. He wanted to ride you back to it."

"To *ride* me?" Jack almost whimpered.

"Yeah. That's the easiest way for them to get around. They're not like angels anymore, because they've—"

"Lost their wings," Jack finished for him, nodding. "So—where did Kundas go?"

"He's . . . ahh . . . in Jeffrey right now. So is Quorshwin. They're fighting over him. Oh, and they're both *really* angry at you."

As if on cue Jeffrey burst through the door and charged at Jack. He left his feet to dive over the bed, hands outstretched to grab Jack around the throat. But Jack *had* been a college halfback, and Jeffrey hadn't. Jack dodged aside to let Jeffrey slam headlong into the bulkhead, then he took off out the door. He turned left and sprinted down the curving corridor.

It really didn't much matter which way he went: Since this was a circular corridor around the control center, either direction would bring him right back here.

He heard Jeffrey bellowing behind him, shouting words in some ancient language he was certain his friend had never learned. It isn't Jeffrey, he reminded himself. *It's two angry demons fighting over one mind.*

Halfway around the circle he stopped, listening to insure that the Jeffrey creature was coming the same way he had, before continuing on. When he heard the heavy footfalls, he took off, quickly making his way back to his room while thinking to Ben, *Would you please get the bed ready to shove up against the door when I come through it?*

Their timing was perfect. Jack bolted back inside his cabin, and Ben slammed the door behind him and jumped back over the bed. Together they pushed it into place. Still, Jack was thinking, this door wouldn't hold long—not against two demons. He wasn't surprised they could gang up in people. He thought again about the Gadarene demoniac who had a legion of demons in him. Jesus had cast all of them out—

"Why not try it yourself?" Ben asked, leaning his full weight against the door as the first heavy THUMP! banged against it.

Should I? Jack thought.

"I'd ask you if you had a better idea—if I didn't already know you *don't*." THUMP! The door bounced open, and the bed bumped back a couple of inches.

Jack shook his head, took a long deep breath, and quoted Paul from Acts 16: "I command you in the name of Jesus Christ to come out of him." He didn't say it loudly. He didn't say it dramatically. But the thumping on the door stopped, just the same.

"Jack?" Jeffrey called out a moment later.

"Jeffrey?" Jack answered, and he looked at Ben in mute appeal.

"They're gone, Jack," Ben answered.

"Really? Where?"

"I don't know. But I can tell you this: When we *do* get their bodies back for them, they are really going to be *livid* at you."

Jack sat down on the bed and sighed. "I can hardly wait."

* * *

Dr. Ragan Podrasky had an appropriate personality for a surgeon. Arrogant, vain, daring, and incontestably eccentric, he wielded his life as he wielded his scalpel: He cut carefully, quickly, and deeply. Those whose lives he impacted either loved him enough to make excuses for him or hated him enough to kill him. No one, however, went away unimpressed. He liked it that way. He'd spent his entire life impressing others. He was, however, above being impressed himself.

Or he had been until today. He stared at the gray-fleshed humanoid on the stainless steel table before him, paralyzed with indecision. *Where do I start cutting?* he wondered. It was certainly a fair question. Still, the others gathered around the table couldn't keep from smiling behind their surgical masks. This was, after all, the great Dr. Podrasky! Even those who loved him got a thrill out of seeing him discomfited.

"Perhaps if we—" one of the other doctors began, but Dr. Podrasky cut him off with a sharp, slicing:

"Silence!" Then he drew himself up to his full height and made this pronouncement: "What we are about to encounter has never, so far as we know, been faced by mankind before. Look at this creature before us! We have been privileged to perform this autopsy—to see with our own eyes!—what has never been viewed by human eyes before. We're about to cut open a spaceman." He took a deep breath, then said, "Begin."

Conscious of the eyes focused upon him, he bent to cut deeply into what should have been the creature's chest, slicing from sternum to navel—if it had *had* a sternum, or *had* a navel. Everyone encircling the table bent over to peer into the gash, and saw that what the creature had instead was—more gray flesh. Above his mask and below his head-covering,

Podrasky allowed his forehead to crease with frown lines. He cut deeper.

More gray flesh. This was the same color and consistency as the outer skin—slightly slimy, cool to the touch, almost green-gray. Podrasky's frown deepened. Where were the organs? Where were the skeletal structures? Where, indeed, was the blood?

"What are you looking at?" snarled the dead patient—and Podrasky froze in terror, his scalpel held like a conductor's baton. When the almost bisected being's eyes sprang open and the large head wobbled up off the table, the rest of the surgical team wasted no time in departing. They were out the door *immediately*. Pans and steel tables and once-sterile instruments went bouncing across the tiled floor in all directions.

Podrasky would have run too, but for one thing: The beast—he had to regard him that way, now that he'd seen the creature's dreadful eyes—had grabbed the surgeon by the lab coat, and jerked him down toward his hideous face. "Did you do this?" the gray alien roared, and Podrasky began apologizing profusely. The creature didn't wait for him to finish. He just bellowed, "Stitch me up!" in a voice that might have come from a buffalo.

Ragan Podrasky did a little bellowing himself: "Nurse!" he roared. "I need some *HELP* in here!"

The nurse who was most in love with him heard it as her summons to destiny. She raced back in the door, and together they threaded, stitched, and sutured until they'd closed the huge gash in the uniformly gray body. They worked stiffly, mechanically, avoiding with great diligence those huge black eyes that stared up at them contemptuously. They took no apparent notice when three other, similar bodies got off their tables and out from under their sheets to walk over and take a look at what was going on. When the job was done, Podrasky stepped back formally, gestured toward the zipper of stitches that laced down the center of the creature's body and—bowed. He found it impossible to speak.

Kundas got off the table and stalked out of the operating room, followed by the rest of this green-gray crew. Podrasky and his nurse wordlessly watched them out the door. Then, the moment it swung shut, they collapsed into one another's arms, embracing, hugging, kissing one another literally for dear life. Then, lest these (apparently) spineless aliens came back to take some savage revenge upon them after all, they dropped to their knees behind a rolling cabinet and waited there the rest of the afternoon. Not until he was certain they were gone did Dr. Podrasky venture out of his surgery. He waited until someone could be found and brought to the door who had actually seen the creatures get into a silvery disc and fly away. Once he was certain they were safe, he stood up, brushed off the invisible dirt from the spotless operating room floor, and sauntered out to tell his story. Of course, he told everyone in the officer's mess that night that while, yes, he *had* talked to the spaceman, he really hadn't been all that impressed. . . .

The base commander found him about 8:30, pulled him to the side, and threatened exactly what the government would do to him if he *ever* revealed any *part* of the story to anyone, ever. The good doctor apparently got the message, for while he married the nurse who had helped him—they left the military to go and open a practice in Wisconsin and lived long and productive lives—they never once mentioned that afternoon's activities again. Not even to each other.

* * *

"They're coming for you now," Ben informed Jack quietly, adding, "Jeffrey's with them."

"I wonder," Jack murmured. "Do you think it might be possible to cast them out of their *own* bodies?"

The door swung open—no longer blocked by the bed. Gork stepped in first, followed by Astra, then Kundas, then several other Grays whose names Jack didn't know. They surrounded him, staring with obvious hatred. Jack reminded himself, you have to *expect* hatred from demons.

Ruzagnon/Baal/Gork spoke first. "You've been a disappointment to us, Dr. Brennen. To me especially, since I took a special interest in your enlistment.

"What did you expect?" Jack shrugged—and pain shot down both his shoulder blades, met at his backbone and continued stinging down into his tail. He'd been sitting on the bed when they came in—now he writhed upon it.

"I suppose," Gork replied calmly, "I'd expected you to take a little more interest in learning our ways, in understanding our feelings. But instead you just seem intent on maintaining your prejudice toward us. We've been trying to teach your race tolerance for a long time, Jack—tolerance for religious differences, tolerance for the views of other cultures, tolerance for the relativity of all truth. You've chosen not to listen."

Jack still twisted across the bedspread. Whichever of the fallen was inflicting this upon him was apparently enjoying it.

"Kundas," Ben told him. It was no surprise.

"You've proved most unhelpful," Gork continued. "You've apparently confused the boy into believing your ridiculous tale about our being—what was it again? Fallen angels? We've tolerated most of this, because—as I said—we are the most tolerant of creatures. Besides, we're not without a sense of humor, and your outdated notions are certainly funny. In fact, they've proved—shall we say—nostalgic to some of us! Yes, Jack, for a time we actually enjoyed you. And you *did* seem to keep the boy engaged with his work. Surprised? Oh yes! Your presence has served to challenge Ben—to push him mentally—to refresh his jaded young mind with some concepts utterly foreign to his upbringing. That's been helpful Jack, and we thank you for it. Kundas, let him breathe a moment."

"Only for a moment," Kundas said flatly.

The absence of pain came with the suddenness and delight of a kiss. It felt—heavenly. Jack stopped squirming, and laid flat on his back to gasp in great draughts of air. Astra sat on the bed next to him and began to run her hand across his sweating forehead. He didn't like that much. When she started to stroke his stomach he liked it even less. He twisted out of her reach, and Astra laughed.

"Unfortunately, Jack, you've chosen to refuse the opportunity to participate in the remaking of your race. You were part of the elite, Dr. Brennen—and you kicked it away. Of course, given *your* view, you're probably commending yourself this very moment for not 'selling your soul to the devil.' Is that right, Jack? Are you? We're not the devil, Jack. But if there *is* a devil you're going to meet him soon. Kundas wants to kill you. Why is that, Kundas?" Gork asked.

"We no longer see any need of his presence with us," Kundas muttered.

"Right," Gork nodded, looking back at Jack. "I've told you before, Dr. Brennen—we *own* your race. Just because you don't want to accept that doesn't alter the facts. We own you—we made you—we bred you, like you breed cattle. And what do your farmers do when an animal is of no further use to them? Do they keep them around as pets, eating up food and giving their diseases to other livestock? Of course not. So . . . may I say that it has been interesting to have you with us. Kundas?"

Once again, Jack was racked with agony. Kundas stepped to the edge of the bed and said, "Did you know you can die with pain itself? Just . . . hurt to death? We're limited in how we might go about killing one of you. We have no weapons, of course. But you know already we can cause you hurt—and that's why I plan to hurt you to death. I'm afraid it may take some time. . . ."

As he flipped about on the bed like a fish in the bottom of a boat, Jack chanced to see Ben's face. It was twisted along with his. The boy was hearing his thoughts, feeling for him, *with* him. *Don't worry about me, Ben,* Jack thought as he fought the pain. Once again he thought of words from his favorite hymn:

Let goods and kindred go, this mortal life also. The body they may kill, God's truth abideth still. And He must win the battle.

The pain intensified. Jack hadn't thought it could do that. He screamed and said good-bye to Gloria, then everything went black.

This wasn't the blackness of death, however. This was the black of the time void. Jack suddenly wasn't hurting anymore. He wasn't *seeing* either. As for the fallen, he could hear them around him, cursing and whining and scrambling to find the door out of this room in the darkness. Before they could get away, however, they all heard a very powerful, authoritative voice speaking from somewhere out of the black.

"Touch not the Lord's anointed," the voice said.

She sounded exactly like Gloria.

Chapter Seventeen

A circle of stones

When they fell back into time, everyone had the same question. Rather than "Where are we?" it was "*When* are we?" Once again the angels had hurled them down into the time-stream, but there was no gauge or monitor or clock face to let them know exactly how far they had been thrown. Instead, everyone turned immediately to Ben, expecting him to read a nearby mind and pick the date and time out of it. Not this time, however. Ben did nothing, he just looked back at them blankly.

"What's the matter?" Gork demanded suspiciously. "Aren't there any minds down there to read?"

Ben gulped, his face reflecting his own consternation. "Oh, there are minds all right. It's just . . . I can't make sense of them."

"What do you mean?" Kundas demanded, edging up close to Ben, intimidating the boy by his nearness. He was still chafing at being prevented from killing Jack. Frustrated in that, he was quite willing to hurt this disloyal teenager in Jack's place.

"I mean," the boy explained patiently, "that I don't understand what's *in* these minds. I can see them clearly, hear them—I just don't know the language they're speaking or the meaning of their symbols."

Gork blinked. Then he glanced around the cabin at the beings there assembled and asked, "Who's flying this thing?" When no one knew, he and the other Grays rushed quickly out of the room and across the hall into the control room. "You come too!" the creature shouted back at the humans amongst them, and Ben, Jack, and Jeffrey looked at one another.

Jack was okay. He had sat up on the bed and was twisting and stretching. In fighting the pain he had cramped his muscles. That discomfort was all that had been left behind in the wake of his ordeal.

Ben looked fit but frightened. This was an entirely new and unsettling experience for him. Always before he had been able to penetrate the surrounding environment through the minds of others. Now that he couldn't, it was like being mentally blind. It shook him so much he had to sit on the bed.

It was Jeffrey, however, who was worst off. In a matter of just a few hours he had been possessed by two demons, delivered of them, watched them torture an old friend, and heard a voice from heaven defending that friend. To one who had steadfastly maintained belief in the Pleiadian Sibling story, these events had been enormously shocking. He had done terrible things in the name of these creatures, convincing himself that he was doing them for the greater good of the race. Now the evidence was accumulating that he had been duped—that all the evil he had done had been, in fact, simply *evil.* He was having to adjust to the idea that the all-powerful

Siblings were not all-powerful at all, and that the "religious disguises" they had told him they wore to interact with mankind were actually closer to the truth than the fiction of their being extraterrestrial life-forms. He had staked his life on that trip to the Pleiades—had that, too, been a hoax? Jeffrey looked around at Ben and raised his eyebrows. The boy nodded apologetically—and shrugged.

Gork stuck his bald head back in the room and shouted, "I *said*, you come *too!*"

The three humans got up and shuffled across the curving corridor and into the control room. "You," Gork pointed at Jeffrey, "sit down and determine our location coordinates, and try to find some radio signals. You," he said, his long, slender finger now pointing at Ben, "start describing what you *can* make out of the minds below us. And you," he finished, now pointing at Jack, "find a place to sit or stand and stay out of the way, but I *want you in here*, where I can see you. Ben," he demanded crisply, "describe what you're seeing!"

Ben took a deep breath as a far-away look settled upon his features. "There is someone nearby—he's male—he's hunting—" Ben paused then. As the pause lengthened to a minute, Gork became impatient:

"That's *all?*" the Gray demanded. "*What* is he hunting? Tell me that at least!"

Ben listened in rapt silence. Then he shrugged and said, "I think . . . whatever's there?"

Gork's hard, shark-black eyes peered down at Ben ferociously. He whirled around to Jack. "Location?"

"We're still over New Mexico," Jeffrey said, "although I don't know if they're calling it that yet."

"Radio?" Gork snapped.

"None at all," Jeffrey sighed. "I wonder if it's been invented yet?"

The fallen creatures on the bridge seemed to exchange a single look with one another, as if taking a silent poll on what to do next. Then Gork looked back at Ben. "Do you need English in order to be able to read thoughts?"

"If people think in words—yes, I guess I do. And while I've never really thought about it much before, I suppose people *do* think a lot in language."

The Gray reached over Jeffrey then and punched coordinates into the console. Jeffrey watched, puzzled. "Europe?" he said at last, then narrowed it down to ask, "England?"

"If the boy needs English, perhaps that's the best place to find it." Already the disc was shooting eastward, crossing virgin American forest in route to the Atlantic Ocean and beyond.

Throughout the trip Ben maintained a shifting monitoring of the minds below them. He looked particularly for any trace of technology, any sense of tool use beyond the most rudimentary implements. He found none. In fact, he found very few minds. To someone accustomed to the babbling of thousands of minds all around him all the time, this America seemed to be an empty, lonely place indeed.

Following instructions, Jack had found a seat. Now he watched with fascination the events unfolding before him. Evidently he was watching with too *much* enthusiasm and not enough worry, for Kundas caught his expression and stepped threateningly before him. "What are you grinning at?" the Gray snarled belligerently.

Abashed, Jack looked away as he answered, "I'm just doing as I've been told. I've not been in here much. It's interesting."

"Correction!" Kundas raged. "It's catastrophic! And it's *your* fault we're in this perilous predicament!"

Jack still didn't meet the creature's bug-like eyes, but he did argue back "I don't see it that way. I didn't bring me on this trip, *you* did."

"Not I," Kundas spat out.

"Well, Ruzagnon-Baal there did," said Jack, gesturing toward Gork's back. "If you need to blame somebody, blame him."

"Oh, I do," Kundas seethed, turning himself to look at Gork's back. "I do indeed hold him responsible. Others will, as well," he added ominously, but Gork made no response. He seemed absorbed in his task.

Passing across the Atlantic Ocean, they slipped into night. Within the space of a few minutes they shot over the Emerald Isle of Eire—emerald indeed at this point in its history, although they couldn't see it from the saucer. Moments later they reached their destination and hovered over London.

At any rate, where London *would* be. It wasn't there. There wasn't a light in the night.

They waited until morning, then landed on the spot where London should have been. They all got out to take a look. It just looked like forest to Jack—rich, ancient forest, with lots of enormous old oaks. And it was a gorgeous morning, for it was fall here and the trees were reaching their peak in color. Reds, oranges, and yellows of every shade added their fiery hues to the backdrop of the sunrise. Already a three-inch thick carpet of fallen leaves spread across the forest floor, and while the top layer was wet with dew, the leaves beneath were crisp. An audible crunch marked every step any of them took. *Morning has broken,* Jack hummed to himself. Was this how all forests had been before the coming of the saw? Jack thought wistfully of the little forest near his house and wondered. Would he ever walk under *its* trees again?

"You're certain these are the coordinates I gave you?" Gork asked Jeffrey.

"You didn't give them to me. You punched them in yourself."

"Ah, yes. Thank you for reminding me of that," Gork said with a brittle smile, and for some reason Jack looked at this being's bald, shield-shaped head and felt sorry for him. "There's the Thames," Gork continued, his gesturing toward the river—"or rather, what will *be* the Thames, once people get around to naming it. Dr. Brennen, you're the scholar amongst us! Do you happen to know when London was settled?"

Jack didn't. He shook his head. "Sorry."

"You will be sorry," the Gray snarled. "I very much hope you *will* be sorry soon." Then Gork turned away to pace toward the river. "The first recorded settlement here was planted by the Romans as they conquered the island in—oh, about forty-three years of the common era—what *you* would call A.D., Dr. Brennen. That's right. Forty-three years after your 'God' was born. Look around! You might see an apostle running around somewhere! Oh, but perhaps this would be a little early. Would this be a little early for visiting apostles, Astra?"

Astra's fury at their predicament was evident. "I *hated* this period!" she seethed. "I *loathed* it!"

Gork looked back at Jack and shrugged. "No help there, I'm afraid. Of course, all we really know is that we're here *before* A.D. 43—perhaps years before? Why, your God might not even be born yet! Ho! I have an idea!" Gork said suddenly, swinging about to face the other Grays. "Come, let us go unto Bethlehem and torch every manger we find!"

Jack shivered—then calmed himself. "If they wouldn't even let you harm *me*, what makes you think they'd let you harm Him?"

Gork wheeled around to face him, snarling savagely, "It was a *joke! Just a little joke!* Why is it you Christians have no sense of humor? Why is it you can never even take a little *joke?* Of *course* we won't go down to Bethlehem! Astra, you want to tell these boys why?"

"You do it," she grumbled.

"Because we were *powerless* in that era!" Gork roared.

"I wasn't," Kundas said quietly.

Astra and Gork turned to look at him. There was clearly tension here amongst the Grays, and Jack looked inquiringly at Ben. The boy shrugged as Gork said, "Oh, that's right. You were with the Asmodean group at that point. Conquering the world . . . "

"Conquering you," Kundas answered. Jack couldn't tell for sure, for he really didn't know this Gray well enough to recognize his expressions yet—but he seemed to be smiling.

"A bit of ancient history," Gork explained. "Astra and I and the peoples we ruled had settled the eastern coast of the Mediterranean. We enabled a series of highly successful civilizations, outstripping all of those around us in trade and technology." He turned his black eyes toward Kundas and continued, his voice dripping acid: "Then certain *loyal* associates amongst us turned traitor, and shifted allegiance to another party!"

"That's how the game is played," Kundas responded, and now Jack was sure. Yes, he *was* smiling. "*I'm* the artisan of the group, Baal. I'm the technician. You boasted about the Phoenicians but you never gave me *credit.* I simply threw my weight to a coalition that would do me honor. And we conquered *you.*"

Gork/Baal looked back at the humans and gestured around at the forest. "So our former friends exiled us here—then sent their legions in to conquer us *again.*" Kundas was chortling. "All we had to resist him were family units of Celts. Ah!" The Gray grinned and raised a finger, "but eventually those poor, savage Celts prevailed!"

"Not through superior technology they didn't," said Kundas, and he was back now to his snarling self. "We were undercut by—" Here he stopped himself, and looked directly at Jack. Then he turned and walked back to the saucer, his feet crunching at every step.

Gork/Baal looked back at the three humans. "Ancient history," he said dismissively. "Ben, read any good minds lately?"

The boy rubbed his face in dismay, then shook his head. "There are people around, but I can't understand them."

"Of course not. Even Old English is years away. That's all right. Astra and I speak all the Celtic tongues. You say there are people nearby. Have any of them found *us?* Anybody hiding in those trees out there?"

"None so far."

"Then let's go find *them,* shall we?" Gork shooed them all toward the saucer like a tour guide running behind schedule. In a moment they were airborne again, making a short hop to the East. There they landed again, and once more disembarked.

"Wiltshire, your twentieth-century Englishmen called it," Gork said, sweeping his arms to take in the surrounding area. "But to the people of this time it was simply called the Circle. This way—"

They followed him up a rise and over it, and Jack immediately saw why. The circle of stones stood some distance away still, but it was by far the most impressive feature on the landscape. "Stonehenge," he murmured under his breath.

"Stonehenge indeed," Gork smiled, "and a great place to meet Druids. By the way, from this point I'd like you to refer to me as the Dagda. You can call Astra the Morrigon."

"Or not," Astra snarled. She seemed terribly unhappy to be here.

"Ben? Anyone around?"

"Plenty," Ben answered. "There's a whole tribe of people watching us from behind that grove over there." He pointed to a cluster of larger trees that stood several hundred yards away.

"Ah, yes, I remember that grove. And how are they viewing us?"

"I don't know their speech," Ben reminded Gork again, "but they saw us land in a boat that flies, and they've apparently taken you for gods."

Gork—or rather, "The Dagda," held out his hand to "The Morrigon." "The rest of you, stay here. Come, my dear. Our subjects await." She grudgingly took his hand, and they walked down the incline toward the grove.

As soon as they saw them coming, people hiding in the trees began to run away. Jack watched the escapees carefully. They were dressed in brightly colored garments and golden jewelry, and many of them had flaming red hair. As the Dagda and Morrigon approached them, a courageous few ventured out of the grove to meet them, but it was clear by the expressions on their faces that they were terrified. Soon the Dagda's voice began rolling up the incline toward them, as Gork spoke to these people in a lyrical tongue that just seemed made to be accompanied by a harp.

A moment later the courageous Druids dropped to their faces. Jack couldn't help it. His lip curled up in disgust to watch these fallen creatures play god. Then he glanced around to see if any of the others had caught his sneer. Ben had—of course. Suddenly Ben's forehead clenched in concern, and he looked sharply back down at the parlay. "Jack?" he said uneasily, then added, "Jeffrey?"

"Yes?" Jeffrey answered brightly, barely able to take his eyes off the encounter down the hill.

"Did the Druids sacrifice humans?"

"They did indeed," Jeffrey replied—and he grinned broadly. This was, of course, absolutely fascinating for him. "You think they'll let us watch?"

"They *might* even let us participate," the boy said tremulously, and he began backing up the hill, for "The Dagda" had just pointed up to them. "Jack!" Ben shouted. "Run!"

Jack heard the command, but it took a moment to respond to it. Too long, for by the time he might have started his feet moving, two of the Grays had a strong grip on each of his arms and were ushering him forward.

Gork was grinning at him as he came. "Ah, here he is," he was saying to the white-bearded figures who watched Jack's approach—"your resident missionary." Of course, since he was speaking in English they couldn't understand—*wouldn't* understand. Jack wondered exactly how Gork had described him to *them.* Astra was smiling at him—wickedly, he thought. Gork was explaining:

"We've managed to fix the dating by counting back through clan leaders. This is about 250 B.C., Jack. Oh, I realize you can't really tell them the *gospel* yet, right, since the 'good news' hasn't yet arrived? And they certainly can't understand your language. But they've agreed to host you tonight as an honored guest of the gods. Perhaps you can recall enough Hebrew to give them an Old Testament lesson, hmmm? They're wise folk, these Druids. Who knows—maybe one of them *knows* a little Hebrew!" At that, Gork cackled and gave a command. The Druids grabbed Jack out of the hold of the other Grays, then all four of the fallen walked back up toward the group. A moment later Jeffrey came running back down the hill and thrust something into Jack's hand. . . .

"They say you'll be needing this," he muttered. Jack looked down. It was a disposable lighter.

By the time Jeffrey ran back up to the top of the hill, Ben and the group of Grays had disappeared over it. Jack and those around him were still watching the rise a few minutes later as the saucer suddenly jumped into the sky—and disappeared.

They'd left him behind.

Jack felt certain that no one in history had ever felt more abandoned. He wanted to scream, to bawl, to curl up in a ball on the ground and die. He was more orphaned than any orphan had ever been, for his parents were more than two thousand years from being born! Surely they weren't actually going to *leave* him in this time period? Could the angels of the Lord have saved him from death just to allow him to be misplaced in the third century B.C.? Was he destined somehow to play a role in this century necessary for the eventual coming of the Kingdom of God? What could it be? All of these things ran through his mind as they watched the silver saucer fly away. From that point onward he had little time for speculation. He was struggling to stay alive from one minute to the next.

The Druids all looked very similar to him—aging but robust men with gray beards and piercing blue eyes. It was the eyes that startled him most. These were, after all, savages—yet their eyes were full of intelligence, hungry for wisdom. Jack knew immediately he would never put anything over on these people. More than that: He knew in a heartbeat that he could grow to love them.

One of them began speaking to him. Was he earnestly describing in that lyrical language his understanding of what had just taken place? He gestured toward the spot where the saucer had disappeared, finishing his statement with a gesture of apparent disbelief—then he smiled. It was a beautiful smile, warm and welcoming, and when he waved his arm expectantly back toward the grove, Jack knew instinctively that he was to walk that direction. When he turned and did so, they all smiled and nodded eagerly, clapping one another on the back.

And if this was a trap? Jack thought. What if it was? What could he do about it? Suppose they were taking him into the grove to sacrifice him to the Dagda and the Morrigon, upon the direct instructions of the gods: Did he have any choice but to accompany them trustingly? As they chattered toward him, gesturing toward this and that as they walked into the grove, Jack nodded and smiled and pondered. A missionary, Gork had called him. He'd been mocking, of course, just as he mocked at the birth of Christ and scorned the very name of the Savior born in Bethlehem. But what else *could* he be to these people? Jack wondered. And how very much like the first missionaries to *any* culture must he feel right now?

And so he walked eagerly into the forest with these Celtic wise men, listening to their speech and trying earnestly to understand their words. Soon they came to a clearing within the grove. Here, a kind of model of the great stone circle out on the plain had been laid out upon the forest floor. The model served as stone benches, and they began taking their seats—apparently as assigned. There was clearly some pattern to their arrangement, for some sat next to one another and others left gaps between them. Jack wisely waited to be seated, remembering that over half this group had fled at the sight of the arriving gods. Sure enough, these began to slip back into the sacred grove, and they, too, took their seats. When the ring began to appear full, the first man to speak to him stood up and addressed them all, gesturing frequently to Jack. This was apparently an introduction, for soon this elder stepped back to his own bench, sat down, and waved his arms for Jack to begin.

Jack cleared his throat. "Well," he said, turning in a slow circle to look at each pair of eyes focused on him. "I . . . ah . . . I can't help but feel I'm . . . I'm about to address a faculty meeting. Somehow you look like a gathering of Ph.D.'s." He smiled at this and looked down. When he looked back up at them they, too, were smiling—mostly in confusion, he decided. "I . . . I do wish I had a translator. I've spoken to groups through translation before, and it's comforting to see faces nodding with sudden understanding, rather than just peering at me like I've lost my mind. But—since that's impossible—why don't I just go ahead and tell you what I think, hmm?" Perhaps his raised eyebrows were a universal signal of inquiry, or perhaps this was a common expression in this culture as well as in his own. In any case, they all seemed to shrug and nod to each other.

"I . . . I can't help but think of my grandfathers—on both sides—who traced their lineage back to Irish sources. I wonder if, somehow, we might all be actually related by blood." They were listening, and Jack was warming to his subject—and it suddenly occurred to him that here he was, doing the very thing he did best. Did it matter that they couldn't understand a word he said? "To be sure, we *are* all related by blood. We bear in each of us the blood of God's children, a universal family to which all races and languages belong. More than that. We are related by the blood of this God's only son, who came to seek and to—who *will* come to seek out each person and save that person into God's kingdom—by His blood. And you? You who precede His coming, who obviously seek diligently after the God of this world so that you may worship Him? I wonder how He will judge you? Will He condemn you because you've been duped by these so-called gods in their silvery sky-boats? Will you become part of those 'spirits in prison' to whom Peter says Christ Jesus went and preached while He was in the grave? Or is that group reserved only for those who wouldn't listen to the long-suffering God, back in the time of Noah?" Jack paused then, wondering at his own questions—and wondering how these people, who couldn't understand a word he said, could listen to him with such rapt attention. Their eyes, so bright with interest and intellect, made him suddenly very sad.

"I hope," Jack said, "that God in His mercy finds a way to open Himself to you. I hope that with all my heart. But—since you can't understand me anyway, I might as well go on and say this—if I am to interpret properly the words *I* have received from God, I have to tell you that there is no other way *to* God except through the sacrificial death of Jesus Christ on a Roman cross—an event I have been *told* will not take place for almost another three hundred years. So what can I say to you? Do I really have any message for you at all?" Jack realized now that he was, in fact, talking to himself. He determined that he wouldn't do that, that he would talk to *them*, whether they understood or not: "Only this. God who made the world, who grew these gorgeous trees and who made you and me and our ancestors—that very God does not fly around in spaceships made by hands. That God does not exchange disguises for every new group of people. That God loves you, and wants to save you from the words of the Dagda—"

"Ah!" several of them said at once, excited at having recognized a word. Then they nodded to one another excitedly, and gestured for him to go on.

Jack couldn't go on. The more he spoke now, he feared, the more he would reinforce the very idea furthest from the truth—that he was an emissary from saucer gods, from the Dagda and the Morrigon and whomever else they'd been taught to worship. He shook his head in frustration—shrugged elaborately—and looked around for a place to sit down.

They were surprised at this. The leader of the gathering gestured for him to continued, but Jack just smiled wearily and looked down. The leader took him by the hand then, and leading him to an empty place in the circle gestured for him to sit. Jack did so, with a sigh—and felt hands from both sides pat him on the back. Then others rose to speak. And speak, and speak, and speak. . . . Once again Jack was reminded of a faculty meeting. But he'd never attended a faculty meeting that had extended without a break from early morning until late afternoon! He couldn't remember it all—had he dozed some? By the time the shadows began to lengthen, his tailbone had become far too well acquainted with this backless stone bench. He had some other needs as well. Didn't any of these Druids have them too?

Apparently not—for night came on, yet there was still no pause in the speeches, nor any break for dinner. Daylight faded, and still they talked. Soon he could see nothing in the utter blackness of the night. Then someone began to sing—or chant, rather—and the whole group took up the chorus. He was aware of people standing up all around him, and then hands reached down to pull him up as well. Then they were moving out of this circle in single file, and helpful hands guided him into his place in line.

Chanting in unison, the line of Druids snaked out of the grove and out under the stars—and Jack looked up in wonder. Few times in his life had he ever been far enough away from city lights to see such a panorama of the night sky. It was grand—glorious. He praised God for it.

He could see a little bit now—by starlight. They were on their way to Stonehenge, walking down to it with stately, measured tread. *Surely they didn't do this every day,* Jack thought to himself. Was this a festival of some kind? He stumbled, and someone behind him caught him. He tried then to watch where he was going—as well as he could, anyway, in such darkness. He was a city boy, he had to confess—accustomed to well-lighted streets. When he tripped again he remembered the lighter in his pocket. *That's why they had Jeffrey bring it to me!* Jack realized, and he pulled it out and flicked it.

Never had he heard such screams of rage! Never had he been so quickly buried under a mass of flying bodies and fists! Never had he been pummeled so mercilessly or raged at so violently, and all because he'd flicked on a flame? They grabbed it away from him, of course—extinguished it immediately—but that didn't extinguish their anger. These gentle souls who had reasoned and debated so formally all day long were now beating him—kicking him—kicking him—

* * *

He jerked awake—but he didn't jerk far. His body was immobilized—he'd been bound. It was daylight, apparently—bright daylight. He wondered what time it was? He didn't have any trouble remembering the events of the night before. His head still hurt from where they'd kicked him unconscious. He *did* wonder what it was that he'd done, exactly, that had caused this response. Well, no, he remembered what he'd *done.* He'd made a flame, and that was obviously a big—

Mistake. *Samhain!* Jack thought to himself. Samhain, the holiday that had been turned into Halloween. He remembered now. Oh, what a big mistake! Samhain, the night of darkness, when all the people were required by the Druids to extinguish all of their fires. The Druids would then lead in the ceremony to light a new, central fire for the entire nation, and each clan would be invited to relight their own household fires from that one. That's why the day-long talk-fest. That's why the unlighted parade down to the circle of stones. That's why they'd kicked the stuffings out of him—because he'd lit a fire on the night of darkness. That was like—cursing out loud in church. No, worse than that. This was a national festival, the New Year celebration. He'd profaned the Celtic New Year, something they might be thinking could cause them disasters in the coming months— "Oh boy," Jack murmured. It was like he'd threatened the President.

His words alerted his guards. He recognized their faces as two of the group from the day before. Today they weren't smiling. They pulled him to his feet with a cruel jerk, then began to kick his bound legs forward. Were they trying to make him hop? Jack hopped, and they stopped kicking. He kept on hopping, his weight supported on each side by these two gentle scholars, turned raging warriors of their faith by their righteous indignation. Jack hopped all the way out of the grove.

They made the same turn toward the right, down toward the circle of enormous stones. It had stood here, Jack knew, two thousand years already—what would it be witness to today? From this distance he could see that there was something in the midst of the circle that wasn't there yesterday—a construction of some sort that rose up out of it. Struggling now to recall all he had read of Celtic observance so as not to break another taboo, he scanned this structure for clues—and remembered. The closer they got, the more clear the outline became. This was a giant "man," woven out of wicker—a cage, of sorts, into which someone would be locked. Then, at an appropriate moment in the ceremony, the wicker man—and its occupant—would be burned. *What an appropriate punishment,* Jack thought ironically, *for someone who had profaned the night of darkness.*

"Touch not the Lord's anointed," Jack mumbled—a little bitterly, he guessed, though he was certainly not bitter toward the angel who'd said it. He was thinking instead of Gork and the others—even Jeffrey—and how they'd been certain to place into his hands the means for him to "sin" on his own. To sin as far as this culture was concerned. "Then again," Jack said aloud, still hopping, "that's what they *always* do!" His two companions frowned at him, and it was too hard to talk and hop at the same time, so he shut up. But his mind was finishing his thought: *The fallen put into our hands the means of our own condemnation.*

They hopped him into the ancient monument, and all the way over to the wicker figure. There was a tiny door open in its side—big enough for them to toss him in, then quickly weave it shut. His guards wasted no time. They went right to it, and made ready to push him in. But first the elder came up to him and started a speech. It would be a long speech, if yesterday was any measure, so Jack figured he had some time for a lengthy prayer of his own.

Lord, he thought, *I don't know why You have me here—or even if You have me here. And I don't know why this has to happen—if indeed it does. I know You rescued Shadrach, Meshach, and Abednego out of that fiery furnace, and this looks like it could be just as hot in just a few minutes. I know, if You should choose, You could rescue me as well. But even if You don't, Lord . . . The only reason I can figure that I'm standing here right now is because I've tried my best to be true to You. So—whatever happens—if I'm coming home to You now, or I'm about to wake up from a dream and turn over to hug Gloria, or whatever—I love You, Lord. Thank You for letting me know You. In the name of Jesus I pray it . . . Amen.*

While he was finished with his prayer, the elder was evidently not finished with his speech. Jack took the opportunity to glance around. A big crowd had gathered to witness his execution—several hundred at least. They were all glaring at him angrily. He tried smiling back at them, but that only seemed to make them angrier. He looked up, then, at this monument surrounding him, and couldn't prevent a tourist slogan from popping into his mind: SEE HISTORIC STONEHENGE, IF IT'S THE LAST THING YOU DO! He smiled at that. Odd, he thought, that he should be smiling in the face of his death. No, he corrected himself, it *wasn't* odd at all. It was the grace of God.

The speech was over. They unbound him, then picked him up and tossed him through the trapdoor of the wicker man. Several women rushed forward quickly to weave it shut, but Jack made no attempt to crawl back out of it. He simply walked to the front of the structure and looked out at the elder, who now stood ceremoniously in front of it.

The man met his gaze with those piercing, sky-blue eyes—and held up the lighter.

Chapter Eighteen

Resurrecting the Reich

Nice touch, Jack thought to himself—setting him aflame with his own lighter. But did the Druid elder know how to work it?

With a press of his thumb the blue-eyed priest proved that, while he might be an ancient, he wasn't an old fool. He'd had all morning to figure it out, Jack realized. Besides, if babies could figure lighters out well enough to set houses on fire, he figured it was probably no great puzzle for the combined brain trust of the Celtic community.

As the flame burst upward, apparently from the Druid's fingers, the gathered host broke into a roar of amazed approval. The priest held the flame up over his head and turned in a slow circle, acknowledging the cheers of his people. Then he returned his attention to Jack. After pronouncing some final sentence upon Jack, he held the flame out toward the wicker.

It never touched the wicker frame. A mighty rumble shook the sky, and he jerked his hand away. In concert with the entire crowd he turned his face upward in time to see a disc of silver flash across the sky above them. They saw just a flash—then it disappeared.

A flood of private conversation greeted the saucer's second appearance in as many days, momentarily eclipsing the ceremony. Many in the crowd looked at Jack as the obvious source of such portents. The Druid evidently got their attention back by making just such a statement, and once again all eyes focused on Jack. Since the lighter had gone out, the old priest once again lit the flame.

Once again the silver saucer buzzed the ancient circle, and this time some of the onlookers took it as a cue to depart. A discussion began between the elder Druid and one of his lieutenants, and Jack wondered if perhaps they were arguing about whether or not to go on. If so, the older Druid won, and once more he flicked the lighter.

Suddenly there was a whole series of appearances and disappearances, coming from every point of the compass, happening at such great frequency that some appearances overlapped others, and each one resulting in an ear-pounding boom. At one point there appeared to be three different saucers in the sky at once, each ripping the fabric of the heavens a little more loudly. By this time the crowd was no longer watching the execution. They were running away in all directions, many screaming in terror.

The elder stood his ground for a few moments longer than the rest, but when the booms would not stop, he dropped the lighter and sprinted out of Stonehenge and up the hillside to the grove. By the time the saucer appeared for good, hovering directly above the wicker man, no one was left inside Stonehenge except Jack. Slowly the silver disc descended to earth, shifting to the side at the last possible moment to avoid crushing the structure and its contents. Jack marveled. What in the world had happened?

It was Astra—the Morrigon—who left the saucer and came to get him out. She didn't look at all pleased by this turn of events, but she did make quick work of freeing him. Dressed in an intricately decorated wool gown of brightest red, she indeed looked the part of an ancient goddess intervening in the spiritual affairs of mankind.

Jack stared at her, incredulous. "Why are you doing this?" he asked.

"It certainly wasn't my idea," she snarled—even as she outwardly continued performing every movement with an air of solemn dignity.

"Nice costume," Jack said as he pulled himself through the hole in the wicker and dropped back down onto the grass.

"Don't waste any more of our time," Astra snapped. "Just go immediately and get onto the ship!" Jack did as he was told, but he watched over his shoulder as he went. She had picked up the lighter and, with a dramatic flourish of both arms, she raised it above her head much as the Druid had done. While there was no one in sight, obviously the fallen believed they were being watched. Stooping gracefully, Astra lit the enormous wicker basket on fire—and stepped back. Turning slowly, she walked back to the saucer. While she never looked back, Jack stood in the portal watching. He couldn't help but shiver as the huge structure burned. Before Astra's foot touched the bottom of the ramp every part of it was aflame. Before she reached the top, it was crumbling. It would have been a terrible way to die.

"Thank You, Lord," he breathed quietly.

"Better thank your angels," said Ben, and Jack noticed then that the boy was standing behind him. Astra shot them both an alien sneer as she took one of the branching corridors. The door whispered shut behind her, and they were airborne. All this happened as Jack was replying:

"The Lord directs them, in any case—but why do you say that?"

"They wouldn't let us leave you."

"But you *did* leave," said Jack. He was smiling—but it was a fake smile. Only now that he was back on board the saucer was he realizing just how betrayed and abandoned he'd felt the day before.

"Time travel—remember?" Ben said. "Kundas tried to take us into another time period—must have tried a dozen times—but each time we fell back out of the black we were still here. It got dangerous—after a time. We were criss-crossing our own path, nearly crashing into ourselves—yes, just like that!" Ben said, pointing to Jack. Jack had been thinking of the old phrase "meeting yourself coming and going." "That's exactly what we were doing."

"But how did the angels—"

"That voice came again: 'Touch not the Lord's anointed.'" Ben searched Jack's face, clearly puzzled but also apparently impressed. The look embarrassed Ben, and he blushed. "I understand what the word means," Ben continued. "I can read how you *feel* about it—but how did the Lord anoint you? And pardon me if this sounds insulting, but—why *you?*"

Good question! Jack thought to himself, not bothering to voice the thought since the boy would read it anyway. *Why me, Lord?* Then the words from Isaiah 61 came to mind, the same words Jesus had read to his hometown synagogue. *The spirit of the Lord God is upon me, because the Lord hath anointed me to preach good tidings unto the meek. . . .* Jack finished quoting the verses in his mind, finishing with what he saw as the bottom line: *that the Lord might be glorified.* He looked at Ben, who was watching him carefully. "That's it, I guess. That's why me. Because I'm here and I'm willing. Haven't you told me all along that *you* picked me to go along on this trip?"

"I always thought I did," Ben murmured. "I'm beginning to wonder if *I* had all that much to do with it."

Jack smiled at an idea that popped into his head. "Ben, have you ever felt like someone might be reading *your* thoughts?"

Without warning, they were dropping again into the time void. Darkness flooded instantly in around them, and Jack closed his eyes against the inevitable sense of vertigo. He grabbed his stomach, fearful at first that he was going to throw up, then remembering just how empty he was from hours of not eating. Neither feeling was at all comfortable. He wondered where they were going now. . . .

"Somewhere besides Celtic England, I hope," Ben muttered.

"Where are the fallen *trying* to go?"

"Somewhere where they hope they can control their own fate. I guess you've recognized by now that they're trying to hide somewhere in time?"

"From whom? The angels?"

"Makes sense to me," came Ben's reply. "But you have to remember that I've watched through the eyes of believers as this ship has been blocked and hurled around by beings you Christians *see*—while others don't. Jeffrey is still convinced they're battling against another race of aliens."

Jack tested his eyes against the darkness. It was too overwhelming. He closed them again. "But what about the voice you say you heard—"

"Oh, Jeffrey's not disputing that he heard that voice. He just thinks it's some kind of trick—a deception of that rival alien race. He's been involved in clandestine operations so long that that's the only conclusion his mind will allow him to draw."

Jack shook his head sadly. Then: "What do *you* think?" he asked Ben.

The boy made no reply, and in the darkness Jack was not able to read his expression. In fact, Jack's question was met with such silence that he suddenly feared Ben was no longer there—

"Oh. I'm here all right."

Jack nodded then, relieved. Still, Ben made no response. Jack wondered why.

"I'm still thinking about what you said."

"Which?"

"That maybe your God is reading my mind. . . ."

It had seemed to Jack that they'd been in the time void a long time. It occurred to him that some words were completely meaningless in this state. *Wouldn't it be hellish,* he thought, *to be caught in such a place forever?*

"Don't even *think* it!" Ben said quickly, anxiety oozing from every word. This was new, Jack thought. The boy usually appeared so confident, so in control— "Of course," Ben snapped, and now Jack could hear that he was so frightened he was near tears. "I seem confident because I know what's going on! But you don't understand how it's been on this ship without you here! I kept wondering each time we dropped into this darkness if we were *in* hell, and if we'd ever get out! And when they kept throwing us back into the same time over and over again—"

They were out. There was light, the ship had power again—there was hope. Jack put his arm around the boy's shoulder, and the teenager sagged against him. "Thank God!" the boy whispered.

"Exactly," Jack whispered back.

The crisis passed. Ben straightened up and got that look on his face that meant he was monitoring thoughts all around them. Then he frowned, and looked at Jack. "You're not going to like this," he said quietly, and Jack didn't already.

"Why? Where are we?" he asked nervously.

"What's the worst time period you can think of? The period where these creatures' intervention could do the most damage to the world?"

The cross! Jack thought to himself in horror. They were going to try to undo the cross!

"No!" the boy said, frowning in surprise. "That's not at all what I thought you would think! We're in Hitler's Germany now, Jack. They're trying to rescue the Third Reich."

"Oh!" Jack grunted in dismay. "*That* worst time in history!" There had been so many. . . .

"Right, but *this* is the worst time to you. And what's worst for *me* is that I don't know German any better than I knew Gaelic—"

Throughout this trip they had never moved from the corridor. Now the ramp was dropping open, and they heard footsteps scurrying around the corridor toward them from both sides. They stepped back against the wall as the portal opened. Then Jack gasped, and slunk back further still. They were underground again. And waiting for them on a wooden landing dock were a dozen black-uniformed Teutons, the pride of Hitler's nation. Jack recognized them immediately from their black-peaked hats and the death's-head insignia: SS stormtroopers. But the sight that actually took his breath away was the most ubiquitous symbol of all in this place: On the red armband, within a circle of white, the black swastika looked like a poisonous spider. Another shock quickly followed. In this place, the occupants of the craft didn't go *out.* The stormtroopers came *in.*

Jack watched their hard faces as they marched up the ramp, and realized they were really not hard at all. In fact they were quite expressive and warm. It was the setting in which their faces were framed that made them look so terrifying—the black uniform, the hat, the armband. These things along with the fact that they all looked so much *alike.* That was it, Jack realized. Like they had all been cloned from a single, handsome-faced blonde, and in the process of reproducing that outward beauty all inner beauty had been bled away. But of course, cloning had been unknown in World War II. *Hadn't it?* Jack thought desperately, sudden fear racing his heart. One of these warriors stopped in front of Jack, thrust his movie-star face into Jack's face and smiled. Sick at heart and weak in soul, Jack smiled back. "Ja!" the man grunted, and laughed. Then he moved on with the others, apparently on a tour of the ship. Jack stood against the wall, humiliated. He couldn't look at Ben. He knew that Ben knew that, in that moment of fear, he had actually *contemplated* saying, "Heil Hitler!"

"I'm scared too, Jack," the boy whispered, graciously setting him at ease.

The Nazis moved on through the ship, German comments shooting back and forth between them. Jack wished now he had concentrated harder in the ninth grade. All he could remember of his German was how to say "good morning, how are you?" to someone called Louisa, and Louisa's reply of "Thanks, good. And you?" He had the feeling that wouldn't get him very far in this place. He was thinking again about the Druids, and how he had functioned there without language. Somehow, even though he had studied German and knew something of this time period, how much more frightening would it be to be abandoned *here*. . . .

"Maybe that's because you *do* know something of the time period—and of the dangers," Ben commented.

"Thanks for cheering me up," Jack growled. "Don't you have any other minds to read?"

"Only Jeffrey's, and he's as scared as you are. The rest of the human minds around us are thinking only in German—when they're not thinking of mathematical formulas or rocket designs."

"Is this place a—weapons research center?" Jack wondered aloud. Ben shrugged, but that made sense to Jack. And what could German rocket scientists do with a machine like this one? They were completing the tour now, coming round the other side, and Jack heard the Germans in intense conversation with Kundas and Gork. He was noting with growing alarm how comfortable the Nazis appeared to feel with the Grays—and how fluently the fallen conversed with them in their own language. As the column swept by them, Jack shot a thought at Ben: *Later, would you please explain to me all you know about the relationship between the Grays and the Reich?*

Before Ben could give him any response, the German who had first approached them slid his arm around Jack's neck. "Kommen sie, bitte," he said, smiling. Even without the choke hold, Jack knew enough to know he'd been invited down the rampway. Since the man had another arm for Ben, the boy came too.

There were swastikas on the wall down here. Jack noticed that first. Against the grays of the live rock from which this tunnel had been carved, it was hard to miss the brilliant red and black banners. They apparently served as a permanent reminder of the purpose toward which all denizens of this underground city worked.

And it was a city. The walls climbed up at least fifty feet into the air, then arched up even higher to meet in vaulted ceilings. Steel girders held the roof in place—probably unnecessary, except as protection against Allied bombing raids. Even live rock wouldn't be able to resist a direct hit. This tunnel extended as far as he could see in either direction—and that was far, for the lines of the place were straight and its lights were strong. Besides this tunnel he could see other openings, transverse tunnels that intersected this one at regular intervals in both directions. Forty feet above them ran a system of conveyers that were, even now, bearing engines from one part of this vast complex to another. A small-gauge train track ran through the heart of the system. A child-sized engine chugged past them, pulling behind it open-bed wagons, currently ferrying workers from one location to another. With trains clacking and conveyer belts clinking and drills and hammers adding their noise from workstations on every side, it was very hard to hear anything that was being said. The troopers ushered them across the platform to board yet another train, this one full-sized but with only a single, standard-sized passenger carriage. They boarded this car and, upon a signal from one of the stormtroopers, it began moving.

Ben and Jack sat in the back of the carriage on opposite sides of the aisle. The Grays sat in front of them, and Jack noticed with interest that no one seemed to be pointing out the sights to them. It was as if each was recognized and welcomed under this mountainside—as if all were guests of long-standing. Remembering the subterranean base in 1990s America, Jack began to wonder whether the Grays were even *considered* guests in this place—if, perhaps, it were the Nazis who were welcome visitors? Of course, there *were* those red and black banners everywhere. But who was to say the fallen had not been a part of that hate-mongering organization since its beginning? Jack glanced across the aisle at Ben in time to see him raise his eyebrows meaningfully. The thought gave him a chill.

The train glided through this section of tunnel and another before turning off down one of the intersecting tunnels. They rolled to the apparent end of it and the track loop, and there debarked. They were standing before a wall inset with several levels of windows—rather like a multi-story building inside a cave. They went inside and up in an elevator to the fourth floor. There they stepped out into a large, elegantly-furnished banquet room. Crisp tablecloths and polished silverplate awaited their arrival. Dinner was served.

Ravenous after going a day and a half without a meal, Jack ate heartily. The cooking equaled anything he'd ever eaten in his lifetime. With each bite he became more convinced that they were at the pinnacle of the Reich—of its scientific community, in any case. And while the food was wonderful and the setting unique, the implications of the visit were terrifying to him.

The fallen did not eat. They waited until their human cohorts were well into their meal—and into their schnapps—before beginning negotiations. What they were negotiating Jack had no idea. Despite that fact, he had no question that that's precisely what these were. He did hope that his own future and freedom were not in some way being bargained away. . . .

At length, Baal/Gork looked down the table at him and addressed him directly: "Dr. Brennen! What do you think of our little munitions factory? We're very efficient here—a very important contributor to the success of the Reich. The Fuhrer regards this facility as a model of what all his factories should be. He's quite impressed with us. I guess I don't need to add—we're rather impressed with him as well."

"I'm a little surprised that he regards you so positively," Jack responded, putting his fork down. "I don't really think you meet his criterion for racial purity."

"On the contrary," Gork laughed. "Herr Hitler regards us as German to the core! We are the dwarfs of German legend, don't you see? The funny little creatures who live and work under the mountain? He loves us. He admires us. He *listens* to us, Dr. Brennen. And why not? We *made* him. We are quintessential German archetypes, equal partners with the Aryan super-race we've played a part in *building*. He believes that. And he listens to us carefully when we speak of that *other* race, that subhuman Semitic species that has controlled the money markets of the world and infested with its agents every government but his own. And if we were to suggest a final solution to him of the 'Jewish Problem,' don't you think he would listen? He has, Dr. Brennen. He has put it into action with that same ruthless, Germanic discipline that has allowed him to conquer Europe!"

"Most of Europe," Jack muttered. "I assume Churchill is still at Number 10, and the RAF is still keeping the Luftwaffe away from the Island?"

"Momentarily," Gork shrugged. Then he smiled that hideous, alien smile, and said "Can you imagine, however, how a Spitfire would match up against our saucer? What about hundreds of our saucers? Do you really think London would survive *that* sort of blitz—whether the Yanks come or not?"

"You're forgetting that it didn't happen that way," Jack shrugged.

"I forget *nothing!*" Gork roared, rising from his place at the head of the table. The Germans had been taking in this conversation with the mild amusement of men who know an enemy is being taunted, even though not understanding the taunts. Now several of them stood up in support of Gork and turned cool, threatening looks upon Jack. "I do know *this.* The past can be changed! The past *can* be changed, because we're here to change it! And you, Dr. Brennen, will be privileged to see our victory! First, you'll see the victory of the old Germanic gods over that desert tribe that forced their God upon the whole civilized world! Then you'll see our triumph over that upstart Jewish God himself! You'll watch us mold this super-race into a race of space-faring shock troops. We *may* even take you with us, Dr. Brennen, upon one of our campaigns of conquest. Then we'll let these fine young gentlemen strip you naked and toss you out with the garbage, into the 'outer darkness' of space. No weeping or gnashing of teeth there, Jack. Your body will just become one eternal popsicle. How's that for a glimpse into the future?"

"I've been in the future," Jack replied slowly. "I'm *from* the future. If you're so certain of your new vision of the future, why is it that you've taken to hiding in the past? Do you really think the angels won't find you here, too?"

Gork's smile was cruel—but also ultimately unconvincing. "With all you've seen, are you going to persist in *believing* in these winged crusaders for justice? You might just as well place your faith in Batman!"

"With all I've seen," Jack answered, "I would be a fool *not* to place my faith in the God who created this universe. Now if you'll excuse me," he stood up, placing his napkin beside his plate.

"No, I will not excuse you!" Gork snarled. "You are excused from nothing. You are remanded into the custody of these fine stormtroopers until such a time as we're certain that our efforts to resurrect the Reich are successful. Isn't that one of your favorite words, Brennen? Resurrection? Watch us put it into effect here, my friend. I'm certain the results of our efforts will bring you much joy!" The Grays rose then from the table, and trooped back to the elevator. When Jack started to follow them, his way was blocked by one of the stormtroopers. The man smiled down at Jack while he did so, but there was nothing in his eyes that suggested he might be merciful in the enforcement of his commands. Jack sat back down, and so did the German, returning to eating with obvious pleasure.

"So, Fritz," Ben said suddenly. "You really enjoy that sausage?"

"*Ja!*" Fritz grinned—then his face fell, and he frowned. Ben glanced at Jack and winked.

Obviously, Jack thought to Ben, *Stormtrooper Fritz here knows English. And I suppose he wasn't supposed to let us know?* Ben winked again, and nodded.

When the remaining troopers had eaten their fill, they escorted Jack and Ben to quarters within this building. These were not cells but were truly guest rooms, each with its own bathroom, and locks on the insides of the doors. Jack noticed quickly, however, that there were also locks on the *outsides* of the doors. Since it was no longer a secret that Fritz could understand their conversations, the big German took great care in explaining to them in heavily accented English that they were not to go anywhere without one of the guards accompanying them. Since the guards would not always be available, there would naturally be times when they would need to remain inside their rooms. "Aside from these simple instructions, then," Fritz finished, "you are completely free!" The guards proceeded then to lock them into their separate rooms.

Jack glanced around. There was a radio—unfortunately it could only receive stations broadcasting in German. There was reading material—once again, nothing in English. Jack laid back on the bed and tried to visualize what was taking place right now. He guessed German rocket scientists were already swarming over the saucer, examining, measuring, testing. How long would it take them to duplicate one? How long after that to put it into production? It seemed inconceivable to Jack that history could be somehow changed, but that they were here—*somewhere*—couldn't be denied. Every time-travel story Jack had ever read or seen had centered somehow around the time-travel paradox. But if this had indeed happened during the last days of the Reich—Gork *had* used the word resurrection, so Jack just assumed these must be the Nazis' last days—and if the German scientists were indeed capable of reproducing saucers quickly enough to change the outcome of the war, then how in the world could he be here? The world he'd grown up in would have been different—wouldn't it?

It would have been helpful to talk these things over with Ben—he assumed the boy was reading his mind at this very moment—but the boy's room was across the hall. The only way Ben could talk back would be through pounding on his door. A moment later Jack heard pounding down the hall, and smiled. *I hear you,* he thought to Ben. *And perhaps if we remain in this attractive guardhouse very long we might need to develop that as a means of your talking back to me. But let's save it until we need it.*

Jack heard one more heavy clump, then the boy left him to his fiction of mental privacy. He got off his bed to investigate the chest of drawers and found clean underwear and socks, along with a robe, pajamas, and towels. In the bathroom a shaving kit had been laid out for him—*if* he cared to experiment with a straight razor. He decided that could wait. But he did relish a nice bath, and it was at least a half-hour later before Jack left the steaming bathroom in pajamas and slippers. The bed looked and felt wonderful, and sleep came quickly. But before he closed his eyes there was time for prayer. He prayed, very simply, "Lord—whatever they're trying to make happen here—please don't permit it. . . ."

* * *

Where was Jeffrey? That question had begun to bother him in the night. Was he still aboard the saucer? Had they taken him off in another direction for a different set of meetings? Was he doing a seminar for German spies on "Spy Techniques in the Future?" Since the guards had informed them that they would eat all meals together, he resolved he would ask Ben first thing in the morning.

As soon as they saw one another, however, the boy shook his head no. After a hearty breakfast Ben asked if they might be permitted to walk down to the saucer and fetch some personal items off. Fritz shrugged to the others, and they all said "Ja," Fritz and another agreed to take this first duty, and since they preferred each other's company to that of Ben or Jack, they hung back and allowed the two visitors to walk before them.

"He's hiding in the saucer," Ben whispered as soon as it was possible.

"Why?"

"Why do you think? He thinks they're going to find out he's a Jew."

"What?" Jack frowned. "He's not a Jew! He was christened as an—"

"Shhhh," Ben whispered.

"He was christened as an Episcopalian as a baby." Jack finished.

"That's what he always told you," Ben shrugged. "Guess you didn't know him as well as you thought you did, hunh?"

That was, of course, precisely what Jack was thinking. He started to speak again and Ben cut him off. "Just—*think it* over to me. That's safer."

Very well then, haven't there been scientists poring over every inch of that vessel? How has he avoided them?

"He hasn't." Jack was confused. "They found him first thing yesterday after we arrived."

Then why haven't they—

"Some of these scientists are Jewish too. And *some* of them—" Ben stopped walking, and turned around to the SS troops behind them. He spoke to Fritz particularly, waving him forward to ask him a question. In case any of these other warriors also spoke English, he leaned up to whisper it.

Fritz flushed. Then he straightened up to his full height, obviously deciding whether to get angry or not. The other stormtrooper watched him suspiciously. Then, abruptly, he laughed. He waved his friend over and whispered something to him quietly. Whatever he said brought on raucous laughter, as much from Fritz as from the other guard. Then he murmured something else. With more laughter and a knowing look at Jack and Ben, the other soldier turned around and went back to the barracks. When Fritz turned back to them, his face wore a very sober expression indeed. "Come," he said quickly. "I'll show you."

He led them off the main tunnel then, into one of the side tunnels, then walked them swiftly into another, much less attractive building and down two flights of stairs. They were now below the floor-line of the main tunnels. There was a low buzz of voices coming from the other side of a door. After a last glance around, Fritz quietly knocked upon it, and the voices stopped. Someone opened it slowly, then at the sight of Fritz nodded assent and threw it open wide.

It was a very large room, and poorly lighted, but Jack could see enough to know immediately what was going on. Perhaps a hundred laborers, scientists, and soldiers were gathered in circle. They were on their knees—praying.

"You want to join us, ja?" Fritz asked, and Jack immediately answered:

"Ja! We do!"

Then Fritz grabbed them each by an arm, and leaned his face down to them. "We *know* who—or what—the gray beings are. We will *never* allow them to succeed!"

At that moment—as if in dreadful answer to their unified prayers—the Allied bombs began rocking the tunnels above.

Chapter Nineteen

The tower to heaven

It was a direct hit. This underground base had been found—or betrayed. And while the steel girders were playing their part in keeping the roof from immediately caving in, the walls were heaving in the face of this man-induced earthquake, and people ran screaming for cover.

Jack and Ben reacted instinctively. They knew exactly where they were in relation to the saucer, and they knew, too, what would be the reaction of the fallen to this potential catastrophe. Even now the engines would be churning to start it up. And if the Grays happened to be already aboard, then it would be gone before they arrived.

No one stopped them. No one stopped anyone else, for everyone had mutual need: protection. Dust was falling from the ceiling where the rock took a direct hit, or scraped against a girder. Lightbulbs were popping, showering anyone below them with glass. Still they ran, for the saucer was in sight, and the ramp was down. They bounded up it with time to spare, for they could hear now the whistle of that one-car train as it steamed at full speed toward this spot. They felt certain it was bearing Grays from elsewhere in these tunnels.

White-coated technicians stood in the doorway, watching the rocking ceiling with terror. "You want to go with us?" Ben asked—but of course they couldn't understand.

"Offen-sie, schnell!" Jack was yelling—hoping he'd just told them to get off quickly. They were looking at him strangely, though, so he pushed one of them down the ramp and shouted, "Schnell!" again.

The rest of them seemed to get the idea then, and they were still scampering out of the craft as the train came screeching to a stop on the tracks beyond the dock, its metal wheels scraping the rails with a squeal to equal a thousand fingernails on blackboards. Grays began tumbling off of it—far more than they had brought. Jack estimated two dozen, then a piece of rock bounced off the top of the craft and he ducked out of the doorway himself. Ben was already turning into his cabin, so Jack followed him inside and they shut the door. There were footsteps in the corridor, curses and screams, and a constant stream of apparent debate in that strange tongue he'd only heard the Grays use a few times since he'd been aboard.

They heard the hatch snap shut. They heard the engines whine upward. Then—blackness.

It seemed like several minutes before either of them said anything. Then when Ben at last spoke, it wasn't to Jack. "Jeffrey? Are you all right?"

"Are we out of that terrible place?" came a muffled response. Jeffrey was clearly under a bed.

"We're in the black again. Can't you tell?"

"I've been in the black for days!"

"Just one day," Jack said. "It was only one day, wasn't it?" he asked Ben, suddenly unsure of himself. They'd been underground, after all.

"Seemed like forever."

"Why didn't you tell me you were Jewish?" Jack asked. "We were best friends! I thought we told each other everything?"

"What was the point?" Jeffrey answered, still from under the bed. "I didn't believe any of it. I figured if I *did* you'd just try to 'evangelize' me."

"I did some of that anyway, as I recall."

"You think I don't?" Jeffrey responded.

"In any case, you fooled me. Didn't you think you could fool these Nazis?"

"A lot more at stake this time, wouldn't you say?" Jeffrey answered sardonically. "I couldn't tell you, Jack. I couldn't tell anybody. I had aunts and uncles *perish* at the hands of these creatures. Knowing that kind of thing scars a kid."

"I guess it would, yeah. But wouldn't Ruzagnon have protected you?"

Jeffrey paused a moment before answering. "I don't know if you may have noticed this, Jack, but—I don't think the Grays are very happy with *any* of us human passengers at the moment."

"The *Grays?*" Jack said. "You're not calling them the Space Siblings anymore?"

"I let go of *that* dream two or three time hops up the line," Jeffrey answered wearily.

"But Ben said you still believed that other aliens were—"

"I *wanted* to believe that, Jack. So much so that I kept on telling my mind I believed it. But whenever the Boss told me he would reserve me a spot at Auschwitz, it just became impossible to view them as 'our older brothers and sisters' anymore."

There was a lag, then, in the conversation, and the two of them became aware of the sniffling at the same moment. "Ben?" Jack said? "What's the matter?"

"Ben?" Jeffrey added, finally climbing out from under the safety of the bed. It was a moment before either one of them could find him.

He was laying on the bed Jeffrey had been under, curled into a ball, whimpering. As Jeffrey tried to put his hands on the boy to soothe him, Ben jumped and shouted, "Don't touch me!"

"Ben?" Jack said again after a moment. "What is it? What's wrong?"

Now the boy released a gush of air, and the sobs began to come—long, hard, heaving sobs. Despite his words the two men sat down, one on each side of him on the bed, and held him tightly. He cried for several minutes before he could speak, and then it was only in snatches between gasps. "You know—I told you—that I didn't—read demons?"

"Yes," Jack said quietly.

"Well—I *can* now. And it's horrible!" Again his body was racked with grunting sobs. Again the two men gripped him tightly, brothering him as best they could. Eventually he calmed down, and rested between them, exhausted.

They were still in the blackness of time fall. Jack wondered where exactly they were headed now, but thought better of asking the boy in his present—

"Babel," Ben said.

"What?"

"I was answering Jack's question about where we're bound."

"Did you say 'babble'?" Jeffrey asked. "Is that what you keep hearing from these demons? Confused babbling?"

"Quite the opposite," the boy said, and it was clear he had at last composed himself. "What I'm hearing makes perfect sense. Amazingly so. Look, Jack, you're the expert on this Bible history stuff—what happened in Babel, exactly?"

Jack had known the answer to that when a third grade Sunday School teacher had asked it, years ago—or in centuries to come, whichever way you wanted to count. "It seems that after the flood, all of Noah's descendants—that is, everyone—stayed in one place: the Plain of Shinar. There they tried to build a tower to reach up to heaven. Eventually God got tired of their arrogance and confused their language."

"That's it, Jack. I can understand the demon's horrible thoughts now, for I can understand their language—the language of the beginning. My guess is that it will make just as much sense to you two when you hear it spoken.

"But I didn't—"

"We're going to the tower of Babel. The fallen have convinced themselves that *this* time they can get it *right*."

Oh, come on! Jack thought bitterly. He just seemed to be moving further and further away from home. . . .

* * *

They stood on a vast plain, looking at the edifice that rose up from the center of it. It dwarfed the world. "You've been to New York, Jack," Jeffrey said with awe in his voice. "What would you say? World Trade Center?"

"I've been to Chicago, too," Jack answered, "and that looks taller to me than the Sears Tower. I always thought it was a ziggurat, though. That's what they taught us in seminary. . . ."

"What's a ziggurat?" Ben asked. A picture of a Babylonian staircase tower jumped into Jack's mind, and he started to explain. "Never mind," the boy said. "I've seen enough."

"Never thought it would have been made of metal," Jack muttered.

"I never thought it was really *made*," said Jeffrey. "I figured the 'tower of Babel' story for one of the more interesting myths in Genesis."

"I thought they used bricks and mortar," Jack went on, continuing his thought.

"Maybe they *did*, the first time," Jeffrey suggested. "This time they've got something better, and they're using it."

"*This* time," said Jack, sounding vaguely dreamy. "Which time *is* this?"

"I meant . . . ah . . . this *attempt* at the old time."

"How many times have there been?" Jack wondered, confused.

"Who knows," Ben sighed. "Do you realize that in the few minutes since they've left us here the Boss and Astra could have already crammed in a thousand years of activity?"

"I just hope they come back," Jeffrey murmured quietly.

Jack was still peering at the tower. "It's a launching platform, isn't it?" he said, and though he voiced it as a question there was no question about it. Clearly, the fallen were using all of mankind to build a launching tower to get them off the planet. "Of course, there's a certain inevitability about all of this," Jack murmured as he watched. "After all—we know the outcome of this story, right?"

"They firmly believe they can change the outcome this time," Ben said soberly. He was still shaken from the experience of being inside so many utterly perverse minds at once. Now, outside of the ship and under a bright blue sky, he was feeling better. But it would be a long time before he would be able to put out of his mind completely the things he had seen in those few minutes. Perhaps never. . . .

"Why do they think so?" Jack wondered aloud. "What experiences have they ever had that convince them they might yet be successful? They always lose!"

"Still, you've got to admire their determination," Jeffrey said. When he glanced over and saw Jack staring at him like he was crazy, he added, "Well, *I* admire it."

"They're insane," Ben explained, and the other two looked at him. He was, after all, an expert on the minds of the fallen.

"You think we might go inside someplace?" Jeffrey asked. "I'm afraid this sun on my head is going to drive *me* insane!"

They couldn't go back into the saucer. They had no idea where it was now. Once they'd arrived in this time period, the quarrel that had erupted amongst the Grays as they were leaving the caverns of the Reich had been resolved violently. As nearly as Ben could make out, about half of the fallen had liked Gork's idea of coming here to Babel and trying again to change time. The other half, following Kundas, wanted to stop repeating the failures of the past and to return to what the humans knew as the present. As soon as they'd arrived on this plain, Kundas and his group had seized control of the craft and expelled the followers of Gork/Baal. Kundas considered these three humans Gork had dragged along for the ride as utterly useless, so they were booted off too. Enraged at such treatment, Gork and Astra had played "god" again before the staring workers—had commandeered chariots—and taken off across the plain toward the tower. Jack, of course, was becoming accustomed to being abandoned. And this time he had company.

There was certainly no lack of a place to stay. Vast brick and mortar dormitories ringed the plain, staffed by people whose only task it was to feed the people who built the tower. All the buildings appeared to be just alike—one way to keep down jealously and pride of possession, Jack figured. He had to wonder if the workers even *claimed* a certain building as "theirs" or not? The distances were so vast that he guessed that at the end of a day, workers just looked around for the closest building and headed toward it.

And of course, they had the certainty that no matter where they went, they would be understood. Everyone on this plain understood everyone else. It was, Jack reasoned, the true realization of the Olympic ideal.

The three of them walked into one of the buildings, sat down at one of the seemingly endless tables, and were immediately served the food of the day. This was a thick, tan paste—pounded yam, maybe? Jack thought, but he wasn't certain. He had no idea who grew the food, or where it was grown, or how it was funneled to this plain and onto the table. Obviously, the system worked smoothly. And like those around them, when it was put before them, they ate it. They drank the water. Then they looked around at one another and shrugged.

"No wonder they work so diligently," Jeffrey smiled. "There's nothing else to *do* here."

"We could talk about Ben's comment."

"Which?" Jeffrey frowned.

"That the fallen are insane," Ben explained. Then he looked at Jack. "What do you want to know?"

"What did you mean?"

Ben shrugged. "They're insane. You can't expect them to see the futility of their quest. They really believe that they are the equal of God. They've convinced themselves of that. And they're certain that if they can just build that tower out there high enough, and can just manage to launch a vehicle off of it, that they'll then be able to fly like they all did once. Never mind that they would have to do it inside metal cans where they once could go wherever they chose in the universe. Never mind that the angels could flip them out of orbit to plunge once more to earth with little more than a *thought.* They won't think of that. They're insane." He finished eating his tan paste.

Jack gazed at him. "You plucked all of that from their minds?"

"The memories are there in each of them. Skipping across the stars. Then the images of rebellion, and warfare, and loss—and hatred. Then those other, horrible memories . . . " Ben began trembling, and Jack put a hand on top of his hand.

"Don't," he said. "Stop thinking about it."

Ben nodded. "I'm very tired," he said, and he rose from the table.

"Me too," Jack agreed. "I think I'll go up and find an empty bunk."

"Not me," said Jeffrey, smiling and stretching. "Of course, I *did* spend all of yesterday under a bed. Maybe it's no surprise to you that I'd like to stretch my legs a little and take a closer look at that construction?" He was climbing out from the bench, and looking back out the arched opening of the building toward the sun-drenched plain.

"See you later, Jeffrey," Jack said, and a moment later his old friend walked back out into the sun he'd supposedly been attempting to escape.

"We probably won't, you know," Ben said. "See him again, I mean."

"I know," Jack nodded. "He's going to try to find Gork again, isn't he, to offer his services?" Ben nodded.

"He wants out of here. He sees that as the only way."

Jack looked Ben in the eye. "*Is* it? What's *our* future here, Ben? To eat, to drink, to wander around? I certainly don't intend to work on that tower."

"You said it yourself, Jack," the boy replied, sounding far more like a worn-out grandfather than a teenager. "We already know the end of this story."

Jack looked back out toward the plain. "We know the end of *this* story, but not the end of *our* story. That's the tragedy of evil, Ben. It's been conquered—*will* be conquered, I guess I should say—but the cost in individual lives beggars the imagination. Think of what the rebellion of these creatures has cost *you*, personally. I know what it's cost me." A vision of his wife and daughter hung stinging in his mind. To shunt it aside he glanced around at this mess hall, thinking how much the long tables reminded him of those long tunnels they'd just left, in the Germany of the far distant future. "Tell me, Ben. You can read the minds of these workers that scurry around us like ants on a mission. Is this vast enterprise *fulfilling* to them? Do they *want* to be building this tower for the fallen? Or is it just the life they've been given, the thing they must do, because there's nothing else?"

"You mean the way people in our generation rush around going to work, building the economy, each trying to find fulfillment in the midst of it?"

"I don't know if that's what I meant or not," Jack said, smiling wanly. "*Is* it the same for them?"

Ben scanned the room. "Some of them feel resentment. Some of them feel pride in the accomplishment. Some of them feel nothing." Ben looked back at Jack and went on, "But the main thing is that none of them know what they're building. Not really. And we do." He looked back down at the cup of water in his hand and said, "I've said it before, Jack, but I need to say it again. I'm sorry I got you into all of this."

"I told you before, I don't think you did," Jack answered quickly. "I think God did. But thank you for reminding me of that, since I was just about to start feeling sorry for myself." A thought flicked across Jack's mind, and while he was trying to phrase how to express it, Ben expressed it for him:

"You want to know where Lucifer is in all of this."

Jack blinked, and nodded. "Do you know?"

Ben trembled. "Yes." When he said nothing more immediately, Jack decided the question was just too overwhelming for the boy, and would have dropped it. But at last the teen continued—in a whisper: "Lucifer is hidden. He's there in all of it, but hiding behind the others. They all answer to him, and he extracts from them horrible tribute. He plays them off against one another. He punishes all their failures, but since he enjoys their pain he also *gains*, somehow, from their failures. He is aware of every conversation—including this one. He persists in believing that he is another god besides God—but he knows he's a prisoner, and those two ideas can't be justified. I said the fallen were insane, Jack. Lucifer's insanity drives all of the rest of them." Ben had to stop then. There were tears in his eyes, just from remembering.

Jack looked down at the table, hurting for the boy. "You read Satan's mind?" he said at last.

"No, no," Ben said quickly, his eyes looking haunted, his young face gaunt and sickly. "A better way of putting it is that he reads *mine*. Constantly." The boy's lip curled up in a sarcastic sneer. "That's a part of my 'gift.'" And now, somewhere inside those haunted eyes, it seemed to Jack he saw the laughing presence of someone else. He shivered in revulsion—and recognition.

"Is . . . is that the reason none of the fallen who lost their bodies in Roswell tried to ride *you?*"

"You've got it," Ben said.

Jack's first thought was to run, to escape, to get away from this boy who read his mind and then reported it all to the Evil One. But he didn't run. What good would that do, when the boy could read his mind wherever he ran? Besides, he was convinced that somewhere in Ben's spirit another, far holier influence was at work. He'd seen evidence of that One, as well. So he sat back on his bench, sighed, and said, "Would it help you to know that *everyone* has that same kind of spiritual battle going on inside them?"

Ben's expression looked passive to the point of being lifeless. "Sometimes it has helped. Sometimes, nothing helps."

Jack reviewed again those strange events that had taken place in the saucer over Roswell, New Mexico, in 1947. One thing puzzled him. "I just don't understand why, when the Holy Spirit evicted those demons from Jeffrey, you weren't freed as well?"

From somewhere out on the plain there came the unmistakable sounds of cannon fire. Everyone in the dining hall jumped, including Ben and Jack. Then understanding swept across Ben's face. He quickly and succinctly shared the facts with his friend: "Kundas is back. Along with the old saucer, he's been accompanied by those new model time-ships from Pearson's plant in Huntsville—six of them."

"But—what's all the shooting about?" Jack yelled, for now there was answering cannon fire booming from somewhere in the sky just above them. It shook the mud walls of the building.

"Kundas failed. He couldn't manage to get any of the time-ships onto the space shuttle. Some of those who had supported Kundas have come back here, wanting to follow Gork again. Others are angry at both of them—there are at least two other Gray factions involved in the shooting, which evidently started in our time. The angels apparently threw them all back here together. The demons are at war, Jack—with one another."

* * *

There was really no safe place to wait out the wars in the heavens. Already several of the great dormitories had come crashing down. Built of mud brick, they'd never been designed to withstand the vibrations of sonic shock waves—and certainly none of them could take a direct hit from an air cannon without exploding into red dust.

Since the most intense fire fight appeared to center around the tower's spire, the hundreds of thousands of workers at its base immediately rushed outward in a concentric ring of humanity. Since they knew that the "gods" were not angry at them, Jack and Ben felt no need to join in this catastrophic panic upon the plain. Aside from collapsing buildings, their biggest fear was being trampled. They stood their ground as the first wave rushed past them, then started walking toward where the people *weren't*—the tower itself. While others ran past, calling upon the ground to rise up and swallow them, they strolled casually forward, watching the fireworks unfold before them. So far none of the demons had proved good enough shots to knock another flying box down—but that certainly didn't keep them from trying.

"Brace yourself—" Jack warned, for another wave came hurtling toward them. They stood their ground, arms folded across their chests. Once again, the wave rushed around them without knocking them down. There was a difference this time, though. As they'd run jabbering past, Jack hadn't understood a thing they said.

"The confusion of the tongues?" he asked Ben as they started walking again.

"It just happened."

It was fifteen minutes later and they were much nearer the base of the tower when both of them at once saw the saucer suddenly streak through the sky and disappear again. They looked at each other in recognition. "They can't get out of this time zone again," Ben said for both of them, adding, "That's Astra and the Boss, of course. They're terrified."

"Why?" Jack asked, shielding his eyes from the sun to peer upward. "Suppose they get blown away, their bodies get blown apart. So what? Won't they just put those bodies back together again, or else find them some new ones?"

"That's not what terrifies them." Ben put his hand on Jack's shoulder and said, "I already told you that Lucifer punishes their failures. *He's* the one they're running from—not Kundas."

The box-like machines screamed through the sky, engines whining, guns blazing. "Which one *is* Kundas?" Jack asked, and Ben pointed the particular craft out. Not surprisingly it was the most aggressive ship in the sky. Knowing the technical bent of its pilot, Jack was not surprised to see it score the first hit on another time-box. The flying trunk was wounded, not destroyed—but a box is not the most aerodynamic of structures. It reacted to the hit by flipping over several times and heading for the plain. Where it hit the ground it plowed a furrow half a mile long—and took out another dormitory. Jack shook his head. "Crazy."

Once again the saucer flashed across the sky. Kundas took off after it, but it disappeared again before he could catch up. Another box was firing at him now, and Kundas returned its fire with savage effectiveness, blowing it into two parts. "Uh-oh," Jack had time to say before he dived headlong into the dirt. One of those parts careened toward the tower.

Jack had never before heard a sound like its impact: metal snapping, masonry being smashed to powder, an entire tower twisting and tilting to the side. At first it looked like the tower might absorb the blow after all—but no. Too much weight had been thrown too far to one side. It began to topple on over, disintegrating from the top down. It was only a matter of a few moments now, to see if any of the debris happened to land on them. Dropping from that height, Jack knew it wouldn't take a very big piece—

Suddenly Jack was being lifted off the ground and floated elsewhere. He knew immediately where. This wasn't an entirely unaccustomed feeling—he had, after all, first been abducted in just this way. This did happen much more rapidly, however, so much so that he could now understand the concept of being "zapped" aboard a flying saucer. Dust and debris bounced off the top of the disc as they dropped once more into the blackness of the time void.

"Ben?" Jack called.

"Right here."

"Who's got us?"

"The old gang."

"Let me guess. The angels wouldn't let them leave without us, right?"

"Wrong. The angels wouldn't let them leave without *you.* This time *I'm* along for the ride."

Chapter Twenty

Atlantean landscapes

They didn't go straight to their new destination. Instead they shot through half a dozen different times, each time changing position on the planet before dropping back into the black soup.

How long have we been doing this? was a meaningless question, and Jack knew it. *Why are we doing this?* could potentially be answered, and Ben tried.

"Kundas is obviously still after us," he said. "Baal and Astra are trying to lose us in time."

"When are they planning to stop?" Jack asked, meaning by that "in what time period?" That was the question Ben answered next.

"Before the flood."

"Noah's flood?"

"It figures *you* would name it after Noah," Ben shrugged. "It's been named for many others in many other cultures. We're not going there directly, though."

"That I'd gathered," Jack said as the lights suddenly came on, the saucer shifted position, and they again went black.

"They've laid a time-trail through the Middle Ages, into pre-Columbian America, back through the twentieth century in Australia, India, and Europe, past the Middle Kingdom of Egypt and over the China of Genghis Khan. Congratulations, Jack. You really get around."

"Is there some way Kundas can track us through all those times?"

"Not that they know of, no. But if you ask me, I think eventually he'll guess."

"Why? What's so attractive in the pre-flood world?"

"You can't guess?" Ben chuckled in the darkness. There were times now when he seemed less and less like the boy Jack had first met . . . .

"No . . . ?"

"Wait till you see it, Jack."

"Why? Have *you* seen it?"

"Only in their minds. But it's something."

Once more they climbed into time, and the lights, engines—life itself—appeared to resume. They had been brought aboard in the central under-deck—the level underneath the control room. Ben summoned the elevator to carry them to the flightdeck, and then got on. When Jack hesitated, Ben waved him aboard. "Come on. They want to see us both."

They stepped off into the presence of a half-dozen Grays, but Jack only recognized two of them. Gork, of course—Baal, did he like to call himself?—and Astra were present. The others seemed very unfamiliar. So did the general attitude with which they were greeted.

"Dr. Brennen," Baal/Gork said warmly—and he extended a long, slender hand. "I'm glad we were able to find you at last."

"At last?" Jack frowned.

"Oh, I realize to you it was only a period of a day or so, but to us it's been—well, many of your human years. Ben!" Baal/Gork said charmingly, taking Ben's hand just as he had Jack's. "What a foolish oversight it was for us to leave the two of you behind! We've missed you. Quite frankly, we've needed you." Baal—he really did seem different enough to deserve a new name, Jack thought—turned back to Jack and said, "Especially you, Dr. Brennen. Oh, I know you and I have had our differences in the past. Mostly my fault, I fear. As for leaving you at Babel—well. After the debacle at the tower we were all just in such haste to get away." He gestured at the other Grays around him. "My associates here and I were on the losing end of that quarrel, as perhaps young Ben has told you?"

"Ah . . . a little bit . . . "

"There will be time, now, to tell you much. But briefly put, let's just say that we've been hounded through century after century by one Kundas—whom I think you know well. And we've found that certain time periods have been—shall we say—*blocked* to us?" *Baal gazed at Jack knowingly.*

"By the angels?" Jack answered.

There seemed to be a flicker of the old Gork in the creature's black eyes, but Baal prevailed. "Precisely," he said. "We generally refer to them as 'the Guardians' ourselves. *If* we must refer to them at all."

Jack nodded, amazed to have heard this fallen being admit their existence at last. "I remember from Germany that you didn't like me mentioning them."

"Quite," Baal said. "But now you're back, we've rescued you off that horrible battlefield, and you may have noticed that we've been zipping in and out of time periods rather freely. We've arrived, at last, in a place and time you doubtless think legendary. We've come home at last to Atlantis."

Jack was sure his eyes widened perceptibly. Did he smile, too? "I . . . uh . . . well . . . "

"I'm not surprised at your reaction. Not at all. You've come from a time that disbelieved its existence as much as the late nineteenth century believed it. Did you ever read Donnelly's book on Atlantis?" As a matter of fact, Jack had—but he'd also read L. Sprague DeCamp's thorough debunking of the legend, and had come to conclude that Plato had made it all up.

"The fact is, Dr. Brennen," Baal continued, "the Guardians so thoroughly drowned it that your scientists are as likely to find it as they are Sodom itself."

Jack blinked. "Then why do you want to go back to it?"

Baal laughed—yet another indication that the old Boss had changed enormously. "That's an excellent question! Of course, I also have an excellent answer for it. We're returning to Atlantis to try to make amends for our errors there. Quite honestly, Dr. Brennen—we messed up."

Jack wrinkled his nose in disbelief and looked over at Ben for support. "But—do you really believe you can *change* it, now? It seems to me by this time you would have given up on that approach!"

Baal laughed again—this time with less humor—and said, "A number of our former associates hold that same view, of course. But Dr. Brennen, think. Just because time has never been changed before, does that mean it absolutely *can't* be? We're so much better *equipped* now to perform our Atlantean experiments successfully! And the tools we have to work with there . . . ? You'll see, Dr. Brennen. You'll *marvel*."

"Can we drop down now?" Astra said snidely—indicating that not *all* of the Grays had experienced a complete personality change.

"Of course, dear," Baal said agreeably, then he turned back to Jack as the saucer descended. "I realize that it was none of your doing. I realize that *all* of this has totally disrupted your life. Nevertheless, I *do* thank you for opening the door for us to return here. Please, feel free to roam where you choose! You have the run of the City of Golden Gates and unlimited access to wherever, whatever, whenever! Just please—stay close."

So that in case we need you again to get out of this place, we'll know where to find you, Jack thought to himself as the saucer touched the ground. He looked over at Ben and saw the boy smiling and nodding. Then the ramp dropped open, and Jack debarked into the first theme park in the history of the world—after the garden of Eden, of course.

They had landed in the courtyard of a palace—perhaps *the* palace. It sat upon a promontory out over a tropic ocean. It was the beach that caught his eye first, and the color of the waters beyond. It appeared as if one sea had been layered upon another—the closest in a crystal-clear aquamarine; the second layer, farther out, a brilliant turquoise; the third layer a rich, royal blue. Wasn't this the way they used to paint the coastlines on ancient maps?

He saw now that the beach really wasn't a beach—not of sand. It was instead a wide, sloping patio of roughened white marble, stretching gradually down from the steps of the nearest buildings to the water. The buildings closest were opulent in the extreme, yet it was clear in a glance that they were only out-buildings to the palace. This rose gracefully up beyond them, drawing the eye inevitably up its multiple stories to the pinnacle. This top-most point, probably fifteen stories in height, was crowned by a broad portico which faced the sea, shaded by awnings that sparkled like gold—and might well *be* gold, Jack realized. He stared up at that high porch and wondered, *How in the world do they get up that high?*

"Elevator, of course," said Ben, and the boy started up the marble slope toward the out-buildings.

"Elevator?" Jack said, running to catch up with him.

"Baal said you would marvel, Jack. Marvel away."

* * *

Marvel Jack did. The crown city of Atlantis—the City of the Golden Gates—was far more splendid than San Francisco would *ever* be. Remarkably, it was also far more convenient. What sense could the word "modern" have in a civilization that predated the pyramids? Yet that was the word Jack wanted to use of everything. Atlantis looked more like the twenty-fourth century than "Star Trek" did. Ben assured him that it was actually 250 B.C. Mind boggling.

He walked down a major avenue that was wider than the Champs Elysee. Exotic plant life graced its central strip, growing up the pillars that divided the street and crossing over above it on arches carved of a light, airy stone he didn't recognize. People moved past him on all types of conveyances—some that appeared to move far faster than any automobile, which made him a little nervous—and yet there was no noise of engines, nor brakes, nor even the sound of wheels upon the road. Other vehicles floated lazily above him, moving people from one place to another with no apparent source of power that he could see. From the high porch that morning he'd watched both large ships and small boats ply the multi-layered seas, none of them using nor emitting any form of steam. *How did they all move?* he wondered. This was, indeed, a dreamworld. This part of it, at least: Jack was determined to find the "other side of the tracks." Twentieth-century chauvinism drove him to it.

For Atlantis was just too perfect. Of course, Plato had said as much. But how could Plato have known? This was not the Garden, of course—although Jack was beginning to wonder if the garden of Eden was nearby. Wherever this was, Jack admitted to himself that he was impressed. More than once in the past few days he had longed to have Gloria beside him. Gloria would love this city—and he would love it far *more* in her company. . . .

Baal had been a wonderful host—whenever he was around. It was clear, however, that he and the other Grays were devoting intense time to some project. While Ben evidently played an important role in this task, it apparently didn't require Jack's presence at all. Whether he would be *welcome* to view it, if he stumbled across it in his wanderings, Jack really didn't know. But in sharp contrast to many other stops along this rambling odyssey, Jack had yet to find a locked door anywhere. Apparently the Atlanteans didn't need them.

One broad avenue intersected another, and that one another, and on and on through the city the pattern repeated itself until Jack felt thoroughly intimidated. No American city matched this one, nor any European or African city he'd visited. He wondered how to obtain the use of one of the flying machines. Perhaps then he would be able to fly over areas where *real* people lived with *real* problems. Weary of his wanderings, and somewhat lonely, Jack turned back toward the palace. By the time he arrived at its gates he'd determined what was really wrong with him.

Jack was bored. For weeks—or had it been months? For centuries, he might as well say, he had been blasting through one adventure after another. Crisis after crisis had assaulted him, and he'd grown accustomed to that level of activity. While a vacation was well and good, and he'd certainly needed one, he was spending so much time alone now that all he could think about was his wife and family. Atlantis was a wonderful place to visit, but he didn't want to live here. More than that, he didn't want to *die* here, and if this truly was the Atlantis of myth then he guessed the end could come at any time. And even if the legendary cataclysm never came, a screaming time-box could suddenly drop into the sky and start firing cannons at the palace. Somehow that seemed more likely. He really wished Ben had time to visit with him some . . . .

Walking across an entryway as big as a New York hotel lobby, Jack got his wish. Ben stood by the elevator, apparently waiting for him. "You got my message, I see," Jack smiled, and Ben smiled back.

"You're still the best friend I have, Jack," Ben answered quietly. "You're the only one around who remembers how it's someday going to *be*."

"Do I? You don't think it'll all be different, once you and Baal finish your project?"

"Who knows?" the boy shrugged, veiling his emotions. Was he different? Jack wondered. Was Ben changing too? "Look," Ben said abruptly, "How about if I show you what we're doing? I know you're curious, and it can't hurt anything. What it's all going to mean to the future, I honestly have to say I don't know. I know Baal's plans and the plans of his colleagues. I've also known those plans to fail miserably in the—past." He grinned.

Jack still felt uneasy. "Is . . . Lucifer pleased with the plans?"

Ben's eyes lidded slightly, but his grin stayed fixed. "Like I say. Who knows? Come on. Let's go look at the tanks."

They got onto the elevator and Ben pressed a sequence of numbers Jack obviously didn't know. Rather than rising, the elevator dropped downward. "So," Jack commented. "Secrets."

"Which you're now in on," the boy said without expression. "Or will be, soon." The door opened. "This way, Jack," Ben said, and he led Jack to the left.

This place felt vaguely familiar—then it registered. Of course. These corridors were exactly like those under the western desert of twentieth-century America! "We all like familiar settings," was Ben's only comment to Jack's thought. They turned a corner, then Ben slowed his pace, stepped aside, and gestured toward the walls. Jack turned—and stared.

This place was like an aquarium. Glassed-in tanks lined both sides. But behind the glass, floating in a substance too reddish to be water, were the bodies of Grays. Many, many bodies.

They walked along slowly now, Jack looking from side to side so as not to miss anything. The questions were tumbling through his mind, but apparently Ben was going to be patient enough to allow him to ask them himself.

Or perhaps they would be answered by what he saw. Floating in a series of tanks he now saw the bodies characteristic of the Whites—large noses, multiple layers of whitish fat skin—"Miz White!" Jack exclaimed.

Ben nodded. "Baal rode one such body to convince you he was an alien White." Jack was certain the boy could have elaborated at length, but instead he just walked on. Jack followed.

They came upon a series of tanks that chilled him, for here he began to see combination beasts—part human, part animal. Especially chilling were those bodies which had goats' hooves, horns, and face, yet a man's chest. "The fawn . . . ," Ben explained, then added "or the great horned beast. The devil."

"And Gork—Baal—wore one of these at the Black Sabbat?"

"You're catching on, Jack."

"And all of these are . . ." Jack stepped away from the glass of the nearest tanks and surveyed the way they had come ". . . genetic experiments?"

Ben drew in a deep sigh, then nodded. "Exactly. They needed bodies, Jack—bodies with which they could interact with mankind. They tried possessing human bodies, but—well," Ben said, unable to meet Jack's eyes, "you know something about possession. That didn't work out."

You know something about possession too, *Ben,* Jack thought—but his young friend skipped over the comment and went on:

"They had to have bodies they could control completely—bodies that wouldn't decay, and that would have the mobility of living creatures."

"Why not robots? Surely this Atlantean civilization could have—"

"They tried that, too. There's a gallery of robot forms nearby. But they were never able to get them to *move* as quickly or as gracefully as living creatures—especially like people. And it was people they needed to manipulate, to steer. So—trying to copy humans—they made these."

Jack looked up and down the line of tanks. "Not very good copies," he muttered.

"The fallen would be the first to agree," Ben said meaningfully. "But you see, at this point in history they didn't have the advantage of what the geneticists of our generation have discovered. Now they do."

Jack looked back at Ben. "Because all of that is now in your mind."

The boy shrugged, obviously complimented. "My mind, and the saucer's computer memory banks. They're remaking themselves in mankind's image, Jack. *We're* remaking them," he corrected himself. There was pride in the boy's voice that Jack had never heard—pride in accomplishment. "They look *good*," Ben smiled.

Jack couldn't hide from Ben the sick feeling that floated up from the pit of his stomach—nor the reason for it. "You realize what you're doing, don't you?"

"Of course I do," the boy snapped. "I'm playing god. Then again," he added, his eyes flashing in accusation, "everyone else I know does!"

"You think I play god?"

"Of course you do! 'The spirit of the Lord is upon me,' you say! What's that if it's not playing god?"

There was something so different in Ben's manner, so false in his bearing, that Jack had to believe this just wasn't the same kid he knew. "Ben," he began—

"Yes," the boy snarled back. "I *am* Ben. This is who I *am*, Jack. That other person you think you saw? That's the person you wanted me to be. I picked the image out of your mind and played it for you—played it *on* you. But *this* is truly Ben!"

The boy protested too much. Nothing could have convinced Jack more that Ben was under another's control. "No it's not. Ben! Can you hear me in there?"

"Go away, Jack," Ben sneered. "Your thoughts made an interesting change for a while, but now they're nothing but repeats."

"Ben," Jack said breathlessly, earnestly. "I know you know that you *could* get rid of your 'gift' if you'd like to. Think of it, Ben! You could be free!"

"Free for what?" the boy said sarcastically. "Free to be like every other kid on the block? Free to know *nothing*? No thanks, Jack. I'll stick with my master."

"You could have a *better* master!" Jack appealed. "One who would help you know the *truth*, and make you free!"

The boy laughed. His words were full of scorn:

"I am my *own* master! You would make me be a slave of His again?"

Again? Jack thought. Then he understood. And it horrified him. Through this boy he was speaking to the Evil One himself. Jack clenched his teeth, fighting down the fear—then remembered that the One in him was greater than the one of this world. "I'm not speaking to you, Lucifer. I'm talking to Ben, and if he can hear me, if he can *read my mind*, I hope he's doing so now!" Perhaps Lucifer needed the boy's "gift" so much he couldn't block Ben from hearing—*You can be free of this, Ben. You can.*

From somewhere inside Ben's body came a squeal of pain and the elongated cry, "How?"

The way you've always known from me, Jack thought earnestly. *By claiming the God of Jesus Christ as Lord and letting Christ push this monster from your mind!*

But the boy who'd cried out was buried again, now, in the teenager who stood arrogantly before him, one hand cocked on his hip. "And what would be the purpose in that? We're antediluvian here, Jack! The cross won't happen for twenty-five millennia!"

"But it *will* happen," Jack said aloud to the beast that had so long remained hidden. "And you—of all creatures—should know it."

This boy who had been his friend met Jack's gaze evenly. No—it wasn't Ben. It wasn't Ben who said, "I can't change, Jack. It wouldn't be *me* any longer if I did. Don't you get it?"

"Ben—"

"Go away Jack. I've made my decision—and you lost." The boy spun around then and walked quickly out of the gallery. Jack shook his head sadly, and looked around at the floating bodies. A question flashed across his mind: If Atlantis was destroyed, how did they preserve these bodies into the twentieth century?

"Don't you get it *yet* Jack?" the boy hollered from well out of sight. "We get them out in the *saucer*, of course! Which—thanks to your getting us around the Guardians, my friend—we've managed to get *here* to pick them up!" The elevator door closed. The boy was gone.

Jack stood thunderstruck in the middle of the hallway. Beyond the glass, it seemed as if the floating bodies grinned at him.

* * *

Jack left the palace immediately and began to walk. He took nothing with him. He cared nothing about anything. He felt certain now, as certain as he'd ever felt about anything, that events in this place were racing toward a conclusion. Ben knew the flood was coming. He'd almost told him as much. And if the fallen truly had—through his help!—accomplished their purpose here, why would they need to stay any longer?

But then, what was *Jack's* purpose here? If indeed the angels—the Guardians—had permitted the saucer into this time period because of him, then—why? Certainly he wasn't here just to accomplish the purpose of a boy he'd loved and trusted. If he was here, it was because God had some purpose for his presence here. And in all his life there had been only one purpose that seemed to be of overriding importance. . . .

It took him hours of walking, but Jack did indeed finally reach the people. There were ghettos in Atlantis, as in every other city he'd seen. And if Atlantis had been the most marvelous of all cities in its gorgeous, upscale heart, then it was the most miserable of all cities in its squalid shanty townships.

He found the people, all right. Acres of them, jammed together in towering tenements that would have scandalized a slum-lord.

When he found them, and when he realized that—like the workers in the German rat-warren and the ants who built the tower of Babel—it was *they* who would suffer the fallout of the fallen's failures, then Jack began to do the only thing he knew how to do, really. He found a corner that seemed particularly congested and exceptionally deprived—and started preaching.

"There is a rain coming that will not stop!" he shouted. "And a flood will follow that will drown the whole world!" That grabbed their attention! Many heads whirled around to look. Thinking of Jonah and the city of Ninevah, Jack reached down to the bottom of his diaphragm and shouted the same message even more loudly: "There's a rain coming that will not stop, and a flood will follow that will drown the whole world!"

A crowd began to collect, and he started to look around for something to stand on. Nearby he spotted a large rectangular trash container, filled to overflowing with refuse that hadn't been picked up for days. He tipped it onto its side and got up onto it, and proclaimed his message again.

"What's rain?" somebody shouted, and Jack was so taken aback by the question that several smaller conversations began amongst the crowd before he answered.

"It's—water from heaven!" he said, pointing upward. "Water that falls from the sky!"

A number of people in the crowd laughed at this, and some went on about their business. Others peered at him as if he were crazy, and asked him, "Where does this water come from?"

"From the clouds!" he said, still pointing upward, and he followed his own finger up to the sky. There were no clouds there, however. It occurred to him that he hadn't seen a cloud since he'd been here, just as somebody asked—

"What's a cloud?"

From that point on Jack struggled, trying mightily to make himself understood but being unable to describe rain to people who'd never seen it. Most of the crowd laughed him off and departed.

He asked one of those who lingered just how they watered their crops—but the man didn't know what crops were, either. The fruit was there on the trees, and the boats went to pick it off. Another watcher seemed a bit more familiar with agriculture, and he explained that the waters rose up from out of the *ground* and watered the earth. Nothing fell from the sky. By the time this fellow left, shaking his head derisively, the rest of the crowd was gone. Jack pulled in a long, deep sigh, and looked around. Then he went looking for another street corner. Just because they didn't know what he was talking about didn't mean that the rains would not come.

He moved through the city this way, stopping at a street corner every few miles and preaching his message again. He got better at answering their questions, better at explaining what rain was in terms they could understand, better at refuting hecklers. He slept on the street and no one disturbed him. Occasionally someone would give him something to eat, but that really mattered little to him.

A certain number had begun to trail along behind him, listening to him say the same things at each corner, and explaining to those around them what they'd heard Jack himself explain. Disciples, Jack thought to himself, and the thought did not make him feel good. After all, what *hope* did he have to share with them? None. Just that the flood was coming.

There was *one* thing he began to say with some regularity, especially to those who appeared most frightened and moved by his message. "When death comes to you," he said somberly: "When you are in the prison house of death—there is One who will come to you to tell you of hope. *That* One is the Son of the God who made you—and *He* has the power to give you new life. Listen to Him!"

Jack felt justified in preaching this message. After all, if anyone could be said to have been "disobedient in the time of Noah," then these people could be. After a couple of days of their following him, however, Jack realized he was wasting resources. He collected together those who seemed to understand his words best, and sent them off to other street corners in the city.

It was about the sixth day of his mission to Atlantis that he first caught sight of the woman—and his heart almost stopped beating within his chest. He stood as was his new custom upon a tumbled-over trash box, telling his bad news to all who would listen. As he spoke his eyes scanned the gathering crowd—and there she was. Gloria. Of course it couldn't be, but it still caused his voice to stick in his throat, and his thoughts to fall completely apart. She was the twin of his beloved—or could it be his angel, come to fetch him away? Either way, when it was clear he couldn't preach his message to this group anymore, he jumped off the box and headed toward her. Alarm grew in her eyes as she realized he was coming her way—that didn't seem like the Angel Gloria. He was afraid she would run away, but she held her ground until he reached her, and frowned when he grabbed her hands. "Are you my angel?" he asked her flatly, certain he already knew her answer.

"What's that?" she asked, her frown deepening, but before he could answer she jerked her hands away and ran off.

"Gloria," Jack murmured sadly as he watched her go.

He didn't have long to mourn her retreat. A moment later both of his arms were gripped by pairs of powerful hands, and he found himself begin hustled down the street on tiptoe. He looked right, then left, then back right again, and was so startled by what he saw that he had to break out laughing. They were both dressed in black business suits, with twentieth-century black ties. "What's this?" Jack gasped, still laughing. "The Men in Black are *here*, too?"

Chapter Twenty-One

A mountaintop experience

Jack was ushered into the office of the chief and plopped down in the chair across from him. He wasn't at all surprised when the chief turned out to be Jeffrey. He would have been far more surprised had it *not* been.

"Get out," Jeffrey said to his two agents. "I'll handle this case myself." The two men went out and closed the door. Jeffrey leaned back in his executive chair and propped his feet on his desk. Then both of them burst out laughing.

They laughed for several minutes before Jeffrey sat up, scooted up to his desk and assumed the proper demeanor for an arresting officer. "Now then, Jack. What's this I hear about your creating a public disturbance?" He picked up some papers off of his desk and said, "I have reports here of you creating an unsettled populace, deputizing unlicensed persons to practice religious teachings, starting an unapproved cult—not to mention littering every street corner you preach on." Jeffrey chuckled, dropped the papers on his desk and leaned back again in his chair. "What are you trying to do?"

"You know what I'm doing, Jeffrey," Jack argued, smiling. "This *is*, after all, Atlantis. It *is*, as we both know, going to disappear into the sea."

"Right. But what's that to you or me?" Jeffrey leaned forward again, propping his hands on his desk. "Of course it's going to happen, but we don't need to be here when it does. Those people *do*. And what are you going to do for them, Jack? Send a radio message to Noah and have him drop by and pick them up?"

"They're people, Jeffrey. They deserve to know the truth."

"Why? What good will that do them? Jack, listen. Give up, okay? Just give it up."

"And if I don't?"

"You know, Jack. I'll have to throw you in jail. Do you want that? I don't. Talk about a terrible place to be when the waters start rising. . . . "

Jack sat back in his chair, depressed. There was, after all, some truth in what Jeffrey was saying. He changed the subject. "How many days have *you* been here?"

"Not days, Jack. Years. Kundas planted me here years ago—although it may only have been minutes for him. He's coming back and taking charge. Could happen any day...." Whether consciously or unconsciously, Jeffrey tilted his chair back to glance out the window at the blue sky.

"Kundas, hunh?" Jack replied. Then Ben had been right about Kundas finding them. Of course he had—Ben was always right. Then Jack frowned: "How did Kundas manage to get into this time period? Did the Guardians let him?"

"Look, Jack," Jeffrey responded, raising his hand and blinking his eyes. "I don't stick my nose into anything that's not my business, and the Guardians—the angels—*whatever* you call them—they're not my business."

"What is your business, Jeffrey?"

"Same as it's always been," the man shrugged, smiling his Dr. Doolittle smile. "I watch out for people who learn too much, and dissuade them from sharing it—that's why *you're* here. And, I also keep in contact with my friends and people who might be of help down the way. That's the *other* reason why you're here, Jack. You're my friend."

What a gorgeous word, Jack thought. Friend. It seemed so long since he'd had anyone regard him that way—honestly, at least. Friend. But could Jeffrey be counted on to be any more honest than Ben had? "And you think I might be of help down the way?" Jack echoed Jeffrey softly.

"You might," Jeffrey said offhandedly. "Or I might help you. Hear me out, Jack. Kundas made me a promise. If I would be a good soldier for him here, he would take me back home again. Of course, I can't believe him—which one of these demons *can* you trust, hunh? But what other choice do I have? None. Right?"

Jack thought about that. "I guess so."

"So why not give up this street-corner preaching and join me? Black suit and all! Then when Kundas comes, I'll take you with me."

Kundas. "You really think Kundas would rescue *me*, Jeffrey?"

Jeffrey sighed, and looked at the ceiling. "I don't really think Kundas will *rescue* me. I just think he might need me someday. And he might need you too. Think about it."

Jack nodded. "I'll do that."

"And stop the street-corner preaching. You do that again and I lock you up, and you can forget about *any* chance of going home. You got me?"

Jack stood up. "I think so. Am I free to go?"

"Yeah," Jeffrey grunted. "Stay in touch, hunh?" They shook hands, and Jack walked out the door and past the surprised guards who had brought him in. He wondered if Jeffrey would have them follow him.

He was stepping out of the office building when he saw her again. Gloria's twin—and she was waiting for him. She glanced back and forth up the street as he crossed over to her. "Are you . . . waiting for me?"

She nodded, curtly. "Can we go somewhere else? I don't like talking here."

"Wherever you want—" he started to say, and she cut him off.

"Outside of the city. Where its green."

That sounded fine to Jack. It seemed even more so when he learned she had a flying car at her disposal. "Where do you come from?" he asked. "Are you from this part of the city?"

"Of course not," she answered, expertly steering the flying car into the sky. "You have to understand, your fame is spreading quickly. I wanted to talk to you alone."

"What . . . about, exactly?" Jack asked. He was trying not to feel like he was feeling. This was a stranger, a woman born many thousands of years before him—and before his wife. She wasn't Gloria. But she did look so much *like* her! Sounded like her too.

"You ask me where I come from—a fair question, and I answered it. Now I want to know where *you* come from, and how you've come to know the things you say." She turned to look at him, effortlessly guiding the flying car toward the green-belt which Jack could now see ran around the landward side of the city. "Will you tell me?"

Jack was entranced by her. "Of course," he said, "although I don't know if you'll believe me." She found a place to set the car down in a park-like wood, and produced from inside it a picnic. He spent the rest of the afternoon telling her his story, from the place of his birth to his most recent conversation with Jeffrey. Not once did she smile.

When he was done she pondered for a long time before replying. "Your words are frightening, of course. And very hard to believe. If Atlantis is to drown, then why haven't our scientists warned us? Nevertheless—if it *is* to be so, then shouldn't some of us be making preparations to survive?"

The question surprised him. "But you won't survive."

"So I've heard you say," she replied. "But how can you possibly know that for the truth? If you really believe this—and I'm absolutely certain you do—then why go around telling people who can't do anything about it in any case? Why let yourself be laughed at? Why risk being put into prison?" She stood up, and walked a few paces away from him. "I find that I'm . . . afraid." She turned back to look at him. "Stay with me."

Jack was astonished. "Stay with—? I . . . I don't even know your name!"

"That's a problem easily enough solved," she said. "It's Clarion"—and she smiled. He melted. It was Gloria's smile. While he was thus befuddled, the woman made her strongest argument yet: "I know you have no home to go to. Why not stay with me? After all—it could be *years* before the destruction of the continent begins!"

"That's true," Jack said. "It could."

Then a raindrop hit him on the head.

* * *

Baal stood before a mirror shifting his new shoulders and rubbing the back of his new neck. It didn't feel exactly right. Things didn't seem to fit as they had before. It was going to take him time to learn how to use these heavier hands and thicker feet. Nevertheless, one thing was certain. He could walk among the people of earth now and never be recognized for what he was. He looked *human.* More than that, he looked *good!* No more flabby white bodies or long, spindly gray ones. Instead he had pecs of steel, long black hair, high cheekbones, and cool gray eyes. He could be a star.

It was a stupid thing to wish for, he knew. Why should he, who had once coursed around the edges of galaxies, care anything at all for the adulation of mankind? And yet he did.

He'd spent so many of these millennia pretending to be a god, demanding worship, requiring people to adulate him that he guessed he'd just become accustomed to it. His purpose for getting off this tiny rock went beyond that of most of his associates—even Astra. He wanted to take a colony of humans to another world and finally *be* a god to them! Of course, he would have to defeat the Guardians, somehow. . . . but even if he couldn't, if he could prove himself to be a *good* god, a *wise* god—wasn't there a chance the Guardians would leave him alone with his plaything? After all, there were so many truly *awful* fallen ones to pursue. Kundas, for example, who thought of nothing but vengeance and destruction. Baal shook his head. What a mistake it had been to refuse Kundas' request to be the Phoenician war god. What *suffering* that had caused to everyone—

Quashior rushed into the room. Finding Baal there, he drew himself up to his full Gray height and snarled, "It's started."

Baal looked at him and frowned—watching himself in the mirror as he did so. Oh yes, he was pleased. "What's started?" he asked.

"If you'd take your eyes off of those mirrors and walk out onto the portico, you'd *see* what's started!"

"A riot, perhaps?" Baal asked, still looking more at himself than at Quashior.

"The rain!" the creature who still wore his old Gray body roared, and now Baal looked at him with both eyes. "That's right, the rain! The breakup of the continent has begun! We're looking at forty days and nights and a worldwide flood, and all you can do is admire your new face in the mirror?"

Baal wasn't at all threatened—not by Quashior. He looked back in the mirror and rearranged the way a black curl turned upon his forehead. "I know what your problem is, Quashior. We hadn't gotten to *your* body yet. But don't worry, we will—"

"When?" Quashior roared. "In another twenty-five thousand years, when we come back to this place to try it all yet again? Listen Baal, I *needed* that body, and I was scheduled before you! But, oh no, the beautiful Baal had to be finished first—"

"Quashior!" Baal yelled, silencing his associate. "Relax! There will be time—if not here then in another time per—"

"I thought our purpose was to *change* the outcome! I thought we planned to throw time back into the face of the High King and His Guardians! If that's our purpose then why not take *action?*"

"And what action would you suggest?" Baal asked calmly, stepping away from Quashior and walking across the vast room toward the doors onto the portico. Sure enough, he could see it was raining. He wondered how the golden awning would fare. Not that it mattered, since in a matter of days this entire palace would be swallowed up . . .

"Simple. I'm taking the saucer and going to find the High King's zookeeper. Let's see if we can't change the future by sinking old Noah and his ark!"

"Wait!" Baal whirled around and shouted, for Quashior had gotten back on the elevator. "You're insane!" he shouted. "We need that saucer to get *out* of this time! What do you think the Guardians will do to you if you even *try* to—" He stopped, for the doors had closed and Quashior was gone. "Astra!" he began to shout, terrified now that Quashior would get away with their only means of escape. "Astra, where are you?" he shouted into the palace speaker system. But for some reason his longtime consort wasn't answering. Baal screamed in frustration. Why hadn't he allowed them to put *stairs* in this palace!

* * *

As soon as Jeffrey saw the first drop on his window pane, he closed up his office and ran up to the roof. He had no illusions about being able to wait out the cataclysm from up there. Rather, he climbed the eight stories in order to collect, at last, on an old promise.

In the years since Kundas had dropped Jeffrey into this time and place, he had only returned twice. Each time, he had landed the time-box on the roof of this building. The last time Kundas had departed he had said clearly, "When the time comes, you and your people are to meet me here." It was raining. This was the time.

Not that Jeffrey had that many agents. He had been selective in enlisting new Men in Black for service. It was his expectation that those Atlanteans selected would accompany him back to the twentieth century and form the nucleus for that secretive force in the present. Loyal, unattached to that new time period, untraceable by any government service and unable ever to return home, they would be the perfect operatives. In fact, Kundas had hinted that this had already taken place—that although he didn't know it, Jeffrey had been working with Atlanteans for years. Maybe that was so and maybe it wasn't: Jeffrey had told too many convenient lies in his lifetime to take anyone's word at face value. It did make enough sense, however, for him to have given his operatives this signal: "When the sky begins to leak, come immediately to the top of HQ and wait."

He was the first one on the roof. He realized his heart was pounding—and not from the climb. The time-box was nowhere to be seen—yet. To give himself something to do while he waited, he walked to the edge of the rooftop and looked down into the streets.

There was panic below. "Thanks a lot, Jack," he snarled under his breath. Had his old friend not been so obsessive about the truth, he felt certain the populace would have been merely curious about this new natural phenomenon. As it was, hardly a soul in the whole western part of the city hadn't heard stories about "the crazy prophet who says the sky will cry and drown us." *Look at them down there,* he thought to himself. They were going crazy.

One—two—three agents burst through the rooftop door and turned to look around for him. He waved them out of the center of the roof and waited, looking up expectantly—confidently. At least, he hoped he looked confident . . .

* * *

Raindrops patterned the ground all around them. Clarion turned her head back to frown up into the sky. “What *are* those?” she asked, pointing upward.

“Clouds,” Jack said without looking. “Please take me back to the city. I need to be with the people.”

“Why?” Clarion asked, turning her huge Gloria eyes on him. “Why go back there now? What can you do for them?”

“I can be with them,” Jack shrugged. It wasn’t much, but it was something. It was the thing a pastor would naturally do. “Please take me back.”

“No!” Clarion shouted. “No, I won’t! That would be a waste, Jack! You and I need to make other plans!”

“You and I?” Jack said, looking back at her. “Ma’am—Clarion—you and I only *met* a few hours ago!”

“You know that’s not true,” the woman said gravely. “You and I never met at all, and you know it. We’ve *always* known each other—always. We were made for each other, you and I, and now that we’ve at last found each other I’m not just going to . . . to throw you back into the sea!”

“But . . . Clarion . . . ”

Suddenly she hopped into the flying car and commanded: “Get in.” Thinking that she had changed her mind, Jack jumped in beside her, and the vehicle shot into the air. She didn’t turn toward the city, though. Instead she headed away from it—flying northward until they reached the coast. “Look down there,” she said, pointing, and Jack looked down to where she was pointing. “Do you see it? Not all of us were unprepared!”

Laying at anchor in a harbor below was a ship—and a huge one. He realized now that he’d seen it before as he’d stood on the portico. He’d wondered by what kind of engine it was powered. . . .

"There it is, Jack—our rescue. It's completely furnished with everything we'll need on our journey, and everything we'll need to reestablish civilization whenever the waters recede. We can sail away on it today, Jack—make babies on it together—repopulate the world! You can be king!"

Jack was hanging on tightly to the struts of this little air-car. He felt like he was going to be sick. "Could . . . could you set this thing down? Maybe . . . maybe we could take a closer look . . . "

Clarion eagerly plummeted the vehicle toward the harbor. Jack hung on for dear life, as the rains grew ever harder.

* * *

Jeffrey breathed a sigh of relief. Where there had been nothing, there was suddenly a box-like vehicle, and the door was opening. Ignoring the awed, appreciative expressions of his agents, he quickly ordered them aboard and followed them inside. Most had made it through the chaotic traffic jams in the streets below. Three had not. Too bad. He walked briskly into the control room and informed Kundas that they were aboard and ready.

Neither Kundas nor any of the other Grays aboard said anything. They just punched up the exterior monitors, engaged flight engines, and shot up into the sky. Stopping abruptly in midair and whirling around 180 degrees, the time-box set its sights on the heights of the palace—and opened fire.

Down in the streets of Atlantis, people pointed upward and screamed. Someone on a street corner stood upon an overturned trash bin shouting, "The gods have come to drown us for our sins!" Nobody stopped to listen. There were no storm drains under the streets, so the water was already rising over the shoe-tops. The rooftops of the buildings were quickly filling up with people, far more people than they had ever been built to sustain. The flat roofs were also filling up with water, since they had no drains either. The first people to die in the cataclysm fell many stories through a collapsing roof. The rain fell still harder.

* * *

"Please!" Clarion begged him. "Please! Get on board!"

Jack stood at the foot of the gangplank, feeling numb. He was drenched through, and Clarion had already been shouting at him that there were dry clothes for him aboard. But the rain wasn't the cause of his numbness. It was everything—everything he had seen and heard, everything he'd experienced and believed, everything that he'd dreamed and despaired. Jack had simply become overwhelmed. It was too much.

Weeks of travel could wear anyone out—even if it were just travel between New York and Cleveland. He'd been traveling—forever. He couldn't remember how many times he'd visited—in point of fact he didn't *know* how many times he had visited. Nor was he at all certain that any of them were real. He'd been around the moon, after all—or thought he had—and then had learned it was all a charade. Couldn't this, too, be a charade? He turned his face up to the sky and closed his eyes, letting the drenching rain wash him.

And what about God? Where was God in all of this? Time and again he had been led to believe that he was God's emissary on a strange journey, God's representative among a host of spiritual outcasts. But could that be, really? This dream-like city, this catastrophic storm—wasn't all of this far more the stuff of nightmares than of life? True, the rain dripped from his nose and poured uncomfortably down his neck, but didn't he have such realistic feelings while dreaming? And hadn't he tried, at times, during nightmares to wake himself up, and been unable?

"Jack! Please!" Clarion was screaming at him. "Get on board *now!*" *So much like Gloria,* he thought. So much it hurt. Still leaning his head back, he wasn't certain but what some tears had joined the raindrops that slid down his cheeks to his chin. Gloria. Gloria was gone. If this was a dream, couldn't Clarion be Gloria? Even if this wasn't a dream, what did it matter? He'd been ripped from his time by creatures of hell, and deposited here to die with the rest—so what did it matter what he did now, really? If he wanted to, he could simply pretend Clarion *was* Gloria. He could climb the gangplank and let her take him below—dry him off and put him to bed. He could sleep. To his heart's content he could sleep, drifting upon the waves of the waters that rolled over Atlantis and drowned it forever. And really—was that his problem? Here before him he had the promise of wealth and family and a whole new life—

Let goods and kindred go—The words of that old hymn suddenly, inexplicably rolled through his mind: *This mortal life also. The body they may kill—God's truth abideth still . . .* "His kingdom is forever," Jack said aloud to himself. He knew, then, that he wasn't getting onto the boat.

"Jack! We have to go *now!*" Clarion shouted. Her words were punctuated by the first thunderclap Jack had heard since the rain had arrived. Except that it wasn't thunder at all. It was air-cannon, and it was coming from over the city.

Clarion jerked her head around to look that way, and uttered an oath—a very unladylike, very Anglo-Saxon oath that caused Jack to jerk in surprise. It wasn't so much that it was so out of character for the Gloria role she was playing—it was that he wondered where she had heard it. "Kundas!" she then snarled—and now Jack *knew* where she'd heard it.

"Astra?" he said, half-smiling.

"What?" the fallen creature snapped, looking back at him.

"Astra," Jack said again, shaking his head. "You really had me fooled."

"I've always had you fooled, Jack. You and all your kind. Now get aboard this ship if you have any interest at all in survival!"

"Why?" Jack shrugged, turning to walk away from the gangplank, parallel to the deck of the ship. "Where's Baal?"

"Maybe searching for a soul to ride by this time—" she muttered petulantly, "his new body blown to shreds." She looked back at Jack. "Who cares about Baal?" she growled, now walking along the railing to match speed with him. "Jack, would you come *on?*"

"Why me?" Jack asked, waving his arms as he continued walking. "What use would you have for *me* in your new regime?"

"You are a highly educated, highly qualified individual from the far future. What you don't know yourself you can learn from the computers and disc libraries stored aboard this craft. The things you can remember and teach to those who follow you will go a long way to establishing a long-lasting, creative dynasty that can ultimately control the world!"

"And other worlds as well?" he asked, smiling.

"Eventually."

Jack nodded. "Of course I won't be around for that."

"Of course not," Astra agreed. "But you can have a very comfortable, profitable life with—"

"No thanks."

She had reached the prow of the ship and had to stop. "Jack, I'm warning you!" she shouted at him as he walked on up the shoreline toward the city.

"Excuse me," Jack called back over his shoulder, "but I've got a few more warnings I need to give myself—"

That old, familiar saucer suddenly burst into being right above them both. From the city they heard sounds of more cannon-fire. Obviously, the battle of Babel had now spilled over here.

"Astra!" came a voice from the saucer. It was one Jack didn't recognize.

"What do you want?" Astra yelled back up.

"Astra, what's the matter with you? Kundas has found us and we've got to go!"

"I figured you'd be gone already," she snarled, almost under her breath.

Jack had business elsewhere, but he couldn't help but linger to see how this turned out. "Is that Baal?" he asked Astra.

"Astra!" the voice called down again, as she looked at Jack and nodded.

"He doesn't sound like himself . . . "

"He *isn't* himself. He's got a new body—" She looked skyward and curled her lip in disdain as she added, "The body of a young Adonis."

Jack found all this remarkable. Was she—jealous?

"Astra," Baal was pleading, "Let me bring you aboard! Quashior is wanting to find the ark and sink it, and you *know* the Guardians won't allow that. Meanwhile Kundas wants to sink *us!* Can't you hear him, blowing apart the city? We've got to get *out* of here if we want to have *any* chance of getting off this planet!"

"We'll *never* get off," Astra mumbled petulantly. *Was this why the gods and goddesses of Greece were always believed to quarrel?* Jack wondered. Had the ancient peoples witnessed what he was watching?

"Astra!" Baal shouted. "I need you!"

"You told me you don't need anybody!" she shouted back up at the saucer. "You've got a brand new body, a brand new look—"

"I had to *break* this new body to come find you!" Baal yelled. Then they all heard Kundas' cannons roar again, and this time they sounded far closer. "Please, Astra! Now?"

Astra/Clarion scratched her new head of long black hair, and looked down again at Jack. "Are you coming with us, Jack? Might as well. Look at that water—it's already up over your pants leg."

Jack looked down. She was right, of course. He guessed that he *could* get back on board. Wasn't that what he'd been hoping for, really? That they'd eventually pick him up again and take him home . . . ?

Then again, what would be the point? For Jack knew this now with utter certainty: They would *never* take him home. Why, then, let these fallen ones use him any more for their own purposes? Why not go ahead and serve out his own purpose here? He wondered briefly if Ben was aboard the saucer too. *If you are, Ben,* he thought up toward it, *remember that you could have your own purpose too. . . .*

Jack looked up at Astra, smiled, and said, "No thanks. Have a nice trip." Then he waved, and started slogging away through the high water.

Astra leaned over the prow of her boat and screamed after him, "You're a real fool, Dr. Brennen. Did you know that?" *Yes,* Jack thought to himself, he guessed he did know that. "Your own *God* is going to kill you, and we won't even have to *touch* you!" *Probably true,* Jack thought—then he amended that to, *Doubtless true. But if the Spirit of the Lord is upon me, I've been anointed to preach good news to the captives.* And if the Scripture was to be believed, in that city, some miles ahead were still some people who would soon be captives. He would go preach to them.

He didn't hear the saucer zap Astra inside, or disappear. But when he looked back over his shoulder a few moments later, both were gone.

In the distance he heard more booming from the guns. From the sky came still more rain. Through knee-high water, Jack walked back to Atlantis.

* * *

The end did not come quickly—not for most. Some were killed by collapsing buildings, but most were not. Some were killed by cannon fire from three strange box-shapes which danced across the sky, throwing flame at one another and the ground. No one could figure out who they were, or what they were doing—why were they fighting over a city about to disappear? Yet still they fought, for all of the first day and most of the second, before one of the boxes was blown from the sky.

The other two fired at each other a while longer, but then one of them crashed, and the other disappeared. The water-choked City of the Golden Gates was left to sink in peace.

By that time most of the people in the city were walking slowly westward—through the green belt, through the suburbs, through the farmlands out beyond. Bearing whatever they could carry on their backs, they were heading for the mountains. Few, however, had any hope of reaching them. The strange prophet who had prophesied the coming of the rain had told them that it really wouldn't make any difference anyway. He'd said that the true God who had made the world had, at long last, lost patience with His creation, and was starting over. As he walked along beside them, he told them of a man named Noah, whom he believed was at that moment somewhere half-way around the world, being saved by that same God.

The responses were always the same when he told this story. "Why not us?" someone would call to him as he trudged along through the rising muck beside them. "Who knows?" he would call back. "Perhaps the Son of God will come and preach to *you!*" Then he would drop back, letting that group pass by, awaiting a new wave of refugees to walk beside and encourage. It seemed that he was doing the best he could do.

At one point a group grew surly with him. "None of this ever happened before you came!" they said, and the prophet had been forced to agree. "Maybe you brought it with you!"

"Maybe we should kill you!" someone else suggested, and they talked about drowning him, since he was drowning *them.*

"Go ahead," the prophet had shrugged, and he'd stood his ground, waiting for them to take him. Somehow, now that they'd thought of it, nobody really felt like *doing* it. The mountains were still a long way off. . . .

Unfazed, and not at all angry, the prophet continued to walk right along beside them.

* * *

Thirty-two days after the first rain had fallen, Jack stood on a little outcropping of rock jutting up from a featureless sea. No one was with him here. Six days before, he had left the last group of pilgrims he'd traveled with, heading up this very mountain. He'd gone back in the direction the city had once been, hoping maybe to meet one last group. When he'd found no one, he'd come back this way and climbed the mountain, only to find himself alone at its peak. Now that peak was but a tiny island, and Jack waited here for death.

He figured he'd done the best he could. He was ready to go—ready for a rest. While he'd frequently fantasized over the last month about the ark floating by and picking him up, he knew that would never happen. It *was* comforting, in a way, to see this massive flood drowning the world. It did confirm some things he believed—some things he had read in God's Word. That encouraged him that all of the other things there were true also. He could wait for God in peace.

It *was* interesting, he reflected, that one of his earliest memories had been of just such a scene. His parents had read to him from *Hurlbut's Story of the Bible* since before he could even talk. They'd told him he had first read words from that book. They didn't need to tell him what his favorite story had been, for he remembered both it and the picture that went with it. Why he'd been so fascinated with it he didn't know, nor did his folks—but he'd loved the story of the flood. He also remembered vividly the picture of people climbing to the tops of high mountains to escape it.

And here he sat. The rain still drizzled down, much more slowly now than it had. Still, it had no place to go, so the water kept rising. Forty days and forty nights the Bible said it rained, but he knew he wouldn't last another week. Jack doubted he would last out the *day*.

Strangely, he felt somewhat rested. All the journeying had worn him out, but these last weeks had passed swiftly, for he'd had something useful to do. He hoped it was useful, anyway. He would leave that for God to decide. And in these last few days with nothing to do but sit on this mountain, he'd actually caught up on his sleep. Even so, he napped frequently. He thought it might be easier to be sleeping when the end came—just to drift off, then drift away. . . .

That wasn't going to happen. At noon the water was lapping his feet. By mid-afternoon he sat precariously on the peak with the water up around his waist. Any minute now he knew a swell would roll over him and carry him under. But Jack was very much at peace with God.

It came—lifting him up off the mountaintop, dropping him back down just a few feet away, but over very, *very* deep water. Jack went under.

As his lungs were filling with water he looked around under water for the mountain he'd just left—not that he wanted to try to swim back to it, rather out of simple curiosity. He noticed his hair was floating on the surface of the water—what little hair there was left. He'd had a knife, and lots of time to kill, and it had felt mighty long and stringy, so sometime yesterday he'd cut it. He was dying, and thinking about a haircut . . . .

Now this was curious: Through the water something came—something white, and very swift. A shark, he wondered idly? Then it came to him, and he realized that, no, this wasn't a shark. It was his angel, Gloria, come to get him, and he smiled and opened his arms to greet her. . . .

The angel said nothing. She grabbed him in her arms and flung him—but not out of the water. Rather, she threw him into the blackness he'd come to know so well on the saucer.

Chapter Twenty-Two

Always another semester

He wasn't asleep. Of that much he was certain. He was not asleep at all when he once again fell into time, but neither was he in heaven. He was, instead, sitting behind a bush in the tiny forest that belonged to his tiny city, and he was coughing up seawater. No, he was throwing up seawater, and thinking to himself that if the angel was going to save him she might at least have waited to give him mouth-to-mouth resuscitation on this side of the void.

Jack coughed and choked and coughed some more, then he gasped his lungs full of air. It hurt—lots of pollution that he hadn't been breathing lately—but it was air. Even better, it was the stinking air of home.

He expected someone to come find him. That seemed fitting, for someone to rush toward him, help him up, take him home, and take care of him. But when he popped his head up from out behind the bush, there was no one around at all. Jack staggered to his feet, cleared his throat again, and started home. He was sure hoping the door wouldn't be locked. He had no idea where his keys might be. . . .

He came through the screen porch. "Jack?" he heard Gloria call from the room above him, and he sighed with contentment. "Jack, is that *you?*"

"Yes, Hon," he called back, almost in tears. "I'm home!"

"Where have you been?" she scolded. "You've been gone for hours!"

Hours? No. Days. Weeks. Months. Who could know how long he'd traveled around with the fallen? Yet only *hours* had passed here?

"We've been looking all over for you!" she yelled down the stairs. "We even went down to the forest to search for you!"

"Sorry . . . !" he called back up to her, his mind elsewhere. He had stepped into the downstairs bathroom and looked at himself in the mirror:

His face was gaunt from weeks of walking and little food. His cheeks were stubbly, if not actually bearded. His hair looked—well, like he'd cut it off with a dull knife and no mirror while sitting on an ancient mountaintop. This was definitely not going to be easy to explain. But—he would try.

"Honey!" she called, coming on down the stairs. "Where *were* you?"

"I'll tell you," he sighed, "but you'd better take a deep breath and sit down first." Then he stepped out of the bathroom.

* * *

It felt good to drive again. Of course, everything felt good. It felt good to sleep in his own bed, it felt good to hug his family, it felt good to eat foods he recognized, and it felt good to talk to friends on the phone, even if they didn't understand why it seemed so meaningful to him all of a sudden.

It felt good to talk to his wife again, even though she was watching him now with real confusion in her eyes. Something had obviously happened to him, that she knew. No one could grow that much beard or lose that much weight in a single afternoon. But exactly *what* had happened to him she was still trying to filter. To be honest, Jack hadn't told her a tenth of it all yet. She was still working hard on the flying saucer part. . . .

* * *

This morning, as he drove back to the seminary, he felt *very* good. It felt good to see these places he drove past, which looked just exactly like they had when he'd last seen them only days ago. There was the convenience store where he bought milk and his daughter stocked up on bubble gum. There was the garage that ripped him off every time they fixed his car, but fixed it so well he kept on taking it back. There was the little church whose pastor consistently put interesting sermon titles on his sign board, which made Jack want to go listen. There was—

There was Ben.

Jack drove past him, trying to ignore him. "He isn't there, he isn't there, he isn't there," he started mumbling to himself. But when, halfway down the hill, he slowed down and looked in his rearview mirror, he saw clearly that Ben *was* there. He turned around and drove back.

Ben got into the car, and Jack did a double take. It was Ben, all right, no question—he had Ben's smile, and Ben's small frame, and Ben's voice when he said, "Hello, Jack." But he no longer appeared to be fifteen. Twenty-two wouldn't have been an unreasonable age to guess. Jack stared at him.

A horn honked behind them—some impatient motorist with places to go and people to meet. Jack found a place to pull off and looked again at Ben. "You've grown up," he said at last.

"In a lot of ways," the young man nodded, and he smiled the most genuine smile Jack had ever seen upon his lips. Jack paused then, just looking at him. Then he frowned, and mumbled flatly, "Where do you need to go this time?"

Ben's smile remained fixed in place. "Oh, I thought I'd ride on to that school with you, if you don't mind."

Jack nodded, and pulled back out onto the road. He wondered why Ben was wanting to go there. Did Lucifer somehow want to monitor the thoughts of the young people preparing to preach? Of course, Jack guessed he did that anyway. He glanced over at Ben, awaiting some comment.

After an awkward moment, Ben nervously cleared his throat and said, "If you're trying to talk with me through your thoughts, you'd best forget it. I don't do that anymore."

Jack's eyes narrowed as he slowed down and signaled to turn left. "You don't?"

"I don't," Ben said triumphantly, "and I *can't*. To put it in your own words, I 'lost that gift.'"

Jack felt a thrill surging through him, the thrill a coach feels when his team starts playing well, or a parent feels when her child excels, or a teacher feels when his students start thinking—or a pastor feels, when people he has preached to respond to the call of God. "Have you . . . "

"'For I will pour water upon him that is thirsty,'" Ben quoted, "'and floods upon the dry ground: I will pour my spirit upon thy seed, and my blessing upon thine offspring; And they shall spring up as among the grass, as willows by the water courses. One shall say, I am the Lord's, and another shall call himself by the name of Jacob; and another shall subscribe with his hand unto the Lord, and surname himself by the name of Israel.'"

Jack was grinning. Hugely. In fact he was having a difficult time steering. Even though he couldn't read Ben's mind, he could understand what the young man was saying. He had a spiritual son in Ben—and Ben had come to announce it. "I should know the reference," Jack said, a bit embarrassed. "What's that from?"

"Isaiah 44:1–5. It continues, 'Thus saith the Lord the King of Israel, and his redeemer the Lord of hosts; I am the first, and I am the last; and beside me there is no God. And who, as I, shall call, and shall declare it, and set in order for me, since I appointed the ancient people? And the things that are coming, and shall come, let them show unto them. Fear ye not, neither be afraid; have I not told thee from that time, and have declared it? Ye are even my witnesses. Is there a God beside me? Yea, there is no God; I know not any.'"

Jack's eyes watered. He shook his head. "When?"

Ben smiled—and Jack noticed it was a very adult smile. "Good question. When *does* salvation take place, Jack? I never forgot what you told me—that it was my decision. And one day, I just decided, 'I don't want to do this anymore. God? Please take this gift away!' And He did."

They drove on, Jack pondering this all in his mind. "And what happened then? How did you get the Evil One to release you? Or did you run away?"

"It's a long story, Jack, and I hope to have plenty of time to tell it to you. But, simply put, once the gift was gone I was no use to them anymore. I was like the girl in Philippi who lost her gift of fortune-telling. What was the point in keeping me around?"

"But didn't they try to kill you?" Jack asked, and Ben was laughing before he got the question out.

"'Touch not the Lord's anointed!'" Ben cackled. "Don't think they didn't try! Finally they gave up—and here I am." He shifted position to look directly toward Jack, and said, "I've finished my diploma, as well as my degree, and I'm ready to get into seminary. I guess you could say I've been waiting around for years for you to get back!"

When the new semester arrived, then, Jack found Ben seated in the first row of desks, pen in hand—waiting. Another child in the ministry. There were many others here as well, however, seated all around him and looking at Jack just as expectantly.

"What's the message of Scripture?" he began. "What message do *we* have to share with this, *our* generation on the earth? Isn't it that the answer to evil's rebellion is no different in this time than in any other?

"The command of Christ is clear. We must keep on telling people of the impending doom of this world—and keep on telling of God's loving solution to sin through the cross—and keep on depending upon the God who loves, and who *promises* He will save His children.

"You know," Jack said, picking up the coffee mug he always carried with him to class, "I wonder if the *angels* ever wonder why He cares so much . . . ?"